THE MARRIAGE LIE

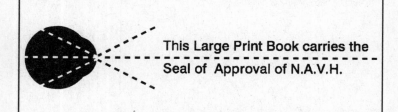

This Large Print Book carries the
Seal of Approval of N.A.V.H.

THE MARRIAGE LIE

KIMBERLY BELLE

THORNDIKE PRESS
A part of Gale, Cengage Learning

GALE
CENGAGE Learning·

Farmington Hills, Mich • San Francisco • New York • Waterville, Maine
Meriden, Conn • Mason, Ohio • Chicago

GALE
CENGAGE Learning·

LIBRARY OF CONGRESS CATALOGING-IN-PUBLICATION DATA

Names: Belle, Kimberly, author.
Title: The marriage lie / by Kimberly Belle.
Description: Large print edition. | Waterville, Maine : Thorndike Press, 2017. |
    Series: Thorndike Press large print core
Identifiers: LCCN 2017002601| ISBN 9781410499677 (hardcover) | ISBN 1410499677
    (hardcover)
Subjects: LCSH: Widows—Fiction. | Aircraft accidents—Fiction. | Secrecy—Fiction. |
    Large type books. | GSAFD: Suspense fiction.
Classification: LCC PS3602.E45745 M37 2017 | DDC 813/.6—dc23
LC record available at https://lccn.loc.gov/2017002601

Published in 2017 by arrangement with Harlequin Books S.A.

Printed in the United States of America
1 2 3 4 5 6 7 21 20 19 18 17

This one's for Kristy Barrett,
bee-autiful inside and out.

1

I awaken when a hand winds around my waist, pulling me head to heel against skin heated from sleep. I sigh and settle into my husband's familiar form, fitting my backside into his front, soaking in his warmth. Will is a furnace when he sleeps, and I've always got some place on me that's cold. This morning it's my feet, and I wedge them between two warm calves.

"Your toes are freezing." His voice rumbles in the darkened room, the sounds vibrating through me. On the other side of our bedroom curtains it's not quite morning, that violet-tinged moment between night and day, still a good half hour or so before the alarm. "Were they hanging off the side of the bed or something?"

It's barely April, and March hasn't quite loosened its icy hold. For the past three days, leaden skies have been dumping rain, and a frigid wind has plummeted temperatures far below average. Meteorologists predict at least another week of this shivering, and Will is the only soul in Atlanta who welcomes the cold by throwing the windows wide. His internal thermostat is always set to blazing.

"It's because you insist on sleeping in an igloo. I think all my extremities have frostbite."

"Come here." His fingers glide up my side, his hand pulling me even closer. "Let's get you warm, then."

We lie here for a while in comfortable silence, his arm snug around my middle, his chin in the crook of my shoulder. Will is sticky and damp from sleep, but I don't care. These are the moments that I cherish the most, moments when our hearts and breaths are in sync. Moments as intimate as making love.

"You are my very favorite person on the planet," he murmurs in my ear, and I smile. These are the words we've chosen instead of the more standard *I love you,* and to me they mean so much more. Every time they roll off his tongue they hit me like a promise. I like you the most, and I always will.

"You're my very favorite person, too."

My girlfriends assure me this won't last forever, this connection I feel with my own husband. Any day now, they tell me, familiarity will fizzle my fire, and I will suddenly start noticing other men. I will stain my cheeks and gloss my lips for nameless, faceless strangers who are not my husband, and I will imagine them touching me in places only a husband should have access to. The seven-year itch, my girlfriends call it, and I can barely imagine such a thing, because today — seven years and a day — Will's hand glides across my skin, and the only itch I feel is for him.

My eyelids flutter closed, his touch stirring up a tingling that says I'll likely be late for work.

"Iris?" he whispers.

"Hmm?"

"I forgot to change the filters on the air conditioner."

I open my eyes. "What?"

"I said, I forgot to change the filters on the air conditioner."

I laugh. "That's what I thought you said." Will is a brilliant computer scientist with ADD tendencies, and his brain is so crammed with facts and information that he's always forgetting the little things . . . just usually not during sex. I attribute it to an unusually busy time at work combined with the fact he's leaving for a three-day conference in Florida, so his to-do list today is longer than usual. "You can do it this weekend when you're back."

"What if it gets warm before then?"

"It's not supposed to. And even if it does, surely the filters can wait a couple of days."

"And your car could probably use an oil change. When's the last time you took it in?"

"I don't know."

Will and I split our household duties neatly down gender lines. The cars and house upkeep are his department, the cooking and cleaning are mine. Neither of us much minds the division of labor. College taught me to be a feminist, but marriage has taught me to be practical. Making lasagna is so much more pleasant than cleaning the gutters.

"Check the maintenance receipts, will you? They're in the glove box."

"Fine. But what's with all the sudden chores? Are you bored with me already?"

I feel what I know is Will's grin sliding up the back of my head. "Maybe this is what all the pregnancy books mean by nesting."

Joy flares in my chest at the reminder of what we are doing — what we've maybe already *done* — and I twist around to face him. "I can't be pregnant yet. We've only officially been trying for less than twenty-four hours."

Once last night before dinner, and twice after. Maybe we went a bit overboard in our first official baby-making session, but in our defense, it was our anniversary, and Will's a classic overachiever.

His eyes gleam with self-satisfaction. If there were space between our bodies for him to beat himself on the chest, he'd probably do it. "I'm pretty sure my guys are strong swimmers. You're probably pregnant already."

"Doubtful," I say, even though his words make me more than a little giddy. Will is the practical one in this relationship, the one who keeps a steady head in the face of my Labrador-like optimism. I don't tell him I've already done the math. I've already made a study of my cycle, counting out the days since my last period, charting it on an app on my phone, and Will is right. I could very well be pregnant already. "Most people give wool or copper for their seventh anniversary. You gave me sperm."

He smiles but in a nervous way, that look he gets when he did something he maybe shouldn't have. "It's not the only thing."

"Will . . ."

Last year, at his insistence, we sank all our savings and a significant chunk of our

11

monthly income into a mortgage that would essentially make us house poor. But, oh, what a house it is. Our dream house, a three-bedroom Victorian on a quiet street in Inman Park, with a wide front porch and original woodwork throughout. We walked through the door, and Will had to have it, even if it meant half the rooms would be empty for the foreseeable future. This was to be a no-present anniversary.

"I know, I know, but I couldn't help myself. I wanted to buy you something special. Something so you'll always remember this moment, when we were still just us two." He twists around, flicks on the lamp, pulls a small, red box from the drawer in the bedside table and offers it to me with a shy grin. "Happy anniversary."

Even I know Cartier when I see it. There's not a speck of dust in that store that doesn't cost more than we can afford. When I don't move to open it, Will flips the snap with a thumb and pulls the lid open to reveal three linked bands, one of them glittering with rows and rows of tiny diamonds.

"It's a trinity ring. Pink for love, yellow for fidelity and white for friendship. I liked the symbolism of three — you, me and baby-to-be." I blink back tears, and Will lifts my chin with a finger, bringing my gaze to his. "What's wrong? Don't you like it?"

I run a finger over the bright white stones, sparkling against red leather. The truth is, Will couldn't have chosen a better piece. The ring is simple, sophisticated, stunning. Exactly what I would pick out for myself, if we had all the money in the world to spend, which we don't.

And yet I want this ring so much more than I should — not because it's beautiful or expensive, but because Will put so much thought into picking it out for me.

"I love it, but . . ." I shake my head. "It's too much. We can't afford it."

"It's not too much. Not for the mother of my future baby." He tugs the ring from the box, slides it up my finger. It's cool and heavy and fits perfectly, hugging the skin below my knuckle like it was made for my hand. "Give me a little girl who looks just like you."

My gaze roams over the planes and angles of my husband's face, picking out all my favorite parts. The thin scar that slashes through his left eyebrow. That bump at the bridge of his nose. His broad, square jaw and thick, kissable lips. His eyes are sleepy and his hair is mussed and his chin is scratchy with stubble. Of all his habits and moods, of all the sides of him I've come to know, I love him most when he's like he is now: sweet, softhearted, rumpled.

I smile at him through my tears. "What if it's a boy?"

"Then we'll keep going until I get my girl." He follows this up with a kiss, a long, lingering press of his lips to mine. "Do you like the ring?"

"I love it." I wind my arm up and around his neck, the diamonds winking above his shoulder. "It's perfect, and so are you."

He grins. "Maybe we should get in one more practice run before I go, just in case."

"Your flight leaves in three hours."

But his lips are already kissing a trail down my neck, his hand already sliding lower and lower still. "So?"

"So it's raining. Traffic's going to be a bitch."

He rolls me onto my back, pinning my body to the bed with his. "Then we better hurry."

2

Tuition at Lake Forrest Academy, the exclusive K–12 in a leafy suburb of Atlanta where I work as school counselor, is a whopping $24,435 per year. Assuming for a five percent inflation, thirteen years in these hallowed halls will cost you more than four hundred grand per child, and that's before they step even one foot on a college campus. Our students are the sons and daughters of surgeons and CEOs, of bankers and entrepreneurs, of syndicated news anchors and professional athletes. They are a privileged and elite tribe, and the most fucked-up group of kids you could ever imagine.

I push through the double doors at a little past ten — a good two hours late, thanks to Will's not-so-quickie and a nail in my tire on the way — and head down the carpeted hallway. The building is quiet, the kind of quiet it can be only when the students are in class huddled behind their brand-new

MacBooks. I've arrived in the middle of third period, so no need to rush.

When I come around the corner, I'm not all that surprised to find a couple of juniors gathered in the hallway outside my office door, their heads bent over their electronics. The students know I have an open-door policy, and they use it often.

And then more come out of the classroom across the hall, their voices rising in excitement, and the alarm I hear in them sticks my soles to the carpet. "What's going on? Why aren't you guys in class?"

Ben Wheeler looks up from his iPhone. "A plane just crashed. They're saying it took off from Hartsfield."

Terror clutches my chest, and my heart stops. I steady myself on a locker. "What plane? Where?"

He lifts a scrawny shoulder. "Details are sketchy."

I shove through the cluster of students and leap behind my desk, reaching with shaking hands for my mouse. "Come on, come on," I whisper, jiggling my computer out of its deep-sleep hibernation. My mind spins with what I can remember of Will's flight details. He's been in the air for over thirty minutes by now, likely roaring somewhere near the Florida border. Surely — *surely* — the crashed plane can't be the one with him on it. I mean, what are the odds? Thousands of planes take off from the Atlanta airport every day, and they don't just fall from the sky. Surely everybody got off safely.

"Mrs. Griffith, are you okay?" Ava, a wispy sophomore, says from my doorway, and her words barely cleave through the roaring in my ears.

After an eternity, my internet browser loads, and I type the address for CNN with stiff and clumsy fingers. And then I pray. *Please, God,* please, *don't let it be Will's.*

The images that fill my screen a few seconds later are horrifying. Jagged chunks of a plane ripped apart by explosion, a charred field dotted with smoking debris. The worst kind of crash, the kind where no one survives.

"Those poor people," Ava whispers from right above my head.

Nausea rises, burning the back of my throat, and I scroll down until I see the flight details. Liberty Airlines Flight 23. Air bursts out of me in a loud whoosh, and relief turns my bones to slush.

Ava drapes a tentative hand across my shoulder blades. "Mrs. Griffith, what's wrong? What can I do?"

"I'm fine." The words come out half

formed and breathless, like my lungs still haven't gotten the memo. I know I should feel sick for Flight 23's passengers and their families, for those poor people blown to bits above a Missouri cornfield, for their families and friends who are finding out like I did, on social media and these awful pictures on their screens, but instead I feel only relief. Relief rushes through me like a Valium, strong and swift and sublime. "It wasn't Will's plane."

"Who's Will?"

I brush both hands over my cheeks and try to breathe away the panic, but it fights to stay close. "My husband." My fingers are still shaking, my heart still racing, no matter how many times I tell myself it wasn't Will's plane. "He's on his way to Orlando."

Her eyes go wide. "You thought your husband was on that plane? Jeez, no wonder you just melted down."

"I didn't melt down, I just . . ." I press a palm to my chest, haul a deep, cleansing breath. "For the record, my reaction was not out of proportion to the situation. Tremendous fear like the kind I experienced produces a sharp spike in adrenaline, and the body responds. But I'm fine now. I'll be fine."

Talking about it out loud, putting my

physiological response into scientific terms, loosens something in my chest, and the throbbing in my head slows to an occasional thud. *Thank God, it wasn't Will's plane.*

"Hey, I'm not judging. I've seen your husband. Totally smoking." She tosses her backpack onto the floor, sinks into the corner chair and crosses legs that are far too bare for uniform regulations. Like every other girl in this school, Ava rolls her skirt waistband until the hemline reaches hooker heights. Her gaze dips to my right hand, still pressed to my pounding chest. "Nice ring, by the way. New?"

I drop my hand onto my lap. Of course Ava would notice the ring. She probably knows exactly what it costs, too. I ignore the compliment, focusing instead on the first half of her reply. "When have you seen my husband?"

"On your Facebook page." She grins. "If I woke up next to him every morning, I'd be late to work, too."

I give her a reprimanding look. "As much as I'm enjoying this conversation, shouldn't you be getting back to class?"

Her pretty pink lips curl into a grimace. Even frowning, Ava is a gorgeous girl. Painfully, hauntingly beautiful. Big blue eyes. Peaches-and-cream skin. Long, shiny auburn curls. She's smart, too, and wickedly funny when she wants to be. She could have any boy in this school . . . and she has. Ava is not picky, and if I'm to believe Twitter, she's an easy conquest.

"I'm skipping lit," she says, spitting out the words in a tone usually reserved for toddlers.

I give her my psychologist's smile, friendly and nonjudgmental. "Why?"

She sighs and rolls her eyes. "Because I'm avoiding any enclosed spaces where Charlotte Wilbanks and I have to breathe the same air. She hates me, and let me assure you, the feeling is mutual."

"Why do you think she hates you?" I ask, even though I already know the answer. Former best friends, Charlotte and Ava's feud is long and well documented. Whatever sparked their hatred all those years ago is by now long forgotten, buried under a million offensive and tasteless Tweets that take "mean girl" to a whole new level. According to what I saw fly by in yesterday's feed, their latest tiff revolves around their classmate Adam Nightingale, son of country music legend Toby Nightingale. This past weekend, pictures surfaced of Ava and Adam canoodling at a neighborhood juice bar.

"Who the hell knows? Because I'm prettier, I guess." She picks at her perfect nail polish, a bright yellow gel that looks like it was painted on yesterday.

Like most of the kids in this school, Ava's parents give her everything her heart could ever desire. A brand-new convertible, first-class trips to exotic locations, a Platinum Amex card and their blessing. But showering their daughter with gifts is not the same as giving her attention, and if they were the ones sitting across from me, I'd encourage them to set a better example. Ava's mother is an Atlanta socialite with the remarkable ability to look the other way every time Ava's father, a plastic surgeon touted around town as "The Breast Guy," is caught groping a girl half his age, which is often.

My education has taught me to see nature and nurture as equal propositions, but my job has taught me nurture wins out every time. Especially when it's lacking. The more messed up the parents, the more messed up the kid. It's really that simple.

But I also believe that everyone, even the worst parents and the most maladjusted kids, has a redeeming quality. Ava's is because she can't help herself. Her parents have made her to be this way.

"I'm sure if you give it a bit more thought, you could come up with a better reason why

Charlotte might be —"

"Knock, knock." The head of the upper school, Ted Rawlings, fills up my doorway. Long and lanky and with a crown of tight, dark curls, Ted reminds me of a standard poodle, one who's serious about pretty much everything except his ties. He must have hundreds of the hideous things, always school-themed and always ridiculous, but on him somehow they only look charming. Today's version is a bright yellow polyester covered in physics equations. "I take it you've heard about the plane crash."

I nod, my gaze flitting to the images on my screen. Those poor people. Their poor families.

"Somebody at this school is going to know somebody on that plane," Ava says. "You just wait."

Her words skitter a chill down my spine, because she's right. Atlanta is a big city but a small town, one where the degrees of separation tend to be short. The chance that someone here is connected in some way to one of the victims isn't small. I suppose the best thing I can hope for is that it's not a family member or close friend.

"The students are anxious," Ted says. "Understandably so, of course, but I don't think we'll get any classroom work done today. With your help, though, I'd like to turn this tragedy into a different kind of learning opportunity for everyone. Create a safe place for our students to talk about what happened and to ask questions. And if Miss Campbell here is correct, that someone at Lake Forrest lost a loved one in the crash, we'll already be in place to provide whatever moral support they need."

"That sounds like a great idea."

"Excellent. I'm glad you're on board. I'll call a town hall meeting in the auditorium, and you and I will tag-team the discussion."

"Of course. Just give me a minute or two to pull myself together, and I'll be right there."

Ted raps a knuckle on the door and hustles off. With lit class officially canceled, Ava picks up her backpack, rifling through it for a few seconds while I dig a compact out of my desk drawer.

"Here," she says, dumping a fistful of designer makeup tubes onto my desk. Chanel, Nars, YSL, Mac. "No offense, but you look like you need them way more than I do." She softens her words with a blinding smile.

"Thanks, Ava. But I have my own makeup."

But Ava doesn't pick up the tubes. She

shifts from foot to foot, one hand wringing the strap of her backpack. She bites her lip and glances at her oxford shoes, and I think under all that bluster and bravado, she might actually be shy. "I'm really glad it wasn't your husband's plane."

The relief this time is a slow build, wrapping me in warmth like Will's sleeping body did just this morning. It settles over me like sunshine on naked skin. "Me, too."

As soon as she's gone, I reach for my phone, pulling up the number for Will's cell. I know he can't pick up for another hour or so, but I need to hear his voice, even if it's only a recording. My muscles unwind at the smooth, familiar sound.

This is Will Griffith's voice mail . . .

I wait for the beep, sinking back in my chair.

"Hey, babe, it's me. I know you're still in the air, but a plane just crashed after taking off from Hartsfield, and for about fifteen terrifying seconds I thought it might have been yours, and I just needed to . . . I don't know, hear for myself that you're okay. I know it's silly, but call me as soon as you land, okay? The kids are kind of freaked, so I'll be in a town hall, but I promise I'll pick up. Okay, gotta run, but talk to you soon. You're my very favorite person, and I miss you already."

I drop my phone into my pocket and head for the door, leaving Ava's makeup where she dumped it, in a pile on my desk.

3

Seated next to me on the auditorium stage, Ted smooths a hand down his tie and speaks to the room filled with high-schoolers. "As you all know, Liberty Air Flight 23 traveling from Hartsfield-Jackson International Airport to Seattle, Washington, crashed a little over an hour ago. All 179 passengers are presumed dead. Men, women and children, people just like you and me. I've called us here so we can talk about it as a group, openly and honestly and without judgment. Tragedies like this one can make us all too aware of the dangers in our world. Of our own vulnerabilities, of just how fragile life can be. This room is a safe space for us to ask questions and cry and whatever else you need to do to process. Let us all agree that what happens in this auditorium stays in this auditorium."

Any other head of high school would hold a school-wide moment of silence and tell

26

the kids to get back to work. Ted knows that for teenagers, catastrophe takes precedence over calculus any day, and it's because he sees everything, good or bad, as a learning opportunity that the students follow him without question.

I look out over the three hundred or so kids that make up Lake Forrest's high-school student body, and as far as I can tell, they're split pretty solidly down the middle — half the students are freaked by the images of an airplane filled with their maybe-neighbors falling from the sky, the other half giddy at an entire afternoon of canceled classes. Their excited chatter echoes through the cavernous space.

One girl's voice rises to the top. "So this is kind of like group therapy?"

"Well . . ." Ted sends me a questioning look, and I dip my head in a nod. If there's one realm Lake Forrest students feel comfortable navigating, it's therapy, group or otherwise. Ours are the type of kids who have their therapists' cells on speed dial. "Yes. Exactly like group therapy."

Now that they know what's coming, the students seem to relax, crossing their arms and slumping back into their plush seats.

"I heard it was terrorists," someone calls out from the back of the auditorium. "That

ISIS has already come out and said they did it."

Jonathan Vanderbeek, a senior about to graduate by the skin of his teeth, twists around in his front-row seat. "Who told you that, Sarah Palin?"

"Kylie Jenner just re-Tweeted it."

"Brilliant," Jonathan says, snorting. "Because the Kardashians are experts when it comes to our nation's security."

"Okay, okay," Ted says, calling everyone back to order with a few taps to the microphone. "Let's not escalate the situation by repeating rumors and conjecture. Now, I've been watching the news carefully, and beyond the fact that a plane crashed, there really is no news. Nobody has said *why* the plane crashed, or who was on it when it did. Not until they've contacted the next of kin." His last three words — *next of kin* — hit the room like a firebomb. They hang in the air, hot and heavy, for a second or two. "And moving forward, let's all agree that there are more credible news sources than Twitter, shall we?"

A snicker comes from the front row.

Ted shakes his head in silent reprimand. "Now, Mrs. Griffith has a few things she'd like to say, and then she'll be leading us in a discussion. In the meantime, I'll be watching the CNN website on my laptop, and as soon as the airline releases any new information, I'll pause the conversation and read it aloud so we'll all have the same up-to-date information. Does that sound like a good plan?"

Nods all around. Ted passes me the mic.

I wish I could say I spent the next few hours staring at my phone, watching for Will's call, but at seventy-six minutes postcrash, only ten minutes into our discussion and a good fifteen before the airline was scheduled to make its first official statement, CNN reports that the Wells Academy high-school lacrosse team, all sixteen of them and their coaches, were among the 179 victims. Apparently, they were on their way to a mid-season tournament.

"Omigod. How can that be? We just played them last week."

"Last week, you idiot. You just said so yourself. Which means they had plenty of time between then and this morning to get on a plane."

"You're the idiot, idiot. I'm talking about how we lost the game that won Wells a tournament spot. Do the math."

"Hold up," I say, the words slicing through the auditorium before the argument can escalate further. "Disbelief is a normal reaction to news of a friend's death, but anger and sarcasm are not good coping mechanisms, and I'm pretty sure every one of y'all in here knows it."

The kids exchange contrite looks and slump deeper into their seats.

"Look, I get that it's easy to hide behind negative emotions rather than confront what a close call our friends and fellow students had," I say, my tone softening. "But it's okay for you to be confused or sad or shocked or even vulnerable. These are all normal reactions to such shocking news, and having an open and honest conversation will help all of us work through our feelings. Okay? Now, I bet Caroline here isn't the only one here thinking back to the last time she saw one of the Wells players. Was anyone else at the game?"

One by one, hands go up, and the students begin talking. Most of the accounts are no more relevant than *same field, same time,* but it's clear the kids are spooked by the proximity, especially the lacrosse players. If they had won that game, if Lake Forrest had been the school with a slot in that tournament, it could have just as easily been our students on that plane. Corralling the conversation takes every bit of my concentration until just after one, when we break for a late lunch.

The students file out, and I pull my phone from my pocket, frowning at the still empty screen. Will landed over an hour ago, and he still hasn't called, hasn't texted, hasn't *anything*. Where the hell is he?

Ted drapes a palm over my forearm. "Everything okay?"

"What? Oh, yes. I'm just waiting on a call from Will. He flew to Orlando this morning."

Ted's eyes go huge, and his cheeks quiver in sympathy. "Well, that certainly explains your expression when I came to your office earlier. You must have had quite a scare."

"Yes, and poor Ava bore the brunt of it." I waggle my phone in the air between us. "I'm just going to see if I can't track him down."

"Of course, of course. Go."

I skitter off the stage and up the center aisle, pulling up Will's number before I've stepped through the double doors. Lake Forrest is set up like a college campus, with a half-dozen ivy-covered buildings spread across an acre campus, and I take off down the flagstone path that leads to the high-school building. The rain has stopped, but leaden clouds still hang low in the sky, and an icy wind whips chill bumps over my skin.

31

I pull my sweater tight around my chest and hustle up the stairs to the double doors, pushing into the warmth right as Will's cell shoots me to voice mail.

Dammit.

While I wait for the beep, I give myself a pep talk. I tell myself not to worry. That there's a simple explanation for why he hasn't called. The past few months have been particularly stressful at work, and he hasn't been sleeping well. Maybe he's taking a nap. And the man *is* easily distracted, a typical techie who can never seem to focus on one thing at a time. I imagine him punching in my number, then forgetting to push Send. I picture him hobnobbing with conference bigwigs by the hotel pool, oblivious to the buzzing phone in his hand. Or maybe it's as simple as his battery died, or he forgot his cell on the plane. I think of all these things, and I can almost taste the joy.

"Hey, sweetie," I say into the phone, trying not to let the worry seep into my tone. "Just wanted to check in and make sure all is well. You should be at your hotel by now, but I guess the reception in your room is crappy or something. Anyway, when you get a second, call me. This crash has got me a little antsy, and I really want to hear your voice. Okay, talk soon. You're my very favorite person."

In my office, I head straight for my computer and pull up my email program. Will sent me the conference details months ago, but there are more than three thousand emails in my inbox and no good system for organizing them. After a bit of searching, I find the email I'm looking for:

From: w.griffith@appsec-consulting
   .com
To: irisgriffith@lakeforrestacademy.org
Subject: FW: Cyber Security for
   Critical Assets: An Intelligence
   Summit

Check me out! I'm Thursday's keynote speaker. Let's just hope they don't all fall asleep, kind of like you do whenever I talk about work. xo

Will M. Griffith
Sr. Software Engineer
AppSec Consulting, Inc.

My skin tingles with relief, and I feel vindicated. The words are right here, in black and white. Will is in Orlando, safe and sound.

I click on the attachment, and a full-page conference flyer opens. Will's head shot is about halfway down, next to a blurb advertising his expertise on all things access risk management. I hit Print and scribble the name of the conference hotel on a Post-it note, then return to my internet browser for the telephone number. I'm copying it down when my phone rings, and my mother's face lights up the screen.

A stab of uneasiness pings me in the chest. A speech pathologist, Mom knows what working in a school environment is like. She knows my days are crazy, and she never disturbs me at work unless there's a life-and-death situation. Like the time Dad hit a pothole with his front bike tire and flipped a three-sixty onto the asphalt, landing so hard he cracked his collarbone and split his helmet clean down the middle.

Which is why I answer her call now with "What's wrong?"

"Oh, sweetheart. I just saw the news."

"About the crash? I know. We've been dealing with it all day here at school. The kids are pretty freaked."

"No, that's not what I meant. Well, not exactly . . . I meant Will, darling."

Something in the way she says it, in the careful and roundabout way she's asking but not asking about Will, soldiers every hair on my body to attention. "What about him?"

"Well, for starters, where is he?"

"In Orlando for a conference. Why?"

The force of Mom's sigh into the speaker pierces my eardrum, and I know how much she's been holding back. "Oh, thank God. I knew it couldn't be your Will."

"What are you talking about? Who couldn't be my Will?"

Her reply gets buried under a student's loud interruption. "Mr. Rawlings told me to tell you they just released a list of names." She screams the words into my office, as if I'm not sitting right here, three feet away, and on the phone. I shush her and shoo her off with a hand.

"Mom, start over. Who's not my Will?"

"The William Matthew Griffith they're saying was on that plane."

Not my husband bubbles up from the very core of me, from somewhere deep and primitive. My Will was on a different plane, on a whole different airline even. And even if he wasn't, Liberty Airlines would have already called. They wouldn't have released his name without notifying me — his wife, his very favorite person on the planet — first.

But before I can tell my mother any of

these things, my phone beeps with another call, and the words on the screen stop my heart.

Liberty Airlines.

4

With a shaking hand, I hang up on my mother and pick up the call from Liberty Airlines.

"Hello?" My throat is tight, and my voice comes out raspy and faint.

"Hello, may I please speak with Iris Griffith?"

I know why this woman is calling. I know it from the way she says my name, from her carefully neutral tone and businesslike formality, and the breath sticks in my throat.

But she's wrong. Will is in Orlando.

"Will is in Orlando," I hear myself say.

"Pardon me . . . Is this the number for Iris Griffith?"

What would happen if I said no? Would it stop this woman from saying the words I know she called to say? Would she hang up and call the other William Matthew Griffith's wife?

"I'm Iris Griffith."

"Mrs. Griffith, my name is Carol Manning of Liberty Airlines. William Matthew Griffith listed you as his emergency contact."

Will is in Orlando. Will is in Orlando. Will is in Orlando.

"Yes." I clutch my stomach with an arm. "I'm his wife." *Am* his wife. *Am.*

"Ma'am, I deeply regret to inform you that your husband was a passenger on this morning's Flight 23, which crashed en route from Atlanta to Seattle. It is presumed that none of those on board survived." She sounds like a robot, like she's reading from a script. She sounds like Siri calling to tell me my husband is dead.

My muscles stop working, and I go down. My torso falls forward onto my own lap, my body bending in half like a snapped twig. The impact knocks the wind right out of me, and the breath leaves me in a great moan.

"I know this must come as a shock, and I assure you Liberty Airlines is here to support you however and whenever you need. We've established a dedicated hotline number and email address for you to contact us anytime, day or night. Regular updates will also be available on our website, www.libertyairlines.com."

If she says anything more, I don't hear it. The phone clatters to the floor and right there, in the middle of my cluttered office, my doorway filling with wide-eyed students, I slide off my chair and sob, pressing both hands to my mouth to stifle the sound.

Two large shoes step into my field of vision. "Oh, Iris. I just heard. I'm so, so sorry."

I look up through my hair at Ted, at his concerned brow under those canine curls, and I weep with relief. Ted is a fixer. He'll know what to do. He'll call somebody who will tell him it was the wrong Will, the wrong plane, I'm the wrong wife.

I try to pull myself together, but I can't, and it's then I notice that my office is crawling with high-schoolers. I already heard them gathering in the hall outside my doorway, low tones and whispered words I wasn't supposed to hear. Words like *husband, plane, dead,* and I know they've heard the news.

No. Just this morning, while I was filling our travel mugs with coffee, Will checked the weather in Orlando on his phone. "High of eighty-seven today," he said with a shake of his head. "And it's not even summer. This is why we will never live in Florida."

Ava watches me with tears in her eyes.

"Will is in Orlando," I say to her, and her face flashes pity.

I'm embarrassed to have her see me like this, to have any of them see me like this, a crumpled, snotty mess on the floor. I cover my face with my hands and wish they'd go away. I wish all of them would just leave me alone. My open-door policy can suck it.

"Here, let me help you up." Ted hauls me off the floor and deposits me on my chair.

"Where's my phone? I want to try Will again."

He leans down, picks up my phone from the floor, passes it to me. Nine missed calls. I taste bile when I see they're all from my mother. None, not even one, from Will.

"Guys, give us a little privacy, will you?" Ted glances over his shoulder. "Shut the door on your way out."

One by one, the kids file out, mumbling their condolences. Ava runs a light finger down my arm on her way past, and I flinch. I don't want her sympathy. I don't want anyone's sympathy. Sympathy would mean what that woman told me is true. Sympathy would mean my Will is dead.

Once everyone is gone and we're alone, Ted drapes a palm over my shoulder. "Is there someone I can call?"

Call! I was about to call the hotel. My gaze

lands on the conference flyer, and I snatch it from my printer, wave it in Ted's face. "This! This right here proves Will is in Orlando. He's tomorrow's keynote. He wasn't on the plane to Seattle. He was on one to Orlando." Hope blooms in my chest.

"Did he check into the hotel?" Ted says, but in a tone that says he's humoring me.

With shaking fingers, I find the Post-it where I scribbled the number and punch it into my phone. I can tell that Ted's holding out little hope, that he thinks this exercise is a futile waste of time, and the blatant mollification that lines his face is too much for me to bear. I stare down at my desk instead, concentrating instead on the marks and scratches that crisscross its surface. The phone rings, then rings again.

After an eternity, a perky female voice answers. "Good afternoon, Westin Universal Boulevard. How may I be of service?"

"Will Griffith's room, please." The words tumble out of me, jagged and raw and way too fast, like an auctioneer hyped on crack.

"My pleasure," the receptionist chirps in my ear. I'm sure she gets crazed spouses on the line all the time, women hunting down their wayward boyfriends or philandering husbands. Westin probably has an entire training manual on how to deal with callers like me. "Griffith, you said?"

"Yes, Will. Or it could be under William, middle initial *M.*" I drag a deep breath and try to calm myself, but my leg is bouncing, and I can't stop shivering.

Ted shrugs out of his jacket and drapes it over my shoulders. I know he means well, but the gesture feels far too personal, and the fabric smells like Ted, fragrant and foreign. I want to rip the jacket off and chuck it out the window. I don't want any man's clothing touching my body but Will's.

The woman clicks around a keyboard for a few seconds.

"Hmm. Sorry, but I'm not finding a reservation for Mr. Griffith."

I choke on a sob. "Check again. Please."

There's a long pause filled with more clicking, more humoring. Dread begins to burrow under my skin like a parasite, slow and steady, eating away at my certainty.

"Are you positive it's this Westin property? We have one in Lake Mary, just north of the city. I can get you the number, if you'd like."

I shake my head, blinking away fresh tears in order to read the hotel information at the bottom of the flyer. "I'm looking at the conference flyer right now. It says Universal Boulevard."

Her voice brightens. "Oh, well, if he's here for a conference, then perhaps I can get a message to the organizer's point of contact. Which conference?"

"Cyber Security for Critical Assets: An Intelligence Summit."

She hesitates only a second or two, but long enough that bile builds in my throat. "I'm very sorry, ma'am, but there's no conference by that name at this hotel."

I drop the phone and throw up into my wastebasket.

Claire Masters, a colleague from the admissions office across the hall, drives me home. Claire and I are friendly enough, but we're not friends, though I don't have to ask why I'm here, buckled into the passenger's seat of her Ford Explorer instead of someone else's car. Early last year, Claire lost her husband to Hodgkin's, and now, whether she volunteered to drive me home or Ted asked her to, the reason is clear. If anyone will understand what I'm going through, it's another widow.

Widow. I'd throw up again, but my stomach is empty.

I turn and stare out the window, watching the familiar Buckhead strip malls fly by. Claire drives slowly, her hands at ten and two, and she doesn't say a word. She keeps her mouth shut and her gaze on the traffic in front of her, and as much as I detest being lumped into her tragic category, at least she knows that the only thing I want is to be left alone.

My phone buzzes on my lap. My mother, calling for what must be the hundredth time. Guilt pricks at my insides. I know it's not fair to keep avoiding her, but I can't talk to her right now. I can't talk to anybody.

"Don't you want to get that?" Claire's voice is high and girlish, and it slices through the silence like a serrated knife.

"No." It takes all my energy to speak around the boulder on my chest.

Her gaze bounces between me, my phone and the traffic before us. "Take it from me, your mother is losing her mind right now."

I wince at her knowing tone, at the way she's putting the two of us on the worst kind of team. "I can't." My voice cracks the last word in two, because talking to Mom would mean saying those awful words out loud. *Will is gone. Will is dead.* Saying the words would make this thing real.

The phone stops, then two seconds later, starts again.

This time, Claire plucks the phone from my lap and swipes the bar to pick up. "Hi, this is Claire Masters. I'm one of Iris's colleagues at Lake Forrest. She's sitting right beside me, but she's not quite ready to talk." A pause. "Yes, ma'am. I'm afraid that's correct." Another pause, this time longer. "Okay. I'll make sure to tell her." She hangs up and places the phone gently back onto my legs. "Your parents are on their way. They'll be here before dark."

I'd thank her, but I can't muster up the energy. I stare out the window and try to picture it, my Will in a field of smoking wreckage, with luggage and debris and charred, twisted chunks of metal scattered all around, but I can't. It seems incomprehensible, as abstract to me as a concept from Dr. Drukker's AP physics class. Will was going to Orlando, not Seattle. He can't be dead. It just isn't possible.

Claire turns onto the ramp for Georgia 400 and floors the gas, and we roar south in blissful, blessed silence.

5

No matter how many times I assure her it's not necessary, Claire walks me up the flagstone path to my front door. I dig through my bag and pull out my keys, sliding them into the lock. "Thanks for the ride. I'm going to be okay."

I open the door and walk through, but when I go to close it, Claire stops me with a palm to the stained-glass panel. "Sweetheart, I'm staying. Just until your parents get here."

"No offense, Claire, but I want to be alone."

"No offense, Iris, but I'm not leaving." Her high-pitched voice is surprisingly firm, but she softens her words with a smile. "You don't have to talk to me if you don't want to, but I'm staying, and that's that."

I step back and let her pass.

Claire glances around the foyer, taking in the honey-colored walls, the gleaming pine floors stained almost-black, the carved railings on the original staircase. She cranes her head around the corner into the front parlor, empty save for a tufted beige sofa we're still paying off — our Christmas gift to each other from Room & Board — then points toward the back of the house. "I assume the kitchen is that way?"

I nod.

She drops her bag by the door and heads down the hallway. "I'll make us some tea." She disappears around the corner into the kitchen.

As soon as she's gone, I latch onto the newel post, this morning's memories assaulting me. The weight of Will's body on mine, heating me with his hands and hot naked skin. His lips in the crook of my neck and heading south, the scratch of his morning beard against my breasts, my belly, lower still. My fingers twining in his hair. The water sluicing down Will's muscled torso as he stepped out of the shower, the brush of his fingers against mine when I handed him a towel. His smooth, warm lips coming in for just one more kiss, no matter how many times I warned him he was in serious danger of missing his flight. That very last flick of his hand as he rolled his suitcase out the front door, his wedding band blinking in the early-morning light, before driving off in his car.

He has to come back. We still have dinner dates and hotel reservations and birthday parties to plan. We're going to Seaside next month, a Memorial Day getaway with just us two, and to Hilton Head this summer with my family. It was only last night that he pressed a kiss to my belly and said he can't wait until I'm so fat with his baby, his arms won't reach all the way around. Will can't be gone. The finality is too unreal, too indigestible. I need proof.

I dump my stuff on the floor and head down the hallway to the back of the house, an open kitchen overlooking a dining area and keeping room. I dig the remote out of the fruit basket, and with the punch of a few buttons, CNN lights up the screen. A dark-haired reporter stands in front of a cornfield, wind whipping her hair all around her face, interviewing a gray-haired man in a puffy coat. The text across the bottom of the screen identifies him as the owner of the cornfield now littered with plane parts and human remains.

Claire comes around the corner holding a box of tea bags, her eyes wide. "You really shouldn't be watching that."

"Shh." I press and hold the volume but-

48

ton until their voices hurt my ears almost as much as their words. The reporter peppers the man with questions while I search the background for any sign of Will. A flash of brown hair, the sleeve of his navy fleece. I hold my breath and strain to see, but there's nothing but smoke and cornstalks, swaying in the breeze.

The reporter asks the old man to tell the camera what he saw.

"I was working on the far west end of the fields when I heard it coming," the old man says, gesturing to the endless rows of corn behind him. "The plane, I mean. I heard it before I saw it. It was obviously in trouble."

The reporter pauses his story. "How did you know the plane was in trouble?"

"Well, the engines were squealing, but I didn't see no fire or smoke. Not until that thing hit the field and blew. Biggest fireball I ever seen. I was probably a good mile or so away, but I felt the ground shake, and then a big blast of heat hot enough to singe my hair."

How long does it take a plane to tumble from the sky? One minute? Five? I think of what that must have been like for Will, and I lean over the sink and gag.

Claire reaches for the remote and hits Mute. I grip the countertop and stare at the scratched bottom of the sink, waiting for my stomach to settle, and think, *What now? What the fuck am I supposed to do now?* Behind me, I hear her scrounging around my kitchen, opening cabinets and digging around inside, the vacuumed hiss of the refrigerator door opening and closing. She returns with a pack of saltines and a bottle of water. "Here. The water's cold, so take tiny sips."

Ignoring both, I move around the counter to the other side and collapse onto a bar stool. "Denial, anger, bargaining, depression, acceptance." Claire gives me a questioning look. "The stages of grief according to Kübler-Ross. I'm clearly in the denial phase, because it makes no sense. How could a man headed to Orlando end up on a westward-bound plane? Was the conference moved to Seattle or something?"

She lifts both shoulders, but her expression doesn't seem the least bit unsure. I may be in denial, but Claire's clearly not. Though she might not say it out loud, she accepts Liberty Air's claims that Will is one of the 179 bodies torn to pieces over a Missouri cornfield.

"It's just not possible. Will would have told me, and he definitely wouldn't have kept up the running dialogue about going

50

to Orlando. Just this morning, he stood right where you're standing and told me how much he hated that city. The heat, the traffic, those damn theme parks everywhere you look." I shake my head, desperation raising my voice like a siren. "He's been so stressed, maybe he didn't know the conference had been moved. Maybe that's where he's been all this time, roaming around the scorching Orlando streets, trying to track down the new location. But then why not call me back?"

Claire presses her lips together, and she doesn't respond.

I close my eyes for a few erratic heartbeats, the emotions exploding like bombs in my chest. What do I do? Who do I call? My first instinct is to call Will, like I do whenever I have a problem I can't figure out myself. His methodical mind sees things differently than mine, can almost always plot a path to the solution.

"You should design an app," I told him once, after he'd helped me chart out an entire semester's worth of drug and alcohol awareness programs. "You'd make a fortune. You could call it *What Will Will Say?*"

He'd patted his lap, smiling my favorite smile. "Right now he says you're adorable and to get over here and give me a kiss."

Now I press my fingers to my lips and tell myself to calm down, to think. There must be someone I can call, someone who will tell me this is all just one huge misunderstanding.

"Jessica!" I pop off the stool and sprint to the phone, resting on a charger by the microwave. "Jessica will know where he is. She'll know where the conference was moved."

"Who's Jessica?"

"Will's assistant." I punch in the number I know by heart, turning my back on Claire so I don't see her creased brow, her averted gaze, the way she's chewing her lip. She's humoring me, just like Ted did.

"AppSec Consulting, Jessica speaking."

"Jessica, it's Iris Griffith. Have you —"

"Iris? I thought y'all were on vacation."

Her comment comes so far out of left field, it takes me a couple of seconds to reboot. Jessica may be a whiz at answering phones and coordinating the schedules of a bunch of disorganized techies, but she's not got the fastest processor in the cache.

"Um, no. What makes you think that?"

"Because you're supposed to be on an all-inclusive, baby-making vacation to the Mayan Riviera. Will showed me pictures of the resort, and it looks ama—" She swallows the rest of the word, then sucks in a breath. "Oh, God. Iris, I must be confused. I'm sure I got the weeks mixed up."

I know what Jessica is thinking. She's thinking he's there with another woman, and I don't even care because what if she's right? What if Will is alive and well and lounging on a beach in Mexico? Hope hangs inside me for a second or two, then fizzles when I realize that he wouldn't. Will would never cheat, and even if he did, Mexico would be the very last destination on my heat-hating husband's list. A cruise to Alaska would be more like it.

"He can't be in Mexico," I say, and it's everything I can do to keep my voice calm, to smother my frustration in a coating of civility. "He's one of the keynotes for the cyber security conference, remember?"

"What conference?"

My eyes go wide. Why would anyone at AppSec ever hire this woman? "The one in Orlando."

"Wait. I'm confused. So he's not in Mexico?"

And Lord help me, this is where I lose it. I suck a breath and scream into the phone loud enough to burn the back of my throat. "I don't know, Jessica! I don't fucking know

where Will is! That's the whole fucking problem!"

Shocked silence all around, from Claire behind me and from Jessica on the other end of the line. It's like silence in stereo, ringing in both ears. I should apologize, I know I should, but a sob steals my breath, and I choke on the awful words that come next. "They — They're saying Will was on that flight that crashed this morning, but that can't be right. He was on a plane to Orlando. Tell me he's in Orlando."

"Oh, my God. I saw the news, but I had no idea, Iris. I didn't know."

"Please. Just help me find Will."

"Of course." She falls silent for a moment, and I hear her clicking around a computer keyboard. "I'm positive I didn't book his flight for today, but I have his log-in creden-tials for the airline accounts. What airline was the plane that crashed again?"

"Liberty Airlines. Flight 23."

Another longish pause filled with more clicking. "Okay, I'm in. Let's see . . . Flight 23, you said?"

I drop both elbows on the countertop, cradle my head in one hand, squeeze my eyes shut, pray. "Yes."

I hold my breath, and I hear the answer in the way Jessica sucks in hers.

"Oh, Iris . . ." she says, and the room spins. "I'm so sorry, but here it is. Flight 23, leaving Atlanta this morning at 8:55 a.m., headed to Seattle and returning on . . . Huh. Looks like he booked a one-way."

My legs give out, and I slide onto the floor. "Check Delta."

"Iris, I'm not sure —"

"Check Delta!"

"Okay, just give me a second or two . . . It's loading now . . . Wait, that's so weird, he's here, too. Flight 2069 to Orlando, leaving today at 9:00 a.m., returning Friday at 8:00 p.m. Why would he book two tickets in opposite directions?"

Relief turns my bones to slush, and I sit up ramrod straight. "Where's the conference? I called the hotel on Universal Boulevard, but it must have been moved."

"Sorry, Iris. I don't know anything about a conference."

"So ask somebody! Surely somebody there knows about the conference your own company planned."

"No. What I meant was, AppSec doesn't have any conferences on the books, not until early November."

It takes me three tries to get my next words out. "And Mexico?"

"The tickets aren't on Delta or Liberty

Air, but I can check the other airlines if you'd like."

There's pity in her voice now, and I can't listen to it for another second. I hang up and Google the phone number for Delta. It takes me nine eternal minutes to make it through the queue, and then I explain my situation to a procession of customer service representatives before I finally land with Carrie, the perky-voiced family assistance representative.

"Hi, Carrie. My name is Iris Griffith. My husband, Will, was booked on this morning's Flight 2069 from Atlanta to Orlando, and I haven't heard from him since he landed. Could you maybe check and make sure he made the flight okay?"

"Certainly, ma'am. I'll just need his ticket locator number."

Which would mean hanging up and calling Jessica back, and there's no way I'm giving up my place in the phone line. I need answers now. "Can't you find him by name? I really need to know if he was on the flight."

"I'm afraid that's impossible." Her voice is singsong and chipper, delivering the bad news like I just won a free meal at Denny's. "Privacy restrictions will not allow us to give out passenger itineraries over the phone."

"But he's my husband. I'm his wife."

"I understand that, ma'am, and if I could verify your marital status over the phone, I would. Perhaps you could drop by your nearest Delta counter with a valid identification, someone there —"

"I don't have time to go to a Delta counter!" The words erupt from the deepest part of my gut, surprising me with both their suddenness and force, and the woman on the other end of the line goes absolutely still. If it weren't for the background noises, computer clicks and human chatter, I'd think she hung up on me.

And then there's a high-pitched squeal like interference on a microphone, and it takes a second or two to identify the sound as my own. I break under the weight of my desperation.

"It's just that he also had a ticket on Liberty Air Flight 23, you know? But he wasn't supposed to be on that airplane. He was supposed to be on yours. And now he's not returning my calls and the hotel doesn't have any record of him or the conference and neither does his assistant, even though she thought he was in Mexico, which he most definitely is not. And now, with each second that passes, seconds where *I don't know where my husband is,* I'm losing more and more of my mind, so please. Take a peek in your computer and tell me if he was on that flight. I'm begging you."

She clears her throat. "Mrs. Griffith, I . . ."

"Please." My voice breaks on the word, and it takes a couple of tries before I find it again. The tears are coming hard and fast now, hogging my air and clogging my throat. "Please, help me find my husband."

There's a long, long pause, and I clasp the phone so tightly my fingers ache. "I'm sorry," she says after an eternity, her voice barely above a whisper, "but your husband never checked in for Flight 2069."

I scream and hurl my phone across the room. It bounces off the cabinet and lands facedown on the tiles, and I don't have to look to know it's shattered.

I spend the rest of the afternoon in bed, fully clothed and bundled in Will's bathrobe, fuming under my comforter. Will lied. He fucking *lied.* No, he didn't just lie, he lied and then backed up his lie with a fake conference, one he corroborated with more lies and a fake full-color flyer that's a masterpiece of desktop publishing. Fury fires in my throat and grips me by the guts and overshadows every other thought. How could Will do such a thing? Why would he go to all that trouble? I am shaking so hard my bones vibrate, mostly because now there's no reason for him to have been on a plane to Orlando.

My parents arrive just before dark, like they said they would. From under my layers of cotton and feathers, I hear their muted voices talking to Claire downstairs. I imagine my mother's horrified expression when Claire tells them about my breakdown at school and the phone calls with Jessica and the Delta agent. I see Mom crane her neck toward the staircase with obvious longing on her face, the way she'd hurriedly wrap up the conversation with Claire so she could rush up the stairs to me. Two seconds after a car starts outside on the driveway, a body sinks onto the edge of my bed.

"Oh, darling. My sweet, sweet Iris." Her voice is soft, but her consonants are hard and pointy — along with her love of meat and potatoes, a stubborn sign of her Dutch heritage.

As awful as it sounds, I can't face my mother. Not yet. I know what I will see if I throw off the covers: Mom's eyes, red-rimmed and swollen and filled with pity, and I know what the sight of them will do to me.

"Your father and I are just heartbroken. We loved Will and we will miss him terribly, but my heart breaks most of all for you. My sweet baby girl."

Tears prick my eyes. I'm not ready to speak of Will in past tense, and I can't bear for anyone else to, either. "Mom, please. I need a minute."

"Take all the time that you need, *lieverd.*" You know Mom is devastated when the endearments revert back to her native tongue.

The bed shifts, and she stands. "Your brother will be here by nine. James was in surgery when they got the news, so they only just left Savannah an hour ago." She pauses as if waiting for a reply, but when she doesn't get one, she adds, "Oh, *schatje,* is there anything I can do?"

Yes. You can bring me Will. I need to wring his neck.

6

I wake up and the first thing I think is *Where's Will? Where is my husband?*

The clock says it's seventeen past midnight. I strain for the sound of water running in the bathroom, for the slap of bare feet on the closet hardwoods, but other than heated air whistling through the vents, our bedroom is quiet.

The day comes roaring back like a head-on collision. Will. Airplane. Dead. Pain steals my breath, stretching from my forehead to my heels.

Terror overwhelms me, and I lurch upright in bed, flipping on the light and sucking deep breaths until the walls stop pushing in on me. I flip down the covers and reach for the divot in the mattress where Will's body lay only yesterday. Without Will in it, our king-sized bed has grown to the size of an ocean liner, swallowing me up with all the emptiness. I run a palm over his pillowcase, pluck at a couple dark hairs caught in the cool cotton. I close my eyes, and I can still feel him, physically feel the heat of his skin, the scratch of his beard sliding across my shoulder blade, the weight of him rolling onto me, my own gasp as he pushes inside. One minute he's here, the next he's gone, like a morbid magician's disappearing act.

And now I'm supposed to believe he's in pieces on a Missouri cornfield? I can't wrap my head around the concept. It's sheer insanity.

Climbing out of bed is like swimming upstream. My body is heavy, my limbs sluggish and stiff, and there's a vise clamping down on my lungs that makes it hard to breathe. I'm still in Will's robe, and it's all tangled and twisted around my body. I loosen the belt, rewrap the terry cloth around my torso and retie everything snug around my waist. It still swims on me, but it's warm and comfortable, and it smells like Will — all of which means I may never take it off.

Downstairs, the kitchen television flashes blue and white streaks in the darkness. Muted coverage of the crash. I stand there for a long moment, staring at a reporter before a field of charred earth and steaming chunks of metal, and it strikes me that he might be enjoying this a little too much. His eyes are too big, his brow too furrowed, everything about him too theatrical. He's waited his entire career for a story like this one; better make it good.

Behind me, the lump on the couch shifts — my twin brother, Dave, in a Georgia Bulldogs sweatshirt and plaid pajama pants. "Been wondering when you'd get down here," he says in his deep, dusky bass that makes him sound like a sports announcer instead of the Realtor he is. He lights up a joint the size of a cigar and sucks in a lungful, patting the cushion next to him.

"I'm telling Mom." Other than crying, it's the first time I've used my voice in almost seven hours, and my throat feels scratchy and sore. I plop down on the couch.

"My husband's a doctor," Dave says through held breath. "It's medicinal."

I snort. "Sure it is."

He offers me a toke, but I shake my head. I'm already a wreck. Probably not the best idea to throw marijuana, medicinal or otherwise, into the mix.

We sit under the cloud of sweet-smelling smoke for a long while in silence, watching the muted images on the screen. The carnage is too much to take in, so I concentrate instead on the reporter's solemn face. He gestures for the cameraman to follow him over to a giant hunk of fuselage, then points to an abandoned child-sized shoe, and I try to read his lips. *What a hungry sticker. Cheese candy. A goat and three trolls.* How do deaf people do this?

The reporter's forehead crumples into rows and rows of squiggles, and Dave shakes his head. "That motherfucker is having entirely too much fun."

Everything you've ever heard about twins is true; Dave and I are living proof. We look alike, we act alike, we share the same habits and gestures. We both have fat lips and bony knuckles, we'll watch any sport but can't stand playing them, and we refuse to eat anything that has the slightest dash of vinegar in it. We even have twin telepathy, this inexplicable connection that lets us know what the other is thinking without either of us saying a word. Case in point? I knew he was gay before he had figured it out for himself.

He stubs the joint out on a teacup saucer already littered with ashes and sets it on the side table. "Just so you know, Ma is a wreck. She's already brought home one of everything from Kroger, and she's got a list a half mile long of all the things she's going to fill your freezer with. If you don't let her coddle you soon, you're going to have enough food here to open a soup kitchen."

"Coddling would make it real." I sigh and press into him, leaning my head on his shoulder. "I keep telling myself it's not. That Will is going to walk through that door on Friday evening, hot and rumpled and grumpy, and I'll get to scream I told you so. I *told* you Will wasn't on that plane. I keep waiting for someone to pinch me, to take me by both shoulders and shake me so I'll wake up, but so far, nothing. I'm stuck in a fucking nightmare."

"Sure as hell feels like it." He picks up my hand, twines his fingers through mine, rolling the ring around with a thumb. "Nice Cartier."

I blink back new tears. "Will and I are trying to get pregnant. You might be an uncle already."

Dave looks at me for a good thirty long and silent seconds. He doesn't say a word, but then again, he doesn't have to. *How long are we going to keep this up?* his eyes say. *This talking about Will like he's still here?*

As long as humanly possible, my answer.

But when it comes to the pregnancy, he doesn't seem the least bit surprised. "What took y'all so long? James and I figured you'd have an entire brood by now."

"Will wanted to wait. He said he wanted me all to himself for a while."

"What changed his mind?"

I have to think about that one for a moment. "I don't know, and honestly, I never thought to ask. I was just so excited he finally came around. He says he wants a little girl who looks like me, but if this is all true, if I really am stuck in this nightmare, I hope it's a little boy who's just like him."

"Even after the conference that wasn't?"

Of course Dave knows about Will's invented conference. I'm sure my mother dragged it out of Claire, then dissected his lie for hours with anybody who would listen. I'm sure she's come up with a long list of theories as to why Will would do such a thing, why he would go to the trouble of creating a conference flyer, why he would book two flights to opposite ends of the country.

But of course I already know the answer. So I wouldn't know where he was going, what he was going to do there, who he was going to see. Any or all of the above.

The helpless fury that had me shaking under my comforter earlier threatens to bubble to the surface, and I swallow it back down. I love my husband. I miss him and want him back. The emotions are so big and wide, they leave no room for anger. I barter with a God I'm not entirely sure I believe in: *Bring Will back, and I won't even ask where he's been. I promise I won't even care.*

"One lie doesn't negate seven years of marriage, Dave. Does it piss me off? Maybe. But it can't erase the love I feel for my husband."

He concedes the point with a one-shouldered shrug. "Of course not. But can I ask you something else without you biting my head off?" He pauses, and I give him a reluctant nod. "What's in Seattle? Besides rain and Starbucks and too much plaid, I mean."

I lift both hands. "Beats the hell out of me. Will grew up in Memphis, and he moved to Atlanta straight out of grad school at University of Tennessee. His entire life is here on the East Coast. I've never even heard him talk of Seattle. As far as I know, he's never been there." I twist on the couch, stare into cat eyes the same dark olive shade as mine. "But what you're really asking is, do I think Will is having an affair."

Dave gives me a slow nod. "Do you?"

My stomach twists — not because I think my husband was cheating on me, but because everybody else surely will. "No. But I don't think he was on that plane, either, so clearly I've not got the tightest grip on reality. What do *you* think?"

Dave falls silent for a long moment, contemplating his answer. "I have a lot of unanswered questions when it comes to my brother-in-law. Don't get me wrong, I adore the guy, mostly because of how fiercely he loves you. You can't fake that kind of love, the kind that, every time you walk into the room, fills his face with so much happiness that I have to turn away — and I'm a gay man. I eat that shit up. So to answer your question, no. I don't think your husband was having an affair."

My heart, which was already hanging by a thread, cracks in two. Not just at Dave's belief in my husband or his talking about him like he's still here, but more so that my brother's love for me is so intense, it extends by default to another person. I curl my palm around his biceps and lay my head on his shoulder, thinking I've never loved Dave more.

"Anyway, what I'm trying to say is, Will came into your life solo. His parents are dead, he has no siblings, he never talks about any other family or friends. Everybody has a past, but it's like his life began when he met you."

Dave is only partly right. Will has a lot of

68

colleagues and acquaintances, but not a lot of friends. But that's because, for techies like Will, it takes a lot for him to open up.

I sit up, twist on the couch to face my brother. "Because he lost track of all his high-school friends except for one, and he's moved off to Costa Rica. He runs a surfing school there or something. I know they still exchange regular emails."

"What about all the others? Friends, old neighbors, workout partners and drinking buddies."

"Men don't collect friends like women do." Dave gives me a look, and I amend. "Heterosexual men don't collect them. They don't feel the need to run with a huge pack of people, and besides, you know Will. He'd rather be at home on his laptop than in a loud, crowded bar any day." It's part of the reason we eloped to the mountains of North Carolina seven years ago, with only my parents and Dave and James as witnesses. Will doesn't like crowds, and he hates people fussing over him.

"Even introverts have a best friend," Dave says. "Who's Will's?"

That's an easy one. I open my mouth to answer, but Dave beats me to the punch. "Besides you, I mean."

I press down on my lips. Now that my

name is off the table, Dave's question has me perplexed. Will talks about a lot of people he knows, but he never really defines them as friends.

Dave yawns and slumps deeper into the couch, and it's not long before he forgets his question and nods off. I sit there next to my snoring brother, watching the horrific images flash by on the television screen but not really seeing them.

I'm thinking about our first anniversary, when I surprised Will with a road trip to Memphis. I'd spent weeks planning it, my version of a *this is your life* tour along all his old haunts, puzzling the stops together from the few stories he'd told me of growing up there. His high-school alma mater, the street where he'd lived until his mother died, the Pizza Hut where he'd worked evening and weekend shifts.

But the closer we got to the city, the more he fidgeted, and the quieter he became. Finally, on a barren stretch of I-40, he admitted the truth. Will's childhood wasn't pleasant, and his memories of Memphis weren't exactly something he wanted to revisit. Once was hard enough. We hung a U-turn and spent the weekend exploring Nashville's honky-tonks instead.

So, no, Will didn't like to talk about his past.

But Seattle? What's there? *Who's* there?

I look over at my sleeping brother, at his chest rising and falling in the darkness. As much as I want to keep Dave's suspicions at bay, to barricade his doubts about Will from my brain, the questions sneak back in like smoke, silent and choking.

How well do I know my husband?

7

When I come downstairs next, it's close to ten in the morning. My family is scattered around the kitchen, drinking coffee and listening to James read news of the crash aloud from a website on his iPad. From where he's seated at the table, Dad coughs into a fist. James stops mid-sentence, and they look at me with a combination of guilt and concern, like four kids I caught stealing from my cookie jar.

"They found the black box?" I say without preamble.

Mom drops the spatula into a skillet of half-cooked eggs and whirls around, looking like she didn't fare much better than I did in the sleeping department. Dark circles spread under her eyes like bruises, and her hair, normally an inspired work of hot-roller wizardry, hangs listless around her puffy face. "Oh, sweetheart." She rushes across the kitchen tile, snatching me into a ferocious hug. "My heart is just breaking for you. Is there anything I can do? Anything you need?"

There are a million things I need. I need to know what made Will board that plane. I need to know what happened to make it fall from the sky. I need to know what his last moments were like, if he went down screaming or without warning, if one moment he was debating peanuts versus pretzels and the next he was dust. I need to know where he is — literally and exactly. Will there be a body to bury?

But most of all, I need Will to be where he said he was going to be. In Orlando.

I untangle myself from Mom's arms. I look to James, since he was the one reading the news. "Do they know why it crashed?"

"It'll be months before they say for sure," James says, his voice careful. He takes me in with his blue-eyed doctor's gaze, methodical and thorough, like he's trying to take my pulse from the other side of the kitchen counter. "How did you sleep?"

I shake my head. I didn't miss the way everyone exchanged looks at my question about the crash, and I sure as hell don't want to talk about my lack of sleep. "Just tell me, James."

He hauls a breath, his gaze sliding over

my right shoulder to Dave, as if asking for permission. Dave must have nodded, because James's gaze returns to mine. "Keep in mind this is just a theory at this point, but the media is speculating a mechanical problem followed by pilot error."

"Pilot error." The words come out sluggish, like my tongue is coated in molasses.

James nods.

"Pilot error. As in, somebody fucked up, and now my husband is dead."

James grimaces. "I'm sorry, Iris, but it sure sounds that way."

Bile rises in my throat, and the room sways — or maybe it's just me.

James hops off his stool and rushes around the counter, steadying me with a palm around my elbow. "Would you like me to give you something? I can't medicate your grief away, but a pill can help take the edge off, at least for the next few days."

I shake my head. My grief, as spiky as it is, feels like the only thing binding me to Will. The thought of losing that connection, even the rawest, sharpest edges of it, fills me with panic.

"I wouldn't say no to a Xanax," Dave says.

James gives me a look, one like *your crazy brother,* then pats my arm. "Think about it, okay? I can write you a prescription for

74

whatever you need."

I give him my best attempt at a smile.

"Come." My mother steers me to the kitchen island, overflowing with food. A platter of scrambled eggs, a mini mountain of bacon and sausage swimming in grease, an entire loaf of toasted bread. For Mom, there's no better way of demonstrating her love than with heavy, hearty food, and this morning, her love is big enough to feed an army. "What would you like?"

I take in the food and the smell hits me, buttery eggs and fried pork grease, doing somersaults in my stomach. "Nothing."

"You can't not eat. How about I whip up some pancakes? I'll make the Dutch kind and load them up with apple and bacon, just the way you like."

Dave looks over from the coffeepot, where he's measuring out the grounds. "Ma, leave her alone. She'll eat when she's hungry."

"C'mere, Squirt," Dad calls out from his seat at the table, patting the chair beside him. "I saved you a spot."

My father is a former marine and a brilliant engineer with an easy smile and a halfway decent jump shot, but his greatest talent is running interference between my brother and me and our mother.

I sink onto the chair and lean into him,

and he slings a beefy arm around my shoulders. My family is not a demonstrative clan. Hugs happen only at hellos and goodbyes. Kisses are rare, and they usually stop just short of skin. So far today I've held my brother's hand, collapsed in my mother's arms and snuggled up to my father. This is what death does. It forces intimacy at the same time it snatches it away.

My gaze falls on the legal pad, covered in Dad's block-letter scribbles. Pages and pages of bullet points, grouped into categories and ranked by level of importance. If Will were here, he and my father would bond over the beauty of this list, a masterpiece of left-brained brilliance. I push aside Dad's reading glasses and scan the papers, a string of knots working their way across my shoulder blades. It seems unfair there are so many tasks to tackle, when all I really want to do is go back to bed and forget yesterday ever happened.

And then I notice a grouping of four or five bullets at the bottom.

"Compensation?" I say, and there's venom in my tone.

"Airlines provide a sum of money to victims' families, Iris. I know it seems harsh, but I'm just looking out for my baby girl. I will make sure you're provided for."

76

As if Liberty Air can fix their shoddy planes and bungling pilots by throwing around some cash. *Oh, we killed your husband? Here, go buy yourself something nice.*

"I'd rather starve to death than touch a penny of their blood money."

"Fine, then don't touch it. Put it in the bank and forget all about it. I'm still going after it for you."

I grab the pen and add my own bullet to the list: *research victims' families' charities.* Someone might profit from Liberty Air's money, but it sure as hell won't be me.

The next page is more of the first, and after a quick scan I flip to the next and then the next, stopping short at what I read across the top: MEDIA. Underneath, my father has created a long and extensive log of calls received, complete with date, time, name of caller and outlet. I don't recognize all the names, but more than a few jump out at me. *People* magazine. The *Today* show. *The Atlanta Journal-Constitution.* Diane Sawyer. *USA TODAY.*

"How did they find me? Our number's unlisted."

Dave settles in at the head of the table with an egg-and-bacon sandwich. "I don't know, but the phone has been ringing off the hook. We unplugged it an hour ago. And last time I looked, there were three news vans parked out front."

"Seriously?"

"Seriously. And you know that photo of you and Will from last New Year's Eve? It's all over the internet."

They could have chosen a worse picture, I suppose. Me and Will in our holiday finest, our faces lit up with goofy grins as he dips me over an arm. I loved it so much I made it my Facebook profile picture, which, now that I think about it, is probably where they got it.

Mom slides a plate with a mini mountain of food in front of me. "Here, *liefje*. Try to eat at least a few bites."

I pick up my fork, cut off a mini slice of sausage and push it around my plate until Mom heads back into the kitchen.

Dad flips to the next page of his list. "Liberty Airlines has established a Family Assistance Center at the international terminal at Hartsfield. A lady by the name of —" he slips on his glasses and consults the paper "— Ann Margaret Myers is your point of contact."

Dave snorts around a giant bite of food. "What kind of idiot plans a gathering for plane crash next of kin at the airport?"

"Liberty Air ones, apparently," Dad says.

"They want us down there so they can, and I quote, *provide comfort and counseling, discuss plans and answer any questions.*"

"Plans?" I say. "What kind of plans?"

"Well, for starters, they're talking about a memorial service as soon as this weekend."

Dad's gentle tone does nothing to stop a familiar anger from sparking like a flash fire. A Liberty Air memorial service feels like an insult, like the neighbor who buys you flowers after they run over your dog. I won't accept their public display of penitence, and I can't forgive their mistake.

"So now I'm supposed to accept help from the people responsible for killing my husband? That's absurd." I shove my plate to the center of the table, and the pyramid of scrambled eggs landslides over the rim.

"I know it seems that way, punkin', but it won't be just Liberty Air. The Red Cross will be there, too, as well as folks whose sole job is to collect information about the crash. I want to hear what they know that we haven't gotten from the TV or newspaper."

"Maybe you can ask them who alerted the media before my daughter," Mom says, slamming the salt and pepper shakers onto the center of the table. "Because that is an unforgivable blunder, and I'd like to tell that person what I think of them."

"Whoever made that mistake will be out of a job, I'll see to it." Dad uses his drill-instructor voice — forceful, booming and unambiguous. He turns, and his expression morphs from fierce to fiercely concerned. "Sweetheart, like it or not, we're going to have to interface with Liberty Air at some point. I can be a buffer if you want me to, or I can stand back and let you handle it yourself. Up to you. Either way, at the very least, we should go down there and see what this Miss Myers has to say, don't you think?"

No, I don't think. I've seen that footage — sobbing family members pushing their way through a sea of cameras, keen to capture their despair for all the world to see. And now Dad is suggesting we become a part of them?

Then again, I have so many questions, not the least of which is *what did you do to my husband?* If this Ann Margaret Myers has an answer for that one, she can plaster my teary, snotty face on the high-definition LED screens at SunTrust Field for all I care.

I push away from the table and head upstairs to get dressed.

On the last night of Will's life, he cooked. Not something out of a box or the freezer section, but a whole-food, homemade meal.

For someone who didn't know how to cut a tomato when I met him, whipping up dinner must have been no easy feat, and it probably took him all day. Maybe something inside him knew what was coming, some otherworldly awareness that his cosmic clock was about to hit zero, but that night — our seventh anniversary — he surprised me with real food, and for the first time ever made by his own hands.

I found him bent over one of my cookbooks in the kitchen, the most amazing smell hanging in the air. "What's going on?"

He whirled around, a twig of thyme dangling from a curl and a mixture of pride and guilt on his expression. "Um, I'm cooking."

I could see that. Anyone could see that. He'd used every pot and pan we owned, and covered the entire countertop, every single inch, with food and ingredients and cooking utensils. Will was covered in flour and grease.

I smiled. "What are you making?"

"Standing rib roast, new potatoes in butter and parsley, and those skinny green beans wrapped in bacon, I forget what they're called."

"Haricots verts?"

He nodded. "I've got dessert, too." He gestured to two chocolate lava cakes in white ramekins, cooling on a rack by the oven. He'd even sprinkled them with powdered sugar. When I didn't respond, he said, "We can still go out if you want to. I just thought —"

"It's perfect," I said, meaning it. I didn't care that the kitchen was a wreck, or that we'd miss our reservations at the new sushi hot spot in Buckhead. Will cooked, and for me. I smiled and leaned in for a kiss. "*You're* perfect."

The meal, however, was not. The roast was overdone, the potatoes were mushy, and the haricots verts were cold, but no food had ever tasted better. I ate every single bite. Afterward, we took the cakes upstairs and devoured them in bed, kissing and licking and growing delirious on chocolate and sex, loving like there was no tomorrow.

But tomorrow came.

8

"Mrs. Griffith, let me begin by expressing my deepest condolences for the loss of your husband."

Dad, Dave and I are sitting shoulder to shoulder, a united front across from our Liberty Airlines point of contact, Ann Margaret Myers, a thin, blonde woman in a punishing ponytail. The tag hanging from her neck identifies her as Care Specialist, and I hate her on sight. I hate her starched pink blouse and the way she's buttoned it up all the way to the notch in her throat. I hate her long, French-tipped fingernails and the way she clasps her hands so fiercely together that the skin turns white. I hate her thin lips and her mud-puddle eyes and her mask of empathy so exaggerated, I have to sit on my hands so I don't punch it off her face.

My father leans both forearms onto the wooden table. "Actually, Ms. Myers, we'd like you to begin with an explanation of how the media learned Will's name before his own wife was told he was on the plane."

Ann Margaret's spine goes ramrod straight. "Excuse me?"

Dad lifts a shoulder, but the gesture is anything but casual. "You'd think an airline would have better ways of informing the next of kin than releasing the passengers' names to the media, but what do I know? I suppose you folks at Liberty Air have a different way of doing things. What I can tell you is that your policy is a shitty one."

"I . . ." Her lips flap around like a stranded fish, and her gaze flits back and forth between me and my father. "You learned about Mr. Griffith from the news?"

The three of us nod, once and in unison.

"Oh, my God, I had no idea. I can assure you, Mrs. Griffith, Mr. Stafford, that is absolutely *not* Liberty Air's policy. Someone over there made a huge, grave error, and I am so very, very sorry."

I know what she's doing. She's distancing herself from both the airline and their mistake, and I'm not buying it. Not even a little bit.

And judging from his scowl, neither is my father. "I appreciate that, Ms. Myers, but I'm sure you can understand that an apol-

84

ogy from you isn't going to cut it. We'd like an explanation, and we want to hear it from the person responsible." He leans back and crosses his arms, commanding, authoritative and in charge. On a good day, my father is someone to be reckoned with. Today he's supreme command.

Ann Margaret is clearly rattled. "I absolutely understand. As soon as we're done here, I will find out what went wrong and then coordinate a face-to-face meeting between that person and your family. Does that sound like an acceptable solution to the three of you?"

Dad gives her a curt nod, but I don't move. To me it sounds like her throwing us a bone, but I'm too tired, too shaken and shattered to say anything without flying across the desk and wrapping my hands around her neck.

The room Liberty Airlines has stalled us in is an airline executive lounge in Hartsfield's brand-new international terminal. It's plush and roomy, decorated in dark jewel tones, with sitting areas and a bar and an entire wall of windows overlooking the concourse. Airplanes lumber back and forth on the other side of the glass like giant missiles, taunting me with murderous intent.

"Has the press found you yet?" Ann Margaret says, and I turn back to the table.

Dave nods. "They've been calling the house all morning, and there are a couple of vans camped out on the street. Some of the reporters even had the nerve to ring the doorbell and ask for an interview."

She shakes her head, disgusted. "We've specifically asked the media outlets to respect the privacy of our families, but not all of the journalists listen. What I can do is make sure you get out of here without having to interact with them. And may I suggest you appoint a family friend to be media contact? That way, you won't have to talk to them until you're ready."

My father adds another bullet to his list, which has grown to a handful of pages.

All around us, people are weeping. A silver-haired man with unshaven cheeks, an Indian woman in a teal-and-silver sari, a black teenager with diamond studs bigger than my engagement solitaire. Tears roll down their cheeks unchecked, and the air in the room pulses with despair. Seeing their sorrow is like watching someone yawn, uncontrollable and infectious. Suddenly and without warning, I'm weeping, too.

Ann Margaret passes me a pack of tissues.

"Ms. Myers," Dad says, "perhaps you could give us a quick update on the crash.

Is there any new information?"

"Please. Call me Ann Margaret, and of course. As you may have heard on the news, both black boxes have been recovered, the flight data recorder and the cockpit voice recorder, and they've been sent on to the National Transportation Safety Board for analysis. I do want to warn you, though. Their final report will likely take months, if not years."

I wince. A month feels like an eternity, but years?

"In the meantime . . ." She pushes a packet of paper an inch thick across the desk and taps a fingertip on a website address printed across the top. "This is a dark website, meaning it's not meant for the general public. There are no links leading to it, and only people who type in the exact address will be able to find it. Liberty Airlines will use it to issue statements and provide updates to friends and family of the passengers as soon as information becomes available. You'll also find a list of contact names, phone numbers and email addresses for every employee on the disaster management team. They are available 24/7, as am I. You are my family, and as such, my very first priority."

I look up. "What do you mean we're your

family?"

She smiles at me, not unkindly. "Every passenger's family receives their own Care Specialist. I'm yours. You are my family. If there's anything at all that any of you need, all you have to do is say so and I'll take care of it."

"Excellent. You can start with giving me back my husband."

Her shoulders fall a good inch, and she tilts her head, reassembling her empathy mask. "I wish I could do that, Mrs. Griffith. I really do."

I hate this woman. I hate her with such an intensity that for a second or two, I actually blame her for the crash. I know Ann Margaret is not the one who performed the sloppy safety check or who banked left when she should have banked right, but I don't believe her *I'm on your side here* attitude, either. If this woman really had my best interests at heart like she claims, she'd tell me what I really want to hear.

"How did my husband get on that airplane?"

It takes Ann Margaret a second or two to register my change of subject, and then she gives me an apologetic smile. "I'm sorry, I'm not sure what you mean."

"What I mean is, did someone actually

see him walk on? Because he was late leaving the house, and even if he didn't hit rush-hour traffic, which he most probably did, he would have had to haul ass through security and to the terminal. He probably would have been the last person on the plane, if he even made it on time."

She shifts in her chair, and she glances at my father as if to request a little help. When she doesn't get any, her gaze returns to me. "Are you asking how Liberty Airlines knows your husband boarded?"

"Yeah. That's exactly what I'm asking."

"Okay. Why don't we just back up a minute, then? All airlines have procedures in place, so mistakes like the one you're suggesting could never happen. Passengers' tickets are scanned at the security checkpoint and then again at the gate, right before they board the plane. Technology doesn't lie. It assures us there are no false positives."

I hear Will's scoff, as clearly and surely as if he were sitting right here, right beside me. If he were, he'd tell this lady that technology lies by design, because it is created and controlled by humans. There are bugs. There are crashes. There are false positives and false negatives, too. So Ann Margaret can try to talk me out of beating this particular horse, but as far as I'm concerned, this horse is far from dead.

My flare of fury settles into one of self-satisfaction. If Liberty Air can make a mistake as grievous as neglecting to call me before contacting the media, then who's to say Will's name on that passenger manifest isn't another? A gigantic, life-altering mistake, but a mistake all the same.

"What if halfway down the Jetway, he turned around and went back out? He could have slipped right past the gate agent while she was scanning someone else's ticket. Maybe she didn't even notice."

"It's possible, I suppose . . ." Ann Margaret looks away, and she doesn't bother to conceal her doubt. She doesn't ask the most obvious question, either — why would anyone turn around and leave? If she did, I'd tell her because it was the wrong flight, headed in the wrong direction. "Perhaps you'd like to speak with someone?"

Now we're talking. I'm already nodding, assuming she's referring to her boss or, better yet, the head of security for Hartsfield.

"Religious or secular? We have Red Cross grief counselors on hand, as well as clerics of every major religion. Which would you prefer?"

Irritation surges up my chest, lurching me forward in my chair. "I don't need to talk to a psychologist. I *am* a psychologist. What I need is for someone to tell me where my husband is."

Ann Margaret falls silent. She chews her bottom lip and glances around at her colleagues, stationed at nearby tables and consoling their inconsolables, as if to say *Now what? They didn't teach us this one at Care Specialist training.* I've stumped her.

"So, what now?" my father asks, ever the planner. "What do we do next?"

Ann Margaret looks relieved to be prompted back on script. "Well, there will be a memorial service this weekend here in town. Liberty Airlines is still working out the logistics, but as soon as I know the time and place, I'll pass it on. I am available to pick you up at your house and escort you to the service if you'd like. It's of course up to you, but there will be media there, and I'll know the way to get around them. And if you're interested, I can help plan a visit to the accident site."

My throat closes around the last two words. *Accident site.* I can barely stand seeing the images on television. The idea of walking among the wreckage, of standing on the earth where 179 souls crashed into it, feels like a vicious punch in the gut.

"There's no hurry," Ann Margaret says,

filling up the silence. "When and if you're ready." When I still don't respond, she consults her papers for the next item on the agenda. "Oh, yes. Liberty Airlines is working with a third-party vendor to manage the process of returning personal effects to the rightful family members. You'll find the form on page twenty-three of your packet. The more detail you can provide here, the better. Pictures, inscription texts, distinguishing characteristics. Things like that."

Will isn't big on jewelry, but he wears a wedding band and a watch. Both were gifts I had engraved with our initials, and both are things I'd want back.

"Again, you're assuming he was on that plane."

My denial, I know, is textbook. I don't believe, therefore it cannot be true. Will is not buried under Missouri soil. He's in Orlando, dazzling conference attendees with his keynote on predictive analytics and bitching in the hotel bar about the heat. Or maybe he's already home, rumpled and tired from wherever he's been all this time, wondering what's for dinner. I picture myself walking through the door to find him there, and a bubble of joy rises in my chest.

"Mrs. Griffith, I realize how difficult this must be, but —"

"Do you? Do you really? Because was it your husband on the plane? Was it your mother or father or daughter or son who was blown to bits all over a cornfield? No? Well, then, you *don't* know, and you *can't* realize how difficult this is for me. For anyone in this room."

Ann Margaret leans into the desk, and her brow crumples. "No, I didn't lose a family member on Flight 23, but I can still feel deep sadness and compassion for you as well as everyone else here today. I share in your anxiety and distress, and I'm on your side. Tell me what you want me to do and I'll do it."

"Give me my husband back!" I shriek.

All around us, tables fall still, and heads turn in my direction. *Solidarity,* their teary faces say. They want their loved ones back, too. If we were sitting close enough, we'd bump fists. It's a shitty, fucked-up society, but at least I'm not the only one in it.

Dave presses a palm to my right shoulder blade, a show of brotherly support. He knows I'm on the verge of a meltdown, and I know his newest, most urgent goal is to get me out of here. "Is there anything else?"

"Yes. It would help greatly if you would provide the name and address of your husband's doctor and dentist. Be assured that all information collected is confidential and will be managed only by forensic personnel under the guidance of the medical examiner. And I'm very sorry to have to ask, but, um, we'll also need a DNA sample."

My father reaches for my hand. "Anything else?" he says through clenched teeth.

Ann Margaret pulls an envelope from her packet and pushes it across the desk. "This is an initial installment from Liberty Airlines to cover any crash-related expenses. I know this is a very difficult time, and these funds are intended to, well, take a little of the pressure off you and your family."

I pick up the envelope, peek at the printed paper inside. Apparently, death has a price, and if I'm to believe Liberty Air, it's $54,378.

"There is more forthcoming," Ann Margaret says.

The anger that's been simmering under the surface since I walked through the door fires into red-hot rage. The flames lick at my organs and shoot lava through my veins, burning me up from the inside out. My hands ball into tight fists, and I sit up ramrod straight in my chair. "Let me ask you something, Margaret Ann."

"It's Ann . . ." She catches herself, summons up a sympathetic smile. "Of course.

Anything."

"Who do you work for?"

A pause. She furrows her brow as if to say *Whatever are you talking about?* "Mrs. Griffith, I already told you. I work for you."

"No. I mean whose name is at the top of your paychecks?"

She opens her mouth, then closes it, hauls a breath through her nose and tries again. "Liberty Airlines."

I rip the check in two, reach for my bag and stand. "That's what I thought."

Ann Margaret is true to her word on one account at least. When we push through the door of the Family Assistance Center, a handful of uniformed Liberty Air agents hustle us through the terminal and out a side door. If any journalists spot us on the way to the car, we don't see them. The agents act as a human shield.

They pile us into Dad's Cherokee and slam the doors, backing away as soon as Dad starts the engine. He slides the gear in Reverse but doesn't remove his foot from the brake. Like me, Dad's still in shock, trying to process everything we learned in the past hour. I lose track of how long we sit there, the motor humming underneath us, staring silently out the window at the concrete barrier of the parking deck, and it's not until I feel Dad's warm palm on my knee and Dave's on my shoulder that I realize that this whole time, I've been crying.

9

All night long, I dream I'm Will. I'm high in the clouds above a flyover state, safely buckled in an aisle seat, when suddenly the bottom drops out of the sky. The plane lurches and rolls, and the motors' screams are as deafening as my own, as terrified as the other passengers' underneath and above and on all sides of me. We heave into a full-on nosedive, careening to the earth with irreversible velocity. I wake up right as we explode into a fireball, Will's terror gritty in my mouth. Did he know what was happening? Did he scream and cry and pray? In his last moments, did he think of me?

The questions won't leave me alone. They march through my mind like an army on attack, blitzing through my brain and lurching me upright in bed. Why would my husband tell me he's going one place but get on a plane to another? Why would he create a fake conference with a fake flyer as fake evidence? How many other times has he not been where he said he would be? My heart gives a kick at that last one, the obvious answer like trying to jam a square peg in a round hole. Will wouldn't cheat. He *wouldn't.*

Then, what? Why lie?

I twist around on the bed, groping in the early-morning light for his empty pillow. I press the cool cotton to my face and inhale the scent of my husband, and memories swell in razor-sharp flashes of lucidity. Will's square jaw, lit up from below by his laptop screen. The way his hair was always mussed on one side from running a hand up it, an unconscious habit when he was thinking about something. That smile of his whenever I came into the room, the one that no one else ever got but me. More than anything, the sensation of how it felt to be whole and to be his, what it felt like to be us.

I need my husband. I need his sleep-warmed body and his thermal touch and his voice whispering in my ear, calling me his very favorite person. I close my eyes and there he is, lying in the bed next to me, bare chested and a finger crooked in invitation, and an empty heaviness fills my chest. Will's dead. He's gone, and now, so am I.

The fresh wound reopens with a searing

hot pain, and I can't stay in this bed — our bed — for another second. I kick off the covers, slip on Will's robe and head down the stairs.

In the living room, I flip the wall switch and pause while my eyes adjust to the sudden light. When they do, it's like looking at a picture of my and Will's life, frozen the moment before he left for the airport. His sci-fi paperback, its pages dog-eared and curling up at the corners, sits on the side table by his favorite chair, next to a mini mountain of cellophane candy wrappers I'm always nagging him to pick up. I smile at the same time I feel the tears build, but I blink them away, because one little word is slicing through my memories like a machete.

Why?

I push away from the wall and head over to the bookshelves.

When we moved into the house last year, Will nixed the idea of a home office. "A techie doesn't need a desk," he said at the time, "only a laptop with a multi-core processor and a place to perch. But if you want one, go for it." I didn't want one. I liked to perch wherever Will did, at the kitchen counter, on the couch, in a shady spot on the back deck. The desk in the living room became a spot for sorting mail, storing pens and paper clips, and displaying our favorite framed photographs — snapshots of happier times. I turn my back to the desk so I can't see.

But inevitably, home ownership comes with a paper trail, and Will stored ours in the living room built-ins. I kneel on the floor, yank open the doors and marvel at a display worthy of a Container Store catalog. Colorful rows of matching three-ring binders, their contents marked with matching printed labels. Everything is ordered and grouped by year. I pull the binders out, laying them across the hardwoods by priority. Where would be the most likely place to find another lie?

A trio of letter trays are stacked at the very left side of the cabinet, and I flip through the contents. Work-related brochures, a yellowed *Atlanta Business Chronicle* with a front-page article on AppSec, tickets for the Rolling Stones concert later this summer. A neat stack of unpaid bills is on top, clipped together and labeled with a Post-it in Will's handwriting: *To Do ASAP.* My heart revs up, pumping too much blood all at once, and I begin to sweat despite the chill in the room. Will isn't dead. He's coming back. The evidence is right here, in his distinct scrawl. A dead person can't go to concerts or knock out to-do lists, and my meticulous husband never leaves a task unfinished.

I sit cross-legged among the papers, sifting through the binders one by one. Bank statements. Credit cards. Loans and contracts and tax returns. I'm looking for . . . I don't know what. A toe-dip into the husband I thought I knew so well, any clue as to why he has suddenly morphed into the kind of man who lies.

An hour and a half later, I come across one. A fresh copy of his will, a version I've never seen before, updated only a month ago, and the discovery hits me like a punch in the gut. He revised his will without telling me? It's not like we have a lot of assets. A heavily mortgaged house, a couple of car loans and not much else. Will doesn't have any living family members, and we don't have children. Yet. Probably. Except for the maybe-baby, our situation is pretty straightforward. I flip through the pages, searching for the reason why.

I find it on page seven: two new life insurance policies Will purchased earlier this year. Together with the one he already had, the payout adds up to a grand total of — I have to look twice to be sure — two and a half million dollars? I drop the papers onto my thighs, my head spinning with all the zeros. The amount is staggering and completely out of proportion to his mid-level salary. I know I should be glad for his preparedness, but I can't help the new questions that poke and prod at me. Why two new policies? Why so much?

"Dare I ask?" I look up to find Dave standing in the doorway. He's wearing his husband's Harvard T-shirt and pajama pants, the fabric rumpled from bed, and yawning hard enough to crack his jaw. By now it's barely seven, and Dave has never been a morning person.

"I'm searching for clues."

"I figured as much." He stretches his long arms up to the ceiling and twists, a noisy wringing out of his spine that makes me think of bubble wrap. "But what I meant is, dare I ask if you've found evidence of another life in Seattle?"

"The opposite, actually. No unusual payments, no names I don't recognize. Only more evidence that when it comes to organization, my husband is completely anal." I pick up the will, flip through to page seven. "Do you have a life insurance policy?"

"Yeah."

"For how much?"

He rubs a hand over his dark hair, making it stand up in tousled tufts. "I don't remember. Just under a million or so."

"What about James?"

"Somewhere around the same, I think. Why?"

"Two and a half million dollars." I shake the paper in the air between us. "*Million,* Dave. Doesn't that seem extraordinarily high?"

He shrugs. "I assume you're the beneficiary?"

"Of course," I say, even as another question elbows its way into my consciousness. Who's to say he didn't purchase others, to benefit whoever's in Seattle?

"Then, yes and no. As I recall, the calculation is something like ten times your annual salary, so, yes, the amount Will insured himself for is steep. But he loved you. He probably just wanted to make sure you're well provided for."

Dave's words start a slow leak of grief, but I swallow it whole. Yes, my husband loved me, but he also lied. "Two of the policies were bought three months ago."

His head jerks up, and his brows slide into a sharp V. "That's either an incredible coincidence or incredibly creepy. I can't decide."

"I'm going for creepy."

He sinks onto a chair and scrubs his face.

"Okay, let's think this through. Life insurance doesn't come for free, and an amount that big would have cost him a hundred bucks or more a month."

I point to the pile of binders, one of them containing this year's bank statements. "Well, he didn't pay for it from our mutual account. I combed through every single statement and didn't find anything but a shocking amount of Starbucks charges."

"Could he have another bank account?"

"It's possible, I guess. But if it's not here, how do I find it?"

"His computer. Emails, bookmarks, history files. Things like that."

"Will never goes anywhere without his laptop. Ditto for phone and iPad."

"Can you log in to his email?"

I shake my head. "No way. Will isn't like us, people who still use the name of their childhood dog as a password. He uses those computer-generated log-ins that are impossible to crack, and a different one for everything."

"Even for Facebook?"

"*Especially* for Facebook. Do you know how often social media accounts get hacked? All the freaking time. Next thing you know, all fifteen hundred of your Twitter followers are getting DMs from you hocking fake

Ray-Bans."

Will would be so proud. They're his words, the ones he preached to me when I told him *rocky321* is my password for everything. Now they roll right off my tongue.

I sigh, looking around at the messy piles of papers and binders. There are no more answers in these, that much is certain. I scoot forward on my knees, begin shoving everything back into the cabinet.

"You know the next place I'd look if I wanted to find my husband's secrets? And I tell you this at the risk of confirming every stereotype you've ever heard about gay men."

I reach for another binder, glancing over my shoulder at my brother, and we say the words in unison.

"His closet."

Will's closet is a neat, orderly world where each item is organized by color and grouped by category. Work shirts, pressed and starched and buttoned. A row of pants with pleats sharp enough to slice bread. Jeans and T-shirts and polos, every hanger matching and perfectly spaced. I pull on the top drawer handle, and it opens to reveal his boxers, rolled into tight Tootsie Rolls and stacked in even rows.

This is Will's domain, and he's everywhere I look. I stand here for a moment, drinking him in like wine, feeling a quivering ache take hold in my stomach. I sense him in the orderliness, in his preference for soft fabrics and rich jewel tones, in the scent of spicy soap and mint. Like I could turn around and there he'd be, smiling that smile that makes him look younger and older at the same time. The first time he aimed it at me in a rainy Kroger parking lot, I liked it so much I agreed to a cup of coffee, even though he'd just rammed his car into my bumper.

"You could have just asked for my number, you know," I teased him a few days later, as he was walking me to the door after our first official date. "Our fenders didn't have to take such a beating."

"How else was I supposed to get your attention? You were driving away."

I laughed. "Poor, innocent fenders."

"A worthy sacrifice." He kissed me then, and I knew he was right.

"You okay?" Dave says now, his tone gentle.

I nod, not trusting my voice.

"Are you sure you want to do this?" He searches my face with a concerned gaze.

"You don't have to help, you know."

"I know, but I want to." He doesn't look convinced, so I add, "I need to."

"Okay, then." He points back toward the beginning, to where Will's sweaters are stacked in perfect piles in the cubbies. "I'll start on that end and you on the other. We'll meet in the middle."

We work mostly in silence. We check every pocket on every pair of pants, shorts and jeans. Dave shakes out every sweater, and I dump out every drawer. We peer inside every single shoe, reach into every single sock. It's a good hour's work, and in the end, we find nothing but lint.

"I know your husband is meticulous, but this is insane. At the very least, we should have found some trash. Old business cards, receipts, some spare change. Is there a spot somewhere where he emptied his pockets?"

"We keep a spare change jar in the laundry room, but as for the other things . . ." I lift both shoulders high enough to brush my earlobes.

My brother and I are seated cross-legged on the closet floor, surrounded by messy piles of Will's clothes and shoes. The closet looks like a tornado came through it, whipping clothes off the hangers and out of the bins and dumping everything onto the floor.

I pick up one of Will's sweaters, a baby-bottom-soft cashmere I bought him last year for his birthday, and hold it up to my nose, inhaling the familiar scent.

In that moment, I feel Will so strongly that it stops the breath in my throat and prickles the hairs on the back of my neck. *Hey, sweetness,* he says in my head, as clearly as if he's standing right beside me. *Whatcha doing?*

I shake the image off, drop the fabric onto my lap. "Now what?"

Dave pauses to think. "His car?"

"It's at the airport."

He nods. "Dad and I will figure out how to get it back. In the meantime, what about social media? When's the last time you checked his Facebook page?"

Dave's question stuns me. Will and I share a home, a life, a past. Our relationship has always been built on trust and honesty. He gives me leeway, and I give him a long leash.

"Never, and stop looking at me like that. Snooping is not something we do, ever. There's never been any reason for either of us to be jealous or suspicious."

Dave inhales, but he doesn't say the words both of us are thinking.

Until now.

James's voice comes around the corner.

"Hey, Dave?"

"In the closet," Dave calls out.

James's laugh beats him to the closet doorway, where he appears clad in head-to-toe lululemon and clutching a white gift bag. His blondish hair is plastered to his forehead with rain and sweat, and his breath comes in quick, hard puffs. "There are so many jokes I could make right now."

Dave rolls his eyes. "Did your run take you by the mall?"

James looks down at the bag like he just remembered he was holding it. "Oh, right. It's for Iris, I guess. I found it hanging on the front doorknob. There's no note."

I take the bag and pull out a brand-new iPhone 6, one of the big ones with more gigabytes than I could ever use, still in the sealed box.

"Why would somebody give you an iPhone?" James says.

"Because she feels sorry for me, and she knows I broke mine." I drop the box back into the bag and hand everything back.

"Do you want me to set it up for you?" Dave says.

"No, I want you to take it back to the store, get a refund and then buy me a different one with my own money."

"Wouldn't it just be more efficient to write

109

this person a check?"

As usual, my brother is right. I do need a new phone, though I'll be damned if anybody but me pays for it. "Okay, but you'll need my laptop to install it. I think it's in a kitchen drawer somewhere. And while you're at it, look up what that thing costs, will you?" I'll have to log on to the school system to find Claire's address, then I can drop her a check in the mail.

"Sure thing."

That settled, James leans a shoulder against the doorjamb, taking in the shambles we've made of the closet. The rows of askew hangers, the mountain of sweaters and shirts on the floor, the clothes hanging out of the drawers like a half-off bin at Target. "Do I even want to know?"

"We're snooping," Dave says.

"And?"

"Nothing. Not even a gas receipt."

Dave's tone is heavy with meaning, as is his expression. A hard knot blooms in my belly at the silent conversation that passes between the two men. *What kind of person leaves nothing, not even a gum wrapper or a forgotten penny, behind? The kind who doesn't want his wife to know what he's up to.* Their words come across so clearly, they might as well have said them out loud.

"He wasn't cheating," I say, my voice as unyielding as I feel. There are some things you know to the very core of yourself, things you would bet your life and very last penny on. This is one of them. "He wasn't."

Dave gestures all around him, to the piles of clothes and shoes. "Sweetheart, no man is this vigilant. There's got to be something going on here."

"Of course there's something going on here. Will got on the wrong plane, flew off in the wrong direction. But not because of another woman. Because of something else."

James opens his mouth to offer up an opinion, and Dave gives him a hard look, one that says *zip it.* I know as soon as they're behind the closed door of the guest room across the hall, they'll be arguing points and discussing theories, and I suppose I should get used to it. My family will not be the first ones to think the worst of Will, that he has another woman — a girlfriend, a wife, the mother of his children — tucked away in a suburb of Seattle.

A stab of fury steals my breath. How could Will do this to me? How could he leave me here all alone, unarmed and clueless, to fight this battle? I want to defend him, I want to defend *us,* but I don't know how. He's left me with nothing but questions.

How am I supposed to prove everyone wrong?

Dave presses a palm to my knee. "We'll keep looking, okay? We'll get on a plane and go to Seattle if we have to. We'll find his something else."

I nod, my heart seizing with love for my twin brother. His offer doesn't come out of a staunch belief in my husband, but mainly out of belief in me. He's willing to search for another explanation only because I'm so adamant there is one.

"You are my second favorite person on the planet," I say, right before dissolving into tears, because it's no longer true. Without Will here, Dave just got moved up to first place.

10

Sunday blooms bright and beautiful, one of those perfect spring days for which Atlanta is famous. Blue skies. Warm sunshine. A crisp breeze carrying whiffs of grass and honeysuckle. The kind of day Will and I loved to spend lazing in Piedmont Park or exploring the Atlanta BeltLine. The kind of day that's too bright and sunny for a funeral.

Liberty Airlines has secured the Atlanta Botanical Gardens for the memorial service, and as I lumber through it in dark clothes and darker glasses, I grudgingly admit the choice is pretty brilliant. With its swooping bridges and reflecting pools and Technicolor Chihuly sculptures everywhere, the park is pretty spectacular. Even better, no journalists are allowed through the gate, and there isn't a zoom lens on the planet that can reach us through the leafy cover. I picture Ann Margaret at the employee meeting, nodding enthusiastically when it was suggested. Who can be bereft when the tulips are in full bloom?

Mom winds her arm through mine, presses her temple to my shoulder. "How are you holding up?"

"I'm okay."

Thankfully, it's not a lie. As soon as we pulled into the garden's parking deck, everything inside me went completely numb, like someone shot me full of Novocain. My body going into survival mode, I guess, and I'm grateful for the reprieve. It sure as hell beats sobbing or throwing up, both of which I spent all day yesterday doing, after Dad handed a solemn-faced Liberty Air representative the items he'd collected from Will's side of the bathroom — his toothbrush, a forgotten fingernail clipping, a few stray hairs. Closure — that's what genetics is supposed to provide for Liberty Air families. But I don't want closure. To hell with closure. I want someone to tell me they couldn't find one piece, not one teeny tiny speck, of my husband on that Missouri cornfield.

Uniformed park employees herd us down bricked pathways into the Rose Garden, a large grassy field set against a backdrop of the Midtown Atlanta skyline. We file into a middle row and take a seat on padded fold-

ing chairs, my gaze picking out a few familiar faces from the Family Assistance Center.
The Indian woman in another sari, this time
white. The black teenager minus the studs,
his face streaked with unchecked tears. The
sun reflects off their wet faces like a beacon,
making me glad for my sunglasses. Especially when I spot Ann Margaret, watching
from the sidelines. Her look of obvious
longing transports me back to the halls of
Lake Forrest, to the pimply-faced girls
desperate to be part of the popular crowd.
We are "her" family, and we're excluding
her. I give her my best mean-girl cold
shoulder and turn away.

The service is an hour and a half of
infuriating, excruciating torture filled with
cheesy songs and a long procession of
speakers, people I've never met before and
will probably never see again. They package
their condolences into ridiculous platitudes,
things like *Let your love be stronger than your
desperation and sorrow* and *Let us concentrate on filling the holes with love and hope.*
Hope for what? I hold my breath and grit
my teeth so I don't scream the words. *Hope
for fucking what?* Thanks to Liberty Air, I
don't have the slightest clue.

Liberty Airlines. Two words I can't utter
without shaking with fury. I hate them for

their sloppy mechanics, their faux concern, their incompetent disaster planners and clumsy crew. If that pilot didn't die in the crash, I'd want to kill him myself.

And where is the pilot's family? Are they here? I study the profiles of the folks weeping all around me, trying to find his wife or husband, their 2.5 loving children. Would they dare to come? Would they be able to face the 178 other families, knowing their loved one made the mistake that brought down the plane?

After the service, we gather for refreshments by a rose arbor better suited to a wedding than a funeral. The flowers won't bloom for weeks, their tight buds only barely there nubs, but the climbing vines with their pale green shoots mock me with their optimism. *Alive, alive, alive,* they scream, while my Will is not.

"Can I get you something to drink?" Dad asks, gesturing to the edge of the crowd, where a uniformed server stands with a tray of icy drinks.

"A Coke," I tell him, even though I'm not thirsty. I figure at least if I'm holding a glass, I can't slug somebody in the gut. But as soon as Dad has slipped into the crowd, I reconsider. "Actually, can we just leave? I really want to go home."

Mom and Dave exchange a look. "Maybe you want to talk to some of the other families?" Mom says.

"No. I really, really don't." As a psychologist, I am a big believer in group therapy, in finding solace with others who have been through a similar tragedy. But doing so with these people here means resigning myself to Will being on that plane, and until DNA tells me otherwise, I'm hanging on to my denial with both hands.

My boss, Ted Rawlings, steps up in front of me. Though I didn't expect to see him here, I'm not surprised. He treats everyone at Lake Forrest, staff and students alike, like one big extended family. Of course he'd be at one of our funerals.

He reaches for my hand, wraps it between both of his. "On behalf of everyone at Lake Forrest Academy, I offer you my deepest, most sincere condolences. I'm so very sorry for your loss. If there's anything I can do, that any of us can do, please, please let me know."

Tears spring to my eyes, not at his words but mostly at his tie — a solemn, staid black so unlike the colorful ones he wears to school. A funeral tie if I've ever seen one. I bet he bought it for the occasion, and the thought makes me unbelievably, inexplicably sad. "Thank you, Ted. That means a lot."

"Take as much time as you need, okay? We'll see you back at school whenever you're ready." He squeezes my hand, then moves on to my mother, becoming the first in an impromptu receiving line. More colleagues and their spouses, a man I belatedly recognize as Will's boss, a few of his coworkers. They file by, repeating much of what Ted just said. The entire Lake Forrest lacrosse team is next, solemn-faced and saying all the right things, but an itchy rash spreads across my skin with each hand I shake. I don't want their sympathy. I don't want their kind words. I only want my husband back.

"Oh, Iris," a familiar voice says, and I'm surrounded by my three best girlfriends, their eyes puffy and bloodshot. Elizabeth, Lisa and Christy huddle around, wrapping me in a hug that smells like flowers and honey and tears.

"He wasn't supposed to be on that plane," I say, pressing my forehead to theirs. "He's supposed to be in Orlando."

There's nothing they can say, no hope they can offer, so instead they scoot in tighter and say nothing at all. The idea that they know me well enough not to plug the silence with platitudes fills me with love at

118

the same time it wrings my heart with a fresh round of grief.

"Thanks for coming," I whisper, right before Mom swoops in. She did this at her and Dad's fortieth anniversary celebration last year, too, moving the line along when someone lingered too long. Now she takes a couple of hands in hers and tugs, her smile so genuine and the move so smooth, nobody but me is the wiser.

A blond man in a pinstripe suit steps up next. "Didn't I see you at the Family Assistance Center?"

"I was there," I say and leave it at that. The thing is, I would have remembered this guy by his height alone. He's shockingly tall, the kind of tall you see prancing up and down a basketball court.

Then again, I was a wreck, and maybe he was sitting down. Either way, he lost someone on that plane, I'm positive of it. His face is molded into something polite and pleasant, but his green eyes give him away. They are haunted, and nothing about this is pleasant.

He offers me a hand. "Evan Sheffield. My wife and baby daughter were on the plane."

I wince, at the same time a shiver of something that feels a lot like relief passes through me. This poor guy lost two people on that plane. Apparently, there are people here who have it worse than me.

"Iris Griffith. My husband, Will . . ." I swallow. I still can't manage to get the awful words past my lips.

Evan gives me a nod, his grimace telling me he understands. Of course, he does. "I wanted to let you know, I'm organizing an association for friends and family of the passengers and crew. I figure if we band together, we'll get a lot more accomplished."

"Like what?"

"Like figuring out what we're supposed to be doing and who we're supposed to be listening to, for starters. I don't know about you, but I don't plan to blindly follow the path my Care Specialist laid out for me. I'm not sure a Liberty Air employee is our best advocate at this point."

"I agree."

"Good." He pulls a business card from his jacket and passes it to me. He points to his name in swirling blue letters. "Shoot me an email with your contact information, and I'll add you to the list. First meeting will be early next week sometime at my firm, Rogers, Sheffield and Shea in Midtown. The address and parking instructions will be included in the email."

I know Rogers, Sheffield and Shea. Everybody in the South knows Rogers, Sheffield and Shea, after they overturned the 2001 conviction of Troy Coles, a Savannah man sentenced to death for a murder he didn't commit. I look back down at his name, a name I now remember as the lead attorney in the case. "You're that Evan Sheffield?"

"Yes, and I'm not the only attorney in the group if that's what you're asking. We've also got a couple of nurses, a sleep therapist and a handful of doctors. If you have a specific talent or knowledge you'd like to volunteer, let me know in the email. It's not mandatory, of course. You can always just come and listen."

"My daughter's a psychologist," Mom says, not able to help herself. "Agnes Scott and Emory educated."

"I'm not sure I'll do anybody any good," I quickly add. "I'm kind of hanging by a thread here."

Evan tries to push up a smile, but it looks more like a grimace. "Welcome to the club. Everybody keeps telling me we'll survive this, but if you ask me, the jury's still out." He inhales, pulling himself together. "Anyway, nice to meet you, and I'll watch for your email."

He moves on, and I watch him give his spiel to the next person, his shoulders slumped with a weariness that I feel down to my bones. Grief is exhausting, and this man lost two people to my one. Where does he get the energy? My gaze travels to a patch of thick, fluffy grass, and I wonder if I could lie on it, just for a minute.

Dave steps up beside me, sliding an arm around my waist, and I lean into him. I meant it when I told Evan I was hanging by a thread — one that's frayed enough to give out any second. I also meant it when I told my mother I wanted to go home. Suddenly, leaving is my newest and most urgent goal. I can't take another person in this parade of mourners.

"Let's go."

Dave points across the grass, where they're setting up giant trays of food on a buffet table. "But —"

"I'm not kidding, Dave. I need you to get me out of here. Now."

Dave looks over his shoulder, craning his neck. "Okay, but Mom just headed off in search of the bathroom, and I don't know where James went." He turns back, gives my hand a quick squeeze. "Hang tight. I'll go round up the troops."

"That'd be great. Thanks."

As soon as he's gone, there's another tug on my sleeve. Before I can stop myself, I whip around, my face tightening into a scowl. *"What?"*

If the man is insulted by my lack of manners, he doesn't let it show. He smiles, a flash of bright white against coffee-bean skin, and holds up a glass of clear, sparkling liquid. "San Pellegrino. You looked like you could use something cold."

"Oh." Guilt surges, and I stretch my mouth into what I hope looks like an apologetic smile. "Sorry, I'm not usually that much of an asshole, but . . ." I take the glass from his hand, tip it in his direction. "Thank you. Really."

"Corban Hayes," he says. "I'm a friend of Will's from the gym."

I sip my water, taking him in over the rim. That this guy spends time at the gym is not exactly news. Tall and lean, with muscles so clearly defined that his veins pop, like black rope standing up on his brown arms. The type of guy who does one-handed pull-ups while chanting *eat clean, train dirty* to anyone who walks by. Will worked out, but he wasn't a gym rat. Weights and treadmills were necessary evils, but only so he could eat as many burritos as he pleased. How good of friends could they have been?

"Will gave me shit for putting the weights up in the wrong place. I gave him shit for being so anal. We've been buddies ever since."

I smile despite myself. "That's Will. He likes order."

"I'll say." Corban's expression sobers, and he shakes his head. "I'm going to miss that guy bossing me around, harassing me to change my passwords every thirty days. My company migrated over to the AppSec security suite last year, and it was the cleanest, quickest software migration we've ever experienced. Will made sure of it, and he didn't bill me for all the extra hours he spent whipping us into shape. I know AppSec was sorry to see him go."

I'm already nodding, already murmuring my thanks for his kind words, when the last ones register. "What do you mean, see him go?"

"To the new job. What's the company's name again? EPM? TPM? Something like that. I assume that's why he was on a plane to Seattle, to finalize the contract, no?"

The glass slips from my fingers, dropping onto the bricks with a loud crash. Heads swing in my direction, and something wet stings my shins.

But instead of lurching backward to avoid the mess, Corban springs forward, clamping a palm around my biceps, right as I feel myself sway. "Steady now."

I open my mouth to tell him to let go, but I can't seem to catch my breath. The air gets stuck halfway down my throat.

"Are you okay? You're white as a sheet."

My lungs have turned to stone. I can't make them expand or contract. I suck little sips of air while black dots dance around the edges of my vision. "Can't . . . breathe . . ."

"That's because you're hyperventilating. Here." He steers me toward a shady bench, parks me there. "Hold your breath. I know it feels wrong, but I promise you it'll help. Hold it for as long as you can, then breathe in through your nose as slowly as possible." He talks me through a few rounds of this, sitting down next to me and demonstrating with puffed cheeks and exaggerated pulls through flattened nostrils, until my lungs release and the dizziness subsides. "Better?"

Slightly. I nod.

He leans over, takes a look at my legs. "If I tell you you're bleeding, are you going to start hyperventilating again?" He doesn't wait for my response, just yanks a paisley pocket square from his jacket and squats on the grass, blotting it on my skin. "I don't think the cuts are deep, but you should still probably get someone to clean them up as soon as you're home."

Vaguely, I'm aware of Corban fussing over me, of a crowd gathering all around us, strangers watching with curiosity and alarm. Somebody slides off my shoe and pours icy water down a shin, and I barely notice any of it.

All along, I've been waiting for someone to tell me these past few days were a mistake, that Will was safe and sound where he was supposed to be, in Orlando. But the conference was a lie, his cover for a difficult truth: that he was headed to Seattle to uproot our lives, to begin the process of starting a new one on the opposite coast. I cover my mouth with a palm, the truth slamming me in the gut. Will had a reason to be on that plane.

Which means I have a reason to give up hope.

Will got a new job in Seattle?

I must say the words out loud, because Corban looks up. "You didn't know?"

My eyes widen. "Of course I didn't know." The words come out like darts, fast and furious. Why else would I be causing such a scene?

Corban pushes up from the ground and settles onto the bench beside me, watching me with eyes black as night. "I didn't realize he hadn't told you yet. If it makes you feel any better, I know he was going to. He was just waiting for the right time."

"When was that, when I came home to find a For Sale sign in front of the house and movers carting out all our stuff?"

"Don't be crazy. You know Will would never let strangers touch his stuff."

I know he's joking, but Corban's words hit me like a fireball shot, sudden and scalding. This guy claims Will was his friend, but he's *my* husband. I feel like a jealous lover, and this feels like an intrusion, like a third person butting into my and Will's relationship, trying to elbow in bed between us. Heat rises in my chest.

"How well do you know Will?" I say, more accusation than inquiry.

Corban's brows rise, then fall into a V. "I told you, we met at the gym."

"Not how. How *well*. It can't be all that well, seeing as he never, not once, mentioned your name. How do I even know you're telling me the truth?"

Corban doesn't look the least bit insulted. He leans back, stretching one of his bulked-up arms along the back of the bench. "Well, I know his dad disappeared when he was seven, and his mom died during his junior year of high school. I know he couch surfed for a month or two until he turned eighteen, social services breathing down his neck the whole time. I know he put himself through college and grad school, and that he was far too qualified for the work he was doing at AppSec. And I know he was bighearted and off-the-charts brilliant, an all-around good guy who fell for the love of his life in a Kroger parking lot."

I fall silent. It took me years to get all that out of Will. He didn't like to talk about his difficult past, and he hated to blow his own horn. That he shared all this with Corban says something about not only the length, but also the depth of their friendship.

"So not all that well," I mumble, and he laughs, proving yet again how well he knew my husband.

And now I'm crying again, both at Corban's obvious affection for Will and at the idea that he had a friend, one he liked and trusted enough to share the most private parts of himself but, for some reason I'll never know, decided to keep that friendship from me. Why would he do such a thing?

Corban presses a palm to the back of my hand for a quick squeeze, pulling away before the gesture can turn anything beyond friendly. "He was going to tell you about the job offer, Iris. Honestly. He wanted you to be as excited as he was. This job was the opportunity of a lifetime. But he was waiting until next weekend, at Optimist, because he didn't want the discussion to detract from your anniversary celebration."

Optimist — yet another fact Corban has gotten right. Will and I have dinner reservations at the Westside hot spot next Saturday, a rare date night with just us two.

"He told me he was going to Orlando. To a conference. He even produced a flyer featuring himself as keynote speaker."

"Orlando, huh?" Corban shakes his head. "That's something I didn't know, though I can't say I'm surprised. This new job came with a promotion and a hefty raise in salary, but Will knew neither would make it an easy decision for you. Two thousand, eight hundred and eighty-four road miles between you and your brother. That's what he kept saying he was up against."

"He wasn't wrong." I draw a shaky breath and wipe my cheeks. "I would have gone, but I would have fought him on it first."

"And who knows? He probably would have let you win."

Corban smiles, and my lips tip up in response, like one of Pavlov's dogs. It happens without me giving them permission.

"You ready?" Dave says from right behind

129

me, and I twist around. My parents and James hover at either shoulder. I give them a quick nod, then turn back to Corban.

He reaches into a pocket, passes me a business card, and I recognize the logo for a local chain of banks. "Call me anytime, okay? Day or night. If you think of any more questions or just want to talk. And for what it's worth, Will was right."

"What about?"

"What the two of you had was worth a million dented fenders."

11

According to Google, ESP stands for Enterprise Security Platform, one of Seattle's top twenty-five Best Places to Work and AppSec's leading competitor. Their client list is long and varied, an impressive list of big names and major brands from the financial, pharmaceutical, aeronautical and manufacturing industries. ESP consultants speak twenty-four languages, work in fifty-seven countries, and spend their free time skiing and biking and diving headfirst off cliffs and mountaintops. It's exactly the type of place Will would want to work if given a chance — successful and hip in an adventurous, granola sort of way. Everything about the company seems perfect for him, save the teeny tiny detail that it's located on the other side of the country.

I click around their website for a bit, scanning employee profiles and checking job boards. Most of the positions I come across are lower level or located in one of the East Coast offices, and I wonder if they already removed the job posting Will filled. The head of Human Resources is a woman named Shefali Majumdar. I click on her profile and jot her contact info onto a Post-it. She won't be in the office on a Sunday afternoon, and my question isn't exactly something you leave in a voice mail. *Hello, did you happen to hire my husband? Yes? Sorry, but it seems he won't be coming.*

"Sweetheart?" Mom says, and I look up to find her standing at the edge of the couch. "Dinner's ready."

I pull up Facebook on my laptop, thinking I'll look through Will's list of friends. Maybe one of their profiles can give me some indication on what to do, where to look next. "Y'all go ahead. I'm not hungry."

"I made mashed potatoes."

My sweet mom. She knows how much I love her mashed potatoes, and I don't have the heart to tell her the smell of them is making me want to throw up.

She perches on the armrest. "At least come sit with us and try, okay? Just a bite or two."

As much as I want to argue the point, she's probably right to be worried. Beyond the bowl of instant oatmeal I wolfed down over the counter on the morning of the crash and the handful of saltines she force-fed me just yesterday, I've barely eaten in the past five days. The therapist in me knows my lack of appetite is the result of shock and depression, that there's a physiological reason for why everything that touches my tongue tastes like cardboard, but still. The last thing I want right now is food. As soon as Mom turned her head, those crackers came right back up.

But now she's watching me with an expression I know all too well, concern mixed with determination, one that says this is a fight she won't give up. With a loud sigh, I slide my laptop to the couch cushion and follow her into the kitchen, where everyone has already gathered.

Mom shoos us to the table. "Sit, sit. I'll be over with the plates in a minute. Boys, give me a hand, will you?"

They do, and Dad swings an arm around my shoulders and pulls me into his side, dropping a kiss on my temple. "How you holding up, Squirt?"

"Hanging in there," I lie.

The truth is, I've called Will's voice mail more times than I care to count just to hear his voice, even though the sound of it kills more than it comforts me. And I can't stop thinking about what I learned from Corban at the memorial — not so much about Will's job offer in Seattle, but more so about the two men's friendship. Why would Will hide that from me? Dave is right; Will was more of a loner than a guy's guy, but he knew enough people to fill a table at KR Steakbar for his thirtieth birthday party. Sure, some of them were married to my girlfriends, but still. The point is, he talked about those men, included them in celebrations like they were buddies.

So why all the secrecy about Corban? Was Will worried I wouldn't like him for some reason? Or did Corban's friendship mean so little to Will that he didn't think to tell me? No, that can't be right. They must have been friends for Will to tell Corban such personal things, things it took Will ages to share with his own wife. I try to piece it all together, to think through the links of what I know — the job, the friendship, Seattle — but I'm too emotionally exhausted. None of it makes any sense.

My gaze lands on Will's spot at the far end of the table. Somebody — Mom, I'm guessing — placed a wicker basket, stuffed to overflowing with sympathy cards, where his plate would be. They've been coming for days now, flowery cards with even more flowery messages, and I can't bring myself to read any of them. I choose a chair at the opposite end and sit down.

"Does that sound all right to you?" my father says, and it's only when no one else answers that I realize he's talking to me.

I look over to find him watching me. "Does what sound all right?"

"That we stay until next weekend." He tilts his head to Dave and James settling steaming plates onto the table, and to Mom beyond them in the kitchen. "We've all cleared it with our work so we can get you through the first week. After that, we'll trade off for as long as you need one of us here."

"I can't ask you to do that."

"Don't be silly," Mom says, her tone a resolute mix of supreme authority and mother-hen concern. "We're staying, and that's that."

She slides a plate in front of me with a serving so massive it hangs over the edges, enough food for three people. She gives me an encouraging grin, and I try not to wince when the smell hits my nose, meat and potatoes and butter. But she's still standing there, so I swallow down my nausea and pick up a bite with my fork.

"Who was that man you were talking to at the memorial? That black guy built like a bouncer," Dave says as I'm lifting the bite to my mouth.

I want to kiss him. Yes, he's asking partly out of curiosity, but he's mostly trying to distract our hovering mother. His strategy works. As soon as she shoots him a questioning look, I slide the food from my fork.

"His name is Corban. He's a friend of Will's from the gym. A good friend, apparently."

Dave is the only one who catches my meaning behind that last word. "You didn't know this before today?"

"No. He also informed me Will was offered a new job at one of AppSec's biggest competitors." I pause, a familiar weight pressing down on my chest. "In their Seattle office."

Every head at the table swings to me.

"The two of you were moving?" Mom says, sinking into the chair across from me. "Since when?"

"Since never. Will and I never discussed it. I only learned of the job offer this afternoon, from Corban."

"Will didn't tell you he got a new job?" Dave's voice has a snap in it, a defensive edge I've heard many times, but never once directed at Will.

It sharpens the edge in mine, as well. "I

136

don't know that the offer was ever actually finalized. In fact, now that I think about it, I'm pretty sure that's why he didn't tell me. Will knew a cross-country move would have been a hard sell, and he didn't want to start the discussion with me until he knew for sure. The point is, this job gives him a compelling reason to be on that plane, as well as a reason not to tell me where he was going. This job was his something else."

Dave and James exchange a look.

"Somebody want to tell me what y'all are talking about?" Dad says from the other end of the table, his gaze bouncing around, from me to Dave to James, then back to me.

I give our parents a quick recap of my search through Will's closet, and how it turned up nothing but lint. "But if I'm right, if Will really was holding off on telling me about the new job, it would explain why we didn't find anything in his pockets. He didn't want me to come across a business card or receipt and wonder what was up."

Mom shakes her head. "Still, it's not like Will to be so sneaky. Why would he apply for a job without telling you?"

"He wouldn't. I'll bet you money he was approached for it through LinkedIn or by a headhunter. Either way, ESP's head of HR will be able to tell me. I'm calling her first thing tomorrow morning."

"Why?" Mom says. I give her a confused look, and she quickly amends. "What I mean is, her answer won't change anything. There are more pressing matters you should be concerned about right now."

"Your mother's right," Dad says. "There's a funeral to plan and a ton of paperwork to be done. The banks will probably work faster if we swing by in person."

"No, Stephen, I meant grieving. Iris needs to concentrate on the grieving process." She turns back to me, reaching over the table for my hand. "Job or no new job, sweetheart, Will got on that plane. He'll still be gone. And as unpleasant as it is, you need to work through your pain now, not push it aside to deal with later. You know this better than anyone."

Her words burn in the corners of my eyes. Logically, I know they're true. But I also know Will's lies are chasing me. I feel their sour breath in my neck and their oily hands on my shoulder blades, shoving me forward, pushing me in a search of the whys. Maybe Mom's right. Maybe my need to map out Will's last moments is a defense mechanism to delay having to deal with the pain. But still. I can't move forward until I fill in the most pressing blanks.

What else do I not know about my husband?
What else did he not tell me?
How many more lies?

Mom gives my hand a squeeze. "I'm just worried about you, sweetie. That's all."

"Thanks." Her concern sends up another surge of tears, one that this time I can't blink away. "I'm a little worried about me, too."

Later that night, after the kitchen is clean and Mom and Dad have headed upstairs for bed, I carry my laptop over to the couch and pull up Will's Facebook page.

My husband was not a big fan of social media. "Why bother?" he'd always say. "It's just a place for people to brag and lie about their lives. Like I'm supposed to believe the biggest asshole from high school is now dating a supermodel? Sorry, but I call bullshit." But like pretty much everybody else on the planet, Will had a Facebook page; he just largely ignored it.

Dave plops down beside me on the couch, throwing his bare feet up on the coffee table and shoving aside a flower arrangement with his toe. Now I know why so many obituaries include the line *in lieu of flowers* . . . They're literally everywhere, solemn springtime arrangements lined up across every horizontal surface, spilling over kitchen counters and mantelpieces, clogging the air with their heady scent.

"Maybe we should donate some of these. What do you think?"

I glance over. "Fine by me. There's a church around the corner and a dozen shelters within five miles."

"Cool. I'll get James to give me a hand."

"A hand with what?" James says, coming into the room with a bottle and three glasses. He holds the glasses by the stems in one hand and pours with the other with a surgeon's steadiness, not spilling a drop. Dave tells him about the flowers, and they agree to distribute the first load in the morning.

"Thanks," I say, taking one of the glasses from James. With my other hand, I gesture to my laptop screen, to the sea of shocked condolence posts jamming up Will's wall. "When did people start treating Facebook as a tool to communicate with the dead? Like this one. *Will, man, so sorry to hear of your passing. RIP, buddy.* Do they really think he's going to see it? He never checked his page when he was alive, much less . . ." Unable to finish, I bury my nose in my wine.

Dave drapes a palm over my wrist. "Stop

torturing yourself, sweetie, and turn off the laptop."

"I can't. I'm looking for clues." I open a screen for Will's list of friends. There are seventy-eight of them, and more than sixty of them are mutual. I scroll to the bottom, to the friends we don't have in common, find a handful of colleagues, one of my girlfriend's exes, a neighbor from down the road, the barista from our neighborhood coffee shop.

Dave leans in, reading over my shoulder. "What kind of clues are you looking for, Inspector Gadget?"

"Clues of the Corban Hayes kind." Dave frowns, and I add, "You know. The banker-slash-bodybuilder I met at the memorial today. The one who told me all those things about Will."

"Because of curiosity, or suspicion?" James says.

I pause to consider my answer, but it doesn't take me long. Yes, curiosity is driving me, but after meeting Corban, I can't shake the feeling there's more I don't know. If there are more people like Corban Hayes out there, I want to speak to them.

"Both."

But I'm not going to find anything here. Will hated Facebook, and there's nobody here I don't recognize or can't place. I slam the laptop closed in frustration.

James leans back into the couch, resting his wineglass on his flat stomach. "Have you checked the cards?"

"What cards?"

He sweeps a palm toward the arrangement on the table and beyond, to vases standing like soldiers at attention on the kitchen bar. "You must've gotten flowers from everyone you know. Maybe there are a couple here from people you *don't* know."

Of course, the cards. The ones Mom arranged in the basket on Will's place mat, the ones I couldn't bear to read. I pop off the couch and fetch the basket from the table.

James refills the wineglasses, and we sip and sift through the condolences, pausing only to point out a painfully bad illustration or an extra corny text, and there are a lot of both. There must be close to a hundred cards here, saccharine messages and religious missives from my and Will's colleagues, old friends and neighbors, aunts and cousins and college classmates, people I haven't seen or heard from in years.

Dave holds up a note card covered in green glitter. "Who are Terry and Melinda Phillips?"

"Aka Melinda Leigh," I say. "Our cousin."

His eyes go wide, and his face spreads into a grin. "The one who came to your wedding in a prom dress?"

I smile at the memory of my brother's face when Melinda walked up the church steps in her frilly blue concoction. "Terry is her third husband. Or is it fourth? I've lost count. And it wasn't a prom dress."

"It was definitely a prom dress, and it was hideous, not to mention two sizes too small." He starts describing the dress for James, the lace and the ruffles and the seams stretched to screaming, while I return to the pile.

A few cards later, I come across something — a name I've never heard of before, printed underneath the generic florist's card message. I twist to face James. "Did you go to Hancock?"

He gives me a funny look.

"This card says *Deepest sympathies for your loss, Hancock High School, Class of '99.* Is that where you went?"

He shakes his head. "I've never heard of the place. Maybe it's Will's alma mater?"

"No, Will went to Central. I know, because I pulled it out of him for that surprise trip I planned to Memphis, on our first anniversary. Remember?"

"The trip that never was." Dave knows Will and I never actually made it to Memphis, and he knows why. And now, I can tell by my brother's expression that he and I are thinking the same thing. *Who went to Hancock?*

And then his eyes go wide, and he pops off the couch. "Be right back." He takes off down the hallway and up the stairs, his footsteps thumping overhead. Next to me on the couch, James settles his glass on the side table, slides his phone from his pocket and begins typing with his thumbs.

When Dave returns a few moments later, a T-shirt clutched in a fist, I recognize it from Will's closet. It's his ratty work shirt, the one he wears around the house for gardening and painting, an ancient thing that's ripped and stained and threadbare around the edges. Its letters are faded, but I know what they say before he holds it up for me to see. *Hancock Wildcats.* I always thought it was just a vintage shirt, a generic one like the kind they sell at Old Navy, but now I make the connection.

Why would Will tell me he went to Central if he graduated from Hancock?

"Haven't you ever Googled your husband's name?" Dave says.

"Of course not. Have you?"

"Yes," Dave and James say in unison.

"Maybe this has something to do with his mother dying," I say, still trying to give Will the benefit of the doubt. "I know he had to move. Maybe he had to change school districts, too."

"Uh, guys?" James grew up in Connecticut, and though he's lived in Savannah for almost a decade, he hasn't quite mastered the use of the word *y'all*. "You said Will was from Memphis?"

I nod, but Dave is more concerned about the card pinched between my fingers. "Does that thing come with a person's name? Or the name of the florist?"

I check it again, shake my head. "FTD .com. I think this is some kind of reference number, though. We can try looking up the order online."

James tries again, this time more insistently. "Guys. I —"

"Or we could just call them," Dave says. "What if we tell them we need a contact for our thank-you cards? I don't know if they'll give it to us, but it's worth a shot."

"We can also try the school. They can put us in touch with someone from the Class of '99."

"Iris." My name comes out like a shot, and if his insistent tone didn't get my attention,

his phone's screen in front of my face does. "Look."

I stare at the Google page, search results for Hancock High School. At the very top, on the very first line of the first listing, is a street address. A chill starts in my chest and creeps down my arms and legs like the start of the flu. *600 Twenty-Third Avenue, Seattle, Washington.*

I pass the phone to my brother and reach for my laptop. "If your offer still stands, I'm booking us on a flight for first thing tomorrow morning."

12

Miraculously, I sleep the entire five-hour flight. From the moment we catch air in Atlanta until the captain dips the nose and aims us at Seattle. My body finally overriding my brain, I suppose, and giving in to my exhaustion. We hit a violent pocket of air on the descent, and my eyes snap wide-open — not frightened but aware. Is that what Will first felt, too? All around us, passengers white-knuckle their armrests, Dave included. I know they're thinking of Flight 23, calculating the odds of two Seattle-bound flights going down in the same week, and I wonder at my own sense of calm. Why am I not frightened like the others? Are my senses that dulled by grief? The plane jostles and squeaks, then evens out, and the passengers melt back into their seats.

Dave reaches across me to shove up the window shade, and the bright light burns my eyes. "Welcome back. I was worried I might have to carry you off."

"Wouldn't be the first time," I say, thinking of the time sophomore year in which Joey Mackintosh showed me how to funnel beer until I passed out in the front yard. Dave threw me over his shoulder and carted me upstairs to bed before our parents returned home from the movies. I press a kiss to his shoulder. "Thank you for being here. I can't imagine doing this all by myself."

"Please. As if I would let you." He gives my arm a quick squeeze, then roots around in his seat pocket, tossing me the bag of Chex Mix he bought in the Atlanta terminal. "Here. Mom told me if I bring you back any skinnier, I'm grounded."

I smile, even though I'm pretty sure he's serious. Mom *would* tell him that, and I *have* lost some weight. After six days of almost no food, my denims hang loose on my hips, my stomach is taut and flat, and my ass — which has never been fat but has certainly never been skinny, either — looks like a shrinky-dink version of its former curvy self. Becoming a widow is good for seven pounds and counting.

I rip open the bag and nibble on one, and when my stomach doesn't revolt at the salty crunch, another, as I get my first glimpse of

Seattle out the window. They don't call it the Emerald City for nothing. Miles and miles of rolling grass, leafy forests and avocado-tinted lakes reaching like long fingers into mossy valleys, made even greener by the infamous rain. Above us, clouds hang low and leaden into the distance.

Fifteen minutes later, we're filing into the Seattle airport with our carry-ons and making our way via shuttle bus to the Hertz counter. Since we don't know exactly what we're looking for or how long we'll need to find it, Dave and I have decided to wing this trip. No car or hotel reservations, no plan, not even a return ticket. Will's head would have exploded at the idea, but the travel websites assured us April's propensity for constant drizzle and arctic winds meant tourists would stay away, and hotel rooms would be plentiful.

We climb into the rental, and Dave starts the engine, gunning the gas until the vents spew warm air at our heads. Atlantans are not built for this kind of cold. The kind that whips across your skin and bites through to your bones, making you feel wet even though you're not. I shiver in the passenger's seat while Dave fiddles with the radio. He settles on a country station, the kind with Willie Nelson and lots of twang, and I pull up the driving directions on my iPhone.

"We need to get over to I-5 and then head north." When Dave doesn't hit the gas, I look over to see him watching me. "What?"

"It's just . . ." He sighs, looking me square in the eye. "Are you absolutely positive you want to do this?"

"You're asking me now?"

He lifts both hands, lets them fall onto the steering wheel. "My timing isn't the best, I'll give you that, but yes. I'm asking you now, when there's still a chance for us to turn this thing around. To go home and forget all about whatever's here in Seattle before it gets in the way of your husband's memory. Because it will, you know. Especially if what we find is bad. Have you considered that it might be?"

"Of course I've considered that it might be bad. In fact, I kind of assume it is. No man rewrites bits and pieces of their lives because those years were squeaky-clean."

He gives me a look that says *touché*. "Okay, so let me ask you this, then — what if whatever we find isn't just bad? What if it's awful? No, what if it's DEFCON-one awful? Without Will here to defend himself or explain, would you still want to know?"

I gaze out over the parking lot and beyond, watching a jet roar skyward while I consider my brother's question. Dave is right; I could still turn this thing around. I could climb out of this car, go back to the airport and try to forget all about Will's past in Seattle. I could concentrate on remembering the good parts of my husband — that nobody could make me belly-laugh harder, that he thought Sunday mornings were made for coffee in bed, that the sloping spot under his left ear seemed made for my nose — and try to ignore the rest. The parts he lied about. The parts of himself he hid. I could go home and get started mourning my husband.

But how do you mourn a person you're no longer certain you know?

I think of possible discoveries that would merit a DEFCON-one rating. That Will has another family, a pretty wife and two adorable toddlers with his square chin and slate-blue eyes, tucked away in a Seattle bungalow. That he's a wanted criminal, a serial killer or a rapist or a terrorist with a long list of murders to his name. Every theory I come up with is ridiculous. Anyone who wants to hide from a secret wife or the law does not put themselves up on Facebook.

Then why all the lies?

I don't have the first clue. But I do know I have to find out.

I twist on the seat to face Dave. "Yes. I still want to know."

"You sure?"

I nod, immediate and decisive. "Positive."

Without another word, he shoves the car into gear, punches the gas, and away we go.

Once Dave has merged onto the highway, I punch in the number for ESP's head of Human Resources and hit the button for speakerphone.

"Good morning, this is Shefali Majumdar speaking."

Except for her name, Shefali sounds as American as apple pie. Her voice is smooth and pleasant, without the slightest trace of an accent I can detect, though once I explain why I'm calling, the awkwardness is hard to miss.

"So basically," she says when I'm done, and there's new hesitation in her tone, "what you're asking me is if I hired your husband?"

"That's correct."

"Who was also one of the passengers on last week's Flight 23?"

"Unfortunately so."

"And he never told you he was interviewing or even looking for a new job?"

"Exactly. I only know because he told a friend he was offered a position at ESP. And that friend told me."

Shefali falls silent, and Dave and I exchange a worried look. I lean back in the passenger's seat and give her a moment to consider my request, my heart thunking against my ribs. I'm prepared to beg, am already gathering up the words in my head, when she begins. "Every human resources manual ever written would say that I can't tell you either way. That applicants for any position have an indisputable right to privacy whether I hire them or not. If your husband didn't see fit to tell you about his job search, then ethically speaking, I can neither confirm nor deny that his search might have led him here."

Disappointment spears me in the gut. I open my mouth to argue, but I've barely made a sound before Shefali cuts me off.

"What I *can* tell you is that ESP hasn't had a senior position opening in more than eight months, and it was for VP of Marketing. Any technical positions we've filled this past year, a software engineer would have been vastly overqualified for."

Dave looks over, his eyes wide. I close mine, her message hitting me like a locomotive. "So you didn't hire him."

Her only answer is silence.

"Did you speak to him recently about a job?"

Shefali pauses, but only for a second or two. "Mrs. Griffith, up until fifteen minutes ago, I'd never heard of him."

Dave and I spend the rest of the drive bickering about what Shefali's words mean.

"Why would Will lie?" Dave says for what must be the fifth time. "Why would he tell Corban about a job he didn't even apply for? One that didn't even exist?"

I give him the same answer as the last time he asked. "Maybe it wasn't Will who lied. Maybe it was Corban."

"That makes no sense. What would Corban have to gain by lying?"

"I don't know." The words come out harsher than I intended because we've been having this same conversation for the past fifteen minutes. I don't have answers for his endless questions. I don't know, I don't understand, and I can't fathom any reason either of them would have for lying.

I'm saved from another round when Dave's phone beeps, indicating we've arrived at our destination. He hits the brakes in the middle of the street, gesturing beyond me out the window.

Hancock High School is a massive complex of brick and mortar in Seattle's Central District, a downtown neighborhood on the confused end of gentrification. It's a neighborhood with multiple personality disorder — housing projects on one block, hulking renovated Victorians on another, boarded-up convenience stores on the next. We park on the street in front of the main entrance and make our way up the cement steps.

Like any other school in the country, Hancock has had to respond to the rash of shootings and stabbings with increasingly drastic security protocols, especially in a neighborhood like this one. Theirs include locked doors, a camera whirring above our heads and a uniformed guard stationed just inside, staring us down. I wave, and he buzzes us in.

"Can I help you?" he says, standing so we can see that he's armed.

I show him my Lake Forrest badge, stamped with the school's emblem and featuring a full-color photograph of me, right above my title as school counselor. Lake Forrest is a small enough school that staff are not actually required to wear them on campus, but I'm suddenly glad I keep mine in my bag.

"My name is Iris Griffith, and I'm a faculty member at Lake Forrest Academy in Atlanta, Georgia. I am looking into the background of one of your alums and was hoping to take a peek in your library. I assume that's where I'd find copies of all your old yearbooks?"

Sure enough, the man points us across the lobby to the main desk. "You'll need a visitor's pass first. Library is down the hall to your left. Can't miss it."

I thank him, and a few minutes later, Dave and I are bellying up to the library's information desk. The woman behind it is barely visible over the piles of books and papers, a leaning tower of brown boxes and a computer screen so old it should be in a museum.

She also looks nothing like a librarian. Her hair is a wild cloud of corkscrew curls, she's covered in leather and tattoos, and it's a good thing this school doesn't have metal detectors, because there's no way she'd make it through one with all those piercings. They line her lobes and nostrils and brows, and when she gives us a smile, two tiny silver balls peek out from under her top lip.

"You're not students," she says, sizing us

up. "Let me guess. Journalists? College recruiters? Neighborhood activists?"

I flash my Lake Forrest badge, launch into my spiel, but she waves me off before I've gotten through the first sentence. "Bummer, I was really hoping you were recruiters. Our seniors are at a sixty-two percent college acceptance rate and holding, and if we don't raise it another ten percent by graduation, I'm going to spend my summer months mowing lawns. Anyhow, what can I do for you guys?"

"We're looking for a copy of your old yearbooks — 1999, maybe a year or two before."

"Who you looking for?"

"My husband." I swallow down a searing pain that I know must melt my features. "His name was Will Griffith."

One of her brows arches at my use of the past tense, but she doesn't ask for details. She pushes to a stand, gestures for us to follow her down to the right, to where an open and bright reading area darkens into the stacks. "Name's India, by the way."

"I'm Iris, and this is my brother, Dave. Thanks for your help, India."

"No problem." She walks fast, her motorcycle boots making dull thunks on the ratty carpet, talking the entire time over her

157

shoulder. "Hancock opened its doors in the '20s, but the first yearbook didn't appear until 1937. I guess it took them that long to get their you-know-what together. Back then we weren't much more than a twelve-room building with a couple hundred students, most of them Jewish, Japanese or Italian." She gestures to the far wall of framed photographs, dozens and dozens of more recent graduating classes, a sea of brown and tan faces punctuated by the occasional light-skinned one.

I stop and scan them for the Class of 1999. The picture's too high for me to pick out Will, but it's the same racial makeup, more dark than light.

India takes a hard right into the stacks, stopping at a shelf packed with hard, burgundy covers, many of them held together by Scotch tape. "What year did you say you were looking for?"

"Graduating class of 1999."

"Oh, that's right. The year we got our first National Merit Scholar, our football team took state and a burst pipe flooded the gym right in the middle of a basketball game." At our raised brows, she lifts a shoulder. "I'm the unofficial school historian. Comes with the territory of running a library, I guess. Anyway . . ." She runs a black-painted fingernail down the spines until she finds the right one, then pulls it out and hands it to me. "Here you go. There are a couple of tables around the corner. Take as long as you need. I'll be holding down the fort up front."

Dave thanks her, and I carry the book with shaking hands to a table at the end of the stacks. The design is classic '90s. Fat gold letters and the outline of a wildcat on satiny maroon, and the few bites of Chex Mix in my belly push up the back of my throat. I shove the book at my brother. "I can't. You look."

We sit, and I study the tabletop's ballpoint graffiti while Dave flips through the yearbook's pages. He stops on a spread of seniors, full-color shots of kids in burgundy caps and gowns, the bright gold tassels hanging alongside smiling cheeks.

Only Will, the only white face on the page, is not smiling.

"Sorry, Iris. It's him." Dave turns the book around so I can see. "William Matthew Griffith."

It's Will, all right. His hair is lighter and his face is thinner, but his eyes are as familiar to me as my own. The sight of him there — *here,* in a Seattle yearbook — hits me like a visceral punch.

159

I press a hand to my churning stomach and try to think through what I know. "Okay, so clearly, the bit about growing up in Memphis was a lie."

"We don't know that. Maybe he only transferred here for his senior year," Dave says, playing devil's advocate. "Hang on, let me get the earlier years." He jumps up from his chair and heads back into the stacks.

But Will's picture is there, too, and in all three, scowling at the camera in a way I've never seen him do, not even when our flight back from Cancun was delayed five times in twelve hours.

Dave rests a hand on the back of my chair, leans in to inspect the pictures. "Why does he look so angry?"

"Because that's what he was. His dad was dead, and his mom was sick. She died his junior year. On top of school and caring for her, he was working two jobs, running the house and paying all the bills." As I say the words, it occurs to me that any or all of this could have been a lie, too. "At least, that's what he always claimed."

Dave sinks into his chair, reaching for the 1999 yearbook, the one where Will was a senior. He taps the white space under his picture. "How come everybody else has a favorite quote and list of extracurriculars, but there's nothing under Will's name. Wasn't he some kind of wrestling champion?" Dave flips to the wrestling page, and there's no Will.

It never occurred to me to question him, but now that I think about it, when would Will have had time for the wrestling team? I press both hands to my churning stomach and swallow down a surge of sick. Who *is* this man I married?

Dave leans back in his chair, running a palm through his dark hair. "Okay, let's think this through — 1999 isn't *that* long ago. I'll bet you at least one of his teachers is still working here. Maybe they'd remember him."

"India might know someone we could ask." I reach for my bag and stand.

Dave gathers up the yearbooks. "You go ahead. I'll put these back and meet you up front."

I find her behind the information desk, sorting returned books onto a rickety cart. She looks up when she hears me coming. "Did you find what you needed?"

"Sort of. I was wondering if any of the teachers who were here in 1999 are still here now."

"Oh, sure. A bunch of them. You wanted to see if one of them remembered your

161

husband?"

I nod.

"Well —" she leans on the cart and thinks for a moment, and then her face brightens "— I'm pretty sure the baseball coach graduated from Hancock in 1999. I don't know if he knew your husband, but he'd be the best place to start." She checks her watch, taps the face twice with a finger. "You have about an hour before practice starts, which means you can probably find him in the gym."

13

Dave and I find a man matching Coach Miller's description in a dim hallway at the back of Hancock High's gym, lugging a metal basket of baseballs into the hall. Above his head, a lone tube light buzzes and hums.

"Are you Coach Miller?" I ask, moving close enough to get a good whiff of his cologne. The man is bathed in it, an overwhelming stench that burns the back of my throat, especially when combined with the other odors hanging in the air, Bengay and sweaty socks.

He looks up, his eyes half hidden under the bill of a Hancock High baseball cap. "Yup."

India wasn't kidding when she said he was built like a linebacker. Coach Miller is massive, six feet and then some of bulky bones and fat-padded muscle under baggy street clothes, jeans and a long-sleeved polo. He ducks back into the room, reappearing two seconds later with another basket, this time filled with mitts.

"The librarian told us you graduated from Hancock in 1999."

"Yeah, that's right." He locks the door with a key he drops into his back jeans pocket. "Who's asking?"

"My name is Iris, and this is my brother, Dave. We were hoping you could tell us what you remember about a former classmate of yours. Will Griffith."

"Nope. Don't know him." He leans down, reaching for one of the baskets.

I slide my phone from my pocket and wake it up, revealing a picture of me and Will. "This is him. William Matthew Griffith. Do you recognize him?"

With a loud sigh, he glances at my screen, then drops the basket and looks again. "Him? That's Billy Griffith."

My heart flips over. "Do you remember him?"

"Everybody who went to Hancock back then remembers Billy Griffith." He cocks his head, and his eyes narrow in suspicion. "Who did you say you were again?"

"Iris Griffith. His wife."

The coach gives a surprised puff, quick and sharp enough to stir up the hair on the left side of my face. "No way."

"Excuse me?"

"It's just . . ." He gives me a slow head-to-toe, lingering on my curviest spots in a way that makes it hard to stand still, then follows it up with a grin, and I'm confused by the incongruity. His gaze was appreciative, but his smile isn't the least bit friendly. "You don't really seem like his type."

Maybe not, but I know this guy's type. The type who, once upon a time, was the one every boy wanted to be and every girl wanted to date. The type who swaggered through the hallways with a ball and an empty backpack, never once thinking beyond next week's game. The type I warn my students at Lake Forrest Academy not to become.

I park my tone in neutral. "How so?"

"Do you have a weapon in your purse or your back pocket? Do you hear voices in your head telling you to, I don't know, light fires and slash tires?"

Indignation burns, hot and sudden, at his question, but I keep my expression in check. "Of course not."

"See? Not his type." He leans down, swipes the basket of balls from the floor. "Now if you'll excuse me, I've got to get ready for practice." Without waiting for a reply, he turns and takes off down the hall.

I shoot Dave a confused look, and he shrugs. Together, we set off after the coach.

"Coach Miller, wait." He doesn't wait, doesn't even slow. His long legs take two steps to my one, and I have to jog to catch up. "Please. I only need ten minutes of your time. I don't know if you've heard, but my husband was a passenger on that plane that just crashed, and I —"

"Look, lady," he says, whirling around so fast I almost slam into him, "I am the last person you ought to be asking about Billy Griffith. I don't like to speak ill of the dead, which means I'm not going to say anything. You do the math."

"I'm not asking you to sugarcoat your memories. I'm only looking for the truth."

He shakes his head, slow and stubborn. "He and I were not friends. We didn't run in the same circles, and we didn't get along. I don't know what else to tell you."

"Tell me what he was like. Tell me how long you've known him and who his friends were and where he lived. Tell me everything you can think of, because . . ." Still shaking his head, Coach Miller takes a step back and then another, his big body gearing up for a retreat, and I can tell I'm about to lose him. I take a deep breath and will myself to keep going, to tell this stranger what I'm really asking. "Because my husband lied, okay? He lied to me about a lot of things. He told me that he was en route to Orlando, not Seattle, when that plane crashed. I had no idea he'd ever even been in this city. All along, I thought he was from Memphis."

What does a Memphis accent sound like? The question slices through my mind, sudden and unexpected. Will didn't have much of a Southern accent, especially not compared to mine, and he never really used any of the slang Southerners are so fond of. Maybe that's just not how they talk in Memphis? I have no idea.

Coach Miller stops moving, and his brows disappear under the bill of his ball cap. "Billy told you he grew up in Memphis?"

"Yes."

The coach leans back, squinting at me down his nose. "Now, *that* sounds like something he would do." He puffs a sigh of defeat, shoves the basket of balls at Dave's chest, doubles back for the mitts and motions for us to follow him. "Practice starts in half an hour, so you'll have to walk with me."

He leads us deeper into the maze of hallways behind the gym, talking over his shoulder. "Like I said before, I remember

Billy Griffith, but not because he was such a great guy. He was the type of guy that when he came walking down the hall, everybody all of a sudden had something very important to dig out of their lockers. You understand what I'm telling you? Anybody who looked him in the eye got singled out, and nobody wanted to get singled out by Billy Griffith. Not even the teachers."

"Why?" Dave says. "What happened if he singled you out?"

"Sometimes a shove or a busted lip, sometimes nothing until days later. That was the scariest thing about Billy, his unpredictability. The only thing you could count on was that he'd turn on you eventually. He was mean and he was angry, and his parents were too busy beating the crap out of each other to care."

His parents. His father, he said, died when he was two. His mother, he claimed, raised him on her own.

"What ages are we talking about here?" I say as we turn the corner onto a row of windowed offices. "How long ago did you know Will — Billy?"

Coach Miller thinks for a moment. "Well, I moved to Rainier Vista the summer before second grade, so what's that? Seven or so?"

168

His answer ties a knot in my throat, because that's when the truth hits home. Memphis was a lie. Not a fib. Not an exaggeration. Not a little white lie or a half-truth. An intentionally false statement meant to deceive. Will *never* lived in Memphis. I'm not certain he ever set foot there. No wonder we spent our first anniversary in Nashville instead.

Rage coils in my belly, writhing only a second or two before it bursts to the blistering surface at the memory of Will's silence on that surprise drive to Memphis. I think about the panic he must have felt at my accidental excavation of his lie, how he must have been scrambling to come up with an explanation, finally settling on the excuse that his Memphis memories were "too painful to relive." I bought it without question, turning the car around without second thought. And now, walking down a dingy, smelly hallway in Will's real alma mater, I feel like a fool.

We stop at an office door, and Coach Miller shoves it open with a giant paw. He ushers us into a tiny and neatly cluttered room, with papers and charts and boxes of sporting equipment stacked in tidy columns along the wall. He takes the basket from Dave, sets it on the floor by the door and offers us a seat in the pair of ratty chairs in front of his desk. I fall onto mine and try to breathe around the fireball in my chest.

Coach Miller sits, digs his heels into the carpet and rolls himself up to the desk, his chair wheels squealing like nails over a chalkboard. He does a little double take when he catches my expression. "You okay?"

Somehow, my voice finds its way outside my head, and it sounds only slightly strangled. "I'm fine. Please, continue."

"Okay," he says, but in a way that tells me he's not totally convinced. He takes off his cap, rubs a palm over his tight curls and sets it back. "Like I was saying, nobody at home was disciplining him, which means he pretty much did whatever he pleased and got away with it, both in school and out. He fought. He stole stuff. He dealt drugs in the hallways and on street corners. He skipped so many classes, I don't know how he ever graduated. Because the teachers wanted him gone, probably."

Coach Miller's revelations are like a string of mini explosions in my head, one on top of the other, leaving me breathless and dizzy.

"Will told me his father died when he was a baby," I say. "He said he had no memory of him."

"Wishful thinking, probably. Mr. Griffith

170

was a mean old drunk. But it was his mother who died, as I recall sometime during our junior year."

I think back to the first time Will told me of her death, the only time I ever saw him cry. Malignant melanoma, he said, caught after it had already metastasized to her brain, liver and lungs. An awful, painful death. "Cancer?"

As soon as I say it, I wish I could go back and fix my tone, make it sound less gullible wife, more certain. Surely, Will couldn't have faked a tale that emotional. No one is that good an actor.

But Coach Miller barks a laugh. "Hardly. She died in a fire."

"Oh, my God," Dave says. "That poor woman. Poor Will."

Coach Miller leans back in his chair, his weight bouncing it around a few times before it finds stillness. "Poor Billy, huh? Let me tell you something. Every kid in our neighborhood was dealing with some kind of crap at home — addictions, arrests, deadbeat dads all over the place — but we were finding a way to deal with them. Billy didn't even try. He just got angry and mean."

Dave and I exchange a frown, and I can tell he's thinking what I am. How does a drug-dealing street punk become a college-educated, loving husband?

I clear my throat against a sudden onslaught of emotions leapfrogging up my chest. Sadness for Will's lonely childhood and his mother's violent death. Resentment for parents who couldn't stop slinging fists long enough to love on their son. Indignation at whatever higher power dealt Will such a crappy hand. Fury I'm only finding out about it now.

"What ever happened to his father?" I somehow manage.

"I heard rumors he's sick, something needing full-time care, but . . ." Coach Miller lifts both hands, lets them fall with a thunk to the desk. "My mom used to keep me updated on neighborhood gossip, but she died a couple years ago."

Dave and I fall silent. When we were young, Mom always told us there were three sides to every argument. Our side, the other side and, somewhere in the middle, the truth. Maybe this is what Dave meant when he asked if I was sure I wanted to know about Will. Without him here to defend himself from Coach Miller's tale, I can't gauge where the middle falls.

But that doesn't mean I'm about to swallow this story whole. Coach Miller is clearly holding on to his grudge with both gigantic fists, and for events that went down almost two decades ago.

He takes in our doubtful expressions and grunts, shoving away from the desk. "Believe me. Don't believe me. Doesn't change the fact that Billy Griffith was a spiteful, sneaky thug who could come up behind you, stab you with a knife and leave before you even noticed the blood. Ask around. I'm sure you'll have a hard time finding anybody to say otherwise. Now I gotta get to practice before those punks destroy my diamond." He stands and stalks past us, forgetting all about the baskets of equipment in his hurry to get to the door. He stops himself halfway into the hall, his big hand gripping the doorjamb. "Do you believe in karma? Because that's the first thing I thought when I heard what happened to Billy."

Dave and I backtrack our way through the corridors of Hancock High, both of us trying to make sense of Coach Miller's story. I wanted a toe-dip into my husband's life. What I got was more like a full-body dunking into arctic waters, and it's left me shell-shocked and numb.

"Did you believe him?" I say as we turn the corner onto a wall of dingy and dented lockers under a giant banner. *Go, Wildcats! Stay Fierce!*

Dave lifts a shoulder, and his mouth scrunches into a tight squiggle I know all too well. He doesn't want to, but he believes at least part of what we heard. "We could check with the local police station. If Will really was dealing drugs, maybe he got into trouble. The police might have it on record."

"I guess." I sigh, my shoulders sagging toward the dingy floor. "And I get that Will wouldn't want to talk about his mother's death. I *get* it. But that story he fed me about her dying of cancer? I cried, Dave. Real tears. He had all the medical jargon down, too. Knew all the symptoms and details of how the cancer progressed. You can't just make something like that up. He must have spent weeks researching melanoma on the web. I mean, you have to really commit to a lie like that one."

At the stairwell, Dave shoves open the door, stepping aside to let me pass. "I'd imagine so."

"And, okay, so his father wasn't the nicest person. That's not something he would have liked to talk about, either. But why not just say they were estranged? Why lie and tell me he never knew him?"

"You're the psychologist here. What would

174

make a person fictionalize the first eighteen years of their life?"

"Or more. After these past few days, I'm no longer assuming anything from the time before I met him. I'm not saying I believe everything Coach Miller said, but he described a deeply troubled kid, and even if only part of his story was true, you don't bounce back from something like that — if at all — without serious therapy. Which is why I need more than just one eyewitness account. I need to talk to their old neighbors, find some more teachers and classmates. Coach Miller can't be the only one who remembers him."

Dave nods his agreement, and we emerge from the stairwell at the front of the building. From his spot by the entrance, the guard gives us a chin lift. "You find what you needed?"

"Yes," Dave says, at the same time I hook a thumb back into the belly of the building, in the direction of the library. "Let's go take another look at the yearbook. Better yet, let's make some copies."

"No need."

"What? Why?"

He flashes me a *zip it* look, leaning in close and talking through gritted teeth. "I'll fill you in in the car."

The guard grunts like he couldn't care either way. "Sign out before you go."

Dave signs us out, and we head out the front door into a biting cold. Sometime while we were inside, steel-colored clouds rolled in on a front that dropped the temperature a good ten degrees. I shiver and tug my coat higher around my neck, but Dave unzips his, pulling the 1999 yearbook from behind his back with a cocky smile.

My eyes go wide. "You *stole* it?"

He purses his lips. "I prefer to think of it as borrowing."

"India won't see it that way. And when she notices it missing, she'll know exactly who took it, too. Our names are on the visitors' log, Dave."

"Stop worrying. Borrowing implies giving it back, as soon as we've made ourselves a copy. We'll put it back before India even notices it's gone."

"You don't know that. What if she does? What if she tracks me back to Lake Forrest?"

He rolls his eyes. "Isn't it difficult, walking around with your panties in such a wad?"

I love my brother, but here's where we're different. I live in a world where rules are meant to be followed, whereas he thinks rules are mostly an inconvenience. Especially the ones that inconvenience him. Dave puts his feet up on chairs and cuts through parking lots and brings his own snacks into movie theaters, all without ever getting caught. It's all about attitude, he would say, and he's not wrong. Dave has a boldness tucked inside him that draws people in and makes them forget he just stepped on their toes in order to push to the front of the line.

At the top of the stairs, the school doors slam open, and a throng of teenagers spills out. They hit the steps and scatter, moving at us with a speed and energy that can only come after being cooped up in a classroom for over eight hours.

Dave grabs my wrist, drags me in the direction of the street. "Come on, before we get trampled."

We're a block away, stepping into the rental, when my phone rings with a number I don't recognize. I press it to my ear. "Hello?"

A woman's voice, high and brisk, greets me. "Iris Griffith?"

"Yes."

"My name is Leslie Thomas. I'm calling from the Family Assistance Center —"

"What happened to Margaret Ann?"

"Ann Margaret," Dave whispers. He starts

177

the car but doesn't shift it into gear.

On the other end of the line, the caller doesn't miss a beat. "Margaret Ann is currently unavailable, but I was hoping I could ask you a few questions."

My attention snags, just for a second, on the name. Ann Margaret or Margaret Ann? Either way, this woman has caught me off guard. "Oh, I . . . Sorry, I'm not really in a place to talk right now."

"This won't take more than a minute or two. I understand that a number of families have banded together and are bringing a wrongful death lawsuit against Liberty Air. Are you one of them?"

Both her question and her tone, high-strung and almost manic, send all sorts of warning bells ringing in my head. Why would anyone at the FAC, an organization that exists under the Liberty Air umbrella, ask such a thing? I frown at Dave, whose brows shoot skyward. *What?* he mouths.

"I . . . I don't know," I say into the phone.

"You don't know if you're one of the families suing Liberty Air?"

"No, I don't know anything about the lawsuit. Who did you say you were again?"

"My name is Leslie Thomas. This morning the *Miami Herald* reported that the pilot was coming off a three-day bachelor party in South Beach and was functioning on only one hour of sleep. If that's true, will you and the other families be charging Liberty Air with manslaughter?"

Something icy steals around my heart, racking my torso with a chill that's not from the cold. The pilot was half-asleep, possibly hungover? The blood drains from my cheeks, and I press a palm to my churning stomach.

Dave frowns. "What's wrong?"

But wait. Why would someone at the Family Assistance Center be telling me this? Aren't they supposed to be protecting the interests of Liberty Air?

"Who are you again?"

"My name is Leslie Thomas."

"And you're calling from the FAC?"

"That's correct."

"Then why are you questioning me like a journalist?"

Silence. I hear her gearing up for another pitch, but it's too late. I already have her number.

"Because you *are* a journalist," I say in an angry hiss. "Which means you're also a liar."

I punch End on my screen and begin filling Dave in, but almost immediately, my phone rings again and from the same number. "Do you know how to block this person?"

Dave takes the phone from my fingers. He's fiddling with the screen when it lights up with a text. I lean across the middle console and frown at the message on my screen.

Go home, Iris.

"Who sent that?" I say.

Dave tries to pull up the number, but it's blocked. His thumbs type out a quick reply.

Who is this?

He hits Send, and we watch my screen for a reply, waking it up with a fingertip whenever it starts to fade to black.

"Why would somebody be telling you to go home?" Dave says.

"I don't know."

"Who else knows you're here?"

"Our parents and James, full stop. I haven't talked to any of my girlfriends since the memorial, and I didn't tell Ted or anyone at school I was leaving, only that I was taking a week or two off."

Dave thinks for a moment. "Well, if it's somebody back in Atlanta, wouldn't they have said *come* home instead?"

I nod, right as another text pings my phone.

Someone who knows what you're looking for, and it's not in Seattle.

14

Across the lake in Bellevue, Dave and I begin at a Best Buy, our best shot of tracing the blocked number on my phone. After that second text came in — *Someone who knows what you're looking for, and it's not in Seattle* — the errand shimmied up to top priority. Neither of us misses the irony. If Will were here, he'd unearth the number in thirty seconds flat.

The kid behind the Geek Squad counter looks to be about twenty or so, the type of guy who Will always claimed gave techies a bad name. Greasy hair. Pimply face. Bushy eyebrows and a prominent overbite. Behind his Coke-bottle glasses, his eyes go comically wide.

"You're asking me to hack another person's phone number?" the geek says, shaking his head. "I can't do that."

"Can't —" Dave gives him a charming smile "— or won't?"

"Irrelevant. I'm only allowed to repair and install."

My brother peels five twenties from his wallet and fans them across the countertop. "Are you sure about that?"

The kid's not sure. His gaze flicks from us to the cash, and the struggle is real. A hundred bucks can buy a lot of gigabytes. He whips his head left and right, taking note of a colleague ringing up a purchase at the register, another hunched over a MacBook at the far end of the counter. When neither of them looks his way, he swipes the bills and my phone from the counter, pocketing both. "BRB," he says, and then he disappears through a door marked Employees Only.

While he's gone, I head over to the computer display and pull up the internet. "What was it Coach Miller called that neighborhood where he lived? Rainier something."

"View? No, that's not right." Dave thinks for a second or two, then snaps. "Vista! Rainier Vista."

"That's it." I look up the neighborhood and scribble a couple cross streets in a notebook I carry in my bag, then do the same with the nearest FedEx and police department.

"While you're at it, find us a decent restaurant. I haven't eaten since Atlanta, and I'm starved."

For my brother, decent means complicated dishes and wine pairings, both of which means dinner takes forever. I shake my head. "We can stop at the first drive-through we come to, but I want to keep moving."

He wrinkles his nose. "You're seriously suggesting we order food at a window and eat it out of a paper bag?"

"Yes, because I still want to see Will's old neighborhood and talk to somebody at the police department before the day's over, and we can't do that if you order the seven-course chef's tasting menu, which I know you will."

"Seriously, Iris. I have to eat something. The low blood sugar is making me light-headed."

"Would you stop being such a drama queen? I already told you, we can —"

"Um, sir?" We look over, and it's the kid, my iPhone in one of his fists. "The text was sent from a messaging app."

"Okay," Dave and I say in unison, and in exactly the same tone. Not okay as in *we're done here,* but okay as in *go on.*

The geek assumes the former. He plunks

down my phone and turns to go.

"Wait," I say. "What about the number?"

"The app encrypts and then destroys the text, as well as where the text originated." He shoves his glasses up his nose with a knuckle. "Think of it as a Snapchat for text messaging. Only, you don't have to reveal any identifying information in order to begin a conversation."

"Meaning?"

"Meaning it's impossible to trace the number. Sorry." He moves down the counter to help an old lady clutching a laptop to her chest.

Disappointment, sharp and instant, stabs me between the ribs. "Now what?" I say, turning to my brother.

Dave sighs, watching the geek go. "Now you owe me a hundred bucks."

I bribe Dave with the rest of my Chex Mix and an eight-thirty reservation at Atmosphere, which, according to Zagat, is one of Seattle's best French restaurants overlooking the Puget Sound. With minimal griping, he steers the rental back across the lake to Rainier Vista.

"Are you sure this is it?" he says, slowing in the middle of the street. "The way Coach Miller described it, I was expecting some-

185

thing much slummier."

I check the street sign against the address in my notebook. "This is the right place, but you're right. It's way nicer than I thought it would be."

Rainier Vista is not Beverly Hills, but it's no slum, either. To our right are small but colorful houses with sweeping front porches; to our left are townhomes and a block-sized park, empty but for a pristine basketball court and a long line of trees. The setting sun lights them up from behind, bare limbs reaching into the leaden sky. I twist on my seat, searching for the promised view, but if Mount Rainier is visible from here, it's tucked behind a thick layer of red-tinged clouds.

Dave pulls over, hitting the button to roll down my window.

"Hi, there," he says, leaning across me to speak to the young couple on the sidewalk. Two kids, barely out of high school, their features hidden under thick hoods. His arm is slung around her shoulders in a gesture that hits me as more possessive than protective. "Do you guys live around here?"

They don't stop walking, don't even turn their heads our way. The girl flicks her eyes in my direction, but her boyfriend hustles her along.

Dave eases the car forward, dialing up the dazzle on his smile. "We're new to the area, and we were hoping you could give us a little bit of direc—" The pair makes a sharp right, veering away from us down a footpath bordering an empty park. "Or maybe not."

"Friendly neighborhood."

Dave puffs an ironic laugh, then looks around, taking in the neighborhood. He points past me, out the passenger-side window and beyond, to a hulking block of what looks to be apartments. "See that simple design and cheap materials? How much you want to bet that's HUD housing, and this neighborhood is a HUD redevelopment?"

"Meaning?"

"Meaning, if I'm right, HUD would have made provisions for the former residents, either to move them to a new neighborhood or guarantee them a spot in the low-income housing here. We've got a fairly decent chance of finding someone who was here before the redevelopment."

"Okay, smarty-pants. So where do we begin?"

"One of those apartment buildings would be our best bet, but judging by the reception those kids just gave us, I'm guessing residents won't take kindly to strangers coming in and asking questions. We'd be better off starting at some sort of community center. If we make friends with the staff, they might be able to tell us who's lived here since before the developers came to town. We can funnel our questions through them."

Dave drives on, making a slow loop through the neighborhood. We pass more of the same, houses of all sizes pressed between parks and playgrounds, with an occasional high-rise jutting out over the rooftops. He points out a sign for the city's light-rail system. "Proximity to public transit, plenty of ramps and open space, and have you noticed all the urban artwork? Definitely a mixed-income neighborhood."

"So where's the community center?"

"If I'm right, it'll be pretty smack in the middle of the development."

We drive around a little more. Dave charts our progress on the map on his phone, driving up and down streets until he swings a sudden left, pointing the rental at a modern glass and stucco building at the end of a one-way road. A Plexiglas sign above the double doors announces it as Neighborhood House. "Bingo."

Dave finds a spot along the street, and we power through a stiff wind up the sidewalk.

A glass-enclosed bulletin board to the left of the door announces an adult financial planning seminar, a jobs lab and the annual literacy drive under a United Way logo.

"Boom," Dave says as we pass. "Social services. Told you it was HUD."

I roll my eyes. "Such a cocky Realtor."

He grins and opens one of the double doors, stepping aside to let me pass.

Inside, Neighborhood House is spacious and bright, a two-story windowed space flooded with natural and LCD light. Two women sit behind the reception desk in the very center, chatting with an elderly black man on the opposite side of the counter. They're young, midtwenties or so, their faces fresh with eager smiles and philanthropic optimism.

"Welcome to Neighborhood House," one of them says, her accent nasal and Midwestern. "Do you know the way or would you like a little direction?"

I step up to the counter, give her a friendly smile. "Hi, and thank you. I'm looking for information on a former resident, and I was hoping you could put us in touch with someone who was well connected in the community back before it was redeveloped."

"I've lived here my whole life," the man says, turning to us with a dentured grin.

"And I know everybody. Who you looking for, sweetheart?"

Now that I'm closer, I see the man is not elderly; he's ancient. Stooped posture and grizzled hair and droopy skin with a labyrinth of lines too deep to be described as wrinkles. And though his eyes are cloudy with cataracts, they're intelligent and twinkling with warmth.

"His name is Will Griffith, though back then he went by Billy. He lived here with his family until sometime in 1999, maybe a year or two longer. I don't know his parents' names, but they —"

"Kat and Lewis," the man says, and he's no longer smiling.

"Was Kat the one who died in the fire?"

"Yes, ma'am. And she wasn't the only one."

Excitement revs my heart, and a tingly warmth rises in my chest. "She wasn't?"

He shakes his head and studies me through squinted eyes. "Who are you, and why are you asking?"

"The son, Billy . . . Will, is my husband. Well, was my husband. He was on that Liberty Airlines flight from Atlanta to Seattle, the one that . . ."

Someone gasps, and right on cue, my throat closes up and my eyes fill with tears, my brain saturated with memories of my husband. Not the new Will, the one who lied about where he was going and where he came from, a past filled with anger and violence. He stays out of the picture, this new man I don't know and can't begin to understand. No, my tears now are for the old Will — the one who used to smack my butt whenever I got out of the shower, the one who asked me to marry him on an ordinary Saturday afternoon, by dropping to his knee in the middle of the breakfast aisle, in the very same Kroger where we began. That's the Will I miss. That's the husband I want back.

"Sorry," I say, ducking my head. I've never been a pretty crier, and I hate crying in public, something I've been doing an awful lot of lately. "I didn't mean to . . ."

One of the women plucks two tissues from a box and passes them over the counter. "Honey, you cry all you want. My God, your husband just died in a plane crash. I think everybody here will agree, you get a free pass."

Her colleague nods in vehement agreement.

Only the elderly man doesn't show a lick of sympathy. His lips, white-line thin, curl down at both ends, and his eyes, which when we first walked in glittered with joviality, are now as dark and stormy as the sky outside. The transformation bottles up my tears.

"You remember my husband, don't you?"

He turns back to the women, slapping a stiff palm to the desk. "Ladies, you have yourselves a nice evening." Without so much as a glance in our direction, he pushes past us for the door.

He's stooped and slow, but he walks with a steady, if not flat-footed gait. I catch up within a few easy strides. "Sir, wait. Please. I'm only asking for a minute or two of your time."

"No, what you're asking is for me to dig up some old and unpleasant skeletons. Skeletons that are better left in the past." Everything about the old man says he didn't like Will then, and now, after I just admitted being married to him, he doesn't like me much, either. He ducks his head and speeds up.

At the exit, he punches a button and a motor whirs, swinging the heavy doors open like they're moving through molasses, only barely faster than the old man. It's enough of a delay that we stop walking.

"Look, I understand Will was a troubled kid, but —"

He lifts a hunched shoulder. "This was the projects. Lots of kids were troubled."

Even after all the lies, the impulse to defend my husband rises inside me like a tsunami, and I bite down on my tongue to hold the wave inside.

"What did he do?" Dave says, coming up alongside me.

The old man grimaces. "I already told you, let old bones lie. Nothing good can come of digging 'em up."

The doors are open now, letting in an icy wind. Sometime in the past few minutes, the skies have begun dumping rain, and it falls in fierce, angry swirls. The man yanks his zipper higher and heads out into it.

Dave and I exchange a look, and he's thinking the same thing I am, that this man is our best bet for information. I jut my chin in his direction, and Dave takes off after him.

"At least let us drive you to where you're going," he suggests as the old man's shuffling down the ramp. "You shouldn't be out in this weather. The sidewalks will be slippery."

The old man is tempted. He pauses, glancing back over a shoulder.

It's enough for Dave to give him an inviting grin. "Our car is warm and dry, and it'll take you anywhere you need to go."

The old man considers the offer for a second or two, his gaze sizing us up. He takes in my leather boots and cashmere scarf, Dave's designer jeans under a Patagonia puffy coat. "Anywhere?"

Dave and I both nod.

The man's scowl fades into something much more calculating. "I could eat."

The old man's name is Wayne Butler, and with his directions, Dave steers the rental to a halal joint on MLK Jr. Way. He takes in the neon signs and the faded red awning, and his shoulders droop, but he doesn't complain, not even when Mr. Butler orders every curry on the menu, then steps aside so Dave can pay.

As soon as we're situated at a table near the window, I use the same strategy that got Coach Miller talking: honesty.

"Mr. Butler, I know you'd rather not go excavating the past, but whatever Will did as a teenager, it can't be worse than what he did to me, his own wife."

"You sure about that?"

I nod, because I know what he wants. Mr. Butler wants me to put myself on his team — a team separate from my husband. I push a chunk of stringy meat around with a cheap fork and gather the words I think he wants to hear.

"My husband — Will — we were married for seven years. He never told me anything about Seattle. I didn't know he grew up here. I had no idea about his home situation. Maybe he was ashamed of his past, or maybe he was just trying to put everything behind him. I don't know. But the thing is, I can't reconcile the man I knew to the man Coach Miller told us about, and I need to do that in order to mourn my husband. I need to know all the parts of him — even the parts he kept hidden, the ugly parts — in order to move on." I say the words, and a slow ache blooms inside my chest.

Something cracks in the old man's demeanor, a slight softening around his eyes and mouth, and relief loosens my muscles. "You talked to Anthony Miller?"

"Yes."

"He's a good man. What did he tell you?"

"He said Will was mean and angry and his home situation was not pleasant. He said there was a fire, and that . . ." It takes me a second or two to muster up the words. "Will's mom — Kat — died in it."

The old man chews a meaty bite. "He told you about the fire, huh?"

I nod.

"I lost everything I owned in that fire, and I'm not just talking about clothes and furniture. I mean letters and baby pictures and the recipes my great-grandmama handed down. My wedding suit and the pearl earrings I gave to my wife, God rest her soul."

I don't bother asking if he was insured. The items he mentioned seem irreplaceable, and besides, after everything I've heard about Rainier Vista at the time, I'm guessing none of the residents were.

"I'm so sorry," I say instead. "That must have been very hard."

He nods, and his mouth settles into a thin line. "Did Anthony tell you who set the fire?"

My heart ticks like a bomb beneath the bones of my ribs. The fire was arson? I try to answer, but I can't speak.

Dave does it for me. "No, who?"

For someone who didn't want to talk, Mr. Butler sure seems to be enjoying the attention now. He leans back in his chair, gesturing out the window with his fork.

"I already told you, this place used to be the projects. Now, I don't know where you folks are from, but by the looks of you, I'd wager neither of you have ever set foot in one. Let me assure you, it's as bad as you think. Gangs, guns, prostitutes and drug runners on every corner. Suffice it to say, we had more than our fair share of troubled kids. But your husband stood out because he was smart. He was smart and he was sneaky, and both of those things together made him dangerous. You never knew he was on the verge of explosion until it was too late."

My gaze flicks to Dave, whose expression is carefully blank. "What are you saying, exactly?"

"I think you know what I'm saying. The police could never prove Will set it, mind, but they were suspicious enough to assign him a case officer. And that fire killed more than just Kat. Two kids died that night, as well."

Dave jerks, and my mouth fills with an all too familiar acid. I turn away from the table and try not to pant, calculating the number of steps to the garbage can in case I can't swallow the sick down. Three, maybe four, tops, but only if I leap over another table. The distraction puts some distance between me and what this man is saying — that Will set a fire that ended the lives of not only two children, but also his own mother. That he was responsible for their deaths. I lean back in the chair and shake my head, a slow side to side.

Not possible.

The old man takes in my posture, reads my disbelief and lifts a lumpy shoulder in a *suit yourself* gesture. "When it came to his parents, your husband got the short end of the stick, that's for certain. Kat and Lewis Griffith could barely take care of themselves, much less another human being."

"Coach Miller suggested there was some violence in the home," Dave says.

"Then he was lying, because there was a lot of violence. A *lot*. But even so, it didn't take long for the fire department to rule it arson. Whoever set the fire used accelerant."

Still.

"It could have been anybody," I say.

My head aches, and I suddenly wish I was back home, letting Mom fuss over me. Why did I have to come out here and kick up this dramatic shit storm? I want to go back in time, unhear everything this man and Coach Miller have told me. It's too much. I no longer want to know.

"True. But the fire occurred at around 2:00 a.m., after a particularly loud and vicious argument between Kat and Lewis ended in them both drinking themselves into a stupor. I'll never forget the screaming and shouting from those two. Anyhow, a container of gasoline was found in the abandoned apartment next door. And Billy, who swore he was asleep in his bed at that time, somehow made it out without a scratch."

I stare at Dave, who's been taking in the news in a way that makes his face shut down. He swipes a palm over his chin and swallows. He doesn't want to believe, but he might.

And even though the psychologist in me knows an abused, neglected kid is sixty percent more likely to get into trouble, I'm not convinced. This is my Will we're talking about. He could have woken up from the noise, or maybe he smelled the smoke. Anybody could have put the gasoline in an abandoned apartment. My Will would never have done such a thing.

"So far the only evidence I've heard has been circumstantial," I say.

"I already told you he was smart. But I'll tell you right now exactly what I told the detectives at the time. What I saw on your husband's face when those firemen carried his unconscious father out of that burning building was disappointment." Mr. Butler slaps his fork to the table and spears me with a hard gaze. "Do you understand what

I'm telling you? He wanted that fire to take them both."

15

I jerk awake when Dave shoves open the curtains with a loud screech. "Rise and shine, princess. It's a brand-new day, and it's raining. Again. Make that still. It's raining still." He turns, his body silhouetted in front of the window like a shadow. "How do people live here?"

I groan, rolling away from the window and the light, and pull the pillow over my throbbing head. After we dropped Mr. Butler back at Rainier Vista, Dave drove us straight to the nearest bar, where he told the bartender to keep the vodka martinis coming until I was good and drunk. With not much more than a couple bites of Chex Mix lining my stomach, it didn't take him long. By the time I reached the bottom of the first glass, the room was already spinning. Things started to get fuzzy somewhere halfway through the second one. I have no memory of the third or how I got from there, a slightly seedy cocktail lounge with bad music and a sticky bar top, to here, wrapped in soft Egyptian cotton.

I push myself up on an elbow and look around the hotel room. Hip and generically modern with a great wall of windows looking out over the water. In the distance is a mountainous horizon, jagged peaks of terrain jutting up into the steel sky. "Where are we?"

He gives me a funny look. "Honey, we're in Seattle, remember? Birthplace of Starbucks and flannel capital of the world, where everybody drives a Subaru. I always thought that last one was an exaggeration, by the way, but it's not. For a city so focused on clean living, you'd think there'd be fewer cars."

"I know Seattle. I meant, what hotel? I hope you didn't have to carry me."

"Hey, that's what brothers are for." He grins.

"I'm sorry we missed last night's dinner reservation."

He plops into an armchair by the window, waving off my apology. "The bar food was actually okay. I mean, it wasn't foie gras, but it was a hell of a lot better than that fast-food curry, which, by the way, was definitely not lamb. But just so we're clear, you're not getting out of feeding me a sit-down breakfast this morning before we go."

"Go where?"

"We can hammer out the agenda at breakfast. We've got places to go and people to talk to, so let's go."

I fall back onto the bed, pulling the covers up to under my chin. "You go. I'm not up to doing anything today."

"This isn't a vacation, Iris. We're on a mission here, remember? Your mission."

"I know, but tomorrow, maybe. Today let's stay in our pajamas, order room service and have a movie marathon."

"I'm already dressed."

I reach one arm out, pluck the hotel TV directory from the nightstand. "I bet they have *Beaches*."

"Come on. I'm not that much of a stereotype."

"Sorry to break it to you, bro, but you are."

He rolls his eyes but doesn't argue the point. "Would you please get out of bed and in the shower? I called around to some old-folks' homes near Rainier Vista, and guess who I found? Your father-in-law. Will's father. I thought we'd start by paying him a visit."

Father-in-law. I roll the word around on

my tongue, and a fresh round of yesterday's hurt throbs in my chest, a hot white pulse that crushes my already trampled heart. And my brand-new father-in-law is not the worst of it. I push up onto an elbow.

"I maybe have had a few too many martinis last night, but I happen to remember every single word that old man said. A woman and two children died in a fire that he's convinced Will set. Maybe Will did it and maybe he didn't, but you know what they say, where there's smoke and all that . . ."

"Well, while you were sleeping off the booze, I did a bit of digging into that fire. I checked the newspapers and read the redacted police report online, and the old man's story was pretty accurate, except he forgot to mention one thing. The police traced the gasoline jug to a store in Portland, which begs the question. How does a seventeen-year-old kid with no car and no money buy gas in a city almost two-hundred miles down the road?"

"Did they mention any other suspects?"

"Only Will's father."

My eyes go wide. "Will's father was a suspect?"

"Of course. The husband is always the first one the police question. Don't you watch

CSI? Especially when he's got loose hands like Will's father did. He was too drunk to remember his alibi, but he had one. A neighbor said he was passed out on their couch when the building went up in flames."

Flames. The word gives me a full-body shiver.

"And the kids?"

"Two siblings, three and five. Fast asleep in the apartment across the hall. Their mother was working the night shift."

My stomach twists with horror for that poor woman. I think of her tucking her babies in that night before heading off to work, telling them she'd be home by the time they awoke, telling herself they'd be safe in their own beds. Their tragedy is every mother's worst nightmare.

I curl around my pillow, burrowing deeper under the comforter. "You know, everything I've learned since the crash is so confusing. Him getting on the wrong plane to the wrong destination. Making up a conference. Meeting this friend Corban he never told me about. All these lies about where he came from and what his childhood was like. I don't understand any of it. Except for the house."

"Your house?"

I nod. "We must have seen a hundred.

205

There was something wrong with every one of them. The kitchen was too dated or the yard was too small or the street was too busy. Nothing was ever perfect enough for Will. Our broker showed us that house more to prove a point than anything else. Like, *see what you can get if you cough up another hundred grand?* But you should have seen his face when we walked in the door." I smile at the memory of how everything about him went completely still but the color in his cheeks, which got more and more flushed with each room we walked through. "By the time we got upstairs, it was a done deal. He had to have it."

A sudden gust of rain machine-gun patters against the window. Dave swings his feet up onto an ottoman, folding his arms across his chest and settling in. "It is a gorgeous house."

I think about the first time we walked up the steps, his face when we pushed through the stained-glass door, how I knew before we walked through, it was a done deal. "We made an offer that same day. Even though it meant mostly empty rooms and a mortgage we could afford only by the skin of our teeth. But now I understand why owning it was so important to him."

"Because the house was a symbol of how

far he'd come."

"Exactly." As I say the word, a familiar anger rises inside me all over again, and I lurch upright in bed. "If he had just told me why he wanted it so badly, I wouldn't have fought him so much. I wouldn't have complained about giving up my Starbucks habit or how we never got to go on vacation so we could buy our dream house. There's not a soul on the planet who would have understood more than me. But he wasn't ever planning to tell me, was he?"

Dave sighs, lifting both hands into the air. "Not this again," he mutters.

"Not what again?"

"We already had this discussion, at length, last night at the bar. You even took a poll. An overwhelming eighty-seven percent of half-drunk hipsters agree that, no, Will was never planning to tell you."

Normally, I'd be mortified by the thought of a hammered me asking people I don't know to weigh in on my marriage. I'm not exactly an uninhibited type, and I don't go around talking to strangers about my business. But I'm too focused on the bigger picture — the fact that my husband not only kept such essential parts of himself from me, his very favorite person on the planet, when we first met, but that he didn't trust me, didn't trust our love, enough to come clean.

"Not about his parents, not about the fire, nothing about his scary, sketchy past. He fed me all that bullshit about growing up with a loving single mother in Memphis, and I swallowed it whole. Did he even go to UT? Does he even have a degree? I have no idea, because I'm the most gullible person in the world!"

"You aren't gullible, honey. You were deceived by the man you loved. There's a big difference."

"I'm a trained psychologist, Dave. I'm supposed to see through people like Will."

"I don't see how any of this is your fault."

"Whatever." I fall back onto the bed, covering my face with the pillow, new tears pricking at my eyes. Up until seven days ago, I was 100 percent convinced I knew my husband. I thought Will told me everything about himself. I thought we told each other everything. And now, I keep unraveling bits and pieces of the former him that lead me back to the same thought: *I never really knew the man I married.*

And now, looking back, I have to question everything. That time we went to San Francisco, a city he swore he'd never visited, and he knew the way with barely a glance at the map. Was it because he'd been there before? When he admitted in a game of Cards Against Humanity that he didn't go to senior prom but refused to tell me why. And when we would go to La Fonda and Will would order *chile rellenos* and *quesadillas con camarones* with perfect pronunciation. Since when did he speak Spanish?

And then it occurs to me that I've lost Will twice now. The first time was when he got on that plane, the second when he posthumously morphed into a stranger. One was swift and shocking, the other more gradual but no less painful. Both wounds are fresh and jagged and deep.

"Tomorrow's a week," I say, my voice muffled. "I will have survived seven whole days without Will."

"I know." Dave is silent for a long moment, and I hear him push out of the chair, moving closer. "Listen, can I ask you something?"

"I'm pretty sure I couldn't stop you if I tried."

"I realize that finding out all this stuff about Will is gutting you."

"It is." A sob pushes up my throat, but I catch it before it escapes.

"But have you considered the obvious?"

"Which is?" I push aside my pillow, and

there he is, my twin brother, staring down at me.

He gives me an encouraging smile. "That maybe he *did* change. Maybe that's why he never told you. Maybe he was looking to start fresh, to press control-alt-delete on his shitty life and start all over with you."

"Okay, then tell me, why did he get on a plane to Seattle?"

The smile drops from his face. My question has stumped him, and even worse, it's stumped me. Why *did* Will get on that plane to Seattle? Suddenly, the idea of hiding out in a hotel room is no longer so appealing. Sighing, I throw back the sheets and haul myself out of bed.

"Thank God," he says as I head off into the bathroom, "because I've seen *Beaches* a million times."

Twenty minutes later, as I'm getting out of the shower, a text from the blocked number pings my phone. Why are you still in Seattle? I mean it, Iris. Go. Home. There's nothing for you there.

I wrap a towel around my torso, shove it under my arms and type out a reply as quickly as my shaking hands will allow. I'm not going anywhere until you tell me who you are. And you were wrong, btw. So far Seattle has been very enlightening.

Two seconds later, another lights up my screen. Don't believe everything you hear.

My pulse ratchets up, and my stomach tightens with something that feels like excitement. Then what should I believe?

I wait, watching the screen until it goes dark, then black.

We find Lewis Griffith at Providence House, a memory care facility for the indigent and the most depressing place on the planet. The floors are grungy, the air is smelly, and the ceilings are low and stained. We find a grim-faced nurse on the second floor, and she points us down a dark hallway. "Room 238, but don't expect him to say much. He's got Alzheimer's, you know."

I thank her, trying to decide if Alzheimer's is the worst or the best way to cap off six decades of a hard life. It's a slow and unpleasant way to go, but at least this way he's not aware of it.

We find him in a closet-sized room that reminds me of a cheap roadside hotel I once stayed at in Guatemala, barely bigger than the bed Mr. Griffith is confined to. There's nowhere for me and Dave to sit, so we stand, shoulder to shoulder and pressed between two flimsy walls, at the foot end of the bed.

I look down at my father-in-law, and a thunderclap rolls through my head. I search his face for pieces of my husband and find only a few. The broad forehead, the square jawline, the slight upward tilt to the eyes. I might find more, if Mr. Griffith didn't look so wrecked, if his skin weren't so waxy and wan, more Madame Tussaud than human, and smothered in brown spots like lunch meat.

I reach for Dave with a shaking hand, and he gives my fingers a squeeze.

"Mr. Griffith, my name is Iris, and I'm your daughter-in-law. I was married to your son, Will. Or Billy. Do you remember him?"

Nothing. Mr. Griffith doesn't seem to hear me. He takes us in with empty eyes.

I pull up a picture on my phone and hold it in Mr. Griffith's line of vision. "This was taken about a month ago."

His forehead creases. A frown?

"Do you remember him?"

Nothing.

"This isn't getting us very far," Dave whispers behind a hand.

I give a subtle shake of my head, slipping the phone in my back pocket. "Mr. Griffith, about fifteen years ago, there was a fire in the apartment where you lived, in Rainier

Vista. Three people were killed. Does that ring any bells?"

Mr. Griffith doesn't nod, but the way his gaze wanders to mine straightens my spine.

"Your wife, Kat, was one of the victims, as were two small children. You and Billy survived unharmed."

His sandpaper lips flap around for a few seconds, like he's trying to speak. Or maybe he is speaking, I don't know. Either way, nothing but air comes out.

"Do you remember anything about that night? The fire? Your wife and son?"

His face curls into a grimace, and his mouth moves around some more. Dave and I grip the metal bed frame and lean in closer, straining to hear.

"Did he just say Billy?" Dave says, looking at me with wide eyes.

My heart rate spikes, and the blood roars in my ears. I'm pretty sure he did. "Mr. Griffith, do you remember Billy?"

For the longest moment, there's nothing but the sound of his wheezing, a breathy whistle sung by rattly lungs. And then he lifts an arm high and slaps the mattress, once, twice, again. His skinny body begins flailing about, limbs writhing, both palms pounding the mattress. Dave and I exchange a worried look.

"Is he okay?" I say.

As if in answer, Mr. Griffith hauls a breath, opens his mouth wide and makes a long, creepy sound somewhere between a moan and a scream.

"Oh, jeez," Dave says, pulling at his collar.

The moaning stops but not the writhing, and only for a second or two, long enough for Mr. Griffith to suck another rattling breath and begin again.

Dave backs away from the bed, moving closer to the door. "Maybe I should go get a nurse."

"You stay here. I'll go." I'll be damned if he's leaving me here alone.

His eyes go wide, and he shakes his head. "No way."

I latch onto his arm and drag him to the door. "Fine. We'll both go."

Mr. Griffith is gearing up for his third round of eerie oms when we stumble into the hall and right into a nurse in pale pink scrubs.

"Oh, thank God," I say. "There's something wrong with Mr. Griffith."

"He's fine. He's just agitated again." She pushes past us and continues down the hall, her crocs squeaking on the dingy linoleum. "Happens all the time."

Again? Dave frowns, and so do I.

"Aren't you going to help him?" I call out after her.

The nurse stops, hauls a full-body sigh and trudges back. She tosses us a dirty look, then disappears into the room. As soon as she's gone, Dave and I exchange glances and make a beeline for the stairs.

"Yeesh, I'm not going to lie," Dave says as soon as we're in the stairwell. "I'm glad to be on my way out of here. This place gives me the creeps. How depressing was that?"

"So is my father-in-law." I hear my words and amend. "Or rather, his illness is depressing."

Dave's expression softens. "His life is depressing, too, sweetie."

I sigh, rounding the landing to the next level. "I know." When it comes to my father-in-law, there are so many depressing things, too many to count.

"We can try him again tomorrow. Maybe bring along some pictures or newspaper clippings that would spark a memory, but for now . . ."

"The police department, I guess. After that —"

"No, I meant with your father-in-law. Shouldn't you, I don't know, do something?"

"Like what? I just found out he existed

yesterday, and it's not like he and Will ever had much of a relationship. I feel sorry for the man, but it seems like he's provided for here."

"Oh, is that what you call it? Do me a favor. Make sure I never end up in a place that smells of canned peas and dirty diapers, will you?"

A niggle of guilt rises in me at my brother's words, along with a flash of irritation he would imply I'm neglecting the father-in-law I didn't know I had. "What do you want me to do?" I say, pushing from the stairwell into the lobby. "Move him into my guest room?"

"Don't be ridiculous. But there's got to be a better place for him than this."

"Mrs. Griffith?" The nurse at the front desk says, thwarting our argument before it can escalate further. She slaps a clipboard to the counter and holds up a pen. "If you don't mind, I have some paperwork for you to fill out."

"Oh. Okay." I frown. "What kind of paper-work?"

"We just want to make sure we have all the information for Mr. Griffith's next of kin, and that you are aware of all of Mr. Griffith's options."

I pick up the pen and flip through the

pages — a contact form, Medicaid forms, privacy and disclosure forms. Pretty standard fare, though I'm not sure why she wants me to fill out any of it. "What's all this for?"

"Providence House is a nursing home, which means we provide generalized care for seniors with all sorts of issues. Our nurses can handle dementia, but we're not specialized in it."

"Then why is Mr. Griffith here?"

"Because the facilities that cater to memory care either don't have Medicaid-funded spots available or long waiting lists for those spots."

"I see." I don't see. Also? I don't like this woman, or what she's implying. "Are you kicking Mr. Griffith out?"

"As long as Mr. Griffith qualifies for Medicaid, he's welcome to stay as long as necessary. I'm only suggesting that should you have a budget for his care, he may be happier in a larger room or even at another facility, one that's better suited to the particular needs of an Alzheimer's patient. I assume, as his daughter-in-law, you would want to make his last months as comfortable as possible."

It all falls together then, and I put the pen on the top of the paper pile. "Are you asking me for money?"

"Of course not. Though we do accept donations."

"Let me guess. Cash only?"

Her lips curl up in a saccharine smile. "A little goes a long way in this place."

By the time we get to the car, I'm shaking with fury. Literally shaking. Full-body tremors that chatter my bones and rattle me from head to toe. "I cannot believe that nurse just squeezed me for money."

Dave hits the remote for the doors and gives me a look over the roof of the car, one that says *I can.*

I fall onto the passenger's seat, pitch my bag onto the floor and slam the door behind me. "And you saw the way that nurse acted upstairs, like calming down a confused, agitated old man was a chore. I don't want to even think about how they are when no one's watching. They're probably too busy watching the *Housewives* in the break room to pay attention to any of the patients. They certainly can't be bothered to mop the floors or spray around some air freshener."

"You're probably not far from the truth." Dave pops the gear into Reverse and swings a long arm over my seat, his gaze bouncing over mine on the way to the back window.

"Which is why I'm really glad you paid that bitch."

16

"Five business days?" I say to the female officer behind the Public Request Unit desk, my voice tipping into a light yell that's only partly from frustration. The Seattle Police Department lobby is a cavernous space of concrete and tile, and the racket of people coming and going makes me wish I'd brought earplugs. "Why does it take five days to make copies of a file from an incident that happened over fifteen years ago?"

"No, five days for us to contact you about your request, and whether or not there will be any charges associated with getting it to you. We'll also let you know at that time if any records or portion of the records are exempt from disclosure. In that case, they'll be withheld or redacted accordingly."

Dave leans an arm on the countertop. "So let me get this straight. Five days until we hear whether or not we'll be able to get a copy of the police report?"

"That's correct."

"Isn't there any way to expedite the process? Like with an extra fee or something?"

The woman lifts a bushy brow that tells him he better not be pulling out his wallet.

Frustration stabs me between the ribs. Five days from now we'll be back on the East Coast, and unless we find another lead before then, no closer to finding out why Will boarded that plane. Five days feel like an eternity.

The officer leans to the left, looking around Dave's shoulder to the man behind us. "Next."

Dave steps into her line of sight. "What do you need from us to get things rolling?"

She passes us a pile of forms and a pen clipped to a clipboard. "Fill these in." She lists again to the left. "Next."

This time we step aside, carrying everything over to a couple of empty chairs by the window. I fall into mine, helplessness pressing down hard enough to make me breathless. "Now what? I'm out of ideas, Dave. Where are we going to look next?"

"Well, we could go back and case the neighborhood again, or maybe try to track down some more classmates. Other folks might have a different story to tell."

"You think so?"

Dave wrinkles his nose. "Honestly? Both options feel like a wild-goose chase to me."

"Yeah. To me, too. And now that we have a copy of the yearbook, I can track down those folks anytime. I don't need to be here to do it. There's got to be something else, something we're missing."

We fall silent, thinking.

I lean back in my chair and replay the conversations with Coach Miller and the old man at the community center, and something about them nags at me. Something one of them said, some detail one of them dropped doesn't sit right, but my thoughts are like a kitten batting at a ball of yarn. Whenever I'm close to catching it, it rolls away.

I imagine the teenage Will waiting outside that burning building, watching firemen carry his parents out, one of them in a body bag. Was he really surprised to see his father alive, like that old man said? Even after everything I've learned about his life here, I can't imagine Will knowingly set the fire in the hope that his parents would become victims. No matter how awful his parents were, they were still his parents, and they weren't the only lives he would be putting at risk by lighting that match. The Will I

222

knew would never do such a thing.

And yet, the old man claimed he wasn't the only one who suspected Will was guilty. Though they couldn't prove it, the police did, too, enough so they assigned someone to keep him out of trouble.

I sit up straight, pointing my pen to the lobby lights. "That's it."

Dave frowns. "What's it?"

"The old man said that Will was assigned a case officer after the fire. That's who we need to talk to next."

"Okay, but how? He never said a name."

"No, but maybe it'll be in the police report."

"It wasn't in the redacted version I read online, but surely something that essential would be included in the full version. You keep working on those." He points to the papers on my lap, rising out of his chair. "I'll go see what I can find out from our friendly lady officer."

I watch him set off across the lobby, heading back to the ten-deep line at the requests desk with all the nonchalance of a Sunday stroll, and something squeezes in my chest — warmth and sunshine and fraternal love. Dave dropped everything to fly with me to Seattle. He left his job, his husband, his life to cart me around this strange city, to pick me up every time new news about my husband knocks me down. I don't know how I'll ever repay him.

As if he feels me watching, he swings back around and makes a writing gesture with his hand. I smile, blow him a kiss, then return to the forms.

I'm starting in on the second page when my cell phone chirps inside my bag, and I scramble to dig it out. After my unfinished conversation with the blocked number, Dave and I agreed I should keep my phone at easy access and the ringer volume high. Whoever the sender is, he likely lived in Rainier Vista at the time of the fire, and he seems to have a very different perspective than what we heard from the old man and Coach Miller. Creepy stalker or not, I want to talk to him. I want to find out what he knows. And so I'm more than a little disappointed when it's my father's name that lights up the display.

"Hi, there, punkin'," Dad says in that easy, steady way of his, and I plug my other ear with a finger so I can hear him. "What's with all the racket? Where are you?"

"In the lobby at the police station. Don't worry, we haven't been accosted or arrested or anything like that. We're just here to request an old police report. It's too much of a story to go into over the phone, but suffice it to say, my husband was a very different person when he lived here. Oh, and it seems I have a father-in-law."

"Huh. Well, I'll be darned. Did you meet him?"

My father has always been the master of understatement, and I can't help but smile. "I did, in fact. And he's not doing so great. He has Alzheimer's, and his nursing home is awful. More drama that I'll fill you in on later." My gaze wanders out the wall of windows, and the pedestrians slogging through the constant drizzle as if it were a sunny day. "Anyway, were you calling to chat or did you need something?"

"I'm calling because your mother's been nagging me to find out when you're coming home, but also to give you a couple of messages."

"Why didn't Mom just call and ask me herself?"

"Oh, you know your mother. She didn't want to be a nag."

"So she just nagged you instead."

"As I said, you know your mother." I laugh, and a smile pokes through his words when he continues, "Now, you got a pen and paper handy?"

I dig an old receipt from the bottom of

my bag and flip it over. "Hit me."

"All righty, let's see . . ." There's a rustling and sounds of paper shuffling, and I picture my father sliding his readers onto his nose and flipping through his list. "Claire Masters from Lake Forrest called to check in, as did Elizabeth, Lisa and Christy, who seemed worried they hadn't heard from you since the memorial. I assume you have everyone's numbers?"

"Yes. I'll shoot them all a text later."

"I'm sure they'll be glad to hear from you. Leslie Thomas said to tell you she's very sorry, and that if you'll talk to her, she has a name you need to hear. Something about a cocktail waitress at a bachelor party, if that makes any sense?"

"It makes total sense, unfortunately. Did she leave a number?"

Dad recites it for me, then moves on to the next message. "Evan Sheffield called, said he was sorry he missed you at the friends-and-family meeting but wanted to make sure you got the updates. He sounded legit. I hope you don't mind, but I gave him your email address."

"That's fine. I promised I'd get it to him at the memorial anyway, and then with all the travel, totally forgot."

"And a man named Corban Hayes

stopped by earlier this afternoon. He seemed like he knew a good deal about you and Will."

"He does. I talked to him at the memorial, too. Remember? He's a friend of Will's from the gym."

"That's what he said. He also brought by a box of things. A couple of books he borrowed from Will a while back, a stack of photographs, a T-shirt from some run they did together, stuff like that. He said he wanted you to have it."

"That was nice of him," I say, right as something else occurs to me. "You didn't tell anybody I was in Seattle, did you?" Not that I imagine any of the callers, Leslie Thomas excluded, would be the messenger hiding behind a blocked number, but still, I have to ask. If my father's been going around telling everyone who called or stopped by where I am, it certainly broadens the suspect pool.

"No, I don't think so. Why?"

"Think, Dad. It's important."

He pauses but only for a second or two. "No, I'm positive I didn't say anything other than that you were away for a few days, and that your mother and I were watching the house. Now, could you please tell me why you're asking?"

Dave sinks into the chair across from me, flashes me an upturned thumb as a sign of victory. I give him a distracted nod, then fill my father in on the texts from the blocked number. That whoever it is knows I'm here, knows Dave and I are here to excavate details from Will's past, even claims to know what I'm searching for and that I'm doing it in the wrong place.

My father's voice goes deep and deadly, a carryover from his military days. "I don't like it, Iris. Whoever is sending those messages could be tracking you from your cell. Which means not only would he know you're in Seattle, he knows you're sitting in the police station lobby."

"Well, at least we're safe here," I say, but my joke falls flat. Dad grumbles while, across from me, Dave's brows slide into a frown. "Seriously, Dad, we're fine. The texts haven't been threatening, just . . . insistent that I go home, which it looks like we're probably doing tomorrow anyway. Seems we've hit a wall here."

"Good. Your mother will be glad to hear it."

Mom's voice carries down the line, as clearly as if she's sitting on his lap. "Hear what, dear?"

"That the kids are coming back tomorrow." She says something else, something I can't quite decipher, and my father sighs. "She wants to know if you've been eating."

"Yes," I say, and it's not quite a lie. I *have* been eating. I just haven't managed to keep much of it down. I steer us back on subject. "Anything else?"

"Yup. Nick Brackman's called four times."

That one gives me pause. Nick is Will's boss, a man I've met only a handful of times at AppSec functions, and so long ago that when he stepped up to me at the memorial, it took me a good few minutes to place him. By the time I figured out who he was, he was already gone. "What did Nick want?"

"He didn't say, but it sounded pretty urgent. He left his cell number and said for you to call him on it the second you get a chance, day or night. He'll pick up no matter the time." My father recites the number, and I jot it onto the receipt. "One more thing, punkin'."

Something about the way his voice dips shoots up a flare of alarm, and I go hot and cold at the same time. "Okay . . ."

He pauses to clear his throat, a delaying maneuver that scoots me to the edge of my chair. "Dad! Just tell me."

"Ann Margaret Myers called this morning." At the name, I grip the chair's arm hard enough to break it in two. "Sweetheart, they recovered Will's wedding ring from the crash site."

Somehow, Dave snags us two first-class seats on the red-eye back to Atlanta, where, according to my father, Will's ring sits in a padded Liberty Airlines envelope on my bathroom counter. According to Ann Margaret, there's not a scratch on it, not even the tiniest of dings. I think of the force that must have ripped the band from his finger, imagine the piece of platinum soaring through the sky and bouncing down the cornstalks like a pinball machine, and yet the ring looks as good as new. A fluke, she called it, kind of like the malfunction that took down that plane.

I sigh and stare out the window, into the night and onto the Seattle tarmac. Whirling yellow lights reflect off the wet surfaces below me, dull smudges of brightness through my swollen eyes and the dark lenses of my sunglasses. I know how ridiculous I must look, wearing sunglasses at ten at night like some wannabe rapper, but it's the only way I could think of to hide my tears. I've been crying ever since Dad told me they found Will's ring, the one with my name engraved on the inside.

These past seven days, I've held out hope. I told myself Will wasn't dead, not really, not until I had proof. Not until they found some tiny part of him at the crash site. I latched onto my hope with both hands, clenching down tight with my fists even as the days passed and the hope slipped through my fingers. And then one phone call from Liberty Air hijacked my hope and took my husband — the love of my life, the future father of my babies — for the second time. But this time the loss feels real, and it burns like a brand pressed to my heart.

Dave wraps my fingers around an icy drink, then presses a tiny blue pill into my palm. "Not only will this little guy knock you senseless, the sleep will be deep and dreamless and last all the way home."

If there's one thing you can count on from an urban, sophisticated gay man, it's good pharmaceuticals. I toss the pill back without hesitation.

And then I turn to the window, press my forehead to the glass and wait for senseless, dreamless sleep to pull me under.

17

Dave and I are halfway up the walk when Mom swings the door open and steps onto the porch in her bathrobe. "*Lieverds!* Welcome home."

We've been on the ground for a little over an hour, and I'm still headachy and groggy from Dave's little pill. But the bigger issue is what Dad told me is waiting upstairs on my bathroom counter. Will's ring is like a living, breathing presence in this house, calling me to it like a beacon. I have a million things to do, a long list of people to call back, yet all I can think about is the ring.

I piece together what I hope is a halfway decent smile. "Hi, Mom."

Her worried gaze tips to Dave, trailing me up the porch stairs. I don't have to turn to know he's gesturing for her to back up and give me some space. Her look of obvious dismay at his message tugs at me, and I remember a Christmas not too long ago, when after too much eggnog she admitted to sometimes feeling like a jilted lover around me and Dave, so covetous is she of our connection. She's wearing the exact same expression now. I reach the top and step into her arms, sinking into a rare bear hug, and her body shakes with what I know is frustration. My mother is a fixer, and my life has turned into a tragedy she can't fix.

"My sweet, sweet baby," she whispers into my hair.

I untangle us, and she leads me into the foyer, where Dad and James stand in their pajamas. Dad swings an arm around my shoulders while James sweeps Dave into an embrace worthy of a three-month rather than three-day separation. I see it, and a twinge of something unpleasant hits me in the solar plexus. Is this how it's going to be now? Bitterness and anger and jealousy every time I see another couple kiss? I swallow the feelings down and make a silent vow. My misery will not begrudge anyone, least of all Dave, his happiness.

"Breakfast will be ready in fifteen minutes," Mom says.

I don't have the heart to tell her I just ate a rubbery egg-and-bagel sandwich on the plane. I snatch my bag from the floor where Dave dumped it and head up the stairs.

"Just going to grab a quick shower. If I'm not down by then, start without me."

She gives me a worried nod.

I haul my heavy body up the stairs and down the hallway to my bedroom, noticing that Mom has scoured the place. The woodwork gleams, the windows sparkle, even the linens have been laundered and the beds made up, the corners tucked tighter than a hospital mattress. I dump everything on the foot end of mine and run a finger up the duvet, breathing in the heady scent of my favorite flower, stargazer lilies, stuffed into bowls and vases everywhere I look. On both nightstands, on the TV table, on the stool by the reading chair by the window. She must have spent a fortune.

In the bathroom, the envelope sits like a hunk of kryptonite on my vanity. I inch my way across the tile and slide my shaking fingers into the padded paper, feeling around until they make contact with a cool slip of metal.

I know it's Will's ring before I pull it out. I know it by the hammered finish, by the weight and the thickness of the metal, the way it slides up my thumb and hugs just the right spot between the joint and the base. My breath catches when I read the inscription, the tiny letters a jeweler in

Buckhead overcharged me to hand engrave: *My very favorite person. xo, Iris.*

A new wave of grief sucker punches me in the heart, a direct hit, and I settle the ring on my thumb, turn on the shower and stumble in fully clothed. I think about the day I pushed it up Will's knobby finger, the ball of emotion that clogged my throat when we exchanged our vows, the way he twirled me around after until my heart felt like it would burst with joy. It was the perfect day, the first in the rest of our perfect lives together. How lucky was I to have found this man, my other half, my very favorite person on a planet crammed with strangers? I knew then our love would last a lifetime.

The lifetime lasted seven years and a day.

I tell myself I should be grateful, that I should cherish every second we had together, but as scalding water batters the top of my head, all I can think is, more.

Dammit, I wanted more.

By the time I strip off my clothes and turn off the water, my skin has bloomed pink, my fingertips have shriveled white and wrinkly, and I've missed breakfast by a good half hour. I picture Mom downstairs in the kitchen, holding a plate of pancakes a foot thick and staring with longing up at the ceiling. I know I should go down there, but I can't. The inertia is as thick and sticky as flypaper. I leave my clothes in a wet heap on the shower floor, wrap my dripping body in a towel and sink onto the vanity stool instead, inspecting my face in the mirror.

Puffy eyes. Dark circles. Fish-belly complexion and sunken cheeks. It seems unfair that losing your husband means also losing your beauty. Haven't I lost enough? Haven't I been given enough shit to deal with? At the very least, widows should get rosy cheeks and glowing skin as a compensation prize.

I'm reaching for my jar of moisturizer when my elbow jostles the Liberty Airlines envelope, revealing another one, a smaller one, lying beneath it. A plain number ten envelope with a bluish tinge, generic and cheap. My name and address are typed in all caps across the front, under the words *Personal and Confidential.* I flip it over, poke a finger under the seal and rip it open.

The sheet of paper inside could have come from a million different notebooks, purchased at a million different stores. But it's the three little words, scrawled in a script as familiar to me as my own, that suck the air from my lungs.

I'm so sorry.

A burst of heat spreads across my chest. I snatch the envelope from the counter and check the postmark. The letter was sent two days ago, on April 8. The crash happened on April 3. That's five days after the crash.

After the crash. *After* it.

And yet this note was written by my husband's hand. I'm positive of it. The angular cursive, the lazy transitions, the too-long tail on the last letter. Even the blots of ink are consistent with Will's favorite pen.

There are a couple of hard knocks on the door, and Dave's voice carries around the corner. "Iris, are you decent?"

It takes me a couple of tries to find my voice. "Come in."

My brother's face appears above me in the mirror, his concerned gaze lasering in on mine. "Was it his?"

At first I think he means the note, even though I just opened it, and there's no possible way he could know. "Huh?"

"The ring. I take it was Will's?"

Oh, right. The ring. I wiggle my thumb, feel the hard metal pushing against my skin. "Yes. It's his."

"Oh, Jesus, I'm so sorry, Iris. I was hoping . . ." Dave steps closer, resting a supportive hand on my still damp shoulder. "I know you were hoping, too."

It's all I can do to nod. He gives me a funny look, and I pass him the paper over my shoulder.

"What's this?"

"A note." My voice is shaky, and so is my body, the emotions coursing through me so fast, my muscles vibrate with it. "I think Will wrote it."

"Okay . . ." Dave dips his head, his eyes scanning the paper. "Sorry about what?"

"I don't know." I hand him the envelope, let him do the math for himself.

It doesn't take him long. He spots the postmark, and his head whips up, his eyes blowing wide. "Who sent you this?"

I shrug. "It's postmarked Fulton County, which means it's local."

Dave sputters for a few seconds before his anger catches wind. "Is this some kind of sick joke?" He shakes the paper above my head, his face turning purple with fury. "This is psychotic. Whoever sent you a note from your dead husband is a psychopath, you know that, right?"

I nod. "But it's definitely Will's handwriting."

"It's postmarked two days ago!" he roars, scowling at my reflection as if *I'm* the one who dropped it in an Atlanta mailbox.

"How could Will have written it?"

"He must have done it before he died."

"Then who sent it?"

Dave's anger ignites my own. "I don't know!" I scream back, the words fueled by fury and frustration. My skin is blistered with it, with the shock of receiving a note in my dead husband's scrawl.

The bathroom plunges into silence.

Behind me, Dave sucks a lungful of air and blows it all out, long and slow, until his shoulders unhunch and his expression loses some of its heat. "Sorry. Sorry, but I'm pissed, okay? I'm going into big-brother protective mode because whoever sent you this did so with one intent and one intent only, and that's to fuck with your head."

I let out a laugh that's not the least bit funny. "Don't tell him, but it's working."

Another hard sigh. "Okay. Let's back up and think this through. *I'm so sorry* is generic enough he could have said it to anyone, but to write it on a piece of paper and hand it to them . . . It has to be someone he knew pretty well. Someone he worked with, maybe?"

"Probably the most likely candidate. If Will wasn't home, he was at the office. Either there, or at the gy—" The word gets swallowed up in a realization, and I twist around on my stool, staring up at Dave head-on. "Corban."

"Who?"

"The friend from the gym. The one who showed up at the memorial with news of the job that wasn't. I don't know if he was lying or misinformed, but there was something off about him, mostly because he knew all these things about Will, when I'd never heard of this guy. Will never talked about him at all. Not once"

"Okay." Dave nods. "Definitely suspicious. So how do we find out if he's the one?"

I pause to think, but the answer doesn't take me long. "I'll call him, ask him to meet me for coffee, get to know him a little better."

"Maybe you didn't hear me just now. I said we. How do *we* find out."

I shake my head. "He won't open up if he suspects even for a second we're onto him, which he will if I bring along a chaperone. I'm a psychologist, Dave. I know how to make people flip over and show me their underbelly. But I have to build trust first, and I can't do that with you glaring at him over my shoulder."

"I don't like it." The anger is back in his voice, and it's laced with *oh hell no*. "If he's our guy —"

"If he's our guy, then having you there will make him clam up for sure. And give me a little credit. I'm not stupid. I'll make sure to suggest a public place, a spot with a million people around. Nothing will happen. I'll be fine. And no offense, but nothing you can say is going to stop me."

My brother thinks about it for a second or two, puffing a trio of short and quick breaths through his nose. "Fine, but only if you promise me that, if he's our guy, you'll let me kick his ass."

I don't tell him there's not a chance, that Corban is built like a tank. I don't remind him of that time in tenth grade, when the PE coach told Dave he fights like a girl. Instead I nod and reach for his hand, thinking never have I loved my brother more.

18

Corban is seated on a bar stool by the window at Octane, a trendy coffee bar and lounge on Atlanta's Westside, when I walk through the door. The place is packed with new age nerds and long-haired hipsters interspersed with a few grad students from the downtown colleges, all of them pounding away at their MacBook Airs. Corban looks up from his phone, greeting me with a smile that is both quick and blinding. "Hey, Iris."

I toss him a wave, then gesture to the counter. "Can I get you anything?"

He lifts a ceramic mug from the bar top, fresh steam rising from the rim. "I'm all good, thanks."

I head to the counter, reciting my order to a dreadlocked girl, and study him out of the corner of my eye. I'd forgotten how dark and . . . shiny he is. His scalp is cleanly shaven and buffed to a high sheen, his arms slick and smooth where they bulge out of his sleeves.

I also can't help but notice he's handsome — the kind of handsome that comes with glossy magazine covers and red-carpet appearances. His clothes are casual, a fitted T-shirt and designer jeans, but he wears them with the elegance of a custom suit, perfect for his lean frame. I was too wrecked the day of the memorial to pay much attention to his looks, but I'm noticing them now, and I'm not the only one. Judging from the hair twirls and liquid looks over coffee cup rims, every female in the place has spotted him and is trying to snag his attention. Their doe eyes narrow when they get a load of me heading in his direction.

I drop my drink on the bar and let him pull me into a hug, soft cotton over muscles hard as steel. He smells like detergent and aftershave, a spicy scent that tickles the back of my throat.

"So great to see you again. How are you holding up?"

Friendly. Empathetic. Sincere. If this is the guy behind the letter, if he's capable of torturing a widow with a handwritten note from her dead husband, he's an Oscar-worthy actor skilled at hiding behind his charm. This doesn't mean I'm letting my guard down. There are plenty of good actors out there, not all of them in Hollywood.

I sink onto a stool, hanging my bag from a hook under the bar. "As well as can be expected, I guess. Thanks for meeting me, and for bringing over the box of Will's stuff. I especially liked the picture CD."

Most were images I'd seen before on Will's phone or on Facebook, but there were a few new shots, candids with Corban surrounded by others at the gym, their faces shiny with sweat, their arms slung around each other's shoulders. Their easy smiles and relaxed postures told me their friendship extended beyond occasional workouts, and seeing them made the hurt throb all over again in my chest. Why did Will keep that part of his life secret from me?

"Will was a good friend. The best," Corban says, his voice and expression mournful — more points in his favor. "I already miss him like hell."

"Me, too." I swallow down the sudden lump in my throat, scolding myself for letting him get me choked up. No way I'm going to let him play me like that, not until I know for certain he didn't send me that note. I curl a hand around my teacup, threading a finger through the handle, and pull myself together.

"The paper said they've begun recovering bodies from the crash site and have already returned some personal items to the families."

I nod, my free hand floating to the spot where Will's ring hangs from a chain, right above my heart, my emotions skidding into dangerous territory, my eyes filling — dammit — with tears.

"Jeez, Iris. I can't even begin to imagine how hard that must be for you." He wraps a palm around my elbow, gives it a quick squeeze. "I'm so sorry."

I'm so sorry. The exact same words on Will's note.

Even though the words are generic, the match dries my eyes like a blast of icy air, and they narrow into a squint I bury in my teacup. Was it intentional? A fluke? The idea that this man would send me that note, then taunt me by saying the identical words to my face, burrows like an insect under my skin. I gulp at my tea, but the hot liquid only fans the flames in my belly. Could Corban really be that cruel? Could anyone?

"Are you okay?"

His concern, as genuine as it sounds, tells me I need to get a hold of myself, of this conversation. I wipe my expression clean and drop my cup back onto the saucer.

"I'm fine. But I asked you here because I wanted to get your take on something." I pause to receive his nod. "I called ESP, the company you told me offered Will a new job. I talked to their head of HR. She didn't know Will, and what's more, she told me the last executive job was filled over eight months ago."

"I don't . . ." Corban's gaze doesn't let mine go, but his dark brows — along with his lashes, the only hairs on his head — dip in a sharp V. "You're telling me that Will didn't get a new job in Seattle?"

"That's right."

"But . . . I don't get it. Why would he feed me that elaborate story about a new job on the West Coast if it wasn't true? Why would he tell me about these hotshot new colleagues he was going to have, all the cool and crazy things they did on their team-building excursions? He told me they were taking him skydiving, and that their office building had a zip line. I mean, those are some pretty specific details. Why would he make all that up?"

"He didn't make it up. I'm pretty sure he got it from ESP's website."

"But the new job, the move to the West Coast, his worries you wouldn't want to leave your family . . . That was all fabrication?"

"Apparently so."

Corban's frown deepens, and his eyes flash with something I recognize as disappointment. His friend, the one he misses like hell, lied to him. He seems so genuinely offended that I decide to switch tracks.

"Did Will ever tell you where he was from?"

Corban tries to shake it off, crossing a denim-clad leg and bouncing his red Converse sneaker under the bar. "Oh, sure. I have a couple of cousins in Memphis, so Will and I were always comparing notes. Turns out we've been to a bunch of the same neighborhood haunts."

"Will is from Seattle."

"Okay." Corban drags out the word like he's humoring me, but his legs go still. "But then he moved to Memphis when he was what, five? Six? I know for sure it was when he was still a kid. Will went to Central, the big rival of the school where my cousins went."

"Will went to Hancock High. In Seattle."

For the longest moment, Corban is speechless, a lapse of silence that amplifies the coffee shop sounds all around us. His face goes slack, like he's run headlong into a door. "Are you sure?"

"Positive. I have the yearbook to prove it."

"So, okay. That's . . ." He runs a palm over his shiny scalp, and I can see his mind working, trying to puzzle the pieces together. That he can't make them fit seems to have him baffled. "Sorry, but I have to ask. Why all the lies?"

"That's what I'm trying to figure out. But if it makes you feel any better, he told them to me, too."

His head tilts. "You thought he was from Memphis, too?"

"Yes."

"Then how'd you find out about Seattle?"

I don't see any reason not to tell him, though I do keep my answer as vague as possible. "I received a condolence card from Hancock Class of '99. One thing led to another."

He takes that in with a curt nod, then falls still for a long moment. "Okay. So on the one hand, I'm more confused than ever, but on the other, in some weird, twisted way, things sort of make sense."

"What are you talking about?"

"Will's behavior lately. He just seemed so . . . distracted and . . . I don't know, off. Moody and super stressed out. A couple of weeks ago, some guy at the gym told him to wipe down the machine, and Will just lost it. He starts screaming and throwing punches, and I had to physically drag him outside and calm him down. I've never seen him lose his temper like that. Now I'm wondering if one thing had to do with the other, like if he was acting funny because of all the lies, or if the lies were to cover up something else. Does that make any sense?"

A flurry of emotions rise in my chest, a familiar hurt leading the pack. "It makes total sense, unfortunately."

"Was he acting stressed with you, too?"

Events from the past month flash across my mind like a slide show. The time I was making dinner while he paced the backyard, his cell pressed to his ear and his face clamped down in a scowl, talking to a person he would identify only as a "colleague." The time I came downstairs to him sitting in his car in the driveway, staring into space for a good twenty minutes. The time I rolled over to find him wide-awake, watching me with an expression I'd never seen before, an emotion I couldn't define. When I asked him what was wrong, his answer was to make love to me.

But AppSec had just acquired the City of Atlanta as a client, and Will's team was working under a tight deadline. He brushed his behavior off as work stress, and at the time, I believed him.

Or maybe I just wanted to.

Now, though? Now I'm certain there was something else going on. Something that made Will get on a plane to Seattle.

"You knew him better than anyone else," Corban says. "What do *you* think was going on?"

I roll his question around my mind for a long moment, coming at it from every possible angle. I think about Will's sketchy past, the destruction he left in his wake back in Seattle. The deadly fire that burned down a block of apartments and landed Will's mother and two innocent children in early graves. His father, alone and bedridden in a state facility for the indigent. And these are only the people I know about. How many others are there?

I swish around the last of my tea, watching the dredges swirl around the bottom of my cup. "I think something — or more likely, someone — from his past came back to haunt him. I think that's why he was acting strange, and why he got on the plane to Seattle."

Corban doesn't answer. I look up and he's gone completely still.

"What?"

"I wasn't going to tell you this, but based on that answer, I feel like I have to." He pauses, holding my gaze with eyes so black, I can't tell his pupil from his iris. "A day or two before the crash, Will called to ask me for a favor. He made me swear on my mother's grave that I would do it."

He stops, and so does my heart. "That you'd do what?"

"I promised that if anything ever happened to him, I'd look out for you."

I return home to a mountain of Lowe's bags climbing the walls of my foyer, and my father on his knees, a drill in his hand and a tool belt slung around his waist.

"What's going on?"

"Floodlights at both doors, that's what's going on." He roots around in one of the bags, pulls out a handful of light switches. "I'll mount these guys on the inside wall, but the outdoor fixtures have motion sensors. Anybody who gets within five feet will find themselves in the spotlight. Literally."

"Is this because of the letter?"

"The letter, the texts and the fact that you live smack in the middle of the twelfth most dangerous city in the country. I'm also changing your locks and putting in extra dead bolts and chains. And an alarm company is coming by later today to hook your system up to their central monitoring system."

Mom comes in from the living room, a book tucked under her arm. "I also asked him to fix the sticky front door, reattach that loose floorboard by the kitchen table and replace that rubber thingy on the leaky hall toilet."

"Valve," Dad says, pushing to his feet. "She asked me to replace the rubber valve. I got enough to replace all of them. You'll thank me when you get your next water bill."

"I'll thank you now, too," I say, and it comes out only a little wobbly, even though what I really want to do is have a good cry that Will never got through his honey-do list. What were the last two that he added, our last morning together in bed? It takes me a second or two to come up with them — the filters on the air conditioners and the oil in my car. I resolve to take care of those myself.

My father bends his knees, putting his eyes on the level of mine. "If you're worried about the costs, punkin', your mother and I will foot the bill. We'd just feel better if you were safe and secure and hooked up to some kind of system, especially now that . . .

Especially now."

I know what he was going to say: especially now that Will's gone. He looks so distraught, not to mention worried, that I wrap my arms around his waist and pull him tight, fresh tears gathering in my eyes. "Now that I'll be living here alone, I'd feel better with a working alarm, too. Thank you. But I don't want you to pay."

"Settled, then." Dad drops a kiss on the top of my head and unwinds us, fishing the drill from where he'd left it in the piles of bags. He hits the button, buzzing the blade around in the air, then takes his finger off the trigger. "Almost forgot. Will's boss left another message while you were gone. By now, his fifth or sixth. I take it you haven't found a chance to call him back yet."

I shake my head. Ever since Will's ring, I haven't given Nick or any of the other callers a second thought.

"You might want to make him a priority, punkin'. I'd imagine he has some financial and logistical issues to discuss, things you won't want to wait too long to tackle. I know it's unpleasant, but you've got a mortgage to pay, and you're going to have to figure out how to do it on one salary."

"Come." Mom slips her hand into my elbow and leads me down the hall. "You call this Nick person, and I'll fix us some tea. Oh, and I have brownies, too, if the boys didn't eat them all."

I look around for Dave and James. "Where are they?"

"They ran to the post office — Dave said something about a yearbook he needed to mail? — and then to meet up with an old friend of James's from med school. Apparently, he sold his practice for the jackpot and now owns a gourmet burger place on Peachtree Street. Seventeen dollars for a hamburger, can you imagine? Anyway, is Earl Grey okay?"

"Perfect, thanks." But Mom doesn't go for the tea bags. She just stands there, watching me. "What?"

"Well, I was wondering if you've given any thought to a funeral. One that's maybe a little more . . . personal than the memorial service Liberty Air put on. That one was perfectly fine, but it didn't really feel like Will, you know? It could have been for anyone."

I nod, because she's right. Despite the pretty setting, the memorial had zero personality. The songs were cheesy, the speakers were unimaginative, and the only time they mentioned my husband by name was during a monotonous reading of the passenger list. Will deserves better than a generic memorial service in a park filled with strangers.

"Want me to come up with some options?" Mom offers. "Take a look at some venues? I wouldn't book anything, of course, not until you approve it."

I smile, a fierce wave of love for my mother warming my insides. "Thank you. I'd really appreciate that."

"Good. It's settled, then. Now, you go call this Nick fellow back. His number's on a sticky by the coffee machine."

While Mom bangs away in the kitchen, I fetch the sticky note, punch the numbers into my cell phone and push Send.

Nick picks up on the second ring. "Nick Brackman."

"Hi, Nick. It's Iris Griffith. Sorry for not calling back earlier, but things have been a little crazy."

"I'll bet. How are you holding up?"

It's the same question strangers recited to me at the memorial, the one I see every time I look into my parents' eyes, word for word the one Corban said to me earlier today. *How are you holding up?* I know they mean well, but does Nick really want to hear that I still sleep in Will's bathrobe even though it smells more like me now, or that I call Will's voice mail twenty times a day, just so I can hear his voice? That my tears wake me most nights, which are only marginally better than the ones where fury makes me scream into my pillow? That the platitudes everybody keeps feeding me, things like *everything happens for a reason* and *Will would want you to be happy* make me want to punch something? That sometimes I feel Will so strongly the air catches in my throat and the hairs soldier up the back of my neck, but when I turn, the only thing I find is the hole where he used to be?

I sigh, collapse onto the couch and tell Nick what he wants to hear. "I'm okay."

The only thing worse than Nick's question, I suppose, will be the day people stop asking it.

"Glad to hear it. If there's anything I can do . . ."

Another platitude, and I bite down on a scream. "Thanks."

"Jessica's boxed up his personal things from the office. It wasn't much. A couple of books, some mugs, a few framed pictures. I think she was planning to swing by with it this weekend."

Surely this isn't what he called to tell me — meaningless clichés and organizational logistics. I give him a curt hum of thanks, a not-so-gentle prompt for his next words.

Either Nick gets tired of stalling, or he takes my bait. "Listen, I have something I need to talk to you about, and I'd really rather not do it over the phone. Do you think we could meet? You name the time and place, and I'll make it work."

"Well, I just got home, and —"

"You live in Inman Park, right?" I don't answer. Nick knows I live in Inman Park. Our address is on the salary stubs he signs every month. "How about Inman Perk in an hour? Best coffee in town, my treat."

After my morning with Corban, I can't contemplate another coffee shop, and after the past few days cooped up either in a hotel room, a car or on a plane, I can't contemplate another second indoors.

"I'll meet you at Inman Perk, but do you mind if we walk the BeltLine? I could use a little fresh air."

"Done. Thanks, Iris. See you in an hour."

As I head out the door to meet Nick, I punch in the number Dad gave me for Leslie Thomas. She picks up on the second ring.

"Before you say a word," she says by way of greeting, "I want to apologize for lying to you the first time I called. I was under an unbelievable amount of pressure to come back with a story. I've only been here a few months, and this was my first chance to prove myself, and I took it too far."

"And now?" My voice is hard, because I don't forgive her. The edges of my anger are still sharp. This woman dangled the name of a cocktail waitress in front of my nose like a carrot. I'm not exactly calling her by choice.

"And now what?"

I sink onto my front stoop, squinting into the sunshine. "Are you still under an unbelievable amount of pressure to come back with a story now?"

She laughs, but it comes across more ironic than funny. "Well, my boss just suggested I pose as another passenger's sister, so you tell me."

I make a neutral sound. This woman lied to me once. Who's to say she won't do it again?

"Listen, all I'm saying is that I feel really shitty for lying, and I want to make it up to you. Throw you the proverbial bone."

"Let me guess. The cocktail waitress's name."

"Ex-waitress, actually. It's Tiffany Rivero, and she served a certain pilot and his rowdy buddies until they cashed out at quarter to three the morning of the crash, and for over six thousand dollars."

My eyes blow wide, both at her message and the amount. "People spend six thousand dollars at a nightclub?"

"They do when they're chugging champagne like it's lemonade, which these guys apparently were. There were also pills being passed around like Tic Tacs."

I suck in a breath, doing the math in my head. Assuming he got the first flight to Atlanta, probably around six or so, he would have gone straight to the airport, meaning he was functioning on virtually no sleep, and that's not even taking into account whatever he consumed.

"We can't know for sure that the pilot was partaking."

"According to Tiffany, he was. Every single one of them was wasted. And here's the kicker — everything she told me, she also told Liberty Air officials. Their response? That she must be mistaken, that there are procedures and protocols in place to make sure no pilot enters the cockpit unless 100 percent sober and alert. They tried to make her think she'd imagined it."

An icy cold blooms in my gut, spreading through it like a cancer. Liberty Air knows about the pilot's alcohol and drug-fueled bachelor party, and they did nothing. They said nothing. I think about the families I saw at the airport and the memorial, of their tears and palpable grief, and a wave of helpless fury threatens to pull me under. Will is dead because of a pilot's irresponsibility and an airline's carelessness.

"Why are you telling me this? I assume this story is about to be blown across every front page of every newspaper and website on the planet."

"True, but my guilty conscience and I wanted you to hear it here first, and to make sure you understood the implications." She pauses, the silence short but weighted, and her jokey tone settles into a serious one. "There's going to be an investigation, Iris, and if this Tiffany chick is legit, if what she says checks out, you and the other families will have Liberty Air by the balls."

19

When I turn the corner to Inman Perk, Nick is standing on the sidewalk, two water bottles dangling from a fist. White-blond hair, super-sized limbs, doughy belly filling out the bottom of his tucked-in polo shirt like a half-inflated inner tube. I must have been worse off than I thought when I couldn't place him at the memorial. Big and bulky, he's not exactly the type of guy you can miss. A pair of pristine Nike sneakers poke out from under his office khakis, from the looks of them, fresh from a shoe box, and I'm suddenly sorry for suggesting we walk the BeltLine in the middle of a work-day.

"Hi, Nick."

"Hey, Iris. Thanks for meeting me. You ready?"

I try to take his emotional pulse, but his eyes are hidden behind dark wraparound sunglasses, his tone and expression guarded.

"Ready as I'll ever be."

The thing is, by now I know that whatever Nick wanted to talk to me about, it can't be good. Why else would he have called six times in half as many days and insisted we meet in person? If I had any doubts, his greeting and body language just now only confirmed it, morphing my suspicion into a dread as dark and sticky as tar.

He passes me one of the bottles, ice-cold and sweating, and we set off for the alley that leads to the trail in painful, stomach-churning silence.

Like on any other sunny spring day, the Atlanta BeltLine, a stretch of parks and trails carved out of the city's abandoned railroad tracks, is bustling. Lululemon-clad moms pushing strollers compete for space with runners and dog walkers and college kids on skateboards. Nick and I fall in line behind them, following the trail north toward the high-rises of Midtown in the far distance.

"This is incredibly difficult for me," he says as we emerge from the shade of the Freedom Parkway overpass, and even though he's starting to sweat through his work shirt, I know he's not referring to our hike. His head is down, his gaze glued to the pavement. "I hired your husband. I

262

groomed him. In the eight-plus years he worked for me, I promoted him six times. Not because I liked the guy, which I did, but because he deserved it."

"Okay . . ." I drag out the word, my heart jumping around too hard, too fast. I feel a "but" coming. It's bearing down on me like an electric thundercloud, sucking every hair on my body skyward.

"I don't know how much you know about our business, but most engineers don't give a crap about where the money comes from. Will was one of those rare breeds that not only cared, he thought about how to bring in more. It's part of why he was so brilliant at his job, because he could design things the customer didn't even know they wanted until he showed it to them." He latches onto my elbow, steers us to the trail's edge to let a trio of bicyclists pass. "The guy was a genius, but I'm sure you already know that."

"I do."

"It's part of the reason why it took us so long. Will was the last person we suspected, the one we never saw coming."

His words squirm under my skin at the same time frustration burns across my chest, and I can no longer bite down on my impatience. "Sorry, Nick, but I slept on a plane last night, and that's after seven nights of hardly any sleep at all. I'm wrecked and exhausted, so please. Can you cut the crap and tell me what you came here to tell me?"

He stops in the middle of the trail, turning his big body to face mine. "There's some money missing from our corporate accounts."

An icy fist hits me in the center of the chest and spreads outward as, suddenly, all the pieces fall together and everything makes sense. It's like one of those psychological tests I give to my students, where you get the gist of the sentence even though most of the words are missing. In this case, the words are *your husband is a thief.*

I fold my arms over my chest, shivering despite the temperature nudging up into the low seventies. "How much money?"

He bounces his meaty shoulders. "Hard to tell, exactly. The forensic accountant is still —"

"Forensic accountant?" The words travel down me like a lightning bolt, melting my rubber soles to the pavement. I'm no finance whiz, but I know the term. Lake Forrest divorces almost always include one, a financial investigator specialized in ferreting out hidden funds. Last year, Jeannette Davis's mother was awarded half of her soon-to-be ex-husband's offshore accounts, thanks to hers.

"As I was saying, until the forensic accountant comes back with her final report, we don't have a number."

"Give me a ballpark."

"Four million, four hundred seventy-three thousand." Nick coughs into a fist. "And counting."

"So. What you're really asking me here is if I've happened to notice an extra four and a half million sitting around in our joint bank account?" The words feel like okra, prickly and slimy on my tongue.

"No, but . . ." Nick grimaces. "I . . . thought maybe you might know something . . ."

My eyes widen. "No. Jesus, no. Of course not."

"My ass is on the line here, Iris. We're planning to go public next year, and my board is holding me accountable. Nobody wants to buy stock in a company whose internal procedures allow an employee to walk away with four and a half million. Please, if there's anything you're not telling me . . ."

"He didn't walk away, Nick. He got on a plane that fell out of the sky." I think about what Leslie Thomas told me, of a hungover pilot half-asleep at the wheel, and a surge of sick rises from my belly.

He winces. "I know that, and I'm sorry as hell about it. But what I'm trying to say here is, I thought of Will as a friend, which is partially why I'd like to keep this between us."

"Meaning?"

"Meaning, that if we get back that money and can straighten out the books, that will be the end of it. It'll stay between us, no questions asked. At this point I don't care about the whys and hows. I just need to recover that money."

"You really think I know where it is?"

He gives me an apologetic smile, but it doesn't soften his next words. "Do you?"

Anger rises up inside me, silent and swift. "You can't seriously be asking me that."

His silence tells me he is. I'm suddenly nauseous, too much tea and Mom's brownie revolting in my gut, and I worry I might throw up on Nick's brand-new sneakers.

"I'm sure it's all a big misunderstanding."

Nick shakes his head, short and definitive. "It's not."

"How do you know that Will's the one who took it?"

"I can't tell you that."

"Four and a half million doesn't just disappear overnight. This must have been going on for years. How does nobody not notice?"

"I can't tell you that, either. In fact, I've probably said too much already. My lawyers are going to have a shit fit when I tell them about this conversation."

Lawyers. Forensic accountants. I roll the Cartier ring up and down my finger with my thumb, an unconscious habit I picked up sometime this past week, fiddling with the ring whenever I think of Will. Maybe it's because of the way he gave it to me, so unexpectedly and intimately, or maybe it's because of his words — *you, me and baby-to-be*. But for some reason, for lots of reasons, touching it has given me comfort.

Until now.

Now I notice Nick noticing, and jutting out above his dark shades, there's a new crease between his brows.

I shove my fists into the pockets of my hoodie. "I don't know anything about the money, and I can assure you it's not sitting in our account."

For the longest time, he doesn't respond. People pass us on all sides, whizzing by on skates and skateboards, and Nick just stands there, filling up half the path with his girth and watching me with a blank expression. I know what he's doing. He's waiting for me to insist it's not true, that his forensic accountant must have made a mistake, that Will Griffith wasn't capable of stealing from him or from anyone, but I can't seem to choke the words out. If my husband was the type of person to once upon a time set fire to an apartment complex filled with sleeping people, who's to say he wouldn't swipe some cash from his employer's account? I stand there across from him, biting down on my tongue and a mounting urge to cry.

Nick takes my silence as the answer it is, giving me a sorry smile before heading back the way we came. "Sorry, Iris, but I'm going after that money, even if that means taking you and a dead man down in the process."

As soon as Nick's gone, I toss the water bottle into a trash can and take off running. It's a gorgeous spring afternoon, and the air is filled with the sounds of a sunny day in the city: leaf blowers buzzing, the musical jangle of dogs on leashes, the low thrum of traffic in the distance and the resounding slap of my sneakers against the pavement. Eight days of little food and no activity has my muscles weak and stiff, and every step feels like punishment, but Nick's words are chasing me, and I need to burn off all the nervous energy twitching in my bones.

Will and I loved the BeltLine. We loved the urban artwork and the skyline views and the miles and miles of parks and green space. We loved exploring it on our matching bikes, old-school types with three gears, metal bells and wicker baskets hanging from the handlebars. Will surprised me with them one year for my birthday.

"You know what this means, right?" I said, climbing on mine and wheeling it up and down the street with a loud whoop.

Will grinned from where he was watching, his hands on his hips, at the top of the drive. "No more Uber bills?"

I laughed. "That, plus if we bike all the way to Midtown and back, the French fries I'm going to eat for lunch will be guilt free."

We took the bikes out whenever we could. On sunny weekends and warm evenings, to restaurants and bars and just because, and we were that obnoxious couple who took up the entire BeltLine because we biked back holding hands.

And now, if I'm to believe everything I've learned today, this same man was a criminal. A liar and a thief, one who in the last month of his life was distracted and moody. One who got into fights at the gym and punched dents into living-room walls. One who Nick and his forensic accountant were onto. It doesn't take a genius to figure out Will was probably feeling squeezed.

I sprint past cell towers and graffitied walls, along townhomes and parks and restaurants, their terraces filling with an early happy-hour crowd. The sun's rays beat down on my head, and I pull over on the side of the trail to peel off my hoodie. As I'm tying it around my waist, the Cartier ring blinks in the golden light.

When I was flipping through our bank statements last week, did I see a line item for Cartier? I squeeze my eyes and try to remember. Surely I would have noticed that kind of charge — designer diamonds don't come cheap. I dig my phone from a zippered pocket, check both my banking and credit card apps. No big-ticket items on any of them. No four and a half million dollars, either.

So how did Will pay for this ring?

The question starts a dull throb behind my breastbone, and I turn back for my car.

The Cartier store is smack in the middle of the Neiman Marcus wing at Lenox Square, nestled between other high-end brands. I hurry down the broad hallway, past Tesla and Louis Vuitton and Prada, wishing I'd made time to change out of my running clothes, maybe do something with my hair.

A uniformed security guard is stationed behind Cartier's heavy glass door. He takes me in through the window with an *are you sure you're in the right place?* stare. I lift my chin and reach for the brass handle, and he jerks forward before my fingers can make contact.

"Good morning, ma'am," he says, whisking open the door. "Welcome to Cartier."

The place screams expensive. Dark wood paneling, plush carpet, glittering jewels floating behind displays of seamless glass. The floral arrangements alone probably cost as much as my monthly electricity bill. Standing among them puts me on edge, like anyone here can see that I'm not one of them, an imposter. I look around, but other than the security guard and a blonde sales-clerk polishing a gold bangle bracelet with a deep red cloth, the store is empty.

She looks up with a generic smile. "Can I help you?"

Her accent is heavy and Russian, and she is every cliché you've ever heard about Eastern European mail-order brides. Tall and thin, bleached blond hair, a few spritzes more than necessary of perfume. Her nails are too long and her makeup is too shiny, and her generous curves are stuffed into a too-short, too-tight suit. She's strikingly pretty, though, even if she doesn't exactly exude warmth.

My gaze dips to her name tag. "Hi, Natashya, my husband was in here recently and bought me this." I hold up my right hand, and her brows rise infinitesimally, suppressed surprise or Botox or a combination of the two. "I was wondering if you could look up the details of the sale."

"Is gift, no?"

"Yes."

"You don't like?"

"No, I love. I just . . ." I hold out my hand, gazing down at the three thick bands of gold and diamonds. I just what? Suspect my husband bought it with stolen money? Think the receipt might hold a clue as to where he stashed the rest of the four and a half million? "I need the papers for insurance purposes."

"Ah. Of course," she says. She settles the bracelet back in the case, locks it and slips the key into a jacket pocket, then gestures for me to follow her to an ornate cherry desk along the right wall. "Please. Have seat."

I sink onto the padded chair across from her.

"What is husband's name?" She pulls a wireless keyboard from a drawer, twisting to face the computer screen.

"William Griffith. He would have been in here two or three weeks ago, I'm guessing."

Recognition alights on her face, an almost-smile. "Lucky you. Handsome man."

"You remember him?"

"I sold him ring."

I try to picture my husband hunched over the shiny cases, his brow furrowed in frustration while busty Natashya helps him select the perfect gift. Eye candy aside, he's never been much of a shopper, and he's always detested the mall. "Why fight the crowds?" he always said. "Everything I could ever need can be bought on the internet and shipped to my front door."

"Your husband did homework. He knew which ring, what size. Quickest sale I ever make."

I take in her words, thinking her scenario makes much more sense. Of course he would have scoured their website before coming, would have even called ahead to make sure they had the ring in stock. He probably had Natashya here waiting at the door with the bag and the credit card

273

machine. Get in, get out, get on with his day.

She punches a button on the keyboard and the printer whirs to life. "Had money to exact penny."

I give her a pleasant nod, then freeze when her words sink in. "Wait a minute. Are you telling me he paid for the ring in cash?"

She glances over but only long enough to dip her chin. "Da."

"How much cash?"

"Twelve thousand four hundred dollars plus tax."

She says it as easily as if she's rattling off the price for a pound of sugar, while I try to come up with something I own that costs that much money. A heavily mortgaged house. A bank loan for a four-year-old car. Not even my engagement diamond, a simple solitaire set in platinum prongs, was that expensive.

The infinity ring suddenly feels too tight, like three rubber bands stretched to snapping around the base of my finger.

"Twelve . . . twelve thousand four hundred dollars?"

"Plus tax." She takes the papers from the printer and presses it into a red leather booklet, checking a number on the screen.

"Thirteen thousand, two hundred and sixty eight."

With or without tax, the amount is staggering.

I watch the receipt roll off the printer and wonder if he bought anything that day besides the ring, if the four and a half million was burning a hole in his pocket. How was he planning to hide that kind of cash? *Where* did he hide that kind of cash? Would it fit in a box under the floorboards? In a safe up in the attic? Or would he need one of those fireproof storage units advertised on billboards along the downtown connector?

And most important: How would I go about finding it?

The salesclerk slides the booklet across the desk. "Tell husband Natashya say hi."

20

Back in my idling car, I open the red leather booklet and flip through the papers Natashya pressed into it. A certificate of authenticity for the ring. The return policy. An invoice and tax receipt. I run the pad of my finger over Will's familiar signature scrawled across the bottom, swallowing a sudden lump. Will may have bought this ring with stolen money, but that doesn't change the fact he bought it for *me*. He braved the mall and selected a gift that would mean something for *me*. For *us*. Pink for love, yellow for fidelity, white for friendship. Him, me and baby-to-be. No matter his past, no matter where he got the money and how he paid for it, this ring is mine. I'll never take it off.

And then my gaze falls on the contact information on the invoice. Below Will's name, below our home address, there's a phone number I don't recognize. It's one of the three Atlanta area codes — 678 — but the digits are otherwise unfamiliar. Definitely not Will's cell, which begins with 404.

His work number, maybe? Will was always calling me from numbers I didn't recognize, and he said the only ones I should ever bother to save were his cell, Jessica's direct line and the main number for AppSec. Now I wish I'd been more meticulous about recording them.

I pull up his contact page on my phone, check the numbers I have for his office against the Cartier receipt. None of them match.

So . . . what? Natashya got the number wrong when she entered it into the system? Will gave her a fake number to avoid being at the receiving end of the store's telemarketing campaign? And then it occurs to me. What if he had a second cell phone I didn't know about? Another life, another wife? The possibility hits me square in the belly, churning to acid in my gut.

Before I can chicken out, I punch the digits into my cell and hit Send, holding my breath as it rings over my car's hands-free system. Once, twice, again. After the fourth, it flips me to voice mail, a computer-generated voice repeating the number and asking me to leave a message. I hang up before I get to the beep.

Now what? I chew my lip, stare out the windshield at people coming and going through the parking lot, and think things through. Maybe the number is nothing but a mistake, but what if it's not? What if it really did belong to Will? A cell phone doesn't come for free. What if I can trace the number? Will it point me to a bank account I didn't know he had, one fat with the stolen AppSec money?

My cell phone buzzes between my fingers, and I jump clear out of my seat. My brother. I suck a monster breath, willing my heart to settle, and answer on the hands-free system. "Just so you know, you scared the pants off me, and now I have to go back inside the mall to pee."

"Just so *you* know, Mom thinks you've fallen into the Chattahoochee. Wait, what are you doing at the mall? I thought you were meeting Will's boss."

"I was." I drop the phone in my cup holder, leaning back into the seat and giving Dave a quick but thorough blow-by-blow of my conversation with Nick. The missing money, Nick's notice of the ring, the way he waited for the words I couldn't choke out: *My husband didn't do it. He's innocent.* "They've lawyered up, Dave. Nick said he'd take Will down if he had to, but he was going after that money."

"Of course he is. Nobody just lets somebody run off with four and a half million dollars. Which means you need to be lawyering up, too. You need to make sure none of this blows back on you."

My spine straightens against the leather upholstery. "Blow back how? I didn't steal a penny." As I say the words, Nick's warning slides through my mind. He told me he'd take me down, too, in order to recover the money, and a chill skates across my skin.

"Maybe not, but if Will used stolen money to buy things you shared — cars, furniture, vacations, those kinds of things — as his wife you could be held accountable. They could come after you, too."

I unfold my right hand from the steering wheel, the Cartier blinking on my finger. "Will paid cash for the ring."

A pointed silence fills my car.

I drop my forehead to the steering wheel, give it a few thumps. "How did this happen? How did I go from happily married to a widow wearing hocked jewels in just a week?"

"Now is not the time to be feeling sorry for yourself, Iris. Now is the time to find and retain the best lawyer in town."

My thoughts zip to Evan Sheffield, the seven-foot attorney I met at the memorial, the one who lost his wife and baby daughter in the crash. I think of him and his shoulders heavy with burden, and the feelings come flooding back. The shock. The fury. The grief. I imagine myself sitting across from him, looking into his sad eyes as I tell him about the missing four and a half million, and the idea makes me dizzy with dread.

"I'll make some calls today," I say, lifting my head to find a valet standing in front of my car, watching me with concern. I give him a weak smile to let him know I'm all right, and he jogs off. "In the meantime, do me a favor, will you? Don't tell Mom and Dad about this, okay? Dad already threatened to pay for the alarm system, and I don't want them to worry any more than they already are."

"Are you sure that's a good idea?" Dave says, right as a text pings my phone. "You can't . . ."

Dave's still talking, but I'm no longer listening. I'm staring at a text from the 678 phone: Hello, Iris. How did you get this number?

My stomach flips upside down. With shaking fingers, I type my answer. How do you know my name? Who is this?

280

A bubble appears under my message, indicating the other person is typing. I hold my breath and wait for the answer.

"Hellooo," Dave says over the car speakers. "Iris, are you still there?"

I mash the button on my steering wheel to end the call, my gaze never leaving the phone. A few seconds later, a text lights up my screen. There was only one other person who knew this number, and he's dead. Do you have what he took from me?

Nausea rises in my throat. Whoever is on the other end is referring to the money. A partner?

ME: I'm not answering any questions until you tell me who you are.

678-555-8214: This isn't a negotiation. I want my money.

ME: What money?

678-555-8214: Tell me where Will hid the money or you'll be joining him.

I take the long way home, winding down Lenox Road in a daze, my phone on the passenger-side floor, where I flung it like a hot potato. I barely notice when the stately

281

condos and perfectly manicured lawns give way to a seedier strip, dark-windowed lingerie shops and gentlemen's clubs of Cheshire Bridge. I putter past in the slow lane, stuck behind slow-moving out-of-towners and Marta buses making frequent stops, fingers gripping the wheel hard enough to snap it in two.

I've never been at the receiving end of a death threat before. Even though it was delivered in the most impersonal way possible, via text and from who knows how many miles away, the words still hit me like an icy fist in my gut.

Tell me where Will hid the money or you'll be joining him.

At a light, I lean over the middle console and check my cell. Still dark and silent, thank God. Whoever the person is on the other end of that 678, I don't doubt for a second that their threat was serious. This person knows Will, knows about the four and a half million, and thinks I know where Will put it. People have killed for a whole lot less.

Two questions enter my mind at once. First: How did the sender know it was me? This person must have already had my cell phone number, but how? Second: If the number wasn't Will's, why would he have given it to Natashya? Why list it on the receipt of something bought with stolen money?

The car behind me beeps, and I look up to see the light has turned green. I leave my phone on the floorboard and hit the gas, falling into line behind a white SUV.

And then another thought makes my hands wrap tighter around the wheel. Could the blocked number and the 678 number be owned by the same person?

I roll that one around in my mind, poking and prodding for holes. The Best Buy geek said the Seattle texts, the ones that showed up as a blocked number on my phone, were sent from a messaging app and therefore couldn't be traced. What if the 678 phone has the messaging app on it? It's entirely possible they originated from the same cell phone.

I take a right on North Highland and follow the two-lane road through the heart of Virginia Highlands. By now it's close to six, and the streets and sidewalks are crammed with rush-hour and dinner traffic. I creep along, trying to convince myself the senders are the same, but I can't. The tone of the texts was too different, the messages too contrasting.

I swerve into a parking lot and dig my

phone off the floor, pulling up the text string from the blocked number. Compared to the threat from the 678 number, these texts seem almost innocuous. Urging me to go home, to not believe what I was hearing about Will from the folks in Rainier Vista. Like whoever it was didn't want me to find out the truth about Will.

I think about who would want to keep me in the dark about Will's past, who would have something to lose or gain if I found out, and the only person I can come up with is . . . Will. Will didn't want me to know, enough so that he lied about his parents, his background, his ties to Rainier Vista and Seattle. Will is the most likely person to have sent those texts.

Which is, of course, impossible. A dead man can't send a text.

And then Corban's words filter through my brain, the ones Will made him swear on his mother's grave: *I promised that if anything ever happened to him, I'd look out for you.* Is Corban the person behind the blocked number, an anonymous protector fulfilling his promise to a dead friend? I let the possibility sink into my brain, but something about it doesn't feel right, something doesn't quite pass the smell test.

And then it hits me. Corban didn't know

about Will's past in Seattle, either. He was just as stunned as I'd been when I found out. Either that, or the man is a world-class actor.

Frustration burns across my chest, and I shove my car into Reverse, swinging it around and punching the gas for the road home. Do I get help? Contact the police and have them trace the 678 number? Maybe I should tell them about Nick threatening to take me down in order to get back the money. Maybe Nick is the one behind the text?

But what if Dave is right? I could be held accountable. And they might try to take the ring. I splay my fingers on the wheel, and the diamonds flash in the sunlight coming through the front windshield. I picture myself rolling it off my finger and dropping it into an evidence bag, and a panicky feeling rises in my throat. I remember Will's soft smile when he put it there, on the morning of the day he died, and my hand tightens into a fist.

They'll have to cut my finger off to get it.

I have an antiquated system. This is what the alarm guy — a potbellied man who tells me to call him Big Jim — says as soon as I walk through the front door. Something about my panels and motion sensors being far too basic for the newer technology, which nowadays works via GSM rather than hardwired telephone lines. He tells me all this in a rambling, roundabout way, using far too many words for the message he's trying to convey.

I interrupt him halfway to nowhere, softening my words with a smile. "Is there a price in there somewhere?"

The grin Big Jim gives me in return is big and wide, revealing teeth as crooked as they are yellow. "There's a price in there, but I was just working up to it gentle-like, so as not to scare you off."

"It's like pulling off a Band-Aid. Just say it really fast and get it over with. It's less painful that way."

"Six hundred bucks." He hands me a handwritten proposal, tapping his mouth with a pen. "That's to install all new equipment, add glass breaks to the rooms on the ground floor, replace your old panels and add another one to your bedroom wall, all of which will qualify your system for our basic package."

My cell phone feels hot in my pocket, the threatening words flashing across my mind. *Tell me where Will hid the money or you'll be joining him.*

"How much for your mac-daddy system?" I say.

One of Big Jim's bushy brows rises up his forehead. "You talking cameras and two-way voice intercoms and panic buttons?"

"Is that the best you've got?"

"Yes, ma'am, top-of-the-line. Also comes with a video monitoring system you can control from your phone or computer."

"Sold."

"But I haven't told you the price."

"Whatever it is, I'll pay it. And if you install everything today, it comes with the added bonus of a home-cooked meal and a hefty tip. From the smell of things, my money's on spaghetti." I give him a *this is your lucky day* smile. "Mom's meatballs are world-class."

He leans back on his heels and cackles. "It's a deal."

I leave him to his work and head down the hallway into the kitchen, where Mom is at the stove, stirring a pot large enough to feed the whole block. She hears me dump my bag on the counter and tosses me a smile over her shoulder.

"Hi, sweetheart. You're just in time. Dinner will be ready in fifteen."

"Perfect." I drop a kiss on her cheek, getting a good whiff of tomatoes and garlic and spices, and my stomach growls at the same time nausea twists it in a knot. "Hope you don't mind, but I just offered to feed the alarm guy."

Mom's face brightens. There's nothing she loves more than sharing her cooking with appreciative strangers, and everything about Big Jim says he appreciates a lot of food. She wipes her hands on her apron and moves to a cutting board on the island, setting to work on a cucumber for the salad. "Where have you been all afternoon? I thought you were just running out for an hour or so."

"Oh, I went to run a few quick errands, but you know how Atlanta traffic is. Rush hour starts at four o'clock some days. It took me forever to make it back." I flip on the water and wash my hands. "What can I do to help?"

She points the end of the knife at a bowl full of shallots. "Slice up one of those, will you?"

Mom begins chatting about her ideas for the funeral, listing off a couple of venues she wants to check out, and relief loosens the muscles knotted across my shoulders. Either Mom didn't notice I was being intentionally vague, or she decided not to push it. But I meant what I said to Dave.

Until I know how airtight Nick's allegations are, I'm not planning to fill my parents in on the missing four and a half million dollars. They're already worried enough, and adding death threats and the possibility of criminal charges into the mix will send them into nuclear territory.

But a bigger reason — and yes, after the events of these past few days, I can see how some might call it an irrational reason, as well — is that I don't want to further tarnish their memory of Will. My parents have always loved Will, and for the exact same reasons that Dave did, because of how plainly and perfectly Will loved me. The thought of watching their expressions turn sour, of seeing judgment flash across their faces every time his name is brought up at Christmases and birthdays, makes my stomach feel heavy, like there's a rock lodged at the very bottom.

Dave comes through the back door with his iPad and a bottle of beer, his designer sunglasses hanging from the neck of his polo shirt. "Why'd you hang up on me?"

The great thing about having a twin is that you're so in sync, and they know what you're thinking without you having to say a word. Until you've got a secret, that is, and then the worst thing about having a twin is that you're so in sync.

The problem is, I know Dave, and I know if I tell him about the death threat, he'll glue himself to my side and never leave. As much as I love my brother, the thought of his constant hovering makes me hot and itchy, my skin stretched too tight.

"I didn't hang up on you," I lie. "We must have gotten cut off or something."

He narrows his eyes. "Then why didn't you call me back?"

"Our conversation was already winding down. What else was there to say? Besides, I was on my way home. I figured we could finish up in person." I pluck a bottle of water from the fridge and turn to face him. "Like now, for example. Let's finish now."

My cell phone buzzes in my pocket, vibrating the skin of my hip and spiking both my pulse and my body temperature. I unzip my hoodie and peel it off, dropping it onto the counter next to my bag.

He cocks his head and studies me, his gaze crawling over my face. "What is up with you? Why are you purple? What are you not telling me?"

"Nothing, Dave. I'm not telling you nothing."

He throws his hands up in the air by his sides. "That doesn't make any sense."

"Exactly, and neither does this conversation."

Mom's sigh is one I've heard a million times before. What sounds like an argument to her is just Dave's and my normal way of communicating . . . except for now. Now we're fussing because he's trying to un-puzzle my secret, and I'm holding the missing piece in my pocket.

"I swear, you two are worse than a couple of toddlers." She shoves a stack of plates into Dave's hands. "Set the table, would you?"

He gives me an *I'm watching you* look, then heads toward the table.

As soon as his back is turned, I slide the phone from my pocket.

678-555-8214: FYI, I know how to get around an alarm system.

UNKNOWN: Why the alarm, Iris? Did something happen?

21

All through dinner, the phone is like a hunk of plutonium pressed against my hip, a silent and deadly thing radiating poison in my pocket. If I had any doubts before that the numbers came from different sources, I certainly don't now. There's no way *I know how to get around an alarm system* and *Did something happen?* came from the same thumbs.

Unless it's someone trying to mess with my mind. The thought sours my stomach, churning the spaghetti and meatballs I just choked down into a nauseating mush, because it's entirely possible. Maybe even the same person who sent the letter in my husband's hand, which my training tells me could have only come from a sociopath.

"Iris, sweetheart, did you hear a word we said?" Mom says from across the table.

I freeze my fork mid-spaghetti twirl, look up from my plate to find her watching me, her brow furrowed with concern. "I'm sorry, what?"

"We were just talking about our plans, and how James needs to head home this weekend."

He confirms this with an apologetic smile. "I have a full day of surgery on Monday, and I really need a day or two at home to get my bearings. I hope you understand."

"You don't have to apologize for having your own life and career. Go. Of *course,* go. I'll be fine."

"I'll come back next weekend, and we'll see where we're at." He says this to the table, but mostly to Dave, and that's when it dawns on me that James is planning to return to Savannah alone. He's leaving my brother here.

I look around at my family, wonder what else of their conversation I missed. "What are everybody else's plans?"

"We're staying," they say, pretty much in unison.

"Don't you have to get back to work?" I say to my parents, then turn to Dave. "What about *your* career? Don't you have showings next week?"

"I'll get a colleague to handle them." He lifts a shoulder, like *no biggie,* but I happen to know he's full of crap. Real estate is a tough business, and the sharks in his office are notoriously bloodthirsty, always nipping at other agents' clients. Guilt nips at my insides.

My gaze goes to Mom, then Dad, both of whom are conspicuously silent. I see a million things in the way they look at me — worry, determination, stubbornness. They've no plans to leave this weekend, either. In fact, Mom looks ready to chain herself to the chair and bolt it to the floor.

"You guys really don't have to stay. I'll be fine."

Mom looks insulted I would even suggest it, and she's shaking her head before I've finished speaking. "Your father and I have already cleared it at work, and we *want* to stay. We're *happy* to, and for as long as you need us."

A warm wave of love for my sweet mom washes up my chest. If she had her way, she'd be moving in and force-feeding me three square meals a day until I am ready to start dating again. Is it weird that I want some time alone? I'm not an introvert. I love my family, and I normally wish they lived closer. New widows usually dread this moment, when the people pack up their things and return to their own lives, leaving the widow alone with her grief. And here I am, trying to talk my family into it.

I put down my fork and say it as gently as I know how. "I love having you here, and as much as I appreciate the four of you gathering around me this past week — and I really do — I'm not going to be around much. I'm going back to work Monday morning."

Mom's brows dip under the weight of her worry. "So soon?"

I nod. "It's what I would tell myself to do, if I were my own patient. To get back to my normal life and routine, to carve out a new normal for myself. And honestly, I'm kind of looking forward to being around kids who are even more screwed up than I am. It might take some of the edge off." When she doesn't crack the slightest smile at my joke, I reach across the table and cover her hand with mine. "Mom, I know what I'm doing. I promise."

She darts a look at Dad, who gives her an *up to you* shrug. She shakes her head, her stubborn expression digging in even further. "I don't like the idea of you being alone."

"I'll meet Elizabeth for dinner or invite her over for a drink. I haven't seen or talked to her, to any of my girlfriends, since the memorial. It'll be good."

"That's a great idea. You do whatever you need to do," Mom says. "I'll keep working on the funeral plans, and now that it's warming up, your window boxes could use some refreshing . . ."

I try for a compromise. "Why don't you go home for a few days, take care of whatever you need to take care of there, then come back later in the week? We'll have the whole weekend together."

"I have a better idea," Dave says, as usual wading in to save me. "Why don't we all meet at Mom and Dad's next weekend instead? It's closer for us, and Mom and Dad won't have to make the drive again."

I give an enthusiastic nod. "Honestly, I wouldn't mind getting out of town for a bit."

"I don't know . . ." she hedges.

"Jules, she'll be fine," Dad says, tossing me a wink. "Won't you, punkin'?"

"Absolutely. And I'll leave straight from school on Friday to put me there by dinnertime."

Outnumbered and outmaneuvered, Mom reluctantly agrees, and Dad steers the conversation to weekend plans. There's a new barbecue restaurant in town he's been dying to try, and maybe we could all go see a movie at the new Cineplex, one where they serve wine and have big chairs that recline like La-Z-Boys. I smile and hum like I love the idea, but meanwhile I'm counting the moments until I'm alone.

There's something I need to do, and I can't do it with any of them here.

After dinner, I dig a blank check and a hundred-dollar tip for Big Jim from my bag, hand both to Dad and head upstairs. The adrenaline that's carried me all day is long depleted, and exhaustion pushes down on me like a lead blanket.

Big Jim is hunched on the floor just inside my bedroom door, packing up his toolbox. I trip over his industrial boot.

"Whoa there," he says, steadying me with a palm around my wrist. "Won't do anybody any good with broken bones."

I don't tell him there's nobody but me now, or that a broken bone hurts a hell of a lot less than a broken heart. I brush myself off and tell him I'm fine.

A brand-new alarm panel hangs on the wall above his head.

"I was just about to call you up here." He pushes to a stand and dusts his hands on the seat of his pants. "You got a minute or two for me to give you the highlights?"

My eyes are burning, my brain is blurry, and my body aches to climb under my covers, but I nod anyway. "Explain away."

"Okay. For now I've set your system to a

default code, but as soon as I'm done here, you should change it to one of your own. You'll use the code to turn the system on and off, as well as make any changes to the panel settings, so make sure it's a combination you know by heart. And see these three buttons here?" He points to a vertical row of squares — universal symbols for police, fire and ambulance. "These here are your panic buttons. There's another two by your bed, tucked behind each of your nightstands. You gotta hold 'em in for a minimum of three seconds, and make sure you mean it because we show up with guns blazing, no questions asked. If it turns out to be a false alarm, you'll be getting a big old bill."

"Got it."

"Good. Now, your duress code is set to straight down the middle of the keypad — 2580. That's another one you'll want to change to your own as soon as I'm done."

"Why would I use a duress code instead of a panic button?"

"In case somebody's holding a gun to your head and watching over your shoulder while you disarm the system."

My eyes blow wide. "That actually happens?"

Big Jim nods, his fleshy jowls bobbing. "Just happened to a young couple in Buckhead. Two armed men surprised the husband as he was coming in from the garage, pistol-whipped 'em both until they forked over all their cash and valuables. Husband used the duress code, otherwise they'd probably both be dead."

"Jesus." I haul a calming breath, but it doesn't work. The idea of someone chasing me into my own home, pistol-whipping me until I fork over four and a half million dollars I don't have, sends an army of ants crawling under my skin.

He points to an 800 number on the inside cover of the keypad. "Call this number first thing after I'm gone and set up your code word. It's an added security measure, and our operators'll ask for it every time they call. If the bad guy is standing next to you, give 'em the wrong word, and that's their signal to send in the cavalry. Don't worry if you forget any of this. It's all explained in detail in the owner's manual, which I'll get you before I leave."

"Give it to my father, will you? He's got your payment, and Mom's holding dinner for you downstairs whenever you're ready."

Big Jim pats his gut and grins. "I'm pretty much always ready."

After he's gone, I toe out of my sneakers, dig my cell phone out of my pocket and collapse onto my bed. There are no new texts, nothing from either number, and I don't know whether to feel relieved or disappointed. Both, maybe. Relief for the one, disappointment for the other.

I pull up the string with the 678 number, the one ending in two threats. Tell me where Will hid the money or you'll be joining him. FYI, I know how to get around an alarm system. No way I'm touching either one of those.

I back up, click on the conversation with the blocked number. Why the alarm, Iris? Did something happen?

I think about who would be worried about me besides the people cleaning my kitchen downstairs — my colleagues, my girlfriends, the friendly neighbors to our left and across the street. None of them would text me from a blocked number. I press my fingers to my eyes and rub. Maybe I'm too tired. Stressed. Wrecked and confused from lying in the bed I once shared with Will. None of this makes any sense.

Before I can think through the pros and cons of engaging whoever is on the other end of the blocked number, my thumbs start typing. Why do you care? Who are you?

The reply pings my screen two seconds later, as if whoever is on the other end has been waiting for me all this time, thumbs pressed to the screen. I'm a friend, and I want you to be safe. Tell me who's after you and why. I want to help.

ME: Don't play games with me. If you knew that I was in Seattle and got an alarm, you know about the stolen money, too.

UNKNOWN: I know about the money. I just wasn't sure that you did.

My heart rides into my throat as I type the next words.

ME: Are you the one who stole it?

UNKNOWN: That depends on who you believe.

The last text comes with a whiplike lash. So far, the only theory I've heard for who took the money is Will, which means . . .
Not possible. A dead man can't send texts.
I'm considering my next move when another text lights up my screen.

UNKNOWN: Please tell me what I can do to help you.

ME: I don't think so. Not until you tell me

who you are.

UNKNOWN: I want nothing more, believe me. But it's better for both of us if I remain anonymous.

ME: Then what's the point? Why bother texting me at all?

UNKNOWN: Because it's the next best thing to actually being there.

22

The law offices of Rogers, Sheffield and Shea are located in the heart of Midtown, high in the clouds looming over Peachtree Street. Their lobby is everything you'd expect from Atlanta's most prestigious attorney firm. Modern furnishings, seamless glass walls providing sweeping views of downtown and a twenty-foot trek to a dark-haired receptionist who could moonlight as a model.

"Iris Griffith here to see Evan Sheffield."

She gestures to a row of leather chairs by the window. "His assistant will be right out. In the meantime, may I get you something to drink?"

"I'd love a water, thanks."

What I'd really love is to get the hell out of here. To take the elevator back down to the parking deck, make a dash for my car and gun the gas for home. It's not so much that I'm dreading what I'm here to tell him, though admitting my husband is a liar and a thief is certainly bad enough. No, my urge to beat a retreat is more fueled by fear. The last time I saw Evan, his eyes were haunted, and they've haunted me ever since.

His assistant leads me into his corner office, where Evan is seated at a round table by the far wall. He's grown a beard since I've seen him last, a scruffy patch of dirty-blond fur that sprouts from the lower half of his face, either a bold middle finger to the corporate world or a testament that the weight of his grief is too heavy a load to bear.

I lift a hand. "Hi, Evan."

His suit jacket is folded over the chair beside him, his sleeves rolled up to just under his elbows. It's an attempt at looking relaxed, but it doesn't work. His back is slumped, his shoulders hunched, and his face, when it spreads into a sorry excuse for a smile, looks bruised and battered. He unfolds his massive body from his chair and reaches a long arm across the table, shaking mine above a bucket of ice and a tray of every brand of bottled water imaginable.

"Good to see you again, Iris. I'd ask how you're holding up, but I hate that question, and besides, I'm pretty sure I already know."

Of course he knows. He knows that the

hole Liberty Air blew into his life is permanent, as is that hollow place inside him. He knows how you can lose hours at a time staring into space and torturing yourself with an endless parade of what-if scenarios. What if she'd gotten stuck in traffic? What if she'd given up her seat for that five-hundred-dollar coupon airlines are always using as enticement for overbooked flights? What if what if what if? He knows these things, so no need to say them out loud.

"Thanks for seeing me on such short notice," I say instead. "I know you had to shuffle some things around."

He waves off my thanks. "You're the psychologist. Is it weird that I wanted to see you?"

I sink into a chair diagonal from him, his blunt honesty loosening some of the knots across my shoulders. "Funny, I was just wondering how weird it would be if I hightailed it for the car."

"Is it my quick wit and sparkling personality?" He pushes up a self-deprecating smile, gestures to his massive frame. "My Herman Munster build and he-man charm?"

"It's your eyes, actually." I brace and look at them full on, and they're just as awful as I remembered. A beautiful mossy green, but they're red around the rims, and the surrounding skin is puffy and crisscrossed with lines I happen to know are from despair. "Looking at them hurts my heart."

He winces, but he doesn't let go of my gaze. "No more than looking into yours hurts mine."

"You must be a sucker for punishment, then."

He puffs a laugh devoid of humor. "It's all relative these days, isn't it?"

There's really nothing to say to that, so I don't say anything at all. I stare out the window instead, watching a pair of hawks swoop and dive against fluffy white clouds. While Dave and I were chasing Will's past around Seattle, a group of thirty or so people boarded a private Liberty Airlines jet and traveled to the crash site. I saw the images on *Huffington Post,* Evan's profile standing taller than the blackened stalks, solemn figures holding hands and hugging in a charred field soaked with the essence of those they lost. I saw them and I thought, *I can't.* What does it say about me — a psychologist, for crap's sake — that they could and I can't?

"One of the lessons I've learned this past week," Evan says, his voice bringing me back, "is that nobody understands what you and I are going through. People think that

they do, and a lot of them want to understand, but they don't. Not really. Unless
they've lost someone like you and I have,
they can't."

Grief wells up like a sudden tide, intense
and overwhelming. Evan has just hit on a
big part of why grief groups are so popular.
We're strangers on the same boat, both
trapped in a sinkhole of sorrow. At the very
least, it helps to know you're not going
under alone.

"It's not just losing Will, it's . . ." I pause,
searching for the right word.

But either Evan's already thought this
through, or his brain is much quicker than
mine. "It's the horror of how."

My nod is immediate. "Exactly. It's the
horror of how. It's where I go whenever I
close my eyes. I see his tears. I hear his
screams. His terror beats in my chest. It's
like I can't stop replaying those awful last
minutes, putting myself in his shoes while
the plane flipped and swerved and fell from
the sky."

I say the words and boom — I'm crying.
This is why I didn't want to come, why no
force on the planet could have made me
step onto that cornfield. Whoever said God
doesn't give you more than you can handle
was full of shit, because this — this grief

that slams me over and over like a Mack truck, this weight of missing Will that presses down on all sides until I can't breathe — is going to kill me.

Evan pushes a box of Kleenex across the table. "I keep forgetting this is my new life. I'll be halfway through leaving a message on Susanna's voice mail, or standing in my boxers in my daughter's room in the middle of the night, her warm bottle in my hand, before I remember. The crib is empty. My wife and baby daughter are dead."

"Jesus, Evan," I say, my voice cracking. I pluck a tissue from the box and swipe it across my cheeks. "A couple days ago, I got a call from some journalist claiming the pilot was sleep-deprived and possibly hungover. Something about a —"

"Bachelor party, I know. I've got somebody in Miami right now, asking around. So far, though, nothing."

"Has he talked to Tiffany Rivero?"

"Who?"

I give Evan a quick rundown of my conversations with Leslie Thomas, and he goes completely still. His expression doesn't change. If it weren't for the purple flush pushing up from under his shirt collar, I'd think he hadn't heard me.

"The story hasn't broken yet, so she might be —"

He pounds a fist on the table, rattling the ice in the bucket. "I *knew* it. I knew these fuckers were hiding something. A plane doesn't just fall from the sky unless . . ." He pauses to pant, three quick breaths that flutter the papers on the table. "If this is true, if there was even a whiff of misconduct by anyone inside that cockpit, I will make it my personal mission to take down that airline and everybody in it. I guarantee you that much."

"The psychologist in me says revenge won't change anything. Your wife and baby girl, my Will . . . they'll all still be dead."

"What does the widow say?"

I don't have to think about my answer, not even for a second. "The widow in me says obliterate the bastards."

"Done. I'll talk to Tiffany personally, fly there myself if I have to." He scrubs a hand down his face, and his fury dissipates as quickly as it came, morphing into sorrow. "God help me, if my girls died because some asshole was too cocky to call in sick . . ."

At the mention of his family, he looks on the verge of tears again, and I know how he feels, like his emotions have multiple personality disorder. Why do they call it grief, when really it's a whole gamut of awful emotions, confusion and regret and anger and guilt and loneliness, wrapped up into one little word?

"I can't keep food down," I hear myself say. Evan's honesty has loosened something up in me, and the words come out on their own accord. "Everything tastes like cardboard, even when I'm starving. I'll eat it, then throw it right back up. And every time I'm hanging over the toilet, puking up my guts, I get this secret little thrill because I think maybe I'm pregnant."

"I take it you and Will were trying?"

I nod. "But not for very long, so the odds aren't exactly in my favor. The nausea is probably psychosomatic or wishful thinking or just plain old heartbreak, I don't know. But I can't help from thinking that if I had a baby, if I had this little nugget of my husband growing inside me, it would make things a little easier."

"I think it would make things a lot easier. Then you'd feel like you had something to live for."

His words trigger a warning in my psychologist's brain. "Are you saying you don't?"

"I'm saying it's awfully hard to remember

that I do sometimes. Especially at 4:00 a.m., when I'm standing in my daughter's dark, empty room, staring into her empty crib while her cries echo in my head."

A surge of sadness for this man jabs me in the center of the chest, telling me that even though my own heart may be broken to bits, things could be worse. I reach across the table, give his big hand a squeeze. The gesture is empathy, sympathy and solidarity, all at the same time.

He pulls his hand out of mine and drops his head into both of his, blowing a long breath out through his fingers. "I'm sorry. You didn't come all the way here to have me cry on your shoulder." He looks up, his mask molded into something semiprofessional. "You said something about needing some legal advice. Does it have anything to do with the crash?"

"No. Yes. Well, sort of, but in a *Twilight Zone* sort of way." I force a laugh, but it comes out loud and abrupt like a sneeze. I follow Evan's lead and become serious. "I need to know if I can be held accountable for my husband's alleged crimes."

His face remains carefully blank. "What kind of crimes are we talking about here?"

"Embezzlement, mostly."

"Mostly, huh?" He fills two glasses with

ice and pushes one my way, offering me one of the dozen bottles of water. I select a can of Perrier, and he pops it open with a hiss. "This sounds like the part where I should warn you our attorney-client confidentiality doesn't kick in until you pay me a retainer." I'm about to ask him if he's serious — I always assumed that was a Hollywood plot device — when he adds, "If we were in a bar, I'd say buy me a beer, but since we're not, a couple of bucks'll do."

I dig five singles from my wallet and slide them across the table.

"Start at the beginning," Evan says, pocketing the cash.

So I do. I tell Evan everything, beginning with the morning of the crash. I tell him about the Orlando conference and the job that wasn't in Seattle. I tell him about how a condolence card led me to Coach Miller and Rainier Vista and the fire. I tell him about the *I'm so sorry* letter and my coffee with Corban and the fact Will asked him to look after me. I tell him about my BeltLine stroll with Nick and how a forensic accountant is ferreting through AppSec's books as we speak, in search of the missing four and a half million. I tell him about the Cartier ring and the texts from both the blocked and the 678 number, and how the threats prompted me to install a brand-new, mac-daddy alarm system. It's a tremendous relief to finally tell somebody, and the words flow without effort, without hesitation. Evan takes them all in with a serious but stony expression, and without scribbling a single word onto his yellow legal pad.

When I'm done, he pushes the pad aside and leans on the table with both forearms. "Okay, so first things first. Liberty Air released Will's name before contacting you?"

"Yes. Only by a half an hour or so, but long enough my mom called me before they did."

"What a bunch of incompetent morons." He shakes his head, and a scowl screws up his face. "You know you can name your price now, right? If you threaten to take their blunder to the press, they'll pay you any amount you want, just to keep you quiet."

Ann Margaret Myers's face flashes across my mind, her mask of exaggerated empathy at the Family Assistance Center when she pushed the check for fifty-four thousand dollars across the desk, her smug-ass smile when she told me there would be more coming.

"I don't want anything from them, least

of all their blood money."

"You say that now, but what about a couple of months down the road, when the bills are piling up and your bank account is down by one salary? What if you *are* pregnant? You're going to need every penny."

"No, I won't. I found Will's life insurance policies a couple of days ago. There are three, and for a total of two and a half million dollars. Financially, I'll be fine."

Evan cocks his head. "Are you telling me you didn't know he had those policies?"

"I only knew about one. The smallest one. The other two he bought without telling me."

"Why do you think he did that, and why for so much? The national average for someone in his shoes — married, no kids — is less than half that amount."

I lift my shoulders up to my ears. "I never thought he'd steal or commit arson, either, so your guess is as good as mine."

"Murder."

"What?"

"If he was the one who set the fire that killed his mother and those two kids, then technically he committed murder."

A chill shimmies its way down my spine.

Evan takes a long pull from his glass, then crunches on a chunk of ice. "Okay, so we've got a couple of things going on here. If his boss is able to prove Will's the one behind the embezzlement, he can come after you now but only if Will used any of that money to pay for things you own together. Georgia is an equitable property state, which means if any of those funds benefited you in any way, AppSec can and will hold you accountable for restitution, maybe even fines. They're going to come after the ring, for sure."

I roll the Cartier as far as it will go up my finger, squeeze my hand into a fist. "Will gave it to me the day he died. They'll have to chop off my finger to get it."

"I'll make sure they don't have to, though more than likely, you'll have to fork up the cash to cover the cost. And if they find out about the two and a half million insurance payout, they'll come after that, too."

"They can do that?"

"I didn't say they'd get it, only that they'd try. And I know it doesn't feel like it, but in terms of your liability in the embezzlement charges, this hidden-past angle is a good thing. We can use it to demonstrate there were a lot of secrets in your marriage, parts of your husband you weren't privy to. His past life in Seattle, the father-in-law you never knew about, all these things are going to work in our favor." He gives me a few moments to digest this news, filling the silence by refilling both of our waters. "Okay. Let's move on to the texts. Did you report them to the police?"

"Not yet. I wanted to talk to you first."

"As much as I applaud your waiting — you wouldn't believe how many convictions I've nailed because some idiot didn't think to consult his attorney first — you've been physically threatened now, twice."

"From someone who wants money I didn't steal and don't have access to. Won't the police have lots of questions?"

"Oh, you can count on it, especially if Will's boss has started up an investigation already. But, Iris, as your lawyer, I do have to ask. Have you told me everything I need to know? I can't help you unless I know all the facts, and I hate walking into anywhere blind."

"Yes, of course. I don't have anything to lie about. Honestly. I've told you everything I can remember."

A niggle of guilt pings me between the ribs, and I look away before he sees. There is one thing I haven't told him, one thing I don't dare to say out loud. It's too far-fetched, and it will make me sound too crazy.

316

"In that case . . ." He slaps both palms to the table, pushes to a stand and flicks his head at the door. "Let's go."

"Go where?"

"To the police station. To file a report."

"What, now?"

He gives me a crooked grin. It's tight and it's forced, but I catch a whiff of the old, playful Evan, before plane crashes and empty cribs sucked the joy out of life. "I won't charge you extra, I promise."

Evan drives us to the station closest to my home, a gray stone building on Hosea Williams Drive, one that seems much too small to be serving a city of more than six million. The inside is like a public bathroom, crowded and dingy and reeking of industrial-strength cleaner mixed with body odor and the stench of fear. Men in rumpled clothes line the lobby's right wall bench, their wrists cuffed to a metal bar. Their oily gazes slide over me, and I shuffle a little closer to Evan.

The desk sergeant, a grizzly-haired man easily in his sixties, greets Evan by name. The acknowledgment is courteous but not the least bit friendly, despite Evan's easygoing manner. He leans an elbow on the desk like it's a bar, explaining the situation and requesting an aggravated harassment form in a tone that makes it sound like the sergeant is an old drinking buddy. The man passes Evan the form without comment.

"He doesn't seem very nice," I whisper behind the paper as Evan and I are sinking into a row of empty chairs by the far wall.

"That's because he hates my guts." Evan doesn't bother lowering his voice. He leans back in the chair, crossing an ankle over his knee, and bounces a *so what* shoulder. "I'm a defense attorney. I make my living defending the same person his buddies just went to a great deal of trouble to arrest. From where he's sitting, I'm batting for the wrong team."

The sergeant purses his lips and nods, but he doesn't look over.

"How am I the wrong team?" I say, stung. "I didn't do anything."

"It'll be fine. Just fill that thing in so we can go make our statement."

I return to the form, and ten minutes later, we're stepping back up to the front desk.

"Detective Dreesch in?" Evan says.

The sergeant doesn't look up from his papers. "Nope."

"What about Detective Willoughby?"

His pen stills against the paper, and after

a great sigh, he leans back in his chair, cranes his neck around the corner. "Detective Johnson's available."

Evan frowns. "Is he new?"

"He's a she, and yup. Fresh from patrol."

"Excellent," Evan says, but in a tone that makes it obvious it's not.

"Wait over there." The desk sergeant aims his pen over our heads, at the row of chairs we just came from, and Evan and I return to our seats.

It's a full forty minutes later by the time he shows us to Detective Johnson, a petite officer with a freshly scrubbed face and pretty features pulled high and tight in a ponytail. Her posture is rigid, and her expression overly serious, a young woman with something to prove and a glass ceiling to bust through. She gestures for us to sit at the edge of her immaculate desk, an anomaly in this cluttered, crowded room, where most horizontal surfaces seem to be hidden under piles of paper files and dirty coffee mugs. She studies my form, looking up with a knitted brow. "Who's the perpetrator?"

"We're hoping you could tell us that from the cell phone number," Evan says before I can draw a breath to answer. Not for the first time, I think how glad I am he didn't send me here alone. I've never done this before, never even had a reason to walk into a police building until Seattle, and now here I am for the second time in a week. I feel completely unequipped for this task.

"Assuming it's not a dump phone," Detective Johnson says. She flips through the copies of the screenshots Evan's assistant printed out, the ones detailing my text conversation with the 678 number. When she gets to the one with the first threat, *Tell me where Will hid the money or you'll be joining him,* she looks up. "What money?"

"Four and a half million in missing funds, allegedly stolen by Mrs. Griffith's husband from his place of employment."

She glances at me but directs her question at Evan. "Where is the husband now?"

"He was a passenger on Liberty Airlines Flight 23. Mrs. Griffith is a widow."

The detective's eyes widen, but as far as I can tell, not in sympathy. "So then, where's the money?"

"My client only learned of the alleged embezzlement yesterday. She's not apprised of where her husband might have stored the funds before his death. It's certainly not in any of their shared accounts. We can confirm all of this with bank statements, of course."

Detective Johnson leans back in her seat, suddenly a lot more interested. "So let me get this straight. Mr. Griffith embezzles millions —"

"Allegedly," Evan interrupts. "As far as I know, no formal charges have been brought."

She gives him an unamused look. "Mr. Griffith *allegedly* takes off with more than four million dollars, then disappears in a plane crash."

"He didn't disappear," Evan says, both his words and tone careful. "He *died,* and in about the worst possible way you can imagine."

"Meanwhile, the money's disappeared, too."

Beside me, Evan grows an inch in his chair. "I don't like what you're insinuating, Detective. Mrs. Griffith lost her husband last week, along with 178 other families who lost husbands, wives, parents and children. Surely you can't be accusing him of what I think you are."

But of course, Evan knows exactly what she's accusing Will of.

And so do I. My heart takes off, fluttering like a bird trapped behind my ribs, because I know, too. It's the same thing I've spent the better part of the past nine days obsessing over. I've come at it from every possible angle, come up with every possibility, and

321

every time, one answer keeps rising to the top like cream.

Evan reads it on my face. He doesn't say a word, but the look he gives me does. It orders me to shut the hell up, to keep whatever I'm thinking to myself.

"I'm not accusing anyone of anything, sir. I'm only trying to get a thorough understanding of the situation so I know what steps we need to take in order to ensure Mrs. Griffith's safety." She turns back to me. "I'd like to hear it from Mrs. Griffith."

"I don't really have anything to add, other than that I found the 678 number on a receipt. Will listed it as his own."

"Does your husband have any reason to be threatening you?"

Evan slaps a palm to the desk and leans in. "Her husband is *dead*, Detective. Remember?"

She doesn't take her eyes off me. "Does he?"

"Absolutely not."

"And you're sure your husband was on that plane." It's neither a question nor a statement but somewhere in between. "You're absolutely positive."

I want to spring over this lady's pristine desk, grab her by the ears and kiss her full on the mouth because, no, I'm not positive.

I've not been positive since the very second Mom called before Liberty Air did. What if it wasn't a blunder but confusion, because Will was behind a computer somewhere, hacking his name on to that passenger manifest?

"No," I say, at the same time Evan barks, "Of course she's positive."

The detective ignores him, her gaze hot on mine. "No, you're not positive, or no, it's not true?"

I swallow, flashing an apologetic glance at Evan, who is shaking his head. "No, I'm not positive."

Evan's lawyer face clamps down, and he latches onto my biceps, hauls me out of my chair and steers me over to the edge of the room, up against an empty spot of wall, pressed between a filing cabinet and a water-cooler.

"I don't even know where to start. No, scratch that. I *do* know. Iris, Will is dead."

"Allegedly," I say, using his own term on him, and he throws up his hands. "Look, I know how weird it sounds —"

"It doesn't sound weird. It sounds certifiably insane. Will's name was on the passenger manifest. They found his ring at the crash site."

"Without a single scratch on it. How does

that even happen? And they still haven't found any of his DNA."

"Because they're still pulling body parts from the earth! Jesus, Iris, think about it! It'll be months before they identify everyone."

"Okay, so what about the texts from the blocked number? Will's the only one who stands to lose anything by me being in Seattle, and he could track my phone to see when I was there and when I got back. And he would for sure know how to text me from an untraceable number. And then there's the letter that mysteriously appeared on my bathroom countertop, in Will's handwriting and postmarked after the crash, telling me he's so sorry. I think he meant for leaving, for making me think he's dead, for breaking my heart."

"The letter didn't mysteriously appear, it was delivered to your house by the United States Postal Service. It could be ten years old, for all we know. Do you know how hard it is to fake your death?"

"I've already done this, you know, had this argument with myself. Over and over and over, a million times in my head. And of course I know how certifiably insane it makes me sound. It's the reason I kept quiet for over a week now, even though I should

have been listening to my gut, which is telling me he's not dead. It's telling me to find
the money, because that's where Will is,
too."

Evan pulls a hand down his face. "I really
wish you told me this before we walked
through the door."

"Why, so you could give me my five bucks
back and tell me to hit the road?" My tone
is teasing, my voice stretched with a smile
— my pathetic attempt at an apology even
though I'm not sorry. If the detective and I
are right, if Will is not dead, then whatever I
say or do to find him is something I'll never
apologize for.

But Evan doesn't crack the slightest smile.
"No, so I could tell you that faking your
death isn't technically illegal, but it's impossible to do without committing a crime.
Beyond the identity fraud and tax evasion,
that money from Liberty Air and Will's life
insurance? If you take it, you'll essentially
be stealing it."

His message sinks my smile. "Oh."

"Yeah. Oh." His gaze fishes over my
shoulder, and his expression goes carefully
blank. I turn and the detective is still at her
desk, watching us with an expression I can't
read. He gives her his back and steps
between us, so that all I see is Evan. "Okay,

new plan. Let's go back over there, explain to Detective What's-her-name that you're a grieving widow with an active imagination and some very wishful thinking, then get the hell out of here."

On the ride back to the office, Evan and I agree to a couple of things. First, to table the *is he or isn't he* argument until either the airline finds biological evidence of Will being on that plane, or I receive another message from the blocked number. I'm also to document every text I receive from both numbers by making screenshots and saving them to a mutual Dropbox account Evan's assistant will set up for us. And finally, Evan will pass the 678 number along to a private detective he's worked with in the past for tracing.

"The Atlanta PD are good," he says, pulling to a stop behind my car in the parking garage, "but they're monumentally over-worked and underpaid. My guy'll be much faster. In the meantime, set your house alarm and call me the second you receive another threat, okay?"

I agree, but I don't reach for the door. "Evan, I want to apologize for what happened back there. I know I should have shared my suspicions long before we sat down with the detective, but who even comes up with that? Not a sane person, that's for sure. Until someone else voiced the idea that Will might still be alive, I didn't permit myself to think it even in my own head, because I didn't want to get my hopes up." I shake my head. "I'm not doing a very good job of explaining, am I? None of this makes any sense."

"No, it makes perfect sense. And you're not crazy, this situation is. For the record, my response was less about an attorney looking out for his client, and more about me trying to muster up genuine happiness for someone who found her husband alive, and then coming up empty. All I found was envy. I know that makes me sound like a miserable, petty asshole, but there it is. I'm a miserable, petty asshole."

"You lost your family. You're allowed to be all those things."

The shadows under his eyes seem darker suddenly, the line of worry indented in his forehead deeper.

We say goodbye, and I yank on the door handle, then think of one more thing. "What was her name?"

"Whose name, the detective's?"

"No." I shake my head. "Your daughter's. What did you and Susanna name her?"

Evan is still for a long moment. "Emma-line." He clears his throat and says it again, offering up the word with a quiet reverence. "Emmaline. We called her Emma."

"Beautiful." I give his arm a quick squeeze, then slide out of his passenger's seat. "I'll think of her every time I hear the name."

23

On Sunday, Mom doesn't want to leave.

"There are two casseroles in the freezer, both big enough to share with half an army," she says. We're standing on my front porch, watching Dad shove the last of their things into the trunk down at the street. Dave and James left yesterday afternoon, and now Mom is milking every last second out of this goodbye. "I thought maybe you'd invite a couple of your girlfriends over this week. Call Lisa or Elizabeth or Christy. Ask them to keep you company."

"Good idea." I'm not quite as enthusiastic as I make it sound. I love my friends as much as any other girl, but after almost two weeks of constant company, I'm looking forward to a little quiet. Grief, after all, is a solitary venture.

"And I froze the soup in individual portions. I thought you could take it in to work for lunch or something. There are cookie balls in there, too, in a plastic bag. Just pop them in the oven whenever you need something sweet."

"Mom, there's enough food in the freezer to last me until Christmas."

"I know, it's just . . ." Worry crumples her forehead. "Are you sure you're going to be okay? I just hate the thought of you here all alone."

"I won't be here most of the time. I'll be at work, and probably pulling extra hours. It's college acceptance season, so I'm sure there's plenty of drama to catch up on."

"It's only five days, Jules," my father calls up the yard. "She'll be fine."

She gears up to protest, and I link my arm through hers and pull her close. "He's right, Mom, I'll be fine. I promise."

She pushes up a watery grin. "I'm supposed to be the one comforting *you,* you know. Not the other way around."

"If it makes you feel any better, I'll promise to be a big fat mess when I see you again on Friday."

She laughs and pulls me into a tearful hug. "Call me anytime, okay? I can be here in three and a half hours."

"I know."

"And you'll look at those venues like you promised? I left the addresses on the kitchen counter."

"I will, I promise."

I walk her down to the car, dole out another round of hugs, and smile and wave until Dad steers their car around the corner. And then I head back up the yard to the house.

The afternoon stretches in front of me like an open, empty road.

I know just how I'm going to fill it.

Back in the house, I slide my phone from my pocket. "Siri, where can you hide four and a half million dollars?"

Siri spits out a list of possible answers, from which I glean that a million dollars in tightly packed ones would fit into a grocery bag, a refrigerator crisper drawer and a microwave. The information is both informative and ridiculous. Why would anyone want a million dollars in one-dollar bills? But, okay, assuming Will packed the money in hundreds or thousands instead, the dimensions would still be manageable. Even with the new alarm, this house isn't exactly the Federal Reserve, and there are only so many places in it to hide a wad of cash that large. Then again, Will is a techie. It would never occur to him to shove cash into a bag and lug it around with him. Any money movement would occur where he felt most comfortable: online.

Okay, so I should be searching for . . . what? An account number scribbled on a scrap of paper? A discarded and forgotten flash drive? The key to a safety-deposit box? I groan at the prospect of searching for an unknown object the size of my pinkie finger.

I decide to start in the attic and work my way down. I dump out boxes and bags, check behind rafters and in suitcases, search in closets and under beds. I move furniture and pull up carpets. I fetch a screwdriver from the kitchen and open every vent, reaching inside as far as my arm will go. I check the freezer and in toilet tanks.

The entire house is an emotional minefield, every room rigged with explosives. Will's jacket hanging on a hook by the back door. His favorite orange juice in the fridge, shoved behind a carton of creamer he never got a chance to put in his coffee. The framed poster we picked out together on a trip to New York City hanging in the hall, the couch pillows he always thought were too many and would toss onto the floor, his razor and a half-empty bottle of aftershave on the rim of his sink. I twist off the cap and press it to my nose, and the familiar scent makes me smile at the same time my eyes build with tears.

Suddenly, I can't breathe. I know the science behind my reaction — that the olfactory bulb is connected to the areas in the brain that regulate emotions and memory — but I still feel assaulted by this surge of Will. I see him. I smell him. I hear his voice in my ear, feel his fingertips sliding down the skin of my back. The sensation is so overwhelming, I actually look for him in the mirror, but there's nothing behind me but wall. Sadness sinks like lead in my belly, and I screw on the cap, carry the bottle to my side of the bathroom and sink onto the vanity stool.

The hundred-watt bulbs above my head are not kind. Greasy hair, sunken skin, a pimple brewing on my chin.

I push to a stand, flip on the shower, return to the bottom drawer where I keep my face masks. I yank it open, and my heart stops, then cranks like a freight train engine starting up, hard and gaining speed. There, on top of the boxes and tubes and tubs is another note, this time scribbled across a bright blue sticky.

Stop searching, Iris. Leave it alone. I can't protect you if you don't.

Chill bumps sprout over every inch of my skin despite the steady puffs of steam surging from the open shower door, and I whirl around, sensing Will as surely as if he's still here, standing right behind me. Who put this here? How? When? I haven't opened this drawer since . . . before the crash? Yes, I'm positive of it.

A slew of emotions screws tight around my chest. Elation. An *I told you so* excitement. A relief so intense it turns my bones to sludge, and my body spills onto the stool.

Will is alive. He *has* to be. This note in his handwriting proves it.

A high and hysterical sound comes up my throat — half laugh, half scream — and I tell myself to get a grip. If I were sitting on my own psychologist's couch, I would explain to myself that in wishing Will alive, I'm idealizing my fantasies and not participating in the reality of his death. That I'm using my denial as a defense mechanism and deferring the work I should be doing — that of grieving my husband. And yet I can't convince myself of any of this, because this time, there's no denying the message.

Stop searching. Leave it alone.

And this time, the note came without an envelope. Which means Will had to have put it here himself.

I snatch my phone from the vanity counter and type the question that's been rolling through my mind like a song on repeat, ever since the very first text. Will, is this you?

My heart clenches like a fist.

The reply comes thirty seconds later. Iris . . .

ME: Iris what? It's a simple question, with a simple yes or no answer. Either you are or you aren't.

UNKNOWN: Nothing about this situation is simple.

A flash of fury rises in me, swift and searing, and I'm suddenly done playing around. I want an answer. If Will is going to go to the trouble to sneak into our house and leave me handwritten notes, the least he can do is admit it's him. My thumbs stab out a reply.

ME: Answer the damn question. Are you or are you not the man who looked me in the eye and promised until death do us part?

I hold my breath and wait for an answer

that doesn't come.

ME: Tell me! Are you?

I stare at the screen, willing the person on the other end to answer.

UNKNOWN: I'm so sorry. I never wanted any of my problems to touch you.

A choked sound erupts up my chest.

ME: I need to hear it. I need for you to tell me.

UNKNOWN: Yes. I'm so sorry, but it's me. It's Will.

His reply releases every emotion I've kept pent-up for these past twelve days. Anguish. Fury. Sorrow. Relief. Despair. They burst from me in ugly, gulping sobs, coming in waves so hard and so fast, I can't catch my breath. My husband isn't dead.

I hit Dial, and as the number rings, it hits me. Will is alive, and yet he concocted an elaborate plan to make everyone — including me, his wife, his very favorite person on the planet — think he's not. He somehow got his name onto that passenger manifest, knowing it would break my heart. I end the call after the third ring.

It comes over me slowly at first, like a storm brewing in the distance. My breath grows shallow and short. My fingertips and toes start to tingle. I stare at the paper between my fingers, and something cold and hard forms in my belly. It snakes through my body and shimmies under my skin and ignites like kerosene in my blood, and suddenly I'm shaking. Will left me on purpose, and for money. Four and a half million dollars of it.

Never has anyone made me feel so worthless.

After my shower, I stomp downstairs in bare feet and wet hair. Sometime under the scalding water, when I was scrubbing my skin hard enough to make it bleed, my fury hardened into determination. Will wants me to stop searching? He wants me to leave it alone? Sorry, but no way I'm stopping now.

In the kitchen, I flip on the water kettle and pull a mug from the cabinet. As I'm scrounging around in the pantry for a tea bag, a trio of new texts ping my phone, rolling from one into the next.

UNKNOWN: I'm so sorry for everything. You

337

have to know, you are the last person on the planet I'd ever want to hurt.

UNKNOWN: I don't want to involve you in my troubles, and I don't want you to have to lie. If the police come looking for me, if they confiscate your phone and find this number, it's okay. There's no way they'll ever trace it. There's no way they'll be able to implicate you.

UNKNOWN: Iris, are you there? Please talk to me.

I clench my teeth, turn off the ringer and chuck the phone into the cutlery drawer.

Once, when Will and I were still dating, he stood me up. There I was in high heels and a slinky black dress at the Rathbun bar, tipsy on lemon-drop martinis and new love, and he forgot we had a date. By then I knew he was a workaholic, and I figured he'd gotten sucked into designing software and lost all track of the time. Six-thirty turned into seven and seven turned into eight. My worry turned into irritation turned into anger. Finally, I slapped two twenties onto the bar and called a cab, firing off a snarky text on the way home. It was a shame he wasn't there for the date, I told him, because it was our last.

He must have checked his phone at somewhere around eleven, because that's when he started blowing up my phone. He apologized. He begged my forgiveness. He suggested we both ditch work the next day so he could make it up to me. He promised to be thorough. I didn't respond to a single message.

But his obvious fluster and steady perseverance got to me, and by midnight I cracked. I texted him that I was going to bed, and we'd talk about it tomorrow.

When he showed up at my door fifteen minutes later, still frantic with worry, I let him in. I tried to stay mad, I really did, but I was soothed by his familiar body against mine, by the thump of his pulse in his neck, by the way his lips were soft but his arms strong as they steered me down the hallway into the bedroom. When the alarm buzzed on my nightstand the next morning, Will and I were still busy, and neither one of us was thinking about work.

But forgetting a date is not the same as choosing money over me, and it's not in the same stratosphere as breaking your wife's heart by faking your death. This time, I will not be soothed.

I leave my cell where it is, tangled in a

dark drawer with the forks and knives and spoons, and fetch my laptop from the table. I need to back up, concentrate on the facts and start at the very beginning. Four and a half million isn't exactly petty cash. You can't just swipe it from the company account without somebody noticing. Maybe if I figure out how he took it, I'll find a clue as to where it is.

I carry my computer over to the couch and type "corporate embezzlement schemes" into the Google search field. A California CFO pocketed almost ninety million. The head of a Chicago meat processing plant ran off with over seventy million. A VP of a West Coast merchandising company stole sixty-five million dollars via a kickback scheme, then gambled all of it away. Closer to home, a Savannah employee benefits manager made off with more than forty million in fraudulent wire transfers.

And then my gaze falls on a story at the bottom of the page, and my heart rate spikes. With shaking fingers, I click on the link, which shoots me to a website profiling the nation's greatest unsolved mysteries.

In the mid-'90s, a man by the name of Javier Cardozo was accused of stealing over seventy-three million from his employer, a Boston mortgage bank. When the police arrived at his house to arrest him, they busted in his door to find the television on and a half-eaten plate of still warm macaroni on the kitchen counter, but no Javier. Both he and the money, every single cent of the seventy-three million, had vanished.

In a year or two, will Will's name be added to this list?

I return to the embezzlement schemes and scroll through the links. From them, I learn two things. First, four and a half million is chump change. I'm sure Nick and the AppSec board think otherwise, but the amount is little league compared to the others I come across.

Second, the money is almost always taken by someone with direct access to the books. A corporate officer, a head of finance, someone who handles billing or payroll. Will was a software engineer. His programming skills may have brought in business for AppSec, but how could he get money out? There had to have been someone else involved. Someone higher up within the company, someone who either paved Will's way or covered his tracks.

Which brings me back to Nick. He didn't mention investigating any other employees, but then again, he was being purposefully vague, and technically, he did threaten me.

He also said his job was on the line, so it's not a long stretch to think he might be desperate. I sigh and sink back into the couch, pushing my computer aside and picking up Dad's legal pad. I flip to a clean page and jot down what I know:

1. Money is missing from AppSec. Four and a half million dollars and counting.
2. Nick thinks Will is the one who took it, and if I'm totally honest, so do I.
3. Will would have had to move funds from AppSec's account to one he controlled, and in multiple transfers spanning many months, if not years.
4. The money is not in the house, but a clue to where Will hid it might be.
5. Nick wants the money back. So does whoever is on the other end of the 678 number, and he's willing to kill for it. Same person?

My heart gives a hard kick at the last one, and blood pulses in my head. Whoever it is hasn't texted again, but it's only a matter of time. You don't send a threat that specific — *Tell me where Will hid the money or you'll be joining him* — and then just fade away into silence. And if I'm to believe him, which I think I should, he knows how to get around an alarm.

The growl of a lawn mower roars outside. A dog starts up across the street. Both spike my pulse, and I retrace my steps after my parents left, when I locked the doors and punched in the code on my gleaming keypad to arm the system. I tell myself I'm fine. I'm tucked safely behind the best alarm money can buy.

Still, my heart doesn't quite settle.

24

The lawn mower sounds like it's coming from just on the other side of my kitchen window. I twist around on the couch, catching a split-second glimpse of a tall, dark figure before he disappears around the corner of the house.

"What the . . . ?"

I pop off the couch and run to the side window, peering through the glass at a shirtless and sweaty Corban. He's got his head down, his shoulder muscles straining as he pushes a mower across a patch of grass that winds around from the side of the house into the back. Beyond him, neat strips of cut grass lie in perfect rows across half the yard. The other half is still wild and unruly, thanks to an unseasonably wet spring and rapidly rising temperatures.

Without thinking, I yank open the back door, and a siren slices through the air. Corban's head jerks up in surprise, and his feet freeze on the lawn. I slam both palms over my ears. "Oh, shit!"

There's no possible way he can hear me above the racket. He leans down and flips a switch on the side of the mower, as if that would help any.

"Hang on!" I take off down the hallway to the front of the house and punch in the code on the alarm pad. The screeching stops instantly, a second or two of blissful silence before the house phone rings.

I snatch the handheld from its stand on the kitchen counter on the way back to the yard, willing my heart to settle. On a bright note, at least I know the alarm works. Any intruder who isn't halfway to Florida by now would have to either be deaf or dead on the floor from a heart attack.

"Hello?"

"We've received an alert for 4538 Ashland Avenue. Do you need us to send the authorities?"

"Oh, no, sorry. False alarm, and totally my fault. I'm still getting used to this thing, and I forgot to turn it off before I opened the door."

"Can you please confirm the error?"

"I thought I just did." I step into a slice of sunshine in the backyard, where Corban is standing, hands to his hips, at the edge of the terrace. I wave an *everything's okay* hand, and he traipses back over to the mower.

"I need to hear the code word, ma'am."

That's right, the code word. The one Big Jim said they'd ask for each time I spoke to them on the phone, the one that lets them know everything is okay. "Rugby."

"Thank you, ma'am. You have a nice day."

I drop the phone onto a stone table and turn toward Corban with an apologetic wave. "What are you doing here?"

Corban looks pointedly behind him, at a strip of freshly mowed grass, then back to me. "I'm mowing your lawn."

"I can see that, it's just . . . My yard service is going to be really confused when they show up here Tuesday morning. They're going to think I'm cheating on them."

Corban gives me an *oh well* grin. "Best to keep those guys on their toes. Men work harder if they think they've got competition."

Before I can respond, he yanks on the cord to start up the mower and gets back to work.

While he's finishing up, I fetch two Heinekens from the kitchen and carry them out onto the terrace, falling into one of the chairs in a patch of late-afternoon sunshine. I inhale the scent of freshly cut grass and taste the tang of beer on my tongue, watching Corban push the lawn mower back and forth across my grass as if it weighed nothing.

He really is a fine specimen of a man. Lean and dark and slick with sweat, his muscles bulked up under his skin. Maybe that's why Will didn't introduce us, because he was afraid of the competition. He must have seen how girls fell all over themselves for Corban at the gym. Maybe Will was afraid I would do the same.

I think of my husband, and my heart gives a happy flutter at the same time the hurt comes flooding back, razor-sharp and every bit just as heavy as before. The reminder sweeps heat through my veins. Will chose money over me, over us. *Good.* Anger is good. Because hurt will make me cry, and once I start, I'm afraid I won't be able to stop.

Corban reaches the end of the lawn, flips a switch, and the backyard plunges into silence.

I pick up the second bottle, wag it in the air. "A beer for your troubles."

"Thanks." Corban pulls a T-shirt from his back pocket and uses it to wipe his face, walking across the newly cut grass. "There's nothing better than a cold beer after mowing. Nothing." He takes it from my hand with a grateful nod, taps the neck against mine. "Cheers."

We both take a long pull from our bottles. Corban sinks into the chair next to me.

"So," I say, "does mowing my lawn fall in the category of looking out for me?"

"Yup, and while I'm here, I might as well take care of anything else you need done. A room that needs painting, maybe, or a drain that's stopped up. I can clean gutters, too. And when's the last time you had the oil changed in your car?"

I feel a twinge at the memory of that rainy morning twelve days ago, when Will asked me the same thing as we spooned in bed, but I swallow everything down, along with another sip of beer. "You're just the complete handyman package, aren't you?"

A self-deprecating smile slides up one side of his face. "It's one of the few pros of growing up with ADD. You learn to do a lot of things when you can't sit still for longer than thirty seconds. Plus, my father wasn't around to take care of things. I was the oldest of five kids, and Mom needed all the help she could get."

My psychologist's training kicks in before

I can stop myself. "That's a lot of responsibility for a kid."

He gives me a one-shouldered shrug. "I didn't mind. I kind of liked bossing the other kids around. Not that my sisters ever listened. Still don't. They're stubborn as mules, just like our mom." His easy smile says he loves them for it.

"Why didn't Will ever introduce us? I mean, he obviously talked a lot about me to you, but he kept your friendship a secret from me. Why do you think he did that?"

If Corban is surprised at my sudden change of subject, he doesn't show it. He leans back in his chair and blows out a long breath.

"I've asked myself that question at least a million times. Will wasn't exactly a spontaneous guy, so I'm sure he had a long list of well-thought-out reasons, but for the life of me, I can't come up with any explanation but one. Maybe our friendship wasn't as good as I assumed it was. I mean, I thought we were tight, but maybe I was wrong."

"And yet you still came all the way over here to mow the widow's yard."

"It wasn't that far. My house is barely outside the perimeter."

I know Corban is joking, trying to make light of whatever moral obligation brought him here from the Atlanta suburbs, but his tone carries an edge that tells me the subject is anything but jovial. He's hurt, snubbed by the fact my husband kept their friendship from me, which in my book makes it even more admirable that he came here today.

"Thank you, Corban. You didn't have to do any of this, but I really appreciate you looking out for me."

"I'm glad to. Because, honestly, now that I know what I know . . ." He glances over, and something flashes across his face, something that makes him look sheepish. "I'm wondering if maybe the problem was me."

I settle my beer onto a stone coaster. "What do you mean?"

"I already told you I thought Will was acting funny. I saw the signs, and I registered them, but I never reacted, not once. Not even when he made me make that promise to watch out for you. Let's be honest. You don't ask a friend to take care of your wife if you're not worried something's about to happen. But not once did I ever sit him down and say, *Hey, man, what's going on with you? Do you need a hand?*" He lifts both shoulders high, then lets them drop. "Looks like I was the shitty friend in this equation, not Will."

I take a long draw from my bottle, but the cold liquid does nothing to budge the sudden lump in my throat. Corban may have been a shitty friend, but what does that make me? What kind of wife doesn't notice when her husband is in so much trouble that the only way out is by faking his own death? An even shittier one. The answer makes me dizzy and unstable, like I've suddenly become unmoored. I plant my feet onto the cement pavers and my palms on the hard seat under me, searching for contact with the earth.

Corban's confession puts us on the same playing field somehow. When it comes to my husband, we've both been betrayed, we've both failed. That's the only excuse I have for what I say next.

"There's some money missing from Will's company," I say, watching a squirrel sway in a neighbor's branch. I can't bear to see the surprise I imagine climbing Corban's face, or even worse — judgment. "A lot of money, actually. Four and a half million and counting, according to his boss. No charges have been filed yet, but it's only a matter of time. The folks at AppSec seem pretty certain it was Will."

There's a long beat of silence. And then

another.

I look over, and Corban is watching me with a face so straight it's deadpan. He holds on to it for another few seconds, and then he presses a palm to his bare stomach and busts out laughing.

"I'm serious, Corban. This isn't a joke."

He gives me a *come on* look. "Will Griffith drove an old jalopy with a hole in the floorboard and a seriously questionable transmission. If he came into some sudden cash, don't you think he would have splurged on a better ride? Or, hell, I don't know, bought himself a wallet that wasn't held together with duct tape?"

"He splurged on jewelry."

"Please. The only jewelry he ever wore was the wedding ring *you* bought him. And before you say anything, his watch doesn't count. I'm pretty sure that thing was made of plastic."

"For me." I twist my hand around, and the Cartier winks in the sunshine. "He splurged on jewelry for me."

Corban's smile drops like a guillotine. "That ring doesn't prove a thing. Will didn't like to spend money on himself, but he would gladly spend it on you. He probably saved up for months, or maybe he financed it. Doesn't matter. The point is, he had a good job. He did well enough for an occasional splurge."

"He paid cash."

"Okay, I'll admit, it doesn't look good, but I don't know . . ." Corban swallows, and doubt pushes across his face like a shadow. "Do you think he took it?"

I lift both shoulders to my ears. "If he did, it's not in our bank account. Not in the house, either."

"Where else could it be?"

I don't answer because, suddenly, the missing-Will part steamrolls me. I may live to be eighty, to pay off this house Will and I bought together, but I'll be doing it alone. His legs won't warm my cold feet, his smiles won't piece together my broken heart. As furious as I am at him for choosing money over me, I'm also flattened and lost without my husband.

"I know," Corban says softly. "I miss him, too."

I nod, trying to drum up some of my earlier anger, but it seems to have abandoned me. The only thing I can manage to muster up is more sorrow. For Will, for me, for Corban grieving a lost friend.

"I owe you an apology, you know."

Corban's head swings my way, his forehead creasing. "What for?"

"I found a note. Two, actually. Both in Will's handwriting, both showed up after the crash."

I've stunned him silent. It takes him a second or two to get his bearings. "What . . . what did they say?"

"The first one said *I'm so sorry.* The second told me I was in danger, and to stop snooping into Will's past. I went to Seattle after the crash. I talked to people who remembered him." I shake my head. "There was lots of drama, none of it good."

"What drama? What happened?"

"Drugs. Arson. Depending on who and what you believe, maybe murder. I met the father I thought died ages ago, not that he was in a state to tell me anything. He has Alzheimer's, and it's pretty advanced. But none of that is my point. My point is, when I met you the other morning for coffee, I suspected you. I thought you sent the notes to . . . I don't know, to trick or torture me or something."

Indignation straightens Corban's spine. "I would never —"

"I know." I pause to give him a smile. "That's why I'm apologizing."

He smiles back. "Forgiven."

"Just like that?"

"Just like that."

We sit for a bit, each of us lost in our thoughts. I lean back in the chair, and Corban does the same, stretching his long legs out before him, closing his eyes to the sun. A shrieking comes from a few houses down — children playing in a yard somewhere — and beyond that, the faint and familiar rumble of traffic.

"So, wait," Corban says, his eyes snapping open with sudden realization, "since I didn't send the notes, who did?"

I don't answer, or maybe I do. Corban studies me with an intense gaze, and from the way his mouth is drawn tight, I can tell he reads my message in the silence.

His eyes go big and round. "No."

I hesitate only a second. I've already started down this path, and after the way he's responded today, my instinct says he can be trusted. "There have also been some texts."

"Saying what?"

"Lots of things. But in the last ones, he admitted it was him."

"No. *No.* That's . . ." He passes a hand over his mouth and shakes his head, a hard back and forth like a dog trying to choke up a bone. "That's not possible. That's insane!"

"Of course it's insane, but so is stealing four and a half million dollars from your employer. You said it yourself, Will was acting funny. What if he was faced with a choice, go to jail or disappear? What if he didn't love me enough to do the right thing?"

As I say the words, my voice breaks and my eyes fill with tears, and I was right before, when I thought that once I started crying I wouldn't be able to stop, because that's exactly what happens. The wound feels ripped open all over again, fresh and jagged, and I wrap both arms around my waist, fold myself double and sob. And it's not the pretty kind of cry, either. It's the kind that sucks the breath from my lungs and screws up my face and turns it all red and snotty. Because this is what it's all about, isn't it? In the end, Will didn't love me enough.

Poor Corban, he looks like he's at a loss. He's a man without a clue what to do with a sobbing pseudo widow, so he just sits there, stiff and uncomfortable, his gaze scanning my face like he's searching for something. Any indication for how to make me stop crying, most likely.

It takes me forever to wind down, for my sinuses to stop streaming and the wails to taper into whimpers. When finally I'm able to suck a long, shaky breath, he passes me his shirt to mop up my face. The cloth smells like grass and cologne and man, and it makes me miss my husband even more.

"There's just one thing I don't understand."

I bark a wet laugh at the irony. "Just one? Because there are a million things I don't understand."

He takes a long last slug of beer, draining his bottle. "If Will's not dead, then where is he? Where'd he go?"

I hike my shoulders to my ears again. "Wherever the money is, of course."

25

That night I don't sleep. Fury pumps like a cactus through my veins, poking me with pointy fingers. Every time I threaten to drift off, it reminds me of my phone downstairs, tangled among the forks and knives, beeping and buzzing with Will's incoming texts.

How many has he sent by now? Ten? Twenty? Forty? I glare at the ceiling, clench my teeth until my jaw aches and tell myself I don't care.

If Dave were still here, I'd pad into his room and bum another one of his magic blue pills. After yesterday — no, after the past two weeks — I could use a night of deep and dreamless sleep, if for nothing else than to keep me away from my phone.

By morning, my brain, soaked with adrenaline and fury, feels numb, and I throw back my covers with relief. I shower and brush my teeth like any normal Monday morning. I dry my hair and put on my makeup. I shove my limbs into a skirt and blouse and my feet into my favorite pair of high heels and teeter downstairs to scrounge up coffee. Normalcy is what I need.

A normal widow would call in sick today. She'd spend the day in bed, wrapped in her dead husband's bathrobe and bingeing on Oreos dipped in peanut butter and hiding from the world. And a normal boss would understand. Ted would reply with a whole slew of platitudes he'd actually mean, telling me to take my time, to not rush things, that my office will be waiting for me whenever I'm ready.

Only, I'm not a normal widow, am I? My husband — the same husband who thirteen days ago dived to his death in a westward-bound 737 — is not really dead, which means I'm also not really a widow.

As the coffee is brewing, I sneak a peek into the cutlery drawer. The phone screen is black. I tap the button with a finger and nothing happens. The battery is dead.

"Ha!" I bark into my empty kitchen, slamming the drawer shut. It feels like a small kind of victory.

What could Will possibly say to make this better? What excuse could he possibly have? And if he went to all this trouble to fake his death, why bother texting me at all? How does he know I won't march into the police station with my phone, fork it over for their detectives to use as Exhibit A?

That last one stops me on the kitchen tiles. Could I really turn in my own husband? Should I? I've always believed that stealing is a crime worthy of punishment, but the thought of my husband, my Will, wasting away behind bars somewhere, squeezes a spiky ball of nausea in my stomach.

And then I think of his mother and those two poor children sleeping in their beds when a fire tore through their building. What if Will was the one who set it? What if he'd gone to prison and we'd never met? How different my life would have been. How empty.

I have so many questions. Maybe I should give him a listen, see what he has to say before making any decisions.

The coffee sputters to a stop, and I pour it into a big gulp-sized travel mug. I grab a granola bar from the pantry, my keys and bag from the counter, and my dead phone from the drawer.

Later. I'll give him a listen later.

High-schoolers swarm the parking lot when I swing into Lake Forrest at fifteen minutes before first bell. They watch me pass from behind designer sunglasses, not even trying to hide their stares and double takes. I'm like a subject for one of their psych experiments, an alien who's just arrived from Planet Widow. They're studying me for signs the aliens have sucked out my brain and replaced it with one of theirs.

Josh Woodruff, a senior, climbs out of the car next to mine, squinting at me over the roof of his hardtop convertible. "Hey, Mrs. Griffith. Are you okay?"

I wince and punch the lock button on my key fob, pulling up my sunniest smile. "Good morning, Josh. Any news?"

His frown clears to a mask of mock modesty, and he begins listing off the college letters he's received — all acceptances and all top-tier schools, but not the one his parents are pushing for. "Still nothing from Harvard, though."

"No matter what they come back with, you should be proud. You've already got an impressive list of schools who want you to wear their jerseys."

He gives me an *I guess* shrug. "Dad's still working his contacts, so hopefully I'll hear back soon."

"Fingers crossed!" I push all sorts of brightness into my answer, though for these kids, luck has nothing to do with it. For them, success is built on two things and two things only — hard work and network. Money is a given, and failure is not an option.

Josh smiles at me in an absentminded sort of way, then stands there until I turn away, toward the high-school building.

The morning air is cool, but the parking lot feels like a giant hill I have to climb in hundred-degree heat. I clack across the asphalt, trying not to work up a sweat in the early-morning sun, but my silk blouse is already sticking to my skin.

"Hi, Bridget. Good morning, Isabella. You ladies are looking extra perky this morning."

They don't look extra perky. They look like two half-asleep teenagers who stumbled into an AP calculus class by accident.

"Mrs. Griffith, are you okay?" one of them asks.

I swallow down a sigh. "Perfectly fine, thank you."

Bridget waves a hand at my torso. "Like, you do realize your shirt is on inside out, right?"

I look down and she's right, dammit. The laundry tag flutters at my waist, and the seams are raw and raggedy. I fold my arms across my chest and try to hold her gaze. "I'll fix it as soon as I'm inside."

"And you're only wearing one earring," Isabella says.

My fingers fly to my ears, my thumb closing in on a bare left earlobe, and a hot flush climbs my face. *Jesus.* No wonder the kids are stopping to watch me lumber across the parking lot, gawking at the poor widow who came to school looking like an unmade bed. I pluck out the other hoop and drop it into my bag, at the same time checking my skirt and sneaking a peek at my pumps. They match, thank God.

"I was in a hurry this morning. Obviously."

"Obviously," they say in unison.

Without another word, I turn and head for the building.

Planning a sensitivity training workshop moves to the top of my to-do list.

Ava is in my office when I walk through the door. I'm not all that surprised to see her here — no one takes advantage of my open-door policy more than Ava — though she's usually slumped in the corner stool, a spot she sits in so often, her name should be stitched across the back like a director's chair. Today, though, she stands stiff and twitchy in the center of the room, her backpack hung over a shoulder, her fingers white where they grip the strap.

And she seems a little out of breath. "Somebody told me you were back, but —"

"Good morning, Ava. How was your weekend?"

She shifts her weight to her other leg and wrings a manicured finger, casting an anxious glance at whoever is standing in the hallway. "What?"

I step around her to the other side of my desk, dropping my bag on the floor before I fall into my chair. Will's picture, the one of him from last year's Music Midtown, smiles at me from next to my computer screen. I open my bottom drawer and chuck it in, frame and all.

"I asked you how your weekend was."

"Oh. Fine, I guess." She chews on her bottom lip, plump and perfectly glossed, her gaze flitting around the room. "Mr. Rawlings told us you wouldn't be back for a while."

I've always liked Ted, but imagining his face at the town hall meeting when he said those words, his furrowed brow and compassionate tone as he implied I was at home falling apart, I can barely contain my cringe. I don't want anyone's sympathy. I don't deserve it.

"I wanted to call," she says, "but I didn't have your number . . ." Ava moves closer to the desk, a conscious step into my field of vision. "And I thought about stopping by, but I didn't know how you'd feel about me just showing up unannounced at your house."

My gaze shoots to hers. "Why?"

Her pretty forehead crumples in a frown. "Why didn't I know how you'd feel?"

"Why would you show up at my house unannounced? Why would you even con- sider it?" The questions come out like angry accusations, and I know I'm being rude and unreasonable, but I can't stop myself. There are too many conversations going on here — with Ava, with her nervously animated hands and my accusing glares, with the phone that's dead in my bag — and my senses are overloaded. It's like I'm watching television and blasting the radio and talking all at the same time. I need for at least one of the noises to shut the hell up.

"Because I . . ." She comes strong out of the gate, then fumbles, her words trailing away into nothing. She backs away from the desk, drops her backpack onto the floor and sits, her back ramrod straight, on the corner chair. Outside my office door, the hallway is quiet, the rest of the kids in class. "I wanted to know how you were doing. I was worried."

It's not just her words that suck the steam from my anger but also her tone, hesitant and unsure. I should apologize. I should open my mouth and tell her I'm sorry for using her as an emotional punching bag, but I can't seem to make myself. I'm too uncomfortable with where this conversation is headed, so instead I flip it back onto her.

"I appreciate your concern. Thank you. So how are things going with Charlotte Wilbanks? Any new arguments I should know about?"

Ava's pretty blue eyes bug, the facial equivalent of *are you* kidding *me*? She doesn't speak for a good ten seconds. "Fighting with Charlotte is just so pointless."

"Good for you. That's a very mature stance to take. What about you and Adam Nightingale? Are you two still an item?"

"Charlotte can have him. All Adam wants to do is play the guitar or have sex, and honestly?" She makes a face. "He's not very good at either." She leans back in her chair, studying me over my desk with a tenderness I didn't know she was capable of. "My mom left."

At first I think I didn't hear her right. "What do you mean she left? Left where?"

"Our house. My dad. She went to live in Sandy Springs with some mechanic named Bruce." She says it like she'd report the weather, flat and matter-of-fact. "Apparently, they're in love or something."

I lean back in my chair, blowing out a breath. "Okay. Wow. That's . . . That must be a huge adjustment for you."

"I'll say. You should see my room at Bruce's house. It's tiny." She gives me a half grin to let me know she's not entirely serious.

"I meant your parents splitting up."

Ava pulls a hunk of hair over her shoulder and winds the ends around a finger. "I don't know. It's not like my dad was the greatest husband or anything. He's hardly ever at home, and when he is, he's always on the phone or behind his computer. I'm not entirely positive he's noticed she's gone. And Mom does seem a lot happier now. She smiles literally all the time."

"Divorce is tough on everyone involved, but you know this is something between your parents, right? It has nothing to do with you."

She nods like she doesn't quite believe me. "You want to know the craziest thing? Mom didn't take anything but the clothes on her back. Not her jewelry, not her car, not even her Birkin bag. Last Christmas she couldn't live without a pink diamond Rolex and now the only thing she wants is fifty-fifty custody."

"It sounds like she's found something much more valuable." I think about Will, about how empty my life is without him in it, about how he's back and blowing up my phone with text messages I don't dare to read, and a pang hits me in the center of the chest.

Ava lifts a bony shoulder. "I guess Bruce is okay."

"I meant you. She might be leaving your father, but it sounds like she's still very much committed to you."

For once, Ava doesn't try to bite down on her smile. She just looks at me and lets it rip, and her happiness lights up her face. She really is a beautiful girl, and I'm about to tell her she should smile more often when the bigger picture occurs to me.

"You seem surprisingly okay with all of this. How come?"

She unwinds her finger, pushes the hair back over her shoulder and straightens her Lake Forrest sweater. "Honestly? Because of you. Because of what happened to your husband. Things like that make you realize what's really important, and it's not another diamond Rolex, you know? Like, life is too short to be focused on all the wrong things."

And just like that, I'm crying. For me, for Will, for Ava and her mother. This is the moment every counselor works for, that aha moment of breakthrough when their student sheds some of the baggage weighing them down, but because of my own baggage, I'm too emotional to say a word.

"Anyway —" she swipes her backpack from the floor and pushes to a stand "— I didn't mean to make you cry. I just wanted you to know that if you need me, I'll be in a tiny bedroom up in Sandy Springs, and I have you to thank for it." Her cheeky grin fades into something more solemn, and her voice goes rough around the edges. "Seriously, Mrs. Griffith. Thank you, and I'm really, really sorry about your husband."

As soon as she's gone, I wipe my tears with my sleeve and call Evan on my desk phone. "Hey, it's me."

"Finally. I must have left you a dozen voice mails. Did you leave your cell at home or something?"

I feel around for my bag on the floor, push it with my foot to the very back corner of my desk, where it tangles with the computer wires. "The battery's dead."

"Well, plug it in, will you? I talked to the waitress."

"What did she say?"

"Nothing, that's the problem. I'm hoping she'll be more forthcoming in person, which is why I'd like to fly down there later this week, you and me both. My size tends to scare people off, and I'm thinking it might help if I show up with another female who also happens to be a psychologist."

"You're probably right. I'm happy to help any way I can."

"Great. My assistant is moving some things around on my schedule. She'll let you know the day once she clears one up."

"Sounds good."

"I also talked to an old buddy of mine whose firm specializes in corporate account-ing fraud, and apparently, it's a well-known secret around town that AppSec's plans to go public keep getting postponed because they can't get their shit together. The VCs have all backed out. They want nothing to do with them."

"What's a VC?"

"Venture capital fund. They invest money in companies like AppSec in exchange for equity. Companies typically use them for an influx of cash as a lead-up to the IPO. In AppSec's case, there were a few enthusiastic investors as recently as three years ago, but only one this past year and that was 100 percent stock, so not exactly liquid."

"I'm a school psychologist, Evan. I have no idea what any of that means."

"It means that Will's boss has lost his marbles if he thinks AppSec will be going public anytime soon. That company is in deep financial distress, and their books are a mess. It's no wonder four and a half million were missing before anyone had any idea it was gone."

The bell rings, and the classrooms spill clumps of rowdy teenagers into the hall. I pull the phone cord long, step around my desk and reach for my office door. It's something I've never done — ever, in the six-plus years I've worked here — and the students notice. They look over with brows light with surprise, right before I shut the door in their faces.

"Okay," I say, returning to my desk chair, "but that still doesn't explain how a software engineer could sneak that much out of the company without anyone noticing. Wouldn't he need someone to sign the checks for him?"

"Not if he moved it electronically. He

probably wouldn't have had to cover his tracks very carefully to get away with it, either, which is both good news and bad. Bad for the thief, but good for the investigators. All they have to do to get it back is follow the paper trail."

"I wouldn't be too sure. Will is a genius, and he wouldn't leave obvious footprints for the investigators."

Especially if I'm right, if Will is hiding out with the money. He'll make sure neither will be easy to trace. In fact, I'm willing to bet I'm the only link left to him, the dead phone in my bag the only clue.

On the other end of the line, Evan shuffles some papers around his desk. "I've got a few calls out. I figure if I can ferret out who AppSec is using as an investigator, it might give me some indication as to where they're looking for the money. In the meantime, what did you do with the Liberty Airlines check?"

"I ripped it in half." I don't mention that if I could have stuffed it down that Ann Margaret's throat, I would have.

"And you haven't claimed any of the life insurance policies, have you?"

"No."

"Good. Don't. As Will's wife, you're going to be the first person they look to as coconspirator, and it's important you don't touch a cent of money that might not be kosher. Will you be okay financially for the foreseeable future?"

I do the math in my head, a quick ballpark of the monthly costs — mortgage, utilities, car and insurance payments — and don't like the answer. Private schools are notoriously stingy when it comes to salaries, and Will's paycheck was double mine. I could sell his car, but Corban was right. It's old and unreliable and probably not worth more than a couple thousand bucks. I'm not entirely sure how I'll manage the mortgage now that my income is down by two-thirds, but I do know this: I'll starve before I sell the dream house Will and I bought together.

"Iris, if you need any help, I'm happy to —"

"I'm fine." I grimace and pump an *I got this* confidence into my tone. "Thanks, Evan, but don't worry. I'll figure something out."

"I just don't want to give them any reason to come after you."

"Understood." This time my tone says the subject is closed.

"Right. While I've got you, is there anything else I should know about? Documents Will asked you to sign, or any big-ticket items other than the ring Will bought with unexplained funds? Cars, vacations, furniture, anything you haven't found reflected on your mutual accounts."

"No, nothing that I can think of. Though I called to tell you why I've let the battery go dead on my cell phone."

"More texts? You're supposed to be uploading the screenshots to the Dropbox account, remember?"

I lean back and look out the window, on to the parking lot of shiny cars and beyond, to the line of trees. "That would mean I'd actually have to touch my phone."

"Are the threats that bad?"

"It's not the threats. It's the texts from the other number, the blocked one. I know who's behind them."

"You do? Who is it?" I pause to gather up the word on my tongue, but Evan is not that patient. "Jesus Christ, you're going to say Will, aren't you?" His neutral lawyer tone has abandoned him, and he sounds skeptical.

"Yes." I say the word, and my heart gives a hard kick. "It's true. It's him."

"How do you know? And by that I mean, *really* know that it's him and not just someone claiming to be him."

"Because I know. Because this is how we

fight. I get pissed and ignore him, and he blows up my phone with excuses and apologies. But, oh my God, Evan, it's really him."

"What did he say?"

"I don't know." I think about the texts, and the emotions rise in my chest, stealing my breath and taking up all the air. "I can't bear to look at his messages. I haven't touched my phone since yesterday afternoon."

Silence stretches, long and leaden, and I feel the need to defend myself.

"You know better than anyone else the hell I've been through these past thirteen days, and now I'm finding out it wasn't real? That it was just some morbid trick so he could run off with a couple million dollars? Uh-uh. Hell, no. I'm so unbelievably furious at him, Evan. I really don't know what to do with myself."

Evan blows out a long breath. "I'm trying to put myself in your place, Iris, I really am, but all I keep thinking is if I suddenly found out Susanna and Emma were alive, there's not one goddamn thing that could keep me from them. Sure, I'd be furious she put me through these past two weeks, but my anger would be far outweighed by relief at finding her alive."

"That's different. Your daughter makes

your hypothetical situation completely different from my reality. Will is an adult, not an innocent child." But even as I say the words, something worms its head up through the anger and resentment, and I find myself stretching out a leg, feeling around for my bag with my foot.

"Love is love. And how will you know if his reasons are forgivable or not if you refuse to look at your phone?" He pauses to let that one sink in, then seems to think of something else. "Hey, I keep meaning to ask. Who told you that blocked number couldn't be traced?"

"What? Oh, some Best Buy geek in Seattle. He said the texts originated from an app, something about a texting equivalent of Snapchat. Once the text is sent, any trace of it is wiped clean."

"Still. Probably wouldn't hurt to have another expert take a look at it. What time are you done there?"

"Officially? Five, but I can leave anytime after three."

He recites an address for a neighborhood near my house, in Little Five Points, and I scribble it onto a sticky. "Ask for Zeke. I'll call ahead and tell him you'll be there around four."

"Okay."

"Oh, and, Iris? Plug in your phone."

26

I check the scribbles on my Post-it against the sign on the window of Sam's Record Shop, a dusty music store in Little Five Points. According to the address Evan gave me, this is the place. I push through the glass door and take a look around.

Sam does a brisk business. Dozens of hippies and hipsters stand around, nodding to a soundless beat on headphones and flipping through old vinyl covers. I squeeze past them, heading for the pretty girl behind the cash register at the far end.

When she spots me, her hot-pink lips slide into a lazy smile. "Hey, how you doin'?"

Her speech is slow and syrupy, and I'm pretty sure she's stoned.

"I'm looking for Zeke. He's expecting me."

She points to a bright yellow door to my right. "Seek and ye shall find."

I thank her and head into the back, which

is little more than a long hallway lined with storage spaces barely large enough to be called rooms. I pick my way down it, peeking into each one, finding stacks of unmarked boxes and plenty of empty take-out containers but no humans.

The last room on the left is jammed with computer parts — consoles and memory boards and semi-assembled laptops. A snake's nest of Ethernet wires and power strips spill across the floor, leading to a stainless-steel table with, behind it, a man who looks more like a surfer dude than a techie. Shaggy hair, half-mast eyes, worn T-shirt over baggy shorts, leather and beads slung around his neck. But he's pounding away at a keyboard, so I assume I'm in the right place.

I knock on the doorjamb, and . . . nothing. I try again, this time harder, and clear my throat. "Hello, Zeke?"

He glances up, but barely. "Depends."

"Evan Sheffield sent me over. I'm Iris Griffith. He said you could help me with my phone."

Without looking away from his screen, Zeke holds out a palm, and I'm already shaking it when I realize the gesture wasn't meant as a greeting. "Your phone," he says, his tone impatient.

Okay, then. I slide it out of my bag and fork it over.

He attaches it to his computer with a cord and goes to work without another word. His fingers fly across the keyboard, and a wave of nostalgia sucker punches me, slamming me with how much I miss Will. The rapid-fire clicking of the keys, the long strings of symbols and numbers rolling across the screen . . . I sink onto the edge of a chair against the wall.

"Somebody at Best Buy told me the number came from an app, which made it untraceable."

Zeke snorts. "And you believed him?"

I bite down on an *obviously.* "Do you think you can trace it?"

"In, like, five minutes, tops." A new text pings my phone, and he glances at the screen. "Dude's persistent, I'll give him that."

I chew my lip and gaze around the room, reading senseless scribbles on a wall whiteboard, taking in the tangles of wires and chargers in a crate on the floor, trying hard to look at anything but my phone. Still. I hear my own voice say, "How many texts are there?"

Zeke stops typing. "Eighty-three."

"Do me a favor, will you? Read me the

last one."

He gives me a strange look but swipes a finger across my iPhone screen. "It says *If I could go back and start all over again, I'd do everything different but you.*"

A sob tries to elbow its way up my throat, and I swallow it down, concentrating on my anger instead. Will is not dead. He's gone by choice. He chose money over me, his supposed very favorite person on the planet. Even if he could go back, even if we could start all over again, would I want to?

But even through the anger mowing away at my insides like a swarm of hungry termites, I know the answer is yes. I shouldn't, but I do, because I think maybe I can change things. Maybe I can make him choose me next time, instead of the money. There's a sucker born every minute out of heartache.

After a few more minutes of ticking away at his keyboard, Zeke looks away from his monitor and to me. "There are, like, thousands of ways to stay anonymous online these days, and this dude used a flawed one." He scribbles something onto a pad, rips off the sheet and hands it to me, along with my phone. An Atlanta address I don't recognize.

"Seriously? That took you what, all of four

minutes?"

For the first time since I walked through his door, Zeke grins, his teeth blinding me in the blue-tinted light. "That's why they pay me the big bucks."

The house is a multi-gabled monstrosity of brick and stone in Vinings, a suburb just outside the northwest perimeter of the city. There are a million houses like it here, in a million neighborhoods just like this one — newly built communities where everything matches. Carefully clipped lawns lined with winding beds of rhododendrons. Twin lanterns on either side of the front door and at least one bay window. Decorative shutters and stout mortar mailboxes down at the curb.

I putter past in my car, checking for signs of life, but as far as I can tell, there are none. The indoor lights are off, but it's also barely dinnertime on a sunny spring day, so why wouldn't they be? There's also no sign of movement, no shadows sliding across the windows. If Will is in there, he's somewhere I can't see him.

Still. Will hiding out in this house doesn't make any sense. If he's got the money, why stop running in an Atlanta suburb? Why not disappear across the border, or at least into the mountains of a neighboring state? Will is too smart, and Vinings is too close to home.

I park around the corner, slip my phone in my skirt pocket and pick my way across a neighbor's backyard on my tiptoes, trying not to sink my heels into their flawless fescue. The landscaping is as young as the house, a few years at best. What trees have been planted are still spindly and bare, providing zero coverage.

I have lost my freaking mind. An open target in broad daylight. The worst Peeping Tom in the history of Peeping Toms — in a skirt and heels, no less.

I come up to the kitchen window and press my nose to the glass. On the other side, a chair is pushed back from the table before an open laptop, its screen dark, next to a plain white mug. This morning's coffee or a late-afternoon cup of tea? There's no telling. Beyond, the kitchen is dark and empty.

I slink around the corner to the back door. A pair of muddy sneakers — men's — lie abandoned next to a pile of newspapers. Whoever lives here runs and recycles, and I add two ticks to the *Not Will* column. Will prefers the gym, and he reads his news online. I shove my way through the shrubs and move on to the next window.

The living room is empty, too, its contents too generic to make any assumptions about the person who lives here. A couch, two chairs, a couple of tables and lamps. I look around for anything personal, photographs or books or discarded items of clothing, but there's nothing. Other than the shoes and the laptop, this place could be a model home.

A light flips on in the hall, and my heart stops, then kicks into high gear. If it's Will, what will I do? Faint into the bushes? Bust through the window? I grip the sill, hold my breath and wait.

Disappointment balloons in my belly, hard and heavy, at the man who walks around the corner. It's not Will, but I recognize him immediately. Tall build and broad shoulders, skin the color of coffee beans. I saw plenty of that skin just yesterday, when he was pushing a lawn mower across my backyard.

I move the pieces in my brain, sliding them around to find where they fit. The house. Will. Corban. If this is the address attached to the blocked number, the one Will's been using to text since he traced me to Seattle, what is Corban doing here? And where's Will? No matter how I try to shove them together, I can't make the pieces connect.

Corban moves farther into the room, and I slide down to the next window, tracking his movements. He's hunched over a cell phone, his thumb swiping at the screen. Whatever he sees there freezes his shoes to the hardwoods, and a frown pushes down on his forehead.

Something inside me goes on high alert, like Ava's fancy sports car that beeps whenever her back bumper gets too close to something solid. The alarm in my head is screaming, telling me I'm backing up to something dangerous. A ravine, maybe, or the edge of a cliff.

Without warning, his head swings up, his gaze whipping to the window.

My window.

As if he knew exactly where to look.

I drop to the dirt, holding my breath and listening for a sign, but I can barely hear above my pounding heart. Did he see me? Is he on his way outside right now? I don't wait to find out. I dig my limbs into the dirt and start scrambling, my heart lodged behind my teeth. Pine straw pricks my hands and skin, and cloth rips in the brambles — my skirt or my blouse or both — but I don't stop. I duck my head and keep going. Twenty feet through the bushes to the end of the house, and then what? As soon as I hit the yard, I'll be seen.

It's either that or pray he doesn't come outside.

A door slams, a dog barks, and that's all I need to know. I burst from the branches, lunge into a sprint and tear across the yard for the car.

I tumble onto my driver's seat and stab my keys in the ignition with shaky, dirt-caked fingers. I chance a peek up the yard as I'm peeling away, and there's Corban standing in the doorway, one hand shading his eyes from the sun.

And smiling.

A few minutes later, I swerve my car between two SUVs in a nearby Home Depot lot and try not to hyperventilate. I'm no longer winded from my sprint across Corban's yard, but my breath still comes in short spurts, and the air feels stuck in my lungs. I puff my cheeks and hold my breath like Corban taught me at the memorial — oh, the irony — and it helps. When I release it, my lungs unknot somewhat.

Corban saw me. Not only did he see me, he could have easily caught up with me. I'm not an athlete, and high heels and a pencil skirt aren't exactly the best gear for a hundred-meter dash. In the time it took me to make it across his yard and into my car, a jock like Corban could have lapped me, twice.

But he didn't even try.

He also didn't look surprised. And he was smiling.

My cell stabs me in the pubic bone, and I dig it from my skirt pocket. I stare at the dark screen, and I recall an information evening Ted and I held for parents a few months ago. The subject was cyberbullying, and we were barely a half hour in when the meeting was hijacked by a couple of helicopter parents who had, unbeknownst to their kids, installed GPS trackers on their teenagers' cell phones. They told us this proudly, as if spying on their kids was a God-given parental right, and I made the mistake of wondering out loud if that was crossing some sort of line. Ted spent the rest of the evening trying to calm everyone down.

But the point is, I know the technology exists.

The trackers these parents talked about were invisible, working undetected in the background. All you have to do is get a hold of the other person's phone long enough to install it, and bingo, you know where they are at all times. The realization rises slowly, repellently, to the surface of my mind, and if it weren't for all those texts from Will, I'd chuck my phone out the window.

And then another realization tightens the breath in my lungs.

The blocked number led me to Corban, not Will.

With shaking fingers, I wake up my phone and scroll through the texts — a whopping eighty-seven in all.

Heartfelt apologies. Detailed explanations and tearful regrets. He says everything right, except for one.

Seventeen times, he tells me he loves me. But not once does he say the words I want to hear. *Our* words. Not once does he tell me I'm his very favorite person, which means the person on the other end of this number also isn't mine.

Which means . . . what? Will is dead? As furious as I am at the idea he'd choose money over me, I don't want to believe it. What about the notes, the ones apologizing and warning me to stop snooping into his past? If Corban is behind the texts, is he behind the notes, too?

I slump my shoulder against the window, the day crashing over me all over again in a sickening wave. I feel it coming. The familiar little tickle in my lungs, a burning at the edges of my eyes, that tightening deep in my throat. All signals I'm on the knife-edge of an impending meltdown.

When the notes and the texts began, I chose to believe Will was on the other end. I *needed* to believe it. When faced with the reality of a plane and a charred cornfield, I chose to look the other way, just like I did in our marriage. So Will didn't like to talk about his past. So there were some holes in his stories. Whenever an incongruity would arise, I convinced myself it was a silly mistake, told myself to overlook it. What mattered, I always thought, was our present.

Only, how can you love a person you don't really know?

The answer breeds and multiplies in my gut, chomping away at the grief, eating it whole and belching it back up in a spiky ball of anger — not just at Will's betrayal but more at myself for falling for it.

Love and sacrifice. Honesty. Trust. We see what we want to see. We gather information, use it or ignore it to shape our own beliefs, to make our own choices, to withhold love or to give it freely.

I toss the phone onto the passenger's seat and shove my car into gear, pointing it back toward the highway.

My husband is dead.

My heart is broken.

My eyes are wide-open now.

Despite rush-hour traffic, I make it back to Little Five Points in under an hour. By now it's closing in on seven, and the sky has faded to a pinkish purple.

Inside, the record store is empty, save for the pretty girl behind the counter. She's counting out money and, when she hears the bell jangle on the door, holds up a finger. I don't wait, shoving through the bright yellow door before she can look up from her pile.

I find Zeke exactly where I left him, still clacking away on his keyboard in the cluttered back room.

"You're back," he says without looking away from his monitor.

I drop my cell onto his desk. "You missed the tracker."

"No, I saw it." He looks up, then rears his head back at my tousled hair and disheveled blouse, my right sleeve ripped in two places. "What the hell happened to you?"

"The tracker happened to me. It would have been helpful if you'd told me it was there."

"You didn't ask."

I can't swallow the sigh that sneaks up my throat. "Can you take it off now, please? And I have another number I need you to trace. It's the 678 number at the top of my text app."

Zeke swipes a finger over the screen, pulls up the messages. There have been four more since the first two, sinister texts promising pain and death if I don't cough up the money. "That's seriously messed up."

"Tell me about it. I was hoping you could tell me who sent them."

"This dude routed the messages through a company site, too, but —" He taps a couple of buttons on the phone and frowns. "Huh. That's weird. Hang on, this may take me a minute."

"While you're at it, is there anything else suspicious or sneaky on there I should know about?"

He digs a charger out of the crate by his feet and holds it out to me. "Throw all your other chargers away, or better yet, bring 'em to me. I'm always in the market for sniffers."

I don't know what a sniffer is, but I drop the charger in my bag anyway.

He returns to my phone, swiping a finger across the screen. "How tight you need this thing to be?"

"Pretend it's your girlfriend's phone."

His eyes gleam, and he gestures to the chair behind me. "Have a seat. You're gonna be here a while."

27

Over the ravioli special at Cafe Intermezzo in Midtown, I fill Evan in on the latest developments. How Zeke traced the phone to a house in Vinings where I found Corban Hayes. How I then hightailed it back to Zeke, who took the tracker off my phone as well as an app that was logging my call and text history. How when I left he was still working his magic on the 678 number, the one that sent the two threats.

"For some reason, it's harder than the other one to trace. Zeke promised to call as soon as he cracked it."

Evan is still in his work suit, an immaculate pinstripe that has to have been custom-made for his extra-long frame, but his jacket is draped over the back of his chair, his collar is loosened, and his sleeves are shoved up his long arms. Together with his mountain-man beard, the effect would be ruggedly charming if it weren't for his eyes, drooping with sorrow at the edges.

"But this other number," he says, reaching a long arm over the table to hand me back my phone, "the blocked one you thought was Will, Zeke traced it to Corban Hayes?"

"No. Zeke traced it to the address of a McMansion in Vinings. But when I looked through the back window, Corban Hayes was who I saw."

Evan's brows blow skyward. "You looked through the back window? Have you gone completely insane?"

"Funny you should ask that, because yes. I have gone insane. Either that, or I'm being haunted by my dead husband. Take your pick."

He plunks both forearms on the table and leans in, hard enough the table wobbles under his weight. "This is not a joke, Iris. If this guy is sending you messages pretending to be your dead husband, there's something bigger going on. You don't want to be anywhere near him, and you definitely don't want to be standing in his own backyard. What if he'd seen you?"

"He did see me."

Evan sits there, his face blank like he's waiting for the punch line.

"Corban saw me. First through the window, and then again when I tore across his yard. It's why I'm such a mess. I got stuck in his bushes." I stick a finger through one of the holes on my sleeve, find a raised scratch across my skin. "Anyway, he didn't chase me. He just stood there and watched me drive away. And here's the creepy part — he was smiling."

"You think the smile is the creepy part."

Normally, I'd laugh at Evan's deadpan expression or the massive understatement or both, but considering the context, I don't find it the least bit funny. Besides, Evan's got a point. Corban's smile was not the only creepy part.

Evan picks up his fork, stabs a ravioli cushion, then drops both to his plate with a clatter. "I don't like it. This guy is pretending to be Will, which means he's devious and dangerous, and he knows too much." Evan shakes his head, picks up his fork. "I don't know what his motives are, but he's a threat. You can't go home. You're not safe there."

"I have a brand-new alarm, the best on the market, according to the guy who installed it. Cameras, panic buttons, the works."

"Alarms won't dissuade a determined criminal, Iris. I've seen it enough times to know this for a fact. You'd be safer some-where else. A friend's house, a hotel, or if you don't have the cash, you're welcome to my guest room."

I don't respond, mostly because I don't know what to say. Attorney/client. Fellow widow. Friend. There are already too many connections here, too many ways our lines can potentially be crossed. As sweet as his offer is, adding roommates into the mix feels like a bad idea all around.

"I can see my offer is freaking you out, so you should know the room comes with its own bathroom and a lock on the door, and that I'm not only asking for you." He lifts his shoulders in a *no big deal* shrug, a stark contrast to his expression. "Whoever said the worst part happens when your family and friends pack up and leave isn't wrong. My house is too damn quiet. It'd be nice having someone around again."

He closes his eyes when he says it, like it's not me he's thinking of, but Susanna and Emma, trying to capture their fleeting im-ages on his mind's eye. I know his offer comes from a good place, but it also comes from a place of love and loss and longing. Already I feel like I'm intruding, and I haven't stepped one foot through his door.

I open my mouth to politely decline, but

Evan must sense it coming, because he cuts me off. "Just think about it, okay? The room's there anytime you want it. And if you don't, at least promise me you'll consider staying with a friend or family member."

I nod and smile my thanks, and Evan returns to his pasta.

"So. Did you ask Zeke if he can track the origin of the spyware?"

"No. I didn't know that was an option."

"I don't know for sure that it is, either, but if anybody can do it, he can. In the meantime — and I can't believe I even have to say this out loud — stay away from Corban Hayes. If he texts again pretending to be Will, do not, I repeat, do *not* engage. If he calls or shows up at your house again, call the cops, and in the meantime, document everything. We'll need it for the restraining order."

My cell phone buzzes on the table, and Dave's face lights up the screen. "It's my brother. Do you mind?"

Evan waves a hand in my direction. "Go for it."

I pick up, sticking a finger in my other ear so I can hear over the restaurant noise. "Hey, can I call you later? I'm at dinner."

"Nope. No way. Do you know how many

messages I've left you? Thirteen, that's how many, and Mom's called me at least twice that, looking for you. She's completely freaked out. Where the hell have you been?"

"Sorry, but you wouldn't believe the last couple of days."

I give Dave a quick rundown of the events since I saw him last — only two days ago but enough drama to fill two months. I stick to the highlights, telling him about Tiffany, the second note, the texts claiming to be Will, Zeke tracking the phone to an address in Vinings.

When I get to the part about Corban spotting me through the window, Dave stops me. "Holy shit, Iris. Did you call the cops?"

"Evan and I were just getting to that part, which is why I need to go. Will you call Mom for me? Tell her I'm fine, and I'll call her in the morning."

"I'll tell her, but you know she's going to keep calling. I suggest you do us all a favor and pick up. Oh, and while I've got you, did you see the email from the Seattle police?"

"No, why? Did it say when we can expect the report?"

"They already sent it."

"The whole thing?"

"The whole thing. The fire, the evidence against Will, everything."

"And? What's it say?"

"Who the hell knows? It's like reading something in Spanish. I only understand every fourth or fifth word. Anyway, take a look at it when you get a chance and call me back. Maybe between the two of us, we can translate all the police-speak."

I look across the table at Evan, dragging a hunk of bread through the sauce on his plate. "I can do better than that."

Evan agrees to take a look at the police report, but only if I show it to him on the laptop screen at my house. Though neither of us actually says it out loud, we both know the reason behind the ultimatum. Evan wants to be sure there's no one lurking in the shadows of my empty rooms, and after today's discoveries and my sprint through Corban's backyard, I want to let him.

My house is a hulking black shadow against the nighttime sky, despite the lights casting a golden glow down at the street.

"I'm not going to lie," I say, searching through my ring for the brass house key. "I feel better with you walking me in. It never occurred to me when I left this morning that I might not be home before dark."

Evan shines his iPhone at my doorknob so I can see. "Yeah. It's pretty spooky."

I push open the door, and the system greets me with a long, shrill beep. I hurry to the pad and punch in the code while Evan pats around for the light switch. He finds it, and the hallway floods with light.

"Alarm's on, which means there's nobody here." I gesture to one of the motion sensors, mounted high in the hallway corner. "Those things are in every room, and the guy who installed them told me they're sensitive enough to work in the dark."

Evan doesn't look convinced. He peers around the corner into the front room, then swings his head the other way. "I'm still going to do a walk-through. You don't mind, do you?"

"Actually, thank you. I'd appreciate it." I flip the dead bolt on the door, reset the alarm and motion for him to follow me to the kitchen, turning on more lights along the way. "Can I get you something to drink? I've got soda and beer and wine, and stronger if you'd like."

He opens the pantry door, shuts it. "I'd love a glass of wine, thanks."

I let him wander around my house, peeking behind doors and rattling knobs and windows while I uncork a bottle of pinot noir. I carry it, along with two glasses, over to the counter and pull up the email from the Seattle Police Department on my laptop. A few minutes later, Evan reappears, looking a great deal more relaxed.

"All clear?"

"All clear." He sinks onto a bar stool, frowns at the screen. "This looks like the incident report."

I push a glass across the counter and lean closer so I can see around his shoulder. "Yeah, so?"

"So really, this isn't telling us anything new. There was a fire that killed Will's mom and a couple of neighbor kids, and the cops found accelerant in the apartment next door, but what happened next?"

I shrug. "What about the case officer? Will was assigned one. Dave and I thought maybe he would know more."

Evan scans the file. "Wyatt Laurie. Does the name ring a bell?"

"No."

"I'll see if I can track him down tomorrow. Did you or your brother check court records?"

"No."

"Those would paint the picture *after* the fire. If there were search warrants or criminal charges filed or, better yet, a case brought to court. That's how we piece together the full story."

Disappointment weights my bones, making my body feel heavy. "Oh."

He glances over, butting my shoulder lightly with his. "Iris, this isn't a bad thing. Police departments can be stingy and slow with their reports, but court records are public, and often they're accessible online." He clicks around with the mouse, and his big fingers punch at the keyboard. "Here we go, the US District Court for the Western District of Washington. What year did all this happen again?"

"1998 or '99."

"Hmm, digital records may not go back that far, but we should be able to find at least a hit or two. Summaries, most likely, but we should be able to come up with at least the outline of a story." He fills in an online form, hits Submit. Two seconds later, the results pop onto the screen. "Bingo. Do you have a printer?"

Evan and I end up on opposite ends on the couch, stacks of printouts spread out on the cushions between us. There aren't that many. A few court records, a handful of news articles on the fire and not much else. So far they've told us nothing new.

Part of the problem is that Evan was right; most of what we were able to find on the internet is incomplete, a paragraph or two summarizing what should be pages and pages of data.

The other part, a bigger part, is that the evidence against Will was sketchy at best. The gas can, purchased in 1997, couldn't be connected to anyone at Rainier Vista. The apartment where the fire began, adjacent to Will's, was unlocked and untenanted, and investigators found more DNA than they could identify. And it didn't help that the investigating officer turned out to be a cokehead who was working his way through Rainier Vista's lineup of hookers. The case was dismissed long before the jury could come to a decision.

I toss the sheet I'm reading onto the couch, the frustration rising swift and thick. "This feels like an exercise in futility. I mean, I began it wanting insight into Will's past, but now . . . Now I'm not so sure. I mean, it's not going to change anything that happened. I just don't see the point."

Evan doesn't look too sure. "If there's one thing I've learned from my job, it's to keep digging until you have the full picture. If you want to know what Will was thinking in the weeks and months and even years before the crash, you need to know the major life events that shaped him as a person." He flaps a page in the air between us. "I'd say the fire qualifies."

I give him a reluctant shrug, and we go back to our reading.

From the printouts, I learn that in addition to the old man Dave and I spoke to at Neighborhood House, the prosecutor's star witness was a woman by the name of Cornelia Huck, a neighbor in 47c, the apartment flanking the abandoned one where the fire was started. Early on in the trial, Mrs. Huck testified she heard Will's parents fighting the night of the fire, but that there were three voices, not two. Two adults and one teenage boy. Mrs. Huck recognized the distinction because she had a handful of kids, though she was careful to point out they were not friends with Will.

At some time after midnight, things quieted down. An hour and a half later, the building was in flames. Mrs. Huck managed to make it out, though she lost everything, and like most of the residents, she was uninsured.

"Do you think Mrs. Huck had an ax to grind?" I say, reaching for my wine. I say the name, and something niggles, a memory pushing at the back of my mind.

"Most definitely. Especially since she was already a little infamous for her regular 911 calls, accusing the Griffiths of disturbing the peace. She said, and I quote, 'she couldn't think straight with all that hollering.' "

"And meanwhile, where are her kids? She mentions them at the trial, but I don't see anything in the reports from the scene of the fire."

"If they're not listed as witnesses or as victims, we can assume they were nothing more than bystanders."

The memory slides into place now, fully formed. Will's high-school friend, the one I never met because he was off in Costa Rica, teaching rich tourists how to surf. His name is Huck. I always assumed Huck was his first name, but now I'm not so sure. One of the neighboring kids?

I lean my head back on the leather, close my eyes and wonder where to begin unraveling the confusion of the past two weeks. With the crash? With Rainier Vista? With the notes and texts? I think back to the morning Will left, when our marriage seemed like the simplest thing on earth. We made each other feel lighter, better, happier. If I'd known all along what I know now about him, would I still feel that way?

I shake my head, shake off the thoughts. "So, now what?" By now it's quarter to ten on a school night, and all I want to do is go to bed.

"I'll sic my assistant on this tomorrow morning, and we'll see what else she can dig up that might be relevant."

"No, I meant about Corban. Should we be contacting the police?"

"And tell them what?"

"Uh, everything I told you tonight. The texts, the tracker, the creepy smile when I drove away."

"A creepy smile isn't a crime, and neither, technically, are the texts."

I sit up a little straighter on the couch. "He's pretending to be my dead husband!"

"Maybe. Right now all we know for sure is that Zeke traced the blocked number to a house where Corban was physically present, and who's to say Will wasn't hiding out in the basement? We don't know that Corban was physically holding the phone that sent the texts, or that he even actually lives there. If anything, you're the guilty one here, for invading his privacy. I know it's frustrating, but I'm just saying, before we go to the police, we're going to need more information."

"Okay, then what about the tracker?"

"Again, we don't know that Corban is the one who put it there. And, unfortunately, this is one area where technology is light-years ahead of the law. Those spyware apps aren't illegal, and unless Zeke can trace the tracker back to Corban using legal means and not his shady hacker ways, we're going to have a tough time proving Corban is guilty of anything."

"Isn't that what the police are for?"

"The police can only take action once sufficient evidence has been obtained, and we don't have that yet. At this point, any suspicions against Corban are just that — suspicions."

"What about a restraining order?"

"We could try for a temporary protective order, but we don't have much to go on. We'd have to show that his behavior has been harassing and intimidating, and that it's caused you to fear for your safety. That's going to be hard to do after you offered the guy a beer for mowing your lawn."

I huff a long sigh.

"Look, I'm not trying to be difficult. I'm just telling you how these things work. Our best course of action is to get a PI on the case first thing tomorrow morning and then come up with a next step based on what he finds. Does that sound like something you can live with?"

I nod, but it's slow and bumpy.

"Good." He slaps both hands to his knees and unfolds his long limbs from the couch. He smiles down at me, shoulders hunched and hands shoved into his pockets. The lawyer version of him is wiped away, and he's back to being the sad-eyed man-boy, the one who, when I look at him too long, hurts my heart. "You sure you're going to be okay here?"

"Of course." An edge of fear shades my voice, and I cover it by dragging my smile wider. From the way his mouth draws tight, I don't think I did a good job.

"If you don't want to stay with me, you can always go to a hotel."

"I'll be fine. I've got the mac-daddy alarm, remember?"

"Right."

Evan offers me a hand and pulls me off the couch, and I walk him to the front door. As he's reaching for the knob, he pauses, turning back with a frown. "Did you ever hear back from Zeke about the 678 number?"

I slide my phone from my pocket, check the screen. "No. Nothing."

"Wonder what's taking him so long. I'll give him a call on the way home. If he's made any headway, I'll let you know. And we'll talk tomorrow about plans to go see

Tiffany."

"Sounds good."

"Okay. Be smart. Keep your doors locked. Don't open up to anyone. Trust your gut. If you have even the slightest suspicion there's something wrong, use the panic buttons. That's what they're for."

"Evan, seriously. I'll be fine."

He relents, yanking on the front doorknob, and a siren splits the air.

"Oh, shit!" I lurch to the pad and punch in the code, and the deafening screech stops. I know from experience what comes next. I run into the kitchen for the phone, which is already ringing.

"Rugby, rugby, rugby," I say by way of greeting. "Sorry! I promise this is the last time."

"Glad to hear all is well, Mrs. Griffith. Have a good night."

I drop the phone onto the charger and make my way back into the hall, my heart settling.

Evan is standing just where I left him, his hands shoved into his pockets, his grin big and wide. "Well, at least we know the thing works."

"My neighbors are going to hate me."

He pulls me in for a quick hug, wrapping me in his praying-mantis arms and his scent of unfamiliar shampoo and aftershave. For a fleeting second, I reconsider his offer of his guest room, and just like that, the hug turns awkward. Too tight, too close, too soon for his chin to be resting on the crown of my head, his hand warm and dry in my neck.

I untangle myself and pull away.

"Be safe, okay?" I nod, and he smiles. "Call you in the morning."

He slips out the door, then waits on the stoop while I flip the dead bolts behind him. He gestures to the alarm pad, and I roll my eyes playfully, punching in the code and giving him a thumbs-up through the glass once the system is armed. Once he's certain I'm safe, he jogs to his car and folds himself in, and a few moments later, he's gone.

I flip off the porch light, then reconsider, flip it back on. If there was ever a night to sleep with all the lights on, every damn one of them, it's tonight. I press my face into the glass panel and look out into the night, at the row of hulking Victorians across the street, their silhouettes looming in the darkness. An occasional upstairs window spills out golden light, but otherwise, all is still.

"I thought he'd never leave," a familiar voice says from right behind me, and my heart stops.

28

I stand very still, a panicky fear roaring in my ears. "What . . . How did you get in here? How did you get past the alarm?"

Corban steps out of the shadows of my front room, dressed like the lead bad guy in a James Bond movie. Indigo jeans, an ebony sweater, black sneakers, all sleek and designer and dark as the shadows outside. He looks like he could scale the walls of my house and drop through a window without making a sound. Who knows? Maybe that's how he got inside.

"I learned a lot from your techie husband, including how to get around an alarm." He makes a tsking sound, and that same creepy smile pushes up his face. It scares me more now than the last time I saw it this afternoon, when I was pulling away from his house. "I told you I knew how. Looks like you should have listened."

It takes a couple of seconds before his

words register over the pounding of my heart, and then another few for me to catch his meaning. Looks like I should have listened to what? And then I understand. Corban is referring to the text from the 678 number: *FYI, I know how to get around an alarm system.* "Hold on. You sent that message? You're the one who's been texting me?"

He lifts both arms to indicate the space around us — my foyer, my house — and I take it as a yes, which means he also sent the other one. The first threat from that same number comes flooding back in razor-sharp focus: *Tell me where Will hid the money or you'll be joining him.*

I look into Corban's eyes, obsidian and more than a little unhinged, and I think he'd do it. He'd kill me and not think twice.

But why? Why send me threatening texts from one number while pretending to be Will with the other? It doesn't make any sense. The roaring in my ears turns hollow, like I'm at the bottom of the ocean.

"Look, I don't know where the money is. I didn't even know about it until a few days ago."

"Of course, you have no idea." His words agree but not his tone. His tone says that I know where the money is, and he'll make good on his threat if he has to.

Sweat blooms between my breasts as I shuffle backward, inching closer to the alarm pad, trying to come up with a way to distract him for three seconds. Three seconds to activate a panic button! What idiot came up with that rule? Three seconds is an eternity when you're panicked.

I back up another half foot. "Honestly, Corban. I turned the house upside down, and it's not here. Look for yourself if you don't believe me."

His eyes narrow, zeroing in on the panel over my shoulder. "You don't seriously think I'm that stupid, do you?"

A rhetorical question if I've ever heard one. I don't answer.

He grabs me by the wrist and pulls me down the hallway, deeper into the house, farther away from the buttons on my alarm pad.

I stumble behind, searching for the imprint of a gun poking out from under his waistband, the shape of a knife strapped under his skintight clothes. As far as I can tell, he's not armed, but he also doesn't need to be. His gym-chiseled body is its own weapon.

He shoves me into the kitchen and swings me around, pressing me up against the lip of the sink. "What's the plan here, Iris? To mourn Will for a month or two, then collect the life insurance and leave town under some *Eat, Pray, Love* I need to 'find myself' new age bullshit?" He serves up his quote marks with a sneer, rage exploding behind his eyes. "Surely the two of you can do better than that."

I don't know what to say, but he seems to be waiting for a response, and the only one I can come up with is "I . . . I don't know what you're talking about."

He makes a disgusted sound. "Where's he waiting for you, South America? Eastern Europe? Mexico?" He snorts, and the sweat on his head glistens under the glow of the kitchen's canned lights. "Scratch that, Mexico is too hot. We both know Will prefers cooler climates."

I shake my head, my heart kicking up another gear. I'm trying to do the math, to piece together the logic behind Corban's string of eighty-seven texts pretending to be my dead husband, and the words coming out of his mouth now. He's talking like Will is still alive.

Yet Corban has tried to trick me before.

For a second or two, I consider the practicalities of going along with his delusions. If he thinks I'm in on this heist with Will, then

playing along might be a halfway decent stalling strategy.

But then Corban takes two steps closer, the thick tangle of veins in his neck pulsing with what I read as rage and hatred, and I chicken out.

"I know the messages were from you. The texts and those two notes. They weren't from Will, were they?"

He laughs, a mean, angry bark. "I always thought it was too much of a coincidence. AppSec closing in on him at the exact time he boards a plane to the one city he detested more than any other place on the planet." He shakes his head. "Nope, never going to happen. Though I do have to give you props. Those tears yesterday were a nice touch. You'd make one hell of an actress."

He steps back, and I skitter around him, moving deeper into the kitchen, but every time I put more than a foot or two of distance between us, Corban closes it with a long stride. It's like a game of cat and mouse, a demented dance around my kitchen island. But now I'm almost to the hall, and I pause, calculating the distance to the back door. If I can get there, all I have to do is open it, and I'll set off the alarm. Can I get there?

He laughs at whatever he sees on my face.

"Have you ever seen a black man run? Don't even bother."

I steer the conversation back to safer ground. "I'm not acting. I'm a grieving widow who found out the man she married was a thief, one who stole four and a half million dollars from his employer."

"Five."

"What?"

"Five million, and *I* stole it. *Me.* I'm the one who came up with the plan. Will only executed it." He puffs up his chest, punching a thumb into the very center. "Do you know how complicated this deal was? How many layers I had to work through to get my hands on the CSS stock? Only someone highly skilled and dangerously intelligent could have come up with a plan that genius. Thanks to me, we walked away with five million dollars."

And yet nobody walked away with the money, did they? Nick caught them.

It suddenly occurs to me that Corban is narcissistic. Probably borderline, as well. Excessive bragging is just one of the personality disorder traits but a classic one, which explains why I didn't see it before. Narcissists are hard to spot, as they're often skilled at hiding their disorder from the world.

"What's CSS?" I say, slipping my palms

into my back jeans pockets. It's a casual move, but also a deliberate one. My phone is there, cold and hard and comforting, against my fingers. I flip the ringer switch to silent. With any luck, he won't know it's there.

"Crunch Security Systems. The shares AppSec acquired in a venture capital payout back in 2013. I'm the one who told Will to move the shares to a company I set up in the Bahamas, and exactly when to liquidate them. He could have never come up with it on his own. He may be a whiz with computers, but he's hopeless when it comes to business."

I give Corban an impressed brow lift, even though I'm only half listening. I need to keep him talking, to put as many words between us as possible.

"But Will must have messed up somehow, because AppSec found out. I talked to Will's boss. He told me they had a forensic accountant tracing the money, and all signs point to Will."

My cell phone vibrates against my hip with an incoming call. Can I swipe to pick up without him noticing?

Corban lifts a shoulder, a *yeah, so*? gesture. "We knew they'd find out eventually."

His indifference stumps me, enough so

that my fingers freeze on my phone. I stand here for a moment, studying Corban's nonplussed expression and pursed lips, remembering the two new life insurance policies and Will's list of household chores that last morning in bed, and the answer falls into place.

I shake my head, unnerved I didn't think of it sooner. "You were going to disappear, weren't you? Both of you, I mean. You and Will were already planning to leave, so when the plane went down at the exact same time the money went missing, you assumed he took off with all of it."

My phone falls still, flipping the caller to voice mail, then starts right up again.

"He *did* take off with all of it. You told me that."

I frown, trying to remember ever saying anything near those words. "I did?"

Corban nods. "When you told me about the note in your drawer, remember? The one Will put there." My heart rate spikes at what he's implying, but before I can process his words, Corban takes two steps closer. I'd back up, but there's nowhere for me to go. I'm already pressed against the counter. "But he made one fatal mistake."

"What's that?" My voice cracks, and I hate myself for sounding so scared.

He grins, werewolf teeth against skin black as coal. "He left his pretty wife here, all alone."

My skin prickles, and I swallow down a spiky ball of nausea.

"You know, I can see what Will sees in you. Beyond the obvious, I mean. You're smart and you're funny, and you've got this thing about you." Corban waves a hand in my direction, his gaze dipping lower, then lower still. "Delicate. Sexy. Will is a lucky, lucky man."

"Was," I say, correcting him. My mind is dull with fear and shock, and I can't think straight. The word comes out slow and sticky.

He crosses his arms, studying me with narrowed eyes. "You know, for a while there I was convinced you were in on his vanishing act. But then you didn't break character, not even when you thought my texts were from him. Either you really didn't know, or you and Will have been one step ahead of me this whole time."

"I'm not lying. I really didn't know."

"Yeah, I'm starting to believe." He pushes away from the counter, stepping closer, then closer still, until the smell of his cologne churns my stomach. "Let's smoke that rat out of his hole. What do you say?"

"What do you mean?"

"I mean he won't answer me." Corban digs around in his pocket for his phone. "But let's see if he'll respond to you."

Before I can say a word, he swings an arm around my neck, pulls my temple flush to his and snaps a selfie. The flash is blinding, and I'm too shocked to do anything other than stare.

While I blink away the white spots in my vision, Corban hunches over his phone, his thumbs typing away. He attaches the picture to an email — no subject line, no message, just a picture of a smiling Corban and a pale and wide-eyed me — and hits Send. Almost immediately, a text pings his phone.

"Good news," he says, flipping the phone around so I can see. "Your husband is alive and well."

Hurt her and I'll slit your throat.

Despite everything, despite my terror that's sharp and pointed, despite this madman who knows his way around an alarm and who I believe when he says he'll kill me, my euphoria is swift and unmistakable.

Will is *alive*.

My phone buzzes, and this time I snatch it from my pocket. Corban doesn't stop me, just leans a hip against the counter and watches, that same creepy smile playing on his lips.

The number is a long string of digits that look like they're coming from a foreign country. I swipe my thumb across the screen and press it to my ear, my voice barely audible above my thudding heart. "Hello?"

"Iris, get out of there."

My sob is thick and immediate. For the past two weeks, I've dreamed of this voice. I've prayed to a God I'm not entirely sure I believe in, bargained with everything dear for just one more chance at hearing it again, and now here it is, finally — *finally* — coming down the phone line, and all I can do is cry.

"Will?"

"Did you hear any of what I just said? Corban is dangerous. He will hurt you or worse in order to get to me. I'm on my way, but in the meantime, get out of there. I don't care what you have to do, just get away and go get help. Can you do that for me?"

Will is on his way! I know there were a lot of other words in there, but *I'm on my way* are the only ones I hear. My husband is on his way home.

"H-hurry."

Corban snatches the phone from my ear. "Yeah, buddy. You better hurry. Your pretty little wife is waiting. Oh, and don't forget my money. This little stunt you just pulled will cost you your share of the funds."

I lunge at my phone, clawing at him to get it back, but he fends me off with ease with a concrete arm.

"She's a spitfire, Billy boy. I'll bet she's a banshee in bed. I'll bet she knocks over furniture and screams like a porn star, doesn't she?"

A wave of sick rolls over in my stomach as I take in Corban's words, the unhinged glint in his eyes. I try to scramble backward, but Corban's hand is an iron vise clamping down on my biceps.

There's commotion on the other end of the line, but I can't make out any of Will's words. Whatever his reply, it deepens Corban's grin.

His gaze lands on me, and a leer prowls up his face. "Don't you worry. I'm sure we'll think of something to do."

29

The doorbell rings less than twenty minutes later, and my heart climbs into my throat. How could Will be here, already? Where was he hiding, in the garden shed? And why ring the doorbell instead of using his key or, better yet, busting through the window in a surprise attack? None of it makes any sense.

Corban checks his watch and frowns. From the looks of his expression, he's thinking much the same.

There's a smattering of sharp knocks, followed by Evan's muffled voice. "Hey, Iris, you still up? I think I left my wallet."

"Busy night," Corban quips, but he's talking through gritted teeth.

I lean my head into the adjoining den, spot a patch of shiny leather sticking out from the stack of court record printouts on the coffee table. Evan's wallet. He took it out of his back pocket to sit down, then must have tossed it there and forgotten about it.

"Now what?" I say.

Corban watches me for a few seconds, working out what to do, how to fix this problem. He's not worried about Evan; I can tell that much. He's worried about me somehow alerting Evan. *I'm* the problem.

"Disarm the alarm from your phone. I don't want you anywhere near those panic buttons."

Evan knocks again, this time harder and with his fist. "Iris, are you in there?"

"Never mind, I'll do it." Corban pulls up the alarm app on his phone — *his* phone, which explains how he got past my alarm — and the pad by the front door gives a trio of staccato beeps. He grabs me by the biceps and pulls me close, his fingers clamping down hard enough to leave a bruise. "Give him his wallet and get rid of him, do you understand? Otherwise I'll break his neck and make you watch."

I nod, swallowing. I don't doubt he could do it, too, despite Evan's size.

"Good girl." Corban turns me around by the shoulders and gives me a hard shove. "Now, go."

There are a number of things I could do here. Slip Evan a sign. Use the distress code when I rearm the system. Bolt out the door and run for my life. But I believed Corban when he said he would hurt Evan and make me watch, and I couldn't bear either. Besides, leaving or alerting the police means I won't get to see Will again.

Which is why I fetch the wallet, plaster on a smile and head down the hallway, tossing as casual a wave as I can manage to Evan through the glass. He looks relieved to see me, though his shoulders stay up by his ears like giant humps swallowing his neck until I pull open the door.

"Where were you?" Evan says. "I tried to call."

"Sorry." Out of the corner of my eye, I catch a flash of movement in the front parlor. Corban slipping into the shadows. "I had my ringer turned off."

"Oh." He lifts a foot as if to take a step inside, but I don't move out of the doorway. I stand there stiffly, holding the door and blocking the entry with my body.

There's a long pause.

I push his wallet into the space between us. "Here. I found it on the table."

He takes the wallet with a curious look, then leans far left and peers through the front room window. My heart stops. Other than the beige sofa, the room is practically empty. If Corban is still standing there, pressed against the opposite side of the wall, Evan will surely see him.

But then Evan straightens, blinking down at me like the only thing he saw was an empty room. "I talked to Zeke. The 678 number is a dead end, unfortunately. A prepay with no name or address attached. There's no way to trace it."

I scrunch up my face, feigning disappointment. "Oh. Okay. Well, thank him for trying. Good night." I push against the door, but Evan stops it with a palm.

"What's up with you?"

I make sure to hold his gaze as I shake my head. "Just beat. I was getting ready to head upstairs to bed."

He cocks his head, frowning slightly. "You look like you've been crying."

"It's been a rough day."

"Oh. Well, if you want to talk . . ." He lets the rest trail while his gaze fishes over my shoulder, craning his head into the house as much as I'll let him, which is not far. Besides my staircase and the lit-up hallway behind me, he probably can't see much. "All right, well, I don't want to keep you. Thanks for this." He holds up his wallet, wagging it as he mouths two words: *You okay?*

I push up a reassuring smile. "You're welcome. Call you tomorrow."

And then I shut the door in his face, flip the dead bolts and head back down the hall.

I'm shaking all over by the time I step into the kitchen. Corban slides from the shadows, holding up a finger. We listen for the sound of Evan's car door banging shut, his motor starting up and the growl of his engine as he drives away.

"Now what?"

Corban's grin is Cheshire wide. "Now we wait."

The clock on the cable box says it's nearing eleven. More than an hour since I pushed Evan's wallet through a crack in the front door, which means I must have been convincing. The police, if he'd alerted them, would have been and gone by now.

But the police didn't come, and we're still waiting for Will.

"Max Talmey," Corban says, stopping his incessant pacing to turn to me, slumped on the den sofa. "Bet you don't know that name, do you?"

I shake my head. I've been awake for what feels like weeks, and now that the adrenaline has burned off, I can barely sit up straight.

Corban hits the end of the carpet and whirls around, punching a fist into the air. "What about Dennis Sciama or Andrea del

Verrocchio? No?"

"No." I stifle a yawn.

"Mentors to Albert Einstein, Stephen Hawking, Leonardo da Vinci, respectively."

"Oh."

It doesn't help that Corban has been talking nonstop. Long, rambling verbiage that goes round and round and nowhere at all . . . except maybe crazy town. I stopped listening ages ago.

"Why is Will getting all the credit? What is wrong with our society that we only acknowledge the quarterback and not the rest of the team? The lead singers and not the band? When in reality, *we're* the brilliant ones here. Without us to lift them up, they'd have never made it out of obscurity."

Corban's narcissistic personality disorder is textbook. A grandiose sense of self, a preoccupation with power and success, an outrageous sense of entitlement and a distinct lack of empathy. The symptoms are all there. In his manic state, he's no longer bothering to disguise any of them.

"Kind of like Neta Snook," I say. What a narcissist wants, more than anything else, is the accolades he feels he deserves.

"Who?"

"The female pilot who taught Amelia Earhart to fly."

"Exactly!" He stabs a finger at my face. "You understand what I'm talking about."

What I understand is that this isn't just about Will taking the money. It's about Will taking the money and running *away.* Corban feels abandoned. He feels rejected and cast aside, and it's this emotion that has triggered his rage.

He resumes his pacing, launching into yet another tirade about how no one seems to appreciate his brilliance. How it was *his* idea to transfer stock and not the more easily traceable money to a company in the Bahamas. *He's* the one who knew when to sell the stock for top-market price. If it weren't for *him,* Will would still be selling dime bags on the street corner. Narcissists love to play the victim.

He stops, looking down at me with a frown. "I'm beginning to think your husband is going to stand us up."

"He wouldn't." I say it with much more confidence than I feel. Will's already proved he loves money more than me. Why not let Corban make good on his threats to rape me? Why not let him get his revenge?

Except he said he was coming. He told me he was on his way.

I'm so sorry, Will says in my head, as clearly as if he were sitting right here, on the couch next to me. For a second or two, I see him driving down a dusty Mexican road, one hand flicking in a wave out the open window.

No, Corban was right about one thing. Will would hate it in Mexico. Too damn hot.

Corban's gaze whips to the back door. "Did you hear that?"

I push myself up on the couch, ears straining. "Hear what?"

"Shh!" He cocks his head, then sticks a finger into the air. "That. Did you hear it?"

I think I might have heard something, a crunching outside the window, maybe, or the snap of a twig, right before a neighbor's dog goes ballistic. His barks spark another, then another, carrying across the neighborhood until the barking comes at me in surround sound. It's like that cartoon scene, when the dogs are alerting each other to a couple of missing dalmatians.

Only this time, they're alerting Corban to someone right outside my window.

I flip around on the couch and cup my hands to the glass, trying to see out, but it's like looking into a black hole, dark and endless. Somewhere in the near distance, the dogs go nuts.

The house line rings.

Corban frowns, and I can tell he's thinking the same thing I am: Why wouldn't Will call on my cell like he did last time?

The phone rings again.

"Should I —"

"Don't move," he barks. He fetches the handheld off the stand in the kitchen and looks at the display. "It's a 770 number." He reads the rest of the digits out loud. "Do you recognize it?"

I shake my head. "I don't think so."

My phone flips the call to voice mail, and the caller hangs up. If there's someone still under the window, I can't hear it over the dogs and the thundering of my heart. Two seconds later, the phone starts up again.

This time, Corban hits the button to pick up on the first ring. "Hello." Not a question but a demand.

Corban's expression changes as distinctly as storm clouds scudding across the sun, turning light to dark. Whoever is on the other line is a surprise and not a pleasant one.

"You've got it all wrong, friend. I'm here as a guest. Iris is —"

The caller cuts him off, and the fact that Corban lets him tells me it's someone Corban is trying to appease. Narcissists are masters at manipulation, and though his silence says he's listening, his movements are preoccupied. His eyes scan the windows, and his body draws in on itself, like a rattlesnake coiling to spring.

"I'd love to do that," Corban says, his tone steering toward cajoling, "but her Ambien just kicked in. I don't know if you've heard, but she recently lost her husband, and she's not handling it very well."

Next door a light flips on, illuminating at least three silhouettes just outside. I blink, and the bodies slide into the shadows.

Corban's voice, when he speaks again, is cold as frozen concrete. "I see."

See what? I don't see a thing. Is it Will outside my window? Where is he? I scan the windows, study Corban's expression, but I don't understand anything.

Corban holds out the receiver, knocks it against my skull. "Tell the cops you're fine, that this is all one big misunderstanding. Tell them I'm here as your guest and to get the fuck off your property." When I can't choke out an answer, he makes a disgusted sound. "Never mind, I'll do it myself. Get the fuck off her property, assholes."

He chucks the receiver onto the floor and sighs. "It seems we have a little problem."

Under any other set of circumstances, Corban's understatement might be amusing, but now his answer sucks some of the steam from my confusion. As far as I can tell, the house is surrounded by police, and Corban is looking at me like he doesn't know what to do with me, which is not good. From where I'm sitting, there's only one way out. A cornered man has nothing to lose. Whoever's on the other side of that glass needs to shoot and do it now.

But would the police do that? Would they shoot an unarmed man? As if Corban is thinking the exact same thing, he lifts both hands into the air and does a slow three-sixty before the window. *Move along, folks,* his smile seems to say. *Nothing to see here.*

I notice every detail of what happens next in crisp, sharp focus. How the bullet hits the window with a hard pop, busting a neat hole in the center of the plate glass. How it whizzes past me with a breathy hiss, a spark of silver and air. How when it hits Corban, his head jerks back, and his blood and brain splatter like a Jackson Pollock painting on me and the wall. How the floorboards quake when his body hits the ground, a two-hundred-plus-pound solid mass of concrete bone and muscle.

And then the back door explodes open, a burst of wood and glass and boot, and an army of uniformed police swarm through. Their guns are drawn, and they're aimed —

every single one — at Corban.

One of them drops to his knees and feels for a pulse, which may be standard procedure but, in this case, completely unnecessary. Corban's eyes are open, but he's missing a big chunk of his forehead.

A female officer crouches next to me. "Ma'am, are you okay?" She runs her hands along my face and neck, her fingers probing into my shaking skin. When she pulls away, her hands are streaked with blood.

"It's n-not mine," I say, but my teeth are chattering, and the words get swallowed up by all the yelling.

A big, dark-haired man behind her is doing most of it. "Which one of you assholes fired?" His face is purple, and he's screaming so hard, spittle sprays in a perfect arc from his mouth. "The suspect was unarmed. Who fired, goddammit?"

The female officer ignores him, reaching around me for the afghan on the sofa and draping it around my shaking shoulders. "We need to warm you up. You're in shock." She twists around, yells into the room. "Can we get an EMT over here?"

The EMTs trot up with a stretcher, but when they get a load of Corban leaking onto my floor, they slow down considerably. One of them breaks away, approaching me with a medical bag. He takes my blood pressure and checks my vitals while snippets of conversations float all around.

The police set up a perimeter around the house, then hunkered down to wait.

The hostage negotiator called Corban on the house line.

The plan was to talk him down.

The order was not to shoot.

And yet Corban took one bullet to the left temple.

No one here is claiming responsibility for firing it.

The answer lurches me to my feet, and I spring over the coffee table, hurling myself through the bodies crowding the room. Hands grab at me, and I shake them off, sprinting out the back door.

"Will!" The dogs start up again, and I yell it even louder. "Will!"

I tear across my backyard to the fence, my head whipping back and forth, my gaze searching in the shadows. I'm frantic, wild and hysterical, desperate to find my husband, who I know — I *know* — is the one who fired the shot.

I cup my hands and scream his name into the sky, even though I know he's not here. By now, Will is long gone.

The realization is like a kick to the gut,

and I double over, wrapping both arms around my middle and wailing. Fury and frustration sweep over me in waves, gaining strength on the replay of tonight's events.

Strong hands clamp on to my shoulders and pull me up and back, turning me into a familiar embrace.

"You're okay," Evan says, his big arms wrapping tightly around me. "I've got you."

30

"Mrs. Griffith," a female voice says. I look up from where my face is buried in Evan's chest to see that it's Detective Johnson standing at the edge of the grass, the detective we spoke to last week at the station. "We have some questions for you when you're ready."

I'm not anywhere near ready. I'm still shaking all over, my muscles tense and slack at the same time, and I feel sick. An adrenaline hangover combined with horror and physical exhaustion. I grab Evan's shirt in both fists and suck a lungful of crisp night air. The backyard spins. "I think I need to sit down."

Evan's demeanor shifts in an instant, switching from friend and consoler to solemn lawyer mode. "My client needs a few moments to collect herself."

Detective Johnson locks eyes with me for the span of a couple breaths. "She's got ten, but have her do it somewhere else. This backyard is an active crime scene, and y'all are contaminating it."

He gazes beyond her to the house, and the dozen or so officers swarming on the other side of the lit-up windows of my den, taking photographs and collecting evidence.

"Let's talk in my car," he says, leading me to the side of the house.

"That's fine," Detective Johnson calls out behind us, "but do not leave the premises. Ten minutes, Mr. Sheffield, and then I'm coming down there to get her. Understood?"

"Understood."

At the front of the house, a long line of police cars and ambulances stand silent and empty on the street, their blue and red lights swirling. A couple of cops stand in a huddle by the mailbox, holding back a pack of curious neighbors. They look up in surprise when they see us coming down the drive, and Evan gives them a quick rundown of the agreement. One of the cops squawks into his walkie-talkie, confirming Evan's tale with Detective Johnson, then waves us on.

"Don't say a word until we're in the car," Evan mumbles.

I press my lips together, letting him pack me into the passenger's seat of his Range

438

Rover. Once I'm in, he jogs around the front to his side, climbs in and slams the door.

"Holy shit, Iris. Why didn't you say anything? Why didn't you give me a sign?"

"Because I was waiting for Will. I talked to him, Evan. He called me on the phone."

"Whose phone?" Evan doesn't seem all that surprised, but he does look concerned.

"My cell."

As I say the words, the realization hits, and I fumble for the phone in my pocket. Will called me, which means I have his number. I can call him back! I pull up the log and hit Redial on the top number. A few seconds later, three melodic beeps come down the line, then a recording in French that is slow and straightforward enough for me to get the gist. The number has been disconnected.

"How can that be? He called me from this number just an hour ago." I hit End, punch Redial, tears of fury and frustration building all over again when I get the same result. "Dammit!" I mash the buttons and try again.

He wraps a palm over my hands, stilling them. "It's okay. We'll figure it out, okay? We'll find him."

I nod, the movement fast and frantic, but the relief is instant. So far, Evan has done everything he's said he would do and more. I release a breath, and my shoulders drop a good three inches. If he says he'll help me find Will, Evan will help me find Will.

Once Evan sees I'm calm, he settles back into his seat. "Okay. Tell me everything, starting the second I left."

The words come out as frenzied as I feel, jumbled and in spurts and starts, tumbling one over the next at breakneck speed. My story is all over the place, but Evan listens without interruption, without even an occasional nod. The entire time, his gaze never leaves my face.

"Will shot Corban. I'm positive of it. He called the police, and when he saw they weren't going to do it, Will took the shot himself."

"Will didn't call the police, Iris. I did."

"What?"

He swipes a hand down his face, his fingers digging into his beard, and nods. "After you handed me my wallet, I couldn't shake the feeling there was something wrong. The whole way home I kept thinking I missed something, some signal you were trying to give me that things weren't right. I was drifting when it came to me. Your alarm wasn't on. Not when you answered the door, and not when you closed it. You didn't arm the system."

"Because we were waiting for Will."

"So you said."

"What, you don't believe me?"

"No, I do. I do believe you, but if you're right, if Will's the one who pulled the trigger, that means he's guilty of a lot more than just embezzlement. Assuming it wasn't one of them, the police are going to treat Corban's death as a murder. They're going to put manpower behind finding his killer."

My mind is depleted by the night's events, from trying to beat back my surging emotions like an exasperating game of Whac-A-Mole, so it takes more than a few seconds for Evan's words to register. But when they do, when the magnitude of his meaning hits, it straightens my spine and skids my voice back into hysteria. "But that's not right! Will killed Corban, because otherwise Corban would have killed me."

"Iris, Corban was unarmed."

"So? People can kill with their hands, especially when they're attached to arms as big as Corban's. And Will knew him. He knew what he was capable of."

"Calm down. I'm on your side, remember? And I'm glad as hell somebody shot that asshole before he laid a finger on you, but you need to slow down long enough to think about where the police are coming from. Especially once they learn Corban was here for the money. That gives Will motive. It makes what Will did murder."

Something heavy and unpleasant washes over me, and I realize with a start that it's disappointment. Ridiculous. What was I expecting here, for Will to come home? For him to apologize and beg my forgiveness, for me to somehow find a way to give it to him, for us to pick up and move on as if nothing has happened? Beyond all the lies and betrayals Will carved into our marriage, five million dollars is still missing, and now there's a man — a horrible, awful, despicable man — murdered. There's no reset button on this thing.

Evan's gaze fishes over my shoulder and sticks. I twist on my seat to see Detective Johnson standing on my front stoop, watching us.

"Her suspicions are already up," Evan says, his gaze coming back to mine. "Whatever you tell her, she's going to be looking for inconsistencies."

"Are you telling me to lie?"

"Hell, no. I'm telling you to think long and hard about what you *do* say."

I give him a squinty look, thinking it still sounds an awful lot like the same thing.

"You don't have much time." Detective Johnson must have given him a sign, because he nods over my shoulder. "Look, I'll plead emotional exhaustion and shock, see if I can hold the big questions off for a day or two, but you're still going to have to give her a statement tonight. She's going to want the basics before she'll release you."

I sigh, trying to settle my thoughts, but there are too many, and I'm too tired. The exhaustion has made me sluggish, like my brain cells are swimming through sorghum syrup. I lean my head on the headrest and close my eyes, just for a second.

A warm palm wraps around my wrist. "Iris, did you hear me?"

"I heard you." I open my eyes and sigh, reaching for the car door. "Let's get this over with."

When you know what to look for, spotting a lie is pretty easy. You see it in the fidgets and sudden head movements or sometimes, when the person is overcompensating, through no movements at all. In how their breathing changes, or how they provide too much information, repeating phrases and offering up irrelevant details. In the way they shuffle their feet or touch their mouths or put a hand to their throats. It's basic psychology, physical signals that the body doesn't agree with the words coming out of its mouth.

So when Detective Johnson asks me what my relationship was with Corban Hayes, I meet her gaze with a perfectly calm face. "He was a friend of Will's from the gym."

The three of us are huddled in my driveway, Evan and I shoulder to shoulder, Detective Johnson scribbling furiously onto a pad. The dogs are finally quiet, but the air is chilly and the street busy.

By now the media has gotten wind of the evening's drama. Their vans line the curb, satellite dishes pointed to the stars. A dozen or so reporters are lined up in front of them, aiming their cameras and microphones up my lawn. Evan shifts his big body in front of mine, doing his best to keep my face off the morning news.

Detective Johnson keeps going like they're not even there. "What time did he arrive?"

"Around ten or so." I keep my tone even and breathing steady, and I answer only the question that is asked. Nothing more, nothing less.

"Why did he stay so long?"

"Because he had this crazy idea that my husband was still alive. He claimed Will owed him money."

444

She raises her brows at the *crazy*. "Last Thursday, when you came to see me with a statement, you agreed. When I asked you if you were positive your husband was on that plane, you said no. You thought he might still be alive, too."

"It's been an emotional couple of weeks."

Tell the truth, but misleadingly — *that* is the key to lying.

Detective Johnson scribbles my answer onto her pad followed by a big question mark. I know her next question before she poses it.

"What about now? Do you think your husband is still alive now?"

I mold my face into a half-amused frown. "That would make me as crazy as Corban, wouldn't it?"

"That's not exactly an answer."

Her response isn't exactly a question, either — one I'm not about to touch.

"Mrs. Griffith, did your husband own a gun?"

"Not that I'm aware of."

"Did he ever go hunting or to the shooting range?"

"You're asking if he knew how to use a gun?"

"Yes."

"Again, not that I'm aware of."

"That's enough. It's late." Evan swings an arm around my shoulders. "I'll call you in the morning to set up a time for the full interview, as soon as Mrs. Griffith is rested."

Detective Johnson doesn't look happy about it, but she relents. Her gaze burns between my shoulder blades as I turn toward Evan's car.

The reporters are ready, and they take off like racehorses released from the gate, sprinting across the lawn with their microphones and cameras bobbing. They shout my name and a jumbled slew of questions I can't decipher.

"No comment," Evan barks, holding them off with an arm, and then he packs me into his SUV. Two seconds later, his engine roars underneath us, and we peel away.

"You should rest," he says as soon as we're around the corner. The radio is on, the volume turned low to some country station, and the car smells like Evan, leather and spice. "I'll wake you when we get there."

I sink deeper into the seat with a loud yawn. "Where's there?"

"My house. And before you say a word, I'm not taking you to a hotel, so don't even ask."

I don't ask. I'm too tired to argue anyway.

I close my eyes, barely even noticing that I'm drifting off.

31

I awaken in a strange room, and it takes me a second or two to remember where I am. Evan's guest room, with its private bath and lock on the door. He was right; the bed is beyond comfortable. I stretch out over the king-sized mattress, wondering how I got here. The last thing I remember was Evan telling me to rest. When my eyes slid shut, we hadn't even made it out of my neighborhood yet.

Last night's events play out in freeze-frames in my mind. A black body sliding from the shadows of my front room. Will's voice in my ear, telling me to get out. Corban's lecherous grin. His brains splattered on my den wall, his skull leaking a thick and gooey puddle onto the carpet. So, so much blood.

Without warning, a wave of nausea pitches up my throat. I lurch out of bed and sprint to the toilet, barely making it on time. My last meal was ages ago, and there's little in my stomach, but I throw it all up, over and over, until all that's left is bile. I flush the sick down, but the dizziness doesn't pass.

Will was there, I'm sure of it. He was, what, twenty feet away? His voice haunts me — *Iris, get out of there. I'm on my way.* Despite Corban's threats and my terror, the only thing I felt when Will's words traveled down the line was relief. Relief that he was alive, that he was coming for me, that finally, after all the heartache and drama, I would see him again.

And now? Now all I feel is a ten-ton weight of disappointment that I didn't and a looming sense of dread for what comes next.

I brush my teeth with a new toothbrush and mini tube of toothpaste on the bathroom counter, select a T-shirt and pair of yoga leggings from the stack of Susanna's clothes Evan left on the dresser for me, then make my way into the hall.

Evan's house is gorgeous. High ceilings, generous moldings, sunny, spacious rooms decorated in neutral colors, each one prettier than the next. I take my time moving down the hall, swinging my head left and right, admiring Susanna's exquisite taste, until I come to a closed door. The last room on the left, and I know whose it is. If I push the door open, I'm certain the walls inside will be painted pink.

By the stairs, I pause at a wall of framed photographs, wedding portraits and vacation snapshots interspersed with more recent baby pictures. A black-and-white shot of a gorgeous dark-haired woman is in the dead center, a tiny infant on her chest. My heart twists for two people I never knew, but mostly for the man I hear banging around downstairs. How does he walk by this picture every day? Does he cover his eyes? Does he look away? I wouldn't be able to stand it.

I pad downstairs, where the scent of something scorched wrings another wave of nausea from my empty stomach. I wait until it passes, then follow the noise into a chef's kitchen, dark cabinets and gleaming stainless appliances. Evan stands behind the island, slicing a red pepper into long, thin strips on a chopping block.

"Hey," I say.

He glances up, then sucks a breath, quick and sudden, through his nose. It's a reflex, one of those involuntary responses to pain, the lung's version of a flinch. I know because it happens to me, too, those memories that slam into me when I least expect them.

"Sorry," I say, already backing out of the room. "I'll go change."

"No. No, that's okay, I'm fine." He clears his throat, shakes his head. "Well, not *fine* fine, but I will be. Soon."

This is why I didn't want to come. Because I'd be stepping into memories that aren't mine, treading onto territory where I don't belong or feel welcome.

"You sure?" I pluck at Susanna's T-shirt. "Because I don't mind."

"No, keep 'em on. Yours are filthy. I figured y'all were about the same size." He waves me in with the blade of his knife, gestures to a seat across the island. "Come on in, sit down. I'm just making dinner."

Dinner? I look around for a clock. "What time is it?"

"Just past six. You slept for almost seventeen hours."

My eyes go wide, and I sink into a stool. "Seventeen hours, how is that even possible? I haven't slept that long since . . . since junior year, when Scott Smith gave me mono. And I did it without one of my brother's little blue pills."

Evan snorts. "If there's one thing I've learned these past two weeks, it's that grief is exhausting."

"I need to call my boss. He's —"

"No need, I already talked to Ted. Your mom, too. She's a trip, by the way. She said to call her the second you get a chance. Ted said to take however long you need."

"What about the police?"

"Detective Johnson was a great deal less understanding. She said if you weren't awake by the morning, she was coming over here to see for herself. I assured her that wouldn't be necessary, that we would drop by the station first thing tomorrow to make a statement."

"Did she give you any news?"

"Some. I thought I'd fill you in over dinner. Then we'll hammer out a plan." He hikes a thumb over his shoulder to the stove, where black steam is rising from a pan like a smokestack. "I'm making enchiladas."

"Okay, but, um . . ." I point, and Evan turns to look. He lunges for the pan, jerking it up off the gas, but it's too late. The contents are already chunks of charred cement.

He dumps it, pan and all, into the sink and turns on the water with a hiss. "New plan. What do you like on your pizza?"

"I want to come stay with you," Mom says into the phone, and I picture her standing in her foyer with her overnight bag, car keys clutched in a fist. "When can I come?"

I'm seated at Evan's kitchen table, watching him scrub the pan with steel wool and elbow grease. He doesn't seem to be making any progress. Every time he rinses the soap off to check, he starts in all over again.

"As soon as I get my house back." Unlike Mom's voice, shrill and verging on hysterical, I'm careful to keep mine even. "It's still a crime scene, and I'm still at Evan's."

When he hears his name, he gives me a chin lift.

"That sweet man," Mom says. "Give him a big hug from me, will you? Tell him I can't thank him enough. Tell him right now."

A warm rush of affection pushes a smile up my cheeks, because Mom's right. Evan Sheffield is a gem. He's one of the good guys. Despite the horrendous calamity that collided our two worlds together, I feel like I've somehow won a prize.

"Mom says she can't thank you enough."

Evan looks up from the sink with a grin, then flips off the faucet and chucks the pan in the trash. "Tell her I like pie. Cherry especially."

I do, and Mom promises to bake him one very soon. She sighs, a long release of stress and relief. "I'm just so glad you're okay."

We chat a bit longer, but I don't tell her

about talking to Will. I'm not ready. I need to hammer out a plan with Evan first; and until I'm certain about what I'm going to say to Detective Johnson, I don't want to involve anyone else, least of all my mother, in either lies or half-truths. I plead exhaustion and promise a longer call tomorrow, and then we hang up.

Evan slides an icy bottle of beer across the table to me and sinks into a chair. "The police found the missing AppSec money."

"All of it?"

"Almost all. Looks like it's short a couple hundred grand." He pauses to take a swig. "They found the statements on Corban's computer."

The realization is like the unveiling of a statue, when someone whips off the sheet and all is revealed. My understanding is that instant. I don't wonder for a second how the money got there, or why.

"Will. He put it there to frame Corban."

Evan shrugs, but his expression says he doesn't disagree. "Corban worked at the bank that handled all of AppSec's transactions. He —"

"Moved the stock to a company he controlled in the Bahamas, then sold it for top price. I know. Corban told me a thousand times. But why would Will leave *all* the

454

money? If he went to all that trouble to steal it, why not leave just enough to implicate Corban and take the rest?"

"Maybe it wasn't only about implicating Corban. Maybe it was also about clearing suspicions. With the money accounted for, the police wouldn't have any reason to look for him."

"Except now they suspect him of murder."

"Maybe. But as far as I can gather, they have very little to go on beyond a trampled-down patch of grass by your shed and the bullet the coroner dug out of Corban's skull. Pretty useless until they can find the gun it came from."

"Which they won't." I don't know what Will did with it, but I know this for a fact: that gun will never be found.

Evan takes a long drag from his bottle and shakes his head. "Before last night, I would have said no way. No way can somebody execute that kind of crime without making a mistake. Nobody is that smart. But your husband just might be, because while all this is going down here, Liberty Air retrieved his briefcase from the crash site. It was pretty wrecked and filthy, and it's been rained on repeatedly, but his laptop was still in one piece. It's being sent to the lab for analysis, but who knows what, if anything, they'll be able to pull off there."

I do. I know what they'll be able to pull off there — nothing. Not one speck of evidence that Will was involved in any way in the AppSec heist. In fact, I'd be willing to bet that every single byte they manage to pull from that machine will prove without a shadow of a doubt exactly the opposite, that Will was an ideal employee who wouldn't dream of stealing a dime.

"Look, I consider you a friend, which means I appreciate the dilemma you're in. If the police find evidence that Will's still alive, if they can pin Corban's death on him, Will is going to prison. No doubt about it. I know after everything, seeing that happen would be devastating."

I nod, waiting for the "but" that's coming at me like a missile.

"*But.* As your attorney, I have to counsel you not to lie. Perjury is a crime, and it's a serious offense. Spousal privilege says you don't have to reveal the contents of the phone call, but if they ask if you've spoken to Will since the crash, and you say something I know to be false, our confidentiality still applies, but I won't be able to defend you."

"I understand. And I wouldn't put you in that position."

"You came awfully close last night." His words are firm, but his tone is gentle.

"I won't do it again."

"Fair enough." He nods, slapping both his hands on the table as if the matter's settled. "So any idea what you're going to say? It'll work in both of our favors if I get a heads-up before we walk into there tomorrow morning."

I picture my husband standing in the shadows by the shed, his face hard with fury, aiming a gun at a man through my window. I picture him pulling the trigger without hesitation, sending that bullet flying down its deadly path, and my stomach sours. Yes, he did it for me, to save me, but still. Will murdered a man, shot him dead and, when it comes down to it, all over a pile of money.

And then I see my husband down on his knee in that Kroger aisle, his face equal parts nervousness and hope, when he said those four little words I'd been waiting to hear. *Will you marry me?* I remember the joy that sparkled inside, the tears that fell down my smiling cheeks as I told him yes. *Yes yes yes.*

Can I really come clean? Can I really tell the police my husband is alive? That he's a murderer?

I close my eyes. "I have no idea."

The doorbell rings, heralding the arrival of dinner. "Think about it and let me know, okay?" Evan says, wrapping a palm around mine before he stands. "You do what you need to do. If I can't be your lawyer, I'll always be your friend."

32

I settle the last from the tray of purple phlox into the soil at my mailbox and pat the dirt all around. It's a glorious Sunday morning, and Atlanta's spring has made a spectacular appearance. Bright sunshine, low humidity and flowers everywhere — in window boxes, lining the streets, in great pink and white bursts on dogwoods and cherry trees. The blooms blanket the city with a layer of yellow pollen, choking me with allergies as thick as my dread.

It's day thirty-three, not that I'm counting, and still no sign of Will.

"There are more than twelve thousand surveillance cameras in this city, and that number keeps growing," Detective Johnson said to me only a few days ago. "You can't make it through a day here without being recorded somewhere."

Her words were as much a promise as a warning. According to Liberty Airlines and the Georgia Department of Public Health, William Matthew Griffith is dead. According to Detective Johnson and the Atlanta Police Department, however, the matter isn't so clear. Corban's killer has not been found. Will's DNA has not been pulled from the wreckage, either.

But since there's a death certificate, there were a flurry of letters going back and forth between the insurance companies and Evan's firm, and last week he handed me a trio of checks with long lines of zeros. I did as Evan advised and deposited them into an interest-bearing account until we know for sure — which, of course, I already do.

But as of today, I'm the only one.

Will covered his tracks well. The police couldn't trace any of the phone numbers back to him. Not from my cell, and not from Corban's. They couldn't find a single file on the recovered computer to implicate Will in the embezzlement. The only reason they have to suspect he's alive at all is me — because I told Detective Johnson the truth. That morning I made my statement was like a cleanse, flushing out all the toxins. I told her everything, starting the morning of the crash. She didn't seem surprised, but until she finds hard evidence either way — alive or dead — she said it's best not to touch a cent of the money.

"Hey, Iris," my neighbor Celeste calls from across the street. She gestures to the flowers I've planted to replace the bushes the police and press flattened. "Looks pretty."

I brush off my hands and push to a stand. "Thanks. Just trying to spruce things up before the place goes on the market tomorrow."

As I say the words, a sharp pain hits me in the center of the chest. Despite the millions gathering dust in a bank account, I'm selling the house. I can't afford the mortgage on my own, and my credit cards are already maxed out paying for the care of Will's father. I've moved him from that horrid facility to a private memory care center, a beautiful building with sunny rooms and a cheerful staff. The monthly bills are killing me, and though Evan assures me money won't be a problem by the time he's done with Liberty Air — Tiffany's story checked out, and she even produced a few damning photographs of the bachelor party in full swing to back it up — the investigation will take months or even years to sort through. My broker assures me there's no better time to sell than now — "It's springtime in a booming real estate market, Iris. You're go-

461

ing to get top dollar" — and it makes me want to shake her.

I'm not selling the house for the profit, you idiot. I'm selling it because I need the cash.

I tell myself it's just a house, an inconsequential and inanimate thing, and losing it can't erase the memories I made here, but it still stings. Despite my half-empty bed, despite the blood that was shed here, I don't want to leave. Only a month ago, Will and I were trying to fill this place with babies.

"Oh, no. You're moving?" Celeste makes a *too bad* face, and her eyes dart around like goldfish. I can practically hear her thinking: *Whatever will we talk about once you're gone?*

I nod. "This place is too big for just me."

Another pang, just as sharp as the first. That morning of the crash, I wanted so badly to be pregnant, and I was, officially, for almost a week. Turns out I was a statistic, one of the one in ten pregnancies that ends in early miscarriage, and the crying jag lasted almost as long. I tell myself it's better this way, that a baby would have united Will and me, inextricably and forever, in a bond much more complicated than marriage. But it still hurts to think about what could have been.

Celeste gives me a bright smile. "We'll sure miss having you around."

I'll bet. The press seems to have finally lost interest in my story, but my neighbors haven't. They ring my doorbell all day long, popping by with casseroles and lasagnas, peppering me with questions about That Night, hoping I'll share a gory detail or two that they haven't already heard on the news. My fifteen minutes of fame have made me the most popular resident in all of Inman Park.

But just like I do now with Celeste, I smile and thank them politely, and then I move along.

Evan calls on my cell as I'm walking into the house. "Hey."

"Hey," I say, and already, I'm smiling. Evan and I talk a handful of times a day, and our conversations always start like this. "What's up?"

"Braves versus the Cards at two, that's what's up. I've got seats behind the dugout. Wanna meet me there?"

Yet another thing Evan and I have in common, a healthy obsession with watching sports. We've discovered over the course of these past few weeks that there are many more interests and quirks we share, happier, more relevant things that bind us beyond the way we lost our spouses. It's strange, when you think about it, how the one thing that brings two people together can be the exact thing keeping them apart. Maybe one day, way, *way* down the line, things between Evan and me could develop into more, but not yet. Not anytime soon. Both of us have a lot more grieving to do.

"Sure," I say. "But it's your turn to buy the hot—" I step into my kitchen, and there he is, there's Will. The air rushes from my lungs.

He's disheveled, and he's lost weight since I saw him last. The lines on his face are deeper, too, slashing across his forehead and cupping the sides of his mouth like parentheses. Even his hair, a dark close-clipped brown, has gone gray around the temples. But he's still as handsome as ever. My body goes numb at the sight of him.

"What happened?" Evan says into the phone, his tone turning serious. "Are you okay?"

"Yes." My throat is strangled, and the word doesn't come out right. It's blurred and formless, even in my own ears.

The line goes quiet. "Is he there? Wait. Don't answer that. Just . . . be careful, and call me later." He hangs up.

I drop my phone onto the counter with a clatter, my eyes never leaving Will's. I grip the marble and wait for the violent spasm of hatred and fury at seeing him again. I brace for it, but it doesn't come. What comes is relief, swift and sudden, and love, like a warm layer of honey around my heart. I still love this man, dammit. I'm still *in* love with him. Despite all the lies and betrayals, I probably always will be.

"God, I've missed you," he whispers.

I run to him, throwing myself at him with a flying leap.

He wasn't expecting it. He goes back on a foot, but he catches me with a loud grunt. His hands wrap around my bottom, mine wrap around his neck, and after that I lose track of who does what. All I know is that he's kissing me, and I'm kissing him back. Thirty-three days is the longest we've ever been apart.

And then I come to my senses.

I scramble out of his grip, rear back with an arm and smack him on the cheek as hard as I can. The flesh-on-flesh sound is loud, almost deafening in the stillness of the kitchen.

Will doesn't move.

I rear back and hit him again, another hard slap where his cheek has already bloomed bright pink, the perfect shadow of my handprint.

Will jerks a little at the contact, but he

lifts his chin and waits for another. It's almost like he wants another blow. Like he welcomes the pain.

When I don't rear back for a third time, his face sags. "You weren't supposed to come looking for me. You weren't supposed to ever find out the truth."

"What is the truth? Because after the past month, I'm thinking pretty much every word out of your mouth was a lie."

He shakes his head. "I never lied about my feelings for you. *Never.* That part is 100 percent true."

A spiked ball of pain lodges behind my heart. I look around the kitchen, at once familiar and strange, at the notes on the fridge and the pictures by the bar and the marble countertops we picked out on a weekend road trip to South Carolina, and blink back tears.

"Yet you still chose the money over me."

He doesn't nod, but he doesn't shake his head, either. "I gave the money back. Remember?"

"You didn't give it back. You planted it on Corban's computer, and for what? So the police would stop looking for you, so they'd think you were dead?"

"I did it for you. I killed Huck for *you.* The police weren't going to do it, not until they saw a weapon, but Huck was a sick bastard, and he would have snapped your neck without blinking, just because he knew I was watching. I couldn't give him that chance."

Huck? I frown. "I thought Huck was living in Costa Rica."

"Huck is Corban. His name is Corban Huck, not Hayes."

And suddenly, it all makes sense. The kid who lived down the hall at Rainier Vista, the son of the woman who testified she heard three voices fighting the night of the fire, is Corban. Corban is Huck. Will's best buddy, who was supposedly running a surfing school in Costa Rica, when he was here, in Atlanta, all along.

The lies just keep on coming.

I cross my arms over my chest, lean a hip against the counter and settle in. "Tell me, Will. The truth this time. I need you to tell me everything."

We end up on the sectional in the den, where never, not even during the worst of our arguments, has there been so much air between us. Only a month ago, we would have talked everything out in the center of the couch, Will propped in the corner with me tucked under an arm. We would have held hands just because our fingers were close, would have soothed our harsh words with a caress or a kiss. But today, four couch cushions and a coffee table separate us like an impenetrable crater.

Will leans forward, his elbows on his knees, straightening a stack of magazines on the table. Busywork while he gathers his words. Next to the pile, two bottles of icy water sweat onto their coasters in a slice of afternoon sunshine. I watch a drop gather on one of them, growing fat and heavy at the bottom, and track it on its downward descent.

"I told myself it didn't matter you didn't know the whole truth about me," Will says, still looking down. "About that part of my life, I mean. Rainier Vista. My parents. I thought it was okay to keep all that from you because I got out. I put it all behind me." He checks my expression, trying to calibrate my reaction, and he must not like what he sees, because he frowns. "You have to know, I'm not that person anymore."

I hold my face and tone steady. "Who set the fire?"

"I had nothing to do with the fire. The fire was all Huck." When I don't respond, Will looks away, pausing as if to give himself a silent pep talk. "But, okay, yeah. I knew what he was up to. I knew and I didn't try to stop him. I didn't go around beating on doors, either, warning people to get out."

"Oh, Will . . ." My voice cracks into a long silence.

He watches me, and there's guilt in his expression. "I know. I *know,* okay? And for the rest of my life, I will hear that mother's screams. I will see those two kids coming out in body bags. But, swear to God, I'm not the one who lit the match."

"Your mother died that night, too."

"That woman doesn't deserve my tears, not after what she did." He doesn't sound angry or bitter, just resigned to the fact that his mother wasn't much of one. "Ditto for the man she married."

"I saw him in Seattle, Will. Your father's not well."

"Do you want to hear that I feel bad for him? Because I don't, and neither should you. And you shouldn't be paying for his care. Any man who'd wake up their kid in the middle of the night just to give him a busted lip doesn't deserve a penny of your money. I've washed my hands of him, of everyone in Rainier Vista."

"Everyone except Huck."

Will shakes his head, and he leans forward on the sofa, planting his elbows on his thighs. "No. I don't know how he found me, but our reunion was not a happy one. He didn't give me much of a choice. He told me I had to move those stocks for him or he'd tell you everything. He was one crazy son of a bitch, but he was brilliant at knowing a person's Achilles' heel. He knew you were mine and how much you meant to me."

I close my eyes briefly, the words coming back to me in a nauseating rush. *Let's smoke that rat out of his hole. What do you say?* Corban may have been the one pulling the strings, but it was Will who committed the crime. First, when he stole from AppSec, then again, when he squeezed the trigger. Just because someone was threatening him, my husband is not without blame.

An old, familiar ache blooms in my chest, but I swallow it down. "Go on," I say, opening my eyes. "So, what happened?"

"You know the rest. Nick found out. I left."

"No, I meant, what did you think was going to happen after you moved those stocks? There's no happily-ever-after with five million stolen dollars sitting in your bank account, Will."

"I know, but . . . I *had* to move the stocks. There was no other option."

"You could have told the truth."

"No. I couldn't." He shakes his head, quick and vicious. "You don't understand. I'd never been with a girl like you. So smart and funny and kind. And so damn beautiful." He looks at me, and his face cracks open. "How could I not fall for you? If for no other reason than the way you looked at me."

"How did I look at you?"

"Like I was good. Like I was worthy."

I nod, because it's true. I *did* think he was good. I thought he was worthy. It never occurred to me he was a thief or a liar or a murderer. What part of the man I loved was real? What part of us?

I'm crying now, the tears coming hard and fast. I've held it together for long enough, and there's no one here but us. There's no reason to hold them in any longer.

"Huck sent me texts pretending to be you."

"I know. It's how I knew he was losing it. It's why I came back."

"You didn't send any of them?"

"Only the first couple, when I tracked you and Dave to Seattle. I knew what you were doing there, and I needed you to stop. When you didn't, when I found out what Huck was up to, I put that note in your drawer

471

because I was worried, but otherwise . . ." He shakes his head. "All from him."

"But why?"

"To fuck with your head or to feel out how much you knew, who knows? Most likely some combination of the two. He wasn't exactly the most rational person on the planet."

"And the crash?"

At the accusation in my tone, Will sits up a little straighter. "I had nothing to do with the crash."

"Then how did your name get on that manifest?"

"I was going to Orlando, remember? I —"

I stop him with a palm. "I talked to Jessica. There was no conference."

"No, but there was this guy." He winces. "For fifty thousand bucks he'd give me a new identity, make me disappear. I was meeting him in Key West."

I think about that morning in bed, the way he surprised me with the ring, his expression as he slid it up my finger, and the tears well up all over again.

I gesture for him to keep going.

Will inhales long and deep, blows it all out. "Anyway, I'd missed my flight, so I was waiting at the gate for the next one when the Liberty plane went down. It was almost too easy. You'd be surprised how many holes there were in Liberty's firewall, how easy it was to buy myself a ticket and get my name on the list of passengers. I didn't realize until afterward that a plane headed to Seattle would open up a whole other can of worms."

I think of Susanna, clutching Emma to her chest as that plane fell from the sky, of Evan's haunted eyes at the memorial. "Those poor people! Their poor families. And for two whole weeks, I thought you were one of them, spread in a million pieces across a cornfield. Do you know what that did to me?"

"I do, and I'm sorry. I can't begin to tell you how much."

I look down, at my hands wringing on my lap, at the two rings my husband slid up my fingers. And then I press a palm to my chest, where his ring still hangs on a chain under my shirt. "What about your ring? What about your briefcase and computer?"

"Planted." He winces. "People will do pretty much anything for money."

People like you, I think, and pain lodges like a spiky boulder in my chest. I demanded the truth, but now I want to slap my hands over my ears and unhear his words. I want to press control-alt-delete and force a

473

restart. The truth is too much. My husband is a monster.

"See?" he says. "You're already doing it."

"Doing what?"

"Looking at me differently. Like you're wondering how you ever could have loved me."

I fall silent, because it's true. That's exactly what I was wondering.

Will looks away, his gaze landing on the framed Rolling Stones photograph I gave him last year for his birthday. "You preach about nature and nurture and those poor little rich kids you work for, and yet you can't put yourself in my shoes. You can't imagine what it's like when your dad's too busy whaling on you to hold down a job and your mom's too drunk to care. Or what it feels like to scarf down a sandwich of rotten mayonnaise and moldy bread and feel relief there's something lining your belly. Your life is so far removed from that kind of hell, you can't even picture it."

His words weigh heavy on my heart at the same time they harden it. Yes, experience has taught me to not blame the child for their parents' questionable behavior. Children are the product of their parents, and crappy or nonexistent parenting skills load down a child with baggage that's no fault of their own. I've said it often enough that Will knows I believe this to be true. He knows I won't think less of him for his parents' failures.

But he also knows I teach my students to move past their baggage by becoming accountable. I teach them responsibility for their own actions and behaviors, to follow the rules and live up to expectations. I told Will this part, too, but just like I had been able to pick and choose what I wanted to believe about him, he was able to pick and choose what he wanted to hear.

"I didn't know about your life because you never told me. You didn't even try. How can I imagine something I don't know anything about?"

Now, for the first time today, Will grows defensive. He lurches to the edge of the couch, and his forehead creases in a frown.

"Come on, Iris. Get real. What would you have said if I'd told you? What if I'd taken you for coffee that very first day and told you Huck and I had a plan, a brilliant, foolproof plan to walk away with more money than we ever dreamed possible. Would you have given me your number? Would you have agreed to a second date?" He shakes his head. "I don't think so."

"What you and Huck did was wrong, Will.

To your parents, to those poor kids and their mother, to AppSec, to me. To our marriage. And what if that plane hadn't gone down? You were just going to fly off to Florida and disappear? Did you stop for a second to think about what that would be like for me?"

"I *only* thought about you. You are *all* I thought about, even after I left. I wanted to make babies and grow old with you, Iris. I wanted us to last forever. But I couldn't rewind things with Huck. He threatened to tell you the truth about me, and then Nick found out about the stocks, and he knew I was the one who moved them. I couldn't stay."

"Because you wanted the money."

His hands fist into tight balls, his knuckles hard and white on top of his thighs. "No! *Not* because of the money. It had nothing to do with the goddamn money."

"Then, why? Why couldn't you stay?"

Will's jaw clenches, and he looks away.

"Tell me why, dammit!"

"Because I'd rather you think I was dead, okay?"

He slings the words like weapons, looking just as surprised to have sent them flying as I am to be on the receiving end. He'd rather I think he was dead than *what*? I wait for him to explain, and his defiant expression collapses into anguish. It distorts his features like a hosiery mask pulled too tight.

"I fucked up so many things, but my legacy was the one thing I wanted to do right. I wanted you to think I died on that plane, so that you'd never know the truth. I wanted you to have honorable, happy memories of the man you fell in love with, the man you saw every time you looked at me. I wanted to *be* that man in your memories."

His words break my heart, and I'm as confused now as I've ever been. People are dead. Millions of dollars went missing. What Will did is wrong on so many levels, and I know I should be boiling over with fury. I know I should feel blame and anger and confusion and, yes, hatred, too.

And yet, looking into my husband's beautiful, wrecked face, I can't seem to summon up anything other than sorrow. An overwhelming sadness for a man who would rather fake his death than reveal the truth.

A sob elbows up my throat, startling us both. "I should hate you. I *want* to hate you. I want to be physically ill because I'm sitting in the same room as you, but I'm not. I don't. I still love you and I despise myself for it."

Will moves closer. He scoots down the

couch until he's on my side, sitting right here, less than a foot away. "I'll always love you."

This is the one thing, the *only* thing, I know is true. Every person has a redeeming quality. Will's is that he is capable of love.

"So, now what?" The tears have started up again, because I already know the answer: *Now he leaves. Now he disappears.*

He loops a finger around mine, running the pad of his thumb over the Cartier he put there, a ring that I should give back, though I know with everything inside of me that I will wear it until the day I die. "Come with me. We'll live on a hillside overlooking the ocean and sleep under the stars. We can disappear, just you and me."

I'm shaking my head before the last word is out. I couldn't leave Dave, could never do that to my parents. I could barely contemplate a move to the other side of the country, much less a disappearance. I know better than anyone what that does to the people left behind.

He smiles, and it's the saddest thing I've ever seen. "It was worth a try."

He runs his finger down my arm, and I shiver. Will is not playing fair, and he knows it. My skin has always been too sensitive.

"Stop," I whisper, but I don't mean it, not

even a little bit.

"I can't stop, and I can't leave." His hands wrap around my waist, mine wind around his shoulders. The movement is natural, like there's nowhere else in the world our hands should be. "Not without saying goodbye to my very favorite person on the planet."

So this is it. This is goodbye. I remind myself of all the reasons I should be glad to see him go. The money. The lies and deceit. His dying father and his dead mother. Corban and the two dead kids. Especially the kids. He is not the man I married. I want to hate him for what he's done.

But then I look into his eyes, and he looks like my husband again, the man who slow-danced with me at the top of Stone Mountain with a dozen tourists watching, who slid rings up my fingers and thanked me when I said "I do," who, the last time I saw him, asked me for a little girl who looked just like me. I see him, and I remember the way he used to be, the way *we* used to be, and my heart breaks all over again.

He kisses me and I let him. No — it's more than that. He kisses me, and I put thirty-three days of heartache and confusion and relief into the way I kiss him back. It's like a first kiss and last kiss and all the kisses in between, and suddenly, I can't come up with a single reason for fighting it, this last goodbye between me and Will. I can't muster even the tiniest pang from this gnarled and painful past month. He wants me. I want him back. I have no fight left.

I take him by the hand, pull him off the couch and lead him upstairs. We lose our clothing on the way, dropping piles of cotton and denim on the stairs, the landing runner, the floor by the bed — our bed.

When we're both naked, he lays me down on the mattress, taking me in with tenderness, with reverence, with love. He runs the back of a finger over the ring — his ring — on a chain on my chest. "Beautiful girl."

I hold up my arms in answer, in invitation.

We make love, and it feels like the most natural thing in the world, and also the most heartbreaking. How many times have we lain here just like this, sweet and salty and familiar? A couple thousand, at least.

And yet this time will be our last.

His mouth is on the move, traveling over my skin. Pressing kisses onto my neck, my breasts, loving every inch of me. I feel the orgasm building, swirling, circling just out of reach, and I close my eyes, fist the sheets in both hands and wait for it.

Maybe it's about revenge, about me wanting to hurt Will in the same way he hurt me, about repaying his betrayal with a betrayal of my own. Maybe it's about justice, plain and simple, about holding Will accountable for the fire and the money and the innocent lives shattered. Or maybe it's a combination of both. My reasons may be muddled, but my next move is crystal clear. I don't for a second doubt that it's the right one.

I open my eyes, and my husband is moving above me. His head is tipped back, his cheeks slack and eyes squeezed shut with pleasure, and I know from all the times before that this is a critical moment. *His* critical moment. It will last another handful of breaths, at least.

I reach around to the back of my nightstand, push the panic button and hold it.

Three seconds, that's all it takes.

ACKNOWLEDGMENTS

Writing is a solitary venture, but this book wouldn't exist without the following folks.

My literary agent, Nikki Terpilowski, who never sugarcoats what needs to be fixed in the manuscript but says it in words that make me smile. Thank you for always being in my corner.

My editor, Liz Stein, for loving this story and taking it on as your own. Your brilliance and tenacity helped shape *The Marriage Lie* into what it is today. And to all the hard-working and dedicated people behind the scenes at MIRA Books, I'm blessed to be on your team.

Laura Drake, critique partner extraordinaire, and early readers Koreen Myers, Colleen Oakley and Alexandra Ratcliff. Andrea Peskind Katz, you were right. You are an *excellent* beta reader, and you volunteered yourself right to the top of my list.

Scott Masterson, whose voice I heard in

my head whenever Evan spoke. Thanks for answering my silly questions and for feeding me one of Evan's best lines.

The fabulous ladies of Altitude, my early readers and cheerleaders: Nancy Davis, Marquette Dreesch, Angelique Kilkelly, Jen Robinson, Amanda Sapra and Tracy Willoughby. Seeing you girls is the best day of the month.

My parents, Diane and Bob Maleski, for their never-ending encouragement and thoughtful feedback. I hope this one makes you proud.

And lastly, my very favorite people on the planet. Isabella, you are a master at coming up with plot twists. Are you sure you don't want to be a writer? Ewoud and Evan, thank you for your patience and encouragement, and sorry about all the takeout. You three have my heart.

■ ■ ■ ■

THE MARRIAGE LIE

KIMBERLY BELLE

■ ■ ■ ■

READER'S GUIDE

QUESTIONS FOR DISCUSSION

1. After the crash, Iris discovers pretty quickly that her husband had been keeping deep secrets from her. Consider his reasoning for not telling Iris the truth. Is it ever necessary or justifiable to lie to someone you love? How much is too much to hide from a partner?

2. Does Iris bear any of the blame for accepting her husband's secrecy about his past? Should she have spotted the holes in his stories sooner in their relationship? In what ways could Iris have been lying to herself?

3. When Iris discovers that Will had a disadvantaged youth in Seattle, she begins to have a better understanding of his need to own a home that would essentially make them house poor. In what other ways do you think his past difficulties af-

fected the life he built with Iris?

4. Do you think Will is a sympathetic character? Do you believe he became a good man, one who had truly left his past sins behind? Is it possible to completely leave the past behind and become a "changed person," so to speak? To what extent does a person's past influence or define one's future?

5. Iris's job as a psychologist plays a pivotal role in her life and in her beliefs, yet she doesn't see her husband's true nature. Why do you think this is? Is love really that blind, or does Iris only see what she wants to see? Have you ever turned the other way and chosen to ignore something? Explain why.

6. Iris has a special bond with one of her students, Ava, a beautiful teenager who, despite all her wealth and advantages, still can't find happiness. What do you think the author's purpose was in creating this character? How does Ava's message relate back to the story of Iris and Will?

7. After the crash, Iris finds a friend in Evan Sheffield. Do you think, had they met in

other circumstances, that they would have become friends? Or was their friendship a result of their shared trauma and grief? How do you imagine their relationship playing out a year down the road? Five years?

8. Did the truth about Corban surprise you? If not, at what point did you begin to suspect his character?

9. Iris says to Will, "I should hate you. I *want* to hate you. I want to be physically ill because I'm sitting in the same room as you, but I'm not. I don't. I still love you and I despise myself for it." Can you understand how she feels? Have you ever loved and hated someone at the same time?

10. In the last scene, even though Iris's reasons for pushing the panic button aren't clear in her mind, she is positive it's the right thing to do. Do you agree? Would you have done the same in her position? In what ways does pushing that button give Iris closure?

A CONVERSATION
WITH THE AUTHOR

You have been married to your husband for twenty years. It must be incredibly difficult to imagine your spouse dying in a plane crash. Did this make the novel difficult to write, or did having a husband make it easier to bring the character of Iris and her agony to life?

Yes, I definitely pulled from my own relationship for this story, especially that intense, giddy love that comes early on in a relationship. That's when you're willing to overlook any signs things may not be as they seem, signs that might stand out to you later in the course of the relationship, and having experienced this firsthand definitely helped me put Iris in that vulnerable place. What was much more difficult for me was the story line around the crash itself. My family flies a lot, and imagining losing one of them in that way — so sudden and unexpected — was not pleas-

ant. To say I didn't enjoy flying while writing this story is a huge understatement.

Our leading lady, Iris, is a complex character you push to the emotional limits as she is confronted with serious dilemmas and difficult decisions over and over. Have you ever yourself, or know someone who has, been in a similar situation to Iris?

Not in a situation as severe as Iris encounters, thankfully, but I think we've all been deceived by someone pretending to be a person they're not. The shock of discovering you were so wrong about a friend or loved one — and in Iris's case, a life partner — will mess with your mind and make you doubt every emotion, thought and decision that comes afterward. But despite all of Will's lies, the one thing Iris never doubted was Will's love, and this knowledge made her journey that much more difficult. What circumstances would force a man to leave the woman he loves behind? Iris had to know in order to move on and, ultimately, to heal.

This is your third book and quite a departure from your first two. Did you take a different approach in writing *The*

Marriage Lie? What was your toughest challenge? Greatest pleasure?

Yes, The Marriage Lie *is much more suspenseful than my first two books, and the story was much more complicated to write. One of my main characters was "onstage" for only the first and last chapter, yet he was driving the book. This meant I needed to weave in plenty of flashbacks and reveal truths about Will through third parties. Though these techniques add depth to the story — what is true, and what is not? — it was a lot to keep track of, and it required much more planning before writing the first word. That said, the actual writing part is always the same — me, my laptop and endless hours in a chair.*

What was your inspiration for the story?

Honestly, the idea found me rather than the other way around. I was writing another story — one I immediately put down when the idea for The Marriage Lie *popped into my head. Or I should say* ideas, *as it was actually two story lines that I weaved into one: the story of a husband with a past full of secrets and what that would mean for a marriage, combined with a plane crash followed by mysterious messages that seemingly come from beyond* the grave. There are enough stories of spouses disappearing in real life (North Dakota governor Mark Sanford comes to mind) that most people automatically assume an affair, but I wanted to take this story in a very different direction. Will and Iris appeared in my head, in love and sweet and sincere, and that image became the first chapter. After that, the story was off and running.

Which character did you enjoy writing the most?

I loved writing Iris and Will, especially the sweet scenes documenting their love for each other, but the character who was loudest in my head was Dave, Iris's twin brother. He's snarky and sarcastic but with a kind, authentic heart, which automatically makes him my favorite kind of character to write.

The book is set in your hometown. In what ways did this make writing the book a more personal experience for you?

I drew on a lot of my personal life in Atlanta for this story. My kids go to a private school, where families like Ava's really do exist, and I definitely had a point to make with her story line. On a lighter note, I got to slip some of

my favorite Atlanta haunts into the story —
neighborhoods and restaurants and even the
new BeltLine. It's like a love letter to my own
city, and it was a lot of fun to write.

**What would you like readers to take
away from this story?**

I really hope it makes readers stop and think
about what they would do in Iris's situation.
Yes, she loved her husband, but she had to
decide if she could live with what he'd done.
In her job and to her students, she preaches
accountability, which meant she had to hold
Will accountable for his crimes, as well.

**Question: Tell us about your writing
process.**

I'm a planner but not a plotter. When a story
spark comes, it usually comes with a pretty
good idea of my major plot points and main
characters. The rest I fill in along the way. I'm
not a fast writer, but the words I produce each
day are generally keepers, and my first draft
is pretty clean. It typically doesn't need tons
of work to get it to the final, polished version.

ABOUT THE AUTHOR

Kimberly Belle is the author of *The Last Breath, The Ones We Trust* and *The Marriage Lie.* She holds a bachelor of arts degree from Agnes Scott College and has worked in fund-raising for nonprofits at home and abroad. She divides her time between Atlanta and Amsterdam.